Beginner's Greek

Beginner's Greek

A Novel

James Collins

LITTLE, BROWN AND COMPANY
NEW YORK   BOSTON   LONDON

Little, Brown and Company
Hachette Book Group USA
237 Park Avenue, New York, NY 10017
Visit our Web site at www.HachetteBookGroupUSA.com

First Edition: January 2008

The characters and events in this book are fictitious. Any similarity to real persons, living or dead, is coincidental and not intended by the author.

"Beginner's Greek," from *Collected Poems* by James Merrill and J. D. McClatchy and Stephen Yenser, editors, copyright © 2001 by the Literary Estate of James Merrill at Washington University. Used by permission of Alfred A. Knopf, a division of Random House, Inc. Quotations from *The Magic Mountain* by Thomas Mann are taken from the Vintage edition, with a translation by John E. Woods.

LIBRARY OF CONGRESS CATALOGING-IN-PUBLICATION DATA

Collins, James, 1958 May 8–
Beginner's Greek : a novel / James Collins.— 1st ed.
p. cm.
ISBN-13: 978-0-316-02155-5
ISBN-10: 0-316-02155-5
1. Married people—Fiction. 2. Adultery—Fiction. 3. New York (N. Y.)—Fiction. I. Title.
PS3603.045425B44 2008
813'.6—dc22 2007011690

10 9 8 7 6 5 4 3 2 1

Q-FF

Printed in the United States of America

To
VIRGINIA DANCE DONELSON

Beginner's Greek

Prologue

When Peter Russell boarded an airplane, he always wondered whether he would sit next to a beautiful young woman during the flight, and, if so, whether he and she would fall in love. This time was no different, except for his conviction that — this time — it really would happen. Of course, he always believed more than ever that this time it really would happen. But he knew. He knew. He was working his way down the aisle of a plane bound for Los Angeles from New York, and he figured, realistically, that the occurrence he envisioned would more likely take place on a long trip. He was pleased to discover that on his side of the plane the rows had only two seats, an arrangement that would promote intimacy, and arriving at his assigned place he found that his row mate had not yet appeared, which would allow his mind to savor the possibilities for at least a few more minutes. He stowed his suit jacket, briefcase, and laptop, and settled into his seat by the window. He opened his paper and then looked to his right, regarding the pregnant emptiness beside him. The clasp and buckle of the seat belt lay there impassively, indifferent to whom they would soon embrace. He looked at the scratchy gray and red upholstery, with its abstract design that vaguely recalled clouds at sunset. Peter remembered being at dinner in college one time and listening to an incredibly pretentious jerk, his best friend, impress everyone with some stuff from the highly selective English seminar he was taking — something about how absence implies presence. ("So I guess I shouldn't worry about cutting class so much." General laughter. Jerk.) Well, Peter had to admit, the most prominent thing about the throne of absence beside him was the presence that it lacked.

A man wearing a beige shirt and jacket stopped at Peter's row. He was short and Eastern European–looking and had a small mustache. He looked at the stub of his boarding pass and at the row number and back again and moved on. Peter was relieved. But who knew? Anyone who sat with him might transform his life in ways he would never expect. The man coming down the aisle, the one with the bulldog face and gold tie clasp, might be the owner of a smelting concern in Buffalo, and he might take a shine to Peter and ask him to become a vice president, and Peter might say yes, and move to Buffalo, where he would find the people more complicated than he expected and where, in an appealing way, the grime would climb like ivy up the walls of the old brick buildings. He would marry someone nice who had worked in New York for a couple of years but preferred Buffalo and being near her companionable, well-off parents, and he and she would live in a spacious Victorian house, with several old trees whose leaves in summer were as big as dinner plates. Or what about the ancient, bent-over gentleman in the three-piece suit? Couldn't he be a great-uncle who had disappeared in Burma decades ago and about whom Peter had never heard but whose identity would be revealed when Peter noticed that his ring bore the same distinctive device as one owned by Peter's grandfather? He would leave Peter his fortune.

The tie-clasp man walked past Peter; the ancient one sat before reaching him. Most passengers seemed to have boarded by now. Yet Peter felt a tingle. Something, he knew, was about to happen. Yes — definitely — a young woman was going sit down next to him, and not just a young woman, *the* young woman: a really pretty, really kind young woman, and they would get to talking, and they would become enclosed, in their pair of seats, in a kind of pod within a pod, suspended far above the earth, and by the time they landed it all would be settled and clear. More happy, happy love! Naturally, he had given this individual a lot of thought. He would add and subtract her attributes. She would be pretty and kind. Then pretty and kind and smart. Then pretty and kind and smart and funny, and, in a general way, perfect. Was that too much to hope? He very well knew that it was. He knew that real people with whom one really shared a real life in the real world had flaws. Aren't the slubs and natural variations what give a fabric its special character? Yes, but he didn't want to fall in love with a fabric. He wanted to fall in love with a young woman, a young woman who was pretty and kind and smart and funny and — well, pretty and kind would do, if only she would also fall in love with him.

Peter stared out the window: a truck was pumping fuel into the plane's belly through a thick, umbilical hose. Peter was a happy fellow, basically. He was in his early twenties and he was good-looking, with an open face and light brown eyes and fine brown hair that flopped over his forehead; he stood a shade under six feet and had a strong, medium-sized frame. He liked his job, basically, and he was doing well; he had friends; he was a decent athlete; he had had a relatively happy childhood. But this love business — so far, it had not been very satisfying. He had been involved with girls he liked; he had been involved with girls he didn't like. In neither case had he ever really felt . . . whatever it was that he imagined he was supposed to feel. He was shy, so that even though he showed determination at work, and playing hockey he positively enjoyed giving an opponent a hard check, he shrank before a girl who attracted him, and this made the search for someone who would make him feel whatever it was he was supposed to feel particularly difficult. Moreover, he wasn't cold-blooded, so he couldn't pursue and abandon girls with the same relish as some of his friends, his best friend in particular; rather, he had a sympathetic streak that, in the matter of making conquests, seemed much more like a weakness than a strength.

Peter watched a crewman begin to uncouple the fuel hose. Then he felt a Presence. It was a female, he sensed. Could this be the very one, could this be She? He turned his head and did see a woman. A woman who was perhaps seventy years old wearing a black wig. In place of eyebrows she had two arched pencil lines, and she had applied a large clown's oval of red lipstick to her mouth. Peter's eyes met hers. Her false eyelashes reminded him of tarantula legs. My darling!

"What row is this?" the woman asked him. Peter told her. She looked at her boarding pass and threw her hands up. "Ach," she said, "my row doesn't exist. There is no such row. It's a row they tell you about for a joke. They skipped it. I have the plane where they skip rows. If my son would visit me, I would avoid this aggravation. But no. The wife — the wife gets dehydrated on the plane. Dehydrated, you know — water?" She looked hard at Peter. "Are you married?" she asked. He shook his head. "Marry a nice girl." She paused a moment to make sure this advice sank in and then turned around and headed back toward the front of the plane.

Peter could see no other passengers in the aisle. A flight attendant strode by closing luggage bins. Peter listened to the engines. Any minute now the plane would begin to pull away from the gate and the monitors drooping from the ceiling would begin to play the safety video. Peter looked at the empty seat beside him. His earlier agitation and euphoria had dissipated, replaced by a hangover of irrational disappointment. He looked at the seat belt, two lifeless arms embracing no one. Of course, all that could be inferred from absence was absence. He now knew who would sit beside him: nobody.

Peter sighed and shrugged his shoulders. Then, like a depressive pulling the covers over his head, he spread open his paper so that it surrounded him and began to read a story with the headline "Council Rebuffs Mayor on Wake-Zones Measure." It was quite interesting, actually. There was an effort to slow watercraft to prevent damage to shoreline structures. Like Venice. Peter had been reading for a couple of minutes when he heard some rushed footsteps coming toward him, the light, tripping footsteps, he noted, of a young person, most likely a female young person. Then, when they had seemed to reach his row, the footsteps stopped. Peter became aware of a form hovering nearby. But because of his newspaper, he couldn't see who it was. He nonchalantly folded the paper back, glanced to his right, and saw that a young woman was hoisting a bag overhead. As she lifted her arms, she revealed a tanned, well-modeled stripe of abdomen. Peter's heart fluttered. He concentrated on his paper. "In New South, Courthouse Towns See Change, Continuity."

The young woman sat down. As well as he could, while pretending to idly look around the cabin, Peter studied her. She appeared to be Peter's age, and she had long reddish blond hair that fell over her shoulders. She wore a thin, white cardigan and blue jeans. What Peter first noticed in her profile was the soft bow of her jaw and how the line turned back at her rounded chin. It reminded Peter of an ideal curve that might be displayed in an old painting manual.

His eye traveled back along the jaw, returning to the girl's ear. It was a small ear, beige in color, that appeared almost edible, like a biscuit. Her straight nose had a finely tooled knob at the end, and her forehead rose like the side of an overturned bowl; her complexion was as smooth and warm-toned as honey. As to her form, she was lanky, with long legs and arms and thin wrists. Her long neck held her head aloft.

Now the young woman turned in Peter's direction, looking for the clasp on her seat belt. The trapezoid created by her shoulders and her narrow waist, the roundness of her bosom, the working of her fingers, so long they seemed like individual limbs, all moved him deeply. Then she raised her head, looked at him, and smiled. The effect was like seeing the sun over the ocean at midmorning, a tremendous blast of light. It was as if the young woman had raised some mythic golden shield whose brilliance would prostrate the armies of the Hittites. She had an oval face, and her large eyes were set wide apart; they were green, as green as a green flame! Peter instructed the muscles at the corners of his mouth to retract in a friendly way, with a hint of flirtatiousness. He imagined the result was like the grimace of someone breathing mustard gas. The girl nodded and looked away, buckling her seat belt and settling herself in.

Before she sat down, Peter noticed, she had thrown a thick paperback onto her seat. He hadn't been able to see the title. Now she opened it and began to read. In her left hand she held back a thick wedge of pages, about two thirds of the book. After a moment, Peter saw out of the corner of his eye that she had let go with her left hand and the book had fallen closed. She sat staring before her, lost in thought. Peter saw the book's cover and was taken aback: *The Magic Mountain*, by Thomas Mann.

To sit next to a beautiful young woman on a flight from New York to Los Angeles is one thing. To sit next to a beautiful young woman on a flight from New York to Los Angeles who is on page five hundred of *The Magic Mountain* is quite another. If you look over to see what the beautiful young woman next to you is reading, and it turns out to be a book about angels, then you can with perfect justification refuse her entry into your life. What could you possibly have to say to each other? The same logic applies even if the book is more respectable, but basically dumb — a harrowing but ultimately life-affirming memoir. And if the book is utterly respectable but still basically dumb, say the new book by a fashionable, overrated English novelist, then the young woman is especially dismissible, since the worst alternative possible is talking to someone who thinks she is clever but isn't. At the same time, if she were reading something that showed that she really was extremely smart — a computer-science journal — then there would be no point in talking to her either: she would be far too intimidating. In sum, an argument could be derived from virtually any reading matter that would allow a young man — scared out of his wits — to persuade himself that it was perfectly sensible, rather than the height of cowardice, to ignore the beautiful young woman who would be sitting next to him for the following five hours. Any reading matter, that is, except *The Magic Mountain* by Thomas Mann. A beautiful young woman reading *The Magic Mountain* — how could he weasel out of this challenge? It was a serious book, but not one suited to a preening intellectual, who would prefer one that was more difficult and less stodgy. A young woman reading *The Magic Mountain* had to be intelligent and patient and interested in a range of different ideas, many of them quite old-fashioned. She would also happen to be reading the only long German novel that Peter Russell himself had ever read.

Needless to say, for all his daydream eagerness, now that he was actually presented with the possibility of falling in love with a beautiful young woman sitting next to him on an airplane, Peter was terrified. Terrified that he might actually get what he'd dreamt of getting and terrified that now, having the opportunity to get it, he would screw up. If he did not find some way to speak to this young woman, and charm her, he would kill himself. If he spoke to her and she, without even looking at him, gathered her belongings and moved to another seat, he would also kill himself. The plane had taken off by this time and drifted slowly, as it seemed, above a thick wadding of cloud. The sound of the engines was loud but had become familiar and functioned as thought-extinguishing white noise. Peter was hanging in the air and for five hours essentially nothing would change. The unvariegated membrane of time that stretched before him would be dimpled only when the flight attendant handed him a beverage and a packet of pretzels. Yet, and nevertheless, notwithstanding all this inertia, tremendous forces of potential energy were gathered in this setting. For without even speaking to her, Peter was convinced, he knew for a certainty, he had not the slightest doubt, that he could spend the rest of his life with the young woman who had happened to sit next to him, and it would be blissful.

He could tell this not simply on account of her appearance, or the book she read, but because of the way she held the book in her hands, the way she tilted her head, the way she lightly set her lips together. All this provided more than enough evidence of her kindness, devotion, wisdom, grace, wit, and capacity for love. Never in his experience had he learned more about a woman's character after thorough, and often quite unpleasant, explorations of it than he had already known within thirty seconds of meeting her. (With men, he had discovered, you needed five seconds.) And now he heard the voice of emotional maturity explain to him, patronizingly, that his assumptions about this young woman were based on a "fantasy." Real life, real marriage, involves a commitment to a real person with all her flaws and individual needs. A real life together was doing the dishes when you were tired and paying the mortgage. He stole another glance at the young woman. He imagined her thumb and forefinger grasping a ballpoint pen and writing out a mortgage check, her hand working like some antique mechanism that was a marvel to the world. Bring on the dishes.

So, as we have seen, however inert the setting might seem to be, tremendous forces were gathered in the cabin of this aircraft. Forces. Tremendous ones. Peter knew that with the smallest effort he could potentiate the situation, with epochal consequences for his life and happiness. It was as if the entire cabin were filled with the tasteless, odorless fumes of powerful romantic-sexual gas, and only a spark was needed to create an explosion; the plane would suffer no damage, the other passengers wouldn't even notice, but the result would change his life.

What would that spark be? Peter was not one of those people who easily strike up conversations with strangers. If there were a subset of that group from which he was even more decisively excluded, it would be that which consists of men who easily strike up conversations with strangers who are pretty girls. His best friend was able to meet the eyes of a girl in line at the movies and smile and casually say something like "So, do you think this really is as good as his last one?" Then they'd be off and running. Peter, meanwhile, expected to address the girl's friend, would stand by, mute.

The young woman sighed, shifted in her seat, stretched a little, and looked up. Here was his moment. He could look over and ask, What takes you to Los Angeles? He could say that. What takes you to Los Angeles? The words circled around and around in his head, like the tigers who turned to butter. What takes you to Los Angeles? What takes you to Los Angeles? What takes you to Los Angeles? He became almost dizzy with their silent repetition. Then something strange happened. This was very odd. Peter was not prone to auditory hallucinations, but he thought that he actually heard the words "What takes you to Los Angeles?" being spoken aloud. Suddenly understanding, he jumped in his seat.

"Oh, I'm sorry," he heard a warm mezzo voice say. "I didn't mean to startle you. I was just wondering: What takes you to Los Angeles?" The young woman had spoken to him, and Peter looked at her and her mild, friendly expression. He noticed, as he had not before, how her philtrum rhymed with the shallow cleft in her chin. It was time for him to say something. He was looking at her; she was looking at him with that mild expression of conversational invitation. His brain clicked and whirred and blinked.

Finally, he managed to say, "Work." (More accurately transcribed as "Grk.")

Now Peter braced himself for the inevitable: What sort of work do you do? New Wave, West Coast jazz pianist. Vintner. Assassin. No, he would have to say that he worked for a Wall Street firm and right now was in the corporate finance department — and therefore was the most boring human being you could possibly meet on a plane flying to Los Angeles. Corporate finance. My God. Well, you see, right now we're issuing some convertible debt for a mid-sized bank . . . In fact, there were aspects of it that were interesting to him, but no regular human being, and certainly no beautiful young woman, would ever want to have a conversation about such a subject or believe that a person so employed was worth talking to about anything. He would tell her what he did, and the remaining four hours and fifty minutes of the flight would pass in silence.

But the young woman didn't ask about his job. Instead, she asked, "Do you like Los Angeles?"

"Do you like Los Angeles?" Another impossible question! He knew that the accepted thing was to hold "L.A." in contempt. Still, you couldn't act too proud of yourself for bashing the place, since that was so conventional. If you made a smug wisecrack about it — "Breast implants? Those people need brain implants!" — you risked sounding like a very tiresome person eager to beat a horse that had already been turned to dust. Yet you couldn't actually say you liked L.A., could you? What pressure. Pro, con? Funny, serious? Knowing, naïve? Good, bad? Yes, no? Zero, one? Up, down? Back, forth? He toggled between responses and finally produced a sort of ingenious synthesis: "L.A. is all right."

He watched the aperture of the young woman's lovely face close ever so slightly and felt a pang in his heart. Two nearly monosyllabic responses did not exactly encourage further conversation. He was losing her. So he said, "I guess I really don't know it very well. I guess you do a lot of driving." This was brilliant stuff! He continued: "I know there's a whole world of young movie stars living in old movie stars' houses and spending millions on thirties French furniture, but that's not what I ever see. From what I see, Los Angeles is like any other city where they have lots of highways and air-conditioning. The tables in the conference rooms where I spend my time have the same executive walnut veneer. Otherwise, I'm in my rented car or at the hotel. I guess there are palm trees. I guess there is this tremendous myth of Los Angeles: you're with your girl by her pool at her huge place, built by a silent-screen star; you are both as beautiful as a youth and maiden in a heroic painting; the beads of water on your skin are glittering in the sun. There's that sealed-in, airless feeling you get that makes you think you're isolated even though millions of people surround you. It's a bright, still Wednesday afternoon, and naturally you don't have anything else to do on a Wednesday afternoon but look great with water beads glittering on you. But the Los Angeles I see, it's like a city in the Midwest in summer, just with palm trees and longer distances to drive.

"I do remember once going to a bar with some people after a dinner meeting. Hi ho, let's have some fun. One of the people who lived out there took us to a place, and some young movie stars were there playing pool. They were all so good-looking that just looking at them was completely engrossing. Anyway, one of them, an actress, took off her gloves — she was wearing these old-fashioned gloves with cross-stitching on the fingers — and set them down by her beer and started to play. She was very good, actually, and she had these long, lithe arms, which she was definitely showing off while she played. She seemed haughty and shallow. Simply from watching them play pool I knew that neither she nor her friends were possessed of any civilization or culture or charity or seriousness. And I thought to myself: God, I wish I were one of them."

He stopped, out of breath and in a state of panic. How could he have kept babbling on nonsensically like this? During his speech, he had been addressing the back of the seat in front of him. Now, fearfully, he looked over at the young woman, and — her expression was not so discouraging! She seemed to have been listening intently. Her eyes were wide and her lips were apart. She almost seemed transported by what he had said. Encouraged, he gave her a smile indicating his appreciation of her receptiveness. She lowered her eyes for a moment and then looked up at Peter and said, "That is the most beautiful, the most inspiring thing I have ever heard in my life." Then she began to laugh. She raised one long-fingered hand to cover her mouth and turned away.

To his surprise, Peter noticed that this response had not caused him to blush hotly; rather, something in the young woman's tone and manner emboldened him.

"Okay," he said, "since it worked out so well for me, maybe you can explain why *you* are going to Los Angeles."

The young woman didn't answer right away. She ran her finger down the lock on her tray table. Looking at the lozenge of her nail, Peter thought about the soft pad on the other side. The pause grew longer. Peter waited. She turned to him with a dimmed smile, as when the edge of a cloud passes over the sun.

"I'm going to visit my sister," she said. "She just had a baby, a girl named Clementine." She laughed. "It's going to be a little strange being Aunt Holly."

Holly.

"My sister's living with my father at his house. It's in the hills behind Malibu. My sister and I lived in L.A. when we were little, but then my parents got divorced when I was three and my sister was five, and my mother took us back to Chicago, where she was from. My father was a director. Once in a while, he still rolls down the hills and goes into town to let some old producer pal buy him lunch. Mostly, though, he spends his time drinking schnapps and reading detective stories." She paused. "He made some okay pictures," she said. She paused again, before continuing. "We're a little cross with my sister. She naturally didn't think it was really necessary to have a husband to go along with the baby. The father is living with somebody else in Hawaii. He's all excited about the kid and was in the room for the delivery. The only thing that surprises me is that he didn't insist on his girlfriend's being there, too." She sighed, then looked at Peter. "Hey, here I am telling you all my family problems and I haven't known you for five minutes."

She smiled and studied him. She was looking at his eyes and he looked back at hers. Then their focus shifted, and they were looking into the other's eyes, rather than just at the surfaces. For that instant, Peter felt that the whole universe simply stopped, as if its entire purpose had been to whip out its material until it had reached this perfect point of equilibrium. They both forced their eyes to dart away, and matter and time took up where they had left off.

Holly insisted that Peter tell her something about his family and his childhood, despite his protests that it was all very dull. He had grown up in New Jersey and had two older sisters, and he was the son of a business executive and a mother who was passionate about three things (aside from her husband): her children, her charities, and her garden. Holly succeeded in forcing Peter to talk about corporate finance and she actually managed to seem interested in it. He even showed her a tombstone ad in the paper announcing a deal he had worked on. Holly, meanwhile, was not really sure about her career; right now she was teaching high school math in the Dominican Republic, and this was inspiring on some days and incredibly depressing on others. She got to New York fairly often because her aunt lived there. They talked about a lot of things. And for periods they were quiet. She read and he looked at spreadsheets. Then one of them would say something, speaking the words aloud as naturally as he or she had thought them. They would talk for a time and then once again fall into a friendly, active silence. As in a painting, the negative space counted.

"Well," Holly said after a long period of quiet, "that's enough of Hans for a while." She turned to Peter. "Have you ever read this?"

"Yes," Peter said. "It's a *Bildungsroman.*"

"Correct."

"Do you like it?" Peter asked.

Holly thought for a moment. "Do I like it? I don't know. It's not exactly one of those books you 'like' or 'dislike.' Reading it, I feel as if I'm attending a very, very long religious ceremony, which sometimes seems ridiculous and at other times is tremendously absorbing and disorienting. But 'liking,' as in 'enjoying,' doesn't really come into it.

"I guess I do like being plunged into this totally serious — even if it does have its ironic bits — profound, ultraprofound consideration of all the big things. Life, love, death, art, freedom, authority. It's like being transported to a different planet. And then, when you think about what eventually really did happen to Europe, it's hard to complain that it's portentous."

"I totally agree," Peter said. "But I have to admit that the thing that struck me most, even though I knew that I was supposed to be thinking about all that big stuff, the thing that struck me most was —"

"Second breakfast," Holly interposed.

"That's right!" said Peter. "That's right! How did you know?"

"Well, come on," Holly said. "Who reads that they have a meal at the sanatorium called 'second breakfast' and doesn't think that, tuberculosis or not, it sounds like paradise? With a mild case like Hans's? It would definitely be worth it."

Two minds with but one thought! Peter felt faint, but he carried on.

"Where are you now?"

"I just finished the snowstorm."

"My favorite part."

"A little gruesome. The dream about the old ladies dismembering a child . . ."

"Yes," said Peter. "But, you know, despite that sort of thing and the incredible thick soup of philosophizing, I was surprised that the book does have moments that are romantic, actually. When Hans is thinking about Clavdia's wrists. And even though she is a complete drag, you can see how she gets under his skin. The love thing, it manages to sprout a few blades through the cement."

Holly turned toward him and tilted her head. "So you're a romantic?" she asked.

Peter blushed. He couldn't answer or look at her. Eventually, clenching his hands together and staring in front of him, he managed to say, "I guess. Kind of."

He could see Holly out of the corner of his eye, still looking at his profile.

"Sorry," she said. "It's not a fair question to ask a male. Sorry. But anyway . . . me, too."

Peter turned to her. "Could I see the book for a second?" he asked. She handed it to him, and he flipped through the section she was reading.

"Here it is," he said. "Here's the line I remember, a couple of pages back. Since it's italicized, it's easy to find." He swallowed and then read. "*'For the sake of goodness and love, man shall grant death no dominion over his thoughts.'*"

"Yes, that's the one," Holly said.

They were silent for a time. Holly's hands were resting in her lap, with the back of one in the palm of the other. Slightly bent and turned upward, her fingers looked like fronds. Eventually, to Peter's relief, for he feared that he had put a permanent stop to the conversation, she asked him what book he was reading now (*David Copperfield*, which he explained that he had never gotten around to as a boy), and after talking about that they ranged over a number of topics: hockey, why famines occur less frequently under a democratic system of government, more about her family, the schools they had attended, the music they liked (a striking conformity of taste in that crucial area), the differences between Third and Second avenues, books, TV shows of their childhood, economic growth rates in Scandinavia and the Netherlands . . .

So while the plane cruised over the flat, unchanging Midwest, the prairies and the desert, Peter was in a state of serenity and bliss. The spark had flashed, but there was no explosion. Rather, all had undergone an invisible change of state like magnetization. As soon as they had begun talking, all the momentousness of the occasion had melted away and he had felt unconsciously happy. He looked out the window and saw the mighty and forbidding Rocky Mountains. Mighty and forbidding? Maybe to Lewis and Clark. He was soaring thirty thousand feet above them.

How did he feel? It was interesting. He felt sort of the way he did when he floated on his back in cold ocean water on a clear hot day and aligned his body with the sun. The cold wavelets lapped up against him; the sun warmed his face, and he felt deliciously stimulated and calm. They had not talked about anything particularly intimate. They had not fused their identities with the force of smashed atoms. They had come together as simply as two flowers intertwining. How happy he felt. And then, once again, that wet-blanket voice piped up in the back of his head, telling him that it was absurd to feel "happy" under these circumstances. He didn't know this young woman at all. In relations with another person, "happiness" is not the by-product of superficial impressions. Rather, "happiness," so-called, in a committed relationship was the result of grueling, arduous, unrelenting effort. Maintaining a committed relationship is hard. It requires courage, forbearance, stamina, sacrifice. A useful comparison would be working in a leper colony. The notion that you could meet a beautiful and sympathetic young woman on an airplane and chat with her about the subtle differences between Third and Second avenues and that this could produce "happiness" that was any more meaningful than the happiness produced by licking an ice cream cone, this notion was, frankly, rather childish. And in any event, if he thought that his life could be "fixed" by another person, rather than by dedication to his own growth, then he was sadly mistaken. Peter knew this argument. He knew it very well. And he knew that he was in love with the beautiful, sympathetic young woman beside him and that his life would be changed forever.

Peter looked at her. She was explaining something to him about Mary Queen of Scots. "So," she said, "she was visiting Darnley's bedside and a couple of hours after she left, the house he was staying in blew up, and it was obviously Bothwell . . ." When Holly talked, she moved her hands, as if she were juggling, a trait that Peter found endearing.

And did not the question of lust come into it? Yes. Usually, desire made him feel more tense than a sapper defusing a bomb. Curiously, in this case he felt different. He didn't feel the incredible excitement mixed with terror that one succumbs to when anticipating the possibility of sleeping with a woman for the first time. Rather, he felt desirous, infatuated, stimulated but not agitated — as if he were anticipating sleeping with a woman for the second time. It all seemed so right, certain and pleasurable. He looked at her hands, now in her lap again, and the V-shaped creases made in her jeans by her crossed legs, and the curve of her hips, which was barely perceptible.

"Hey! You're not listening," Holly said.

"Uh . . . uh . . . yes, I was! Uh . . . Ridolfi . . . you know . . . Ridolfi—"

"Well, you seemed to be thinking about something else."

~

The pressure in the cabin changed. The captain had made the announcement that they were beginning their descent. A general stirring rippled through the passengers, sounds of clasps opening and closing and papers being redistributed. The atmosphere had changed literally and figuratively. The shadows, figuratively, were getting longer and there was a little chill in the air and the sun was setting earlier — all announcing to Peter the end of the warm, fat, unchanging summer days that had been his for the past few hours. Their time was up.

Accordingly, the moment had come to ask Holly her full name, her address, and her phone number, and to ask her if he could call her sometime. All that. Yet it seemed so contrived, and embarrassing and horrible and jarring, to introduce a "dating" note into their sweet communion: Can I call you? Yuck. They belonged together like the ocean and the shore. To present himself to her as a guy who wanted to buy her dinner at a Mexican restaurant would ruin the state of grace they had miraculously achieved. But there was no way around it, he would have to say something. He tried to put the words together in his mind and finally he settled on a formulation. He took a deep breath. He cleared his throat.

"I guess we're going to land soon," he said. "I wonder if, when you're back in the city sometime —"

"No, look," she said, "how long will you be here?"

"Uh . . . I'm sorry?"

"How long are you going to be in Los Angeles?"

"Um, until the end of the week, actually."

"Do you think you'll have any evenings free?" Holly asked.

"I think so —"

"Then would you like to come out to my father's for dinner some night?"

Peter detected vulnerability in Holly's eyes. Her voice had the slightest quaver. His own nervousness was immediately replaced by a desire to reassure her.

"That would be great!" he said. "I would love to do that!"

"Great!" Holly said.

"How should we —"

"Why don't you call me and tell me what night is good? I can promise you that whenever it is we won't have any plans."

"Okay, sure," said Peter. He made a searching movement with his hands and glanced around for a moment. "Oh, my book, it's in my briefcase, up in the thing . . ."

They both looked about them.

"Here," said Holly, "let me borrow your pencil." Peter had been making notes with one of those plastic mechanical pencils, and he handed this to Holly. She opened her book and wrote something on the title page, which she then tore out. "Here you go," she said. "There's the number."

Peter looked at the page. Under the title she had written "Holly" and a phone number below it.

"Good. Thanks," Peter said. He folded the paper and put it in his shirt pocket.

"You can call us basically anytime," said Holly. "My father gets up at five, but Alex and I are night owls, and with the baby, who knows."

"Okay. I may have a dinner thing tomorrow," Peter said, "but the next night? I don't know how late I might have to work, but I'm pretty sure there isn't anything —"

"That sounds good," said Holly.

"Anyway, I'll give you a call."

They exchanged a couple of eager, flirtatious glances.

The plane landed and Peter and Holly collected their things and walked down the aisle together. Walking down the aisle together, he thought. Someday, he would mention this to her. They passed by the food courts and tie shops on the way to the baggage claim area, where they waited for the carousel to begin to turn. Finally, its great scales shuddered into motion, and Peter watched the passengers' mostly rather sad-looking suitcases process before him. They were made of black and red synthetic fabric and had large silver plates with Frenchified brand names; they had wheels and plastic handles, and they were full, Peter was certain, of heartbreakingly banal possessions, underpants with dead elastics. Then, curling into view, there came a boxy suitcase made of leather the color of butterscotch sauce. "Oh," Holly said, "there's mine." Peter heaved the suitcase off the carousel for her.

"Do you see yours?" Holly asked. Peter looked and immediately saw his garment bag. His heart sank as he watched it approach, unstoppably. He knew that as soon as it reached him, Holly and he would part. "There it is," he said, and picked up the bag. Now the two looked at each other once more. He knew it: as soon as she left his sight, the world would close up over her, the way a pond closes up over a pebble that's thrown into it, and she would be lost. He would even begin to wonder if she had ever existed.

"I guess I better get my rental car," he said.

"Dad ordered a car for me," said Holly. "I guess it should be outside."

They looked at each other. The carousel continued to turn. A couple of times, they both began and halted a movement to embrace. Then Holly lightly pressed the fingers of her right hand against the breast pocket of his suit jacket, which was right above the breast pocket of his shirt, which was right above his heart.

"Call me about dinner," she said. "Dad can make his specialty. I hope you like goat."

"I do! I mean, I'm sure I would, if I'd ever eaten it."

Holly dropped her arm down and he caught her fingers in his left hand, held them for a second, and let them go.

So long, he said. Bye, she said. She picked up her suitcase and walked away, turned once after she had gone a few yards to smile back at him, continued on; and then Peter lost her in the crowd.

Peter took a deep breath. He closed his eyes for a moment and tried to fix a picture of Holly in his mind. Then he slipped two fingers into his shirt pocket and felt the page from the paperback; then he patted his jacket in that spot a couple of times. He stood still a moment. And now he had to begin to collect his thoughts. He checked that he had everything. His laptop, his briefcase, his garment bag. He slung the laptop case over his shoulder and picked up the other two, the regulation battle array for the traveling businessman. He started off, looking for the signs that would point him to the rental car agencies. The trail wasn't well marked, and he got turned around a couple of times, and when he finally did find the right place he looked at his watch and realized he better call the Los Angeles office and his own office to check messages. So he put down all his stuff and got out his primitive cell phone. A meeting had been changed. Back in New York, somebody needed some numbers. Now he had to decide: it would actually be a waste of time to call the person in New York. But he would look efficient if he called from the airport. So he did, and he and his colleague had a pointless discussion that nevertheless made them both feel better about having "touched base." Peter had, he thought, conveyed proper on-the-ballness. He made two other arguably unnecessary calls. Taking a small notebook out of his briefcase, he used the plastic mechanical pencil to scribble some reminders to himself and then clipped the pencil inside his shirt pocket. It didn't occur to him that Holly had just held that pencil, for by now his mind was like a set that had been struck and entirely rebuilt for a new scene. He couldn't think about Holly when he was thinking about all the expectations he had to meet over several different time horizons.

Most immediately, there were the logistics of renting the car and driving to his hotel, a nontrivial challenge in this city. Then there was his schedule for the next couple of days. He had it all recorded in several places, but he could not help going over it again and again, re-solving the same problems of how he would get from one meeting to another on time, girding himself for the possibility that a client might actually ask him a question, refiguring some calculations. Lurking behind these thoughts were worries about a couple of matters that he knew he hadn't attended to properly. Still further forward in time, he had to consider how the results of this trip would play in New York. And then there were the projects that were to come to fruition within the next few months. And, finally, while he stood there in line for his rental car, his thoughts leapt all the way ahead to the rest of his life and career.

At the counter now, he listened as the attendant in her tie and vest explained that there was a problem with his reservation. He accepted the offer to go bigger for the same amount and signed in all the appropriate places. Before moving on, he checked again: garment bag, laptop, briefcase. Wallet. Credit card back in wallet. Contract in inside jacket pocket. Map from the rental-car counter. The drive into Los Angeles was not too bad. Stuck in traffic, he remembered something else he needed to do and awkwardly jotted that down on his map. He got off at the right exit, although he suddenly had to cross several lanes of traffic to do so. He found the huge intersections nerve-wracking. Twice, coming from both directions, he overshot his hotel. But finally he arrived.

He checked in. The clerk handed Peter a large envelope that had been hand-delivered, documents and binders sent over from the Los Angeles office, and, following a well-practiced script, he described some of the hotel's special services and its various breakfast offerings. "I very much hope you enjoy your stay with us," the clerk said. In his room, Peter hung up his jacket. Sitting on the bed, he returned more calls. On one, he had to dance around a bit. Then he lowered his back on the bed. He took a deep breath. He squeezed his eyes shut. And then, as if there had been music playing all this time, particularly beautiful music, which he had been too distracted to notice, Holly came into his mind. Now he swelled with a simple, single feeling. All his worries melted away. A picture of Holly appeared. She was standing on a scrubby, dusty California hillside and the late afternoon sun caressed her face. She was smiling at him. Maybe . . . he wondered . . . would she have gotten home? . . . maybe he could call her right now?

Lying there on his back and staring at the ceiling, Peter became aware of the left side of his chest, the place under his shirt pocket. He felt the pressure of Holly's fingers there. He wondered . . . he wondered if he could possibly feel the weight of a folded piece of paper in his shirt pocket? Of course not. He lay on his back looking at the ceiling and thinking about Holly, about the page from *The Magic Mountain*, the title page, on which she had written "Holly" and her father's phone number. He lay on his back staring at the ceiling and thinking about these things. He was preparing to lift his right hand and retrieve the page. He paused before doing so. He paused a little longer.

Then he did lift his right hand and inserted the index and middle fingers into his shirt pocket. The starched oxford cloth felt surprisingly rough and sharp. He waggled his fingers inside the pocket; he didn't feel a piece of paper. He waggled his fingers again, and then he put his hand down by his side. Still lying on his back and staring at the ceiling, he took a couple of deep breaths. All the blood seemed to drain from his body. The piece of paper was gone.

He knew that within seconds his heart would race and his nerves crackle; for the moment, though, he felt the odd, stunned serenity of a condemned man. Now, using both hands to keep the pocket open, he looked inside. He turned the pocket inside out. The piece of paper was lost, there was no doubt about that. Peter would surely conduct a frantic and thorough search. Like a drunk desperate to find enough change for a drink, he would turn out all the pockets of his clothes, where he would find all those little pieces of paper that he had accumulated during his trip. "Not valid for flight." He would rifle through the documents in his briefcase and then, with steely patience, turn them over one by one. He would slide his hands around the various plastic sleeves of his laptop case, finding errant pens and business cards. He would retrace his steps to the front desk and then to his car, where he would unfold and refold and unfold his rental car contract and open the trunk. Then, returning to his room, he would in one last frenzy strip out every article of clothing in his garment bag and search through all the pockets and every pleat and cuff. He would even look in the pockets of the shirts that were still in the plastic bag from the cleaners. Magicians did things like that, didn't they? The card you picked would appear inside another sealed deck, or an apple?

All of this would be completely useless, he knew, but he would do it. He stared at the ceiling. He closed his eyes. He could see the printed words on the page clearly. As for the handwriting, he could remember its general look and the space it took up, but he could not picture anything specific, except the name: "Holly."

Holly.

1

For its entire history, the firm of Beeche and Company, which could trace its origins to New Amsterdam, had engaged solely in one commercial activity: trading. At no time had it cultivated or mined or manufactured any good; it acted, rather, as merchant, factor, broker, financier. At its beginnings, it imported the axes that it traded for wampum, which it traded for beaver skins, which it sold for export. Later on, it bought corn and wheat from the farms of the north and sent its ships laden with them to the Caribbean, where they exchanged their cargo for sugar, rum, molasses, and indigo, which, on the ships' return, Beeche re-exported to the east and west; sometimes, the eastbound ships, after first calling in Britain or France, traveled down to the African coast and then sailed back across the Atlantic with cargo that was human. Beeche was among the first in New York to trade commercial and government paper, and as the years passed it added the securities of banks, then of railroads, then of manufacturers, to its repertoire. By the turn of the last century the firm had grown into a large financial enterprise with thousands of employees, branches throughout the world, and a dozen divisions. Yet its basic business remained the same: trading for its own benefit and brokering the trades of others. No Beeche had touched a plow or a hammer for centuries, nor had he employed anyone who did.

Unlike its competitors, Beeche was still owned by its founding family; no partners had been invited in, nor had shares been sold to the public. Moreover, the Beeches had passed the company down roughly according to the right of primogeniture (although there had been times when women had run it — Dorothea Beeche famously made a killing in the Panic of 1819), so the ownership had remained concentrated. Since it was a private firm, no outsider could easily judge what Beeche and Company was worth, but it typically ranked at the top as an underwriter, and it was legendary for its ability to make huge bets and refuse to fold when the markets (temporarily) turned against it, so its capital must have been very substantial.

Apart from the firm, there were, of course, other sources of Beeche wealth, and their value was even harder to determine. The Beeches, for example, had acquired land continuously, and it was said that they had never sold an acre, but the extent of their holdings was unknown, as they had long since stopped using their own name in making a purchase. Then there were the collections of antiquities, paintings, sculpture, furniture, manuscripts, tapestries, books. Always patrons of American cabinetmakers and silversmiths, the Beeches also took shopping sprees in Europe that had preceded those of other Americans by a couple of generations. One of the Beeches had made a practice of providing liquidity to embarrassed maharajahs by buying their jewels; in the 1940s and 1950s, another had accepted paintings in lieu of rent from impoverished artists living in Beeche properties in lower Manhattan. Nor was it possible to say how much money the Beeches had given away. From the earliest Spastic Hospital through settlement houses on the Lower East Side to the newest program to eliminate malaria, they had exerted themselves philanthropically, usually with the right hand kept ignorant of what the left was doing.

Yet while precision might be elusive, it could be said with confidence, in a general way, that the Beeche fortune was vast.

The incumbent Beeche was named Arthur (as most of his predecessors had been). His legacy, with all its attendant powers and duties, had come to him at the age of forty. He was now fifty-three. One wet morning in June, Arthur Beeche was being driven from his house on Fifth Avenue to Beeche and Company's headquarters on Gold Street. He had left at his usual time, four-fifteen, and at that hour the trip took ten minutes. Rory, the chauffeur, had minded Arthur since he was a little boy and, on account of his employer's generosity and good advice, and his own shrewdness, he had acquired his own fortune. Right now he was making a big bet on volatility, as he told Arthur on the way downtown. They arrived at the Beeche Building, an enormous new edifice. The rain had made black patches and streaks on its slate cladding. Rory opened the car door for Arthur and scampered to open the door of the building. Although he was a large man, Arthur moved in a kind of shimmer, as if an invisible force were conveying him a finger's width above the ground. "Good morning, Mr. Beeche," said a security guard. Arthur smiled and said, "Good morning, Ignazio." He shimmered over to his private elevator, and Ignazio pushed the button for him; the doors opened instantly. "How's your little boy doing?" Arthur asked. "The first-grader."

"Oh! Good, Mr. Beeche," said Ignazio. "Very good."

"Did he get glasses?"

"Yes, sir. It's a big help."

"That's swell," said Arthur. "But the other children don't tease him?"

"Oh no. Maybe a little, but not so bad."

"I'm glad to hear such a positive report," Arthur said, entering the elevator. "See you tomorrow, Ignazio. Take care of yourself."

"Yes, sir. You too, sir," said Ignazio. "Don't fight the tape!"

Arthur laughed. This was a little joke of theirs. "I'll try not to!" he replied.

When Arthur got off on the seventy-seventh floor, a beautifully groomed woman, Miss Harrison, was there to meet him. She carried a folder full of correspondence. As they walked toward his office, he and Miss Harrison talked quietly about how Asia had closed. They passed by some empty desks, through a well-furnished anteroom, and then into Arthur's office proper. It was large and decorated in the expensive but reserved style of a masculine upstairs sitting room in one of Arthur's houses. There were three large paintings and several smaller ones. Arthur changed these regularly, enjoying the chance to study his pictures during his long hours at work.

He sat at his desk, which was bare of any papers. Miss Harrison placed the folder in front of him. She brought his attention to several matters. "Thank you, Miss Harrison," he said, and she withdrew.

Arthur Beeche was six feet three inches tall and was powerfully built. He had a large head with a flat brow; his black hair had always been rather thin and, combed straight back, enough of it now remained only to cover his skull. The most striking thing about Arthur's appearance may have been his mouth, which was incongruously sensitive-looking for the thick superstructure of his jaw and cheekbones. Today he wore a gray suit with a thin, faint red check, cut in the English style.

Arthur was thinking about something that he had not been able to get out of his mind since he first put the suit on that morning: his tailor had died. This event saddened and preoccupied Arthur.

He was, naturally, concerned about finding someone who would make his clothes as skillfully. But he wasn't thinking about that. The news was taking an emotional toll on Arthur, for his tailor had been a particular friend.

Sam Harrison (someone at Ellis Island had given his father, a Russian Jew, the same name as Arthur's aide, who was a Harrison of Virginia) had become a Communist in the 1930s and had remained one. The greatest tragedy of the twentieth century, to his mind, had been the Normandy invasion. By the time the Allies had finally opened the second front, Sam always insisted, even Stalin had come to think that the Soviets could defeat Hitler alone, which would have secured all of Western Europe for the dictatorship of the proletariat. The very rich men of affairs among Sam's clients took pleasure in it when he ranted against capitalism: the irony and humor of being abused by your incredibly expensive Communist tailor was delectable. Meanwhile, the idle men of fashion who patronized Sam all more or less agreed with him.

While Arthur's fellow plutocrats treated Sam with amused, condescending patience, Arthur talked with him frankly and seriously. He didn't relish the incongruity of paying someone to make his suits who, theoretically, would just as soon have seen him guillotined; his mind didn't work that way. He disagreed with Sam and said so forthrightly, taking Sam's opinions at face value, and Sam treated Arthur's with the same respect, and as a result, as they argued over the years, they became better and better friends. What especially bound them together, though, were their discussions on a topic that was dearer to Sam even than politics: his wife, Miriam. He had married when he was twenty and his bride was seventeen, and he thought then, as he thought now, that Miriam was the most beautiful woman in the world (and he was not deluded in this). He had three sons and two daughters and many grandchildren and even a couple of great-grandchildren: he had loved them all and they had all made him proud (well, one of his daughters had married that pisher, but they got rid of him). But most of all, there was Miriam, a tall woman with long auburn hair and a sweet voice and even sweeter disposition. Sam loved her.

Now, Arthur had also loved his wife. They had fallen in love when he was twenty and she was seventeen, but, unlike the Harrisons, they were not married until several years later (and for that occasion, Sam had made Arthur a new morning coat for free). Without question, that had been the happiest day of Arthur's life. As he said his vows, his voice cracked and he wept. He and Maria (pronounced with a long "i") had been married for sixteen years, and he loved her throughout all that time and he loved her now. But she had died of cancer at age forty (at her most beautiful, Arthur and others believed). As he had been purely happy on his wedding day, so he was in pure despair on the day that Maria died. If the sun had burnt out and the seas dried up, Arthur might have been mildly troubled. Maria's death made him distraught.

The person who best understood what had happened to Arthur was Sam Harrison. "It's a tough break, kid," Sam had said. Arthur had trembled.

"You know, Sam," he had said hoarsely, "I have to travel a lot. The worst thing about it was always leaving her. But it was almost worth it because of how wonderful it was to see her again." Arthur had been unable to speak for a moment. "Now I won't see her again." He had looked at Sam and saw the loose skin under his chin quiver and his eyes, each studded with a mole at the lower lid, begin to water. Sam held Arthur's arm. *"Yeetgadal v'yeetkadash sh'mey rabbah,"* he had whispered. *"B'olmo d'vero keerutey."* Arthur had not understood the words, nor had he fully grasped the significance of an atheistic Marxist's uttering a prayer, but he appreciated the sentiment.

Sam and Arthur had always talked about Miriam and Maria, and they continued to long after Maria's death. Years later, Arthur would ask Sam about Miriam, and Sam would grin and say, "Well, the other day . . ." But he would pause and look at Arthur, who would look back at him in the three-way mirror. Then Sam would say, "You're still thinking about her." And Arthur would say yes, and he would tell Sam some memory he had recently had about Maria — the soup in Madrid, her salamander brooch.

Maria was dead. They had had no children; Arthur himself had been an only child. His father was dead and now old Sam Harrison was dead. Arthur rose and looked out the window. The rising sun gave the rain clouds a dull glow. More cars had appeared. In a typical office building, even on a floor at this height, you could hear traffic, especially the slithering sound of tires on wet asphalt; typically, on a stormy day on a floor this high, the wind created spooky sonic reverberations and the building actually swayed. Arthur's office was different. He heard no traffic or wuthering wind, and he felt no swaying. In his office, all was quiet, still. From his vantage he could see a dozen other buildings, and he thought about all the people who would soon be arriving for work. They constituted a lot of energy, activity, money. A lot of life. Arthur did not wonder what it was all for. It seemed obvious to him what it was all for. His own life was busy and full. He had good friends; his mother was still alive and he was close to her. But he felt heavyhearted and alone.

~

A few hours later on that same June morning, a meeting was taking place on the fifty-ninth floor of the Beeche Building. It was in the small conference room, the one with no windows. One of the participants in the meeting, indeed its central figure, was a young man named Peter Russell. Peter was thirty-two years old; he had been working for Beeche and Company since his graduation from college, and he had advanced nicely. Despite the doubts he sometimes entertained about the value of his work, he had enjoyed it, he had enjoyed his success, and he had enjoyed his high pay.

On this morning, though, Peter was quite unhappy. In fact, he was at this moment the unhappiest he had ever been during his entire time at Beeche. The meeting, which he had gone into with enthusiasm, had become a savage, grotesque spectacle in which he was the victim. His tormentors had poured hot lead down his throat, cut off his private parts and stuck them in his mouth, and now, while he was still alive, they were tying each of his limbs to four different horses before sending the horses galloping off in four directions. Peter had fixed his face with an interested, wry expression while he listened to his colleagues, but he knew he was blushing bright red and that he was fooling no one. He felt sweat trickling down from his armpits.

It had all come about like this. A few weeks earlier, after a couple of his patrons had been shifted to different offices around the world, Peter had found himself working for a boss whom he didn't know well. The things he'd heard about Gregg Thropp were not encouraging. Thropp was a short, stocky fellow, and he displayed all the Napoleonic traits so common among those of his physical type. He was driven, ambitious, self-important. When he walked, he moved his stubby legs so fast that even the long-legged had to work to keep up. Peter could see for himself that Thropp was insulting and rude to those below him. Others had warned him that Thropp was a devious, lying, backstabbing worm.

Yet toward Peter, Thropp hadn't acted badly at all. To the contrary! Thropp had treated Peter with courtesy. He'd shown Peter respect in meetings. He'd given Peter credit when it was due him and encouraged and praised him, calling him "Champ." Oh, sure, sometimes he could be pretty blunt, but it was hard to see what was so bad about Gregg Thropp. Peter had come to trust Thropp so much that he even went into Thropp's office one day to show him something that had made Peter especially proud. He had played an important part in a couple of notably profitable transactions that had come to fruition when he was working for Thropp but that had been initiated previously. On this day Peter had discovered a small square envelope in his interoffice mail; inside, there was a handwritten note from Arthur Beeche himself! The note read as follows:

> *Dear Mr. Russell,*
>
> *Please accept my congratulations on your fine work in the reinsurance and Italian bond matters. Well done!*
>
> *Yours very truly,*
> *Arthur Beeche*

> *P.S. I hope you will join us soon for one of our entertainments.*

Well, as one might imagine, Peter had been bowled over. A personal note from Arthur Beeche! What was more, it looked as if Peter was in line to receive an invitation to dinner at Beeche's house. Arthur entertained often, and his dinners were legendary for the quality of the food and drink and for the glamour of the guests. A few people from the firm were usually included, and to receive your first invitation was an important honor. You were supposed to act nonchalant about it, but Peter had been so amazed and pleased that he'd taken the note into Thropp's office and showed it to him.

"Well, well, well!" Thropp had said. "The Champ scores!" He had stood up and begun to lift and lower his arms in front of him, an absurd-looking motion for one so short. "Come on! The wave! The wave!" Thropp did this a few times before he started laughing too hard to continue. When he had recovered, he had looked at Peter earnestly.

"I'm proud of you, Peter," Thropp had said. "I really am. One thing you can sure say about Arthur Beeche is that he has his eye out for talent. You've done good work and you deserve to be noticed. Congratulations."

Thropp had held out his hand and Peter shook it.

"When I'm working for you," Thropp had continued, "and it looks like that'll be any day now, you won't screw me, will you?"

They had both laughed.

Thropp wasn't such a bad guy!

A few days later, Thropp had wandered into Peter's office, looking thoughtful. "Say, Peter," he had said, "you know your idea about securitizing home equity? I'd like to have a meeting on it."

"Really?" said Peter. "But, God, it's such a big thing, and it was just something I was fooling around with. I don't think it's anywhere near ready for a meeting."

"Oh, it wouldn't be a big deal. Just Huang, Kelly, Matt, you know, people like that."

"But —"

"I've been thinking about it. There are a lot of possibilities. Let's kick it around. Be a good thing for the team. Get some juices going."

So it had been agreed that in a few days a meeting would be held at which Peter would give a presentation on his idea. This was the aforementioned meeting, which had descended into a bloodthirsty dance of death.

Peter had gotten a jolt as soon as he had entered the conference room. First of all, the place was already full, which was suspicious.

Then he noticed that he didn't see Huang, Kelly, Matt, or any of his other friends. Where was T.J.? T.J. should have been there! Peter barely knew some of the attendees. More troubling still, a man and woman from Upstairs were sitting in a corner of the room, away from the table. The man, a trim, fortyish black guy, was wearing his jacket even though everyone else was in shirtsleeves. The woman, in her fifties, sat there with an imperious, pre-bored expression. Peter had never met them, but he knew who they must be. He set up his computer and its connections; he noticed that his hands were shaking.

Thropp had begun the meeting. "Welcome, everyone." He nodded toward the man and woman. "Rich, Andrea, thanks for taking the time to come down." He rubbed his hands together. "Well, now, we're all here to listen to Peter tell us about his new idea. Peter has been quite mysterious about it, playing it close to the vest, so I can't tell you much about what he's cooked up. He tells me it has the potential to be something very big. I'd usually want to spend some time going over a presentation like this myself, but Peter was so insistent on having a meeting that I said okay just to get him off my back!" Mild chuckles.

Thropp turned to Peter with a smile and gestured to him. "Go ahead, Peter," he said. "It's your meeting."

This isn't right, Peter thought. His heart began to pound. "Thank you, Gregg," he said with a quaver.

What he had to say was very preliminary, he explained, and he had only a few slides to show. Then he had gone through it all: What is the greatest source of wealth in the country? The equity people have in their houses. Over the past twenty years, the debt on people's houses had been securitized, providing a great benefit to borrowers and investors — and the firms in the middle. In Peter's view, the mortgage market looked shaky. Would there be a way of securitizing home equity? Say a homeowner could sell some of the equity in his house. There could be individual transactions (after all, each mortgage is individual), and you could bundle up those equity stakes just as in the mortgage-backed market. Think of the advantages: home buyers would have an alternative to debt; homeowners could pay down debt and benefit from a rise in prices without selling their houses or borrowing more; they could diversify, buying equity in houses in different markets from their own. With the home equity securities would come hedging opportunities: people could short their own houses if they were in a bubble, and there would be any number of derivative plays. It would spread risk around, make the market more efficient. Then imagine the money you could make if you were the first to come up with such a product.

Peter liked his idea even though it was at only the fantasy stage, and as he spoke he couldn't help but become more enthusiastic about it; this excitement combined with his anxiety made for a great agitation within him, as he allowed himself to think that he might possibly have carried others along.

He hadn't. After he finished, saying, "Well, that's about it. As I mentioned, it's all very preliminary," there was silence. A cough. A rustle of papers. Some taps of a pencil. Another cough.

Thropp spread out his hands. "Reactions? Rajandran?"

Rajandran was one of Thropp's liege men, and Peter didn't know him well; he spoke with great precision, polishing every phoneme. "Well, I am sure we all agree that Peter has some interesting ideas." He smiled. It was amazing how white his teeth were. "But it seems to me that he's missed the boat on this one." Rajandran rattled on for several minutes, enumerating all the reasons everything Peter had said was absurd. The basic premise was nonsensical. The problems with execution would be horrendous. Peter completely misunderstood the market, the simplest model would show that. And on and on. Someone — some mysterious person — had obviously briefed Rajandran on what Peter was going to say and then instructed him to prepare an informed rebuttal. Peter glanced at Thropp, who was rocking in his chair and trying to suppress a smirk. Peter thought he could hear him humming.

As soon as Rajandran finished, before Peter could even begin to respond, someone else piped up. "You know, of course, Peter, that a futures market for housing prices was tried in London and was a complete disaster." Another case of advance research!

"Yes," Peter said, "but, really, there was a marketing problem —"

"Marketing problem!" his antagonist said sarcastically. "You want the firm to spend billions of dollars to redo the economics of housing — and you think a few ads will make the difference?" A snicker traveled the room.

A third henchman joined in. "What about the owner's balance sheet?"

And then each member of the trio simply began to fire away: "Look at the piss-poor reaction to the Chicago Merc product." "Wouldn't insurance make more sense?" "Is it stochastic?"

Peter tried to answer (". . . preliminary, something that would need to be looked at, I can't be sure, um, uh . . ."). And then he just sat there listening, trying to look unfazed despite his red face and the sweat trickling down from his armpits. Finally, the bloodlust of his tormentors seemed to have been sated.

"Anyone else?" Thropp asked. When no one spoke, he turned to Peter. "Well, Champ, I guess you're a few bricks shy of a load."

The man and woman from Upstairs had whispered to each other and gotten out of their seats and were now leaving. They gave a nod to Thropp, who said, "Rich, Andrea, we'll try to give you a better show next time."

Peter's head throbbed. He felt rage and shame. He knew that he was putrefying before everyone's eyes. A nauseous odor was beginning to arise from him, the putrescent stench of failure. From this moment on, people would slip by him quickly in the halls; they would respond to his phone messages and e-mails in the most perfunctory way; they would edge toward the walls when they found themselves in the same room with him. Even if some of them knew that Peter had been set up, they would treat him as one infected with the plague; it was enough that somebody very senior had wanted to lay a trap for him and that he had fallen into it.

"Okay, everybody," Thropp was saying. "That's it." Then he turned to Peter with hooded, menacing eyes. "My office. Five minutes."

When Peter presented himself at Thropp's office, he found Thropp rocking in his chair with his folded hands on his stomach; he wore gold cuff links the size of quarters.

"Ah, Russell, come in," he said.

Peter stood in front of the desk. Thropp didn't invite him to sit.

"Quite an interesting meeting," Thropp said.

Peter nodded.

"Yes, quite interesting," Thropp said. "Tell me, Russell, do you like walnuts?"

There was a large bowl of walnuts sitting on Thropp's desk, but this non sequitur bewildered Peter. He shrugged.

"Go ahead and pick out a couple," said Thropp.

Indifferently, Peter picked up two walnuts.

"Take a look at them."

Peter did so.

"Now give them to me," Thropp said.

Peter handed the walnuts to Thropp, who looked at them for a moment while rolling them around in his right hand.

"Do you know what these are?" Thropp asked.

Peter shook his head.

"These are your nuts, Russell," Thropp brayed. Still holding the walnuts in his right hand, he squeezed them so hard that his fingers turned white. "And I've got 'em, right here!" Then he leaned back and laughed. "Oh, it was wonderful!" he said, laughing even harder. " 'Home equity securities!' " He could hardly speak. " 'Home equity securities!' " Stretching out his thumb and pinkie, he held his hand up to his head like a phone and put on a deep voice. " 'Hello, I'd like to buy one hundred shares of 487 Maple Drive.' " Thropp was laughing so hard now that tears came to his eyes. "And the look on your face when Raj got going! Oh God! Beautiful!" He laughed and laughed and wiped his eyes. "Oh, it was wonderful," he said finally, as his laughter subsided in a sigh.

"I'm happy to have been able to give you so much pleasure," said Peter. "But I wonder if I could ask why you've done this?"

"Why? Why?" Thropp's eyes narrowed and his face went black with malice. "I'll tell you why: I despise you." He snorted and began to grind his teeth. "Peter Russell, so bright and attractive, everybody says. Such a hard worker, such nice guy. Top decile. Everything going for him. It makes me want to puke. Before I'm through, nobody will think you're worth your weight in cockroach dung!" Thropp cackled. "But, oh, did you ever fall for it when I came on all lovey-dovey! Think of it, you come in here" — now he put on an effeminate voice — " 'Oh, Greggy, yoo-hoo! Look-see, I've got a note from Arthur Beeche!' " He fluttered his eyelashes and flapped his hands with loose wrists; then his voice became vicious again. "I'm going to destroy you, Russell." He laughed with depraved glee. "I'm going to destroy you!"

Peter waited a moment before speaking.

"Okay, Gregg," he said patiently. "What I'm hearing is that you despise me. Is that right?"

"Yep."

"I'm also hearing, Gregg, that you hope to destroy me."

"Uh-huh."

"I see, I see." Peter said. He furrowed his brow and thought for a moment. "Gregg, I wonder if the real issue isn't that my skill set may not be the one you're looking for. Under the circumstances, I'm wondering — and I'm just throwing this out — I'm wondering if it would make sense for me to transition to another spot. I'm thinking about the team, here."

"You aren't going anywhere. I've been looking forward to this too much."

"I think, Gregg, that there might be others in the firm who —"

"Nobody's going to save your ass, Russell. Furlanetto — you've crawled up her sphincter, right? Well, she's in Switzerland for the next two years. And Mulvahey? He's jumped ship."

This news startled Peter.

"You didn't know that, did you? Yeah. It'll be out in a day or two. So when you try to run to Mommy or Daddy, there ain't gonna be no Mommy or Daddy."

Peter looked glum.

"Poor little Peter Russell," Thropp said. "His ass is grass, and I'm the cow." This didn't sound quite the way Thropp had wanted, and he paused quizzically before continuing.

"Now, Russell, here's the situation. I can't get rid of you right away because I do have to cover my rear, and anyway the damn lawyers will say I've gotta have cause. So I need to make you look so bad, like such an idiot, that the only question people will ask is why I let you last so long. It'll take some time, but the nice thing is that I'll get to watch you suffer." Thropp allowed for a dramatic pause. "I've come up with a little plan that, if I do say so myself, is brilliant. I'm going to give you a new assignment." He paused again, smiling malevolently. "I'm sending you off to work for Mac McClernand." Enjoying himself, he watched as this news sank in.

Mac McClernand. Oh no, not Mac McClernand.

McClernand was a burnt-out case whose continued employment at Beeche and Company was a mystery. Working for him was career death: you would either be lost in one of his labyrinthine schemes, never to reappear, or the association would so damage your reputation that you would be forced to leave.

Peter began to speak, but Thropp raised his hand.

"Nothing to say about it, my friend. Sent the memo already. Mac's expecting you to report for duty today. He's tickled pink about it. That's exactly what he said, 'I'm tickled pink.'" Thropp chortled. "Oh, this is going to be fun!"

Peter indulged Thropp's laughing for a moment or two, then spoke. "Congratulations, Gregg. It's a plan of such diabolical genius that only you could have devised it. The world has never known such villainy! Yes, Gregg, it's a clever plan, very clever. Unfortunately, it contains one fatal flaw."

"Oh, yeah? What's that?"

"I actually haven't figured it out yet, but it'll come to me."

Thropp laughed with still greater hysterics.

"Is that all?" Peter asked.

"Not quite. Have you seen this?" Thropp held the walnuts, one between the thumb and forefinger of each hand, displaying them to Peter like a magician. He put the nuts on the desk, rubbed his hands, then picked one up, interlaced his fingers, and worked the nut so that it was between the heels of both his palms. He squeezed, cracking the shell, and then burst out laughing again.

"How do you like that?" Thropp greedily picked some meat out of the walnut and ate it. Slivers of shell stuck to his chin.

Peter turned and began to leave.

"Hold on! Got to do the other one!" Thropp called after him. The sound of his laughter followed Peter far down the corridor.

It was a long walk back to Peter's office. His mind raged with emotion and competing impulses. He would go above Thropp. But to whom? He would annihilate the bastard. But how? He would quit. But he had an employment contract; and besides, Beeche was the only place he wanted to work. And in two weeks, he was getting married.

Peter reached his office. Various numbers blinked on his big screen as indexes and rates changed around the world. On his computer monitor, he saw that he had a dozen e-mails. He pushed a button and they all came up, tiled one under the other. Then he noticed the large black diamond on the display of his phone: he had messages. He looked at the clock and saw that it was nearing ten o'clock. At exactly two minutes to ten, it was crucial that he be on the line to Frankfurt.

The phone rang; he could tell by the ID that it was his fiancée, Charlotte Montague.

He picked up the phone and said, "Hi there."

"Hi, Peter!" said Charlotte. "How are you?"

"Oh . . . uh . . . I'm okay." Peter didn't feel like talking about his presentation, and he could already tell that Charlotte must be preoccupied with a wedding crisis, so this wasn't the moment anyway. "How are you doing?"

"Well," said Charlotte, "I'm fine. But the reason I called was that Mother is being completely unreasonable about the cheese. The French people just won't understand about serving it before dinner."

Oh. The cheese. This was serious. Peter didn't mind, really. He knew what was expected of him in his role as bridegroom: listen patiently, show your interest, respond with sympathy, say "yes." With the wedding only two weeks away, Charlotte's nerves were frayed, naturally, as were her mother's. Charlotte kept talking, and Peter had to admit that his mind had begun to wander, as he remembered the meeting and his encounter with Thropp, as he watched the lines skitter on the screen before him, and as he, inevitably, imagined what it would be like to be marrying the woman he really wished he were marrying.

Charlotte talked on. "Scalloping . . . Bartók." Bartók? Then Peter could tell from her tone that she was bringing her own remarks to a close and that he would have to comment. Experience had taught him that in these situations, it was best to leave a few brain cells behind to listen, even as the rest of his mind withdrew.

These scouts gave their report, and Peter said, "God, Charlotte, of course you're completely right about the cheese. I mean, I wouldn't know, but I'd trust you on that more than your mother! Anyway . . . oh, I think that scalloping, you know, might be kind of fussy? And I really like the plan for the music, so I agree with you, we should stick with what we have. I mean, I'm sure it's a beautiful piece —"

"Oh, good," said Charlotte, "I knew that you'd feel that way."

By carefully calibrating his responses, Peter hoped to show that he had given each issue due consideration and was not simply agreeing with Charlotte in order to humor her. The Bartók had raised a genuine concern: Charlotte was impressionable, and if one of her interesting musical friends suggested Bartók for the church, as seemed to have happened, there was a chance that it would be Bartók.

"Well," Charlotte was saying now, "I'd better run. I'm sorry I won't be able to join you tonight."

"Me too."

"Duty calls."

"I know! Don't worry about it. We all understand."

"I'll be sorry to miss Jonathan's reading." Peter's best friend, Jonathan Speedwell, was a writer, and he was giving a reading that night from his new book of stories. Peter and Charlotte had planned to go to it and have dinner with Jonathan and his wife afterward. But Charlotte had to go to an event for her work. Charlotte liked Jonathan a lot and flirted with him in a girlish, free-spirited manner with which she did nothing else. "Did you see the review today in the paper?"

As if Peter had time to read book reviews. "No," he said. "Was there one?"

"Oh, yes! I've got it right here. Let me read it to you —"

"Charlotte —" Charlotte, I've got to make a call, Peter was about to say. The flashing numbers. Frankfurt. But he was too late.

"Let's see," Charlotte said. "Oh, here we are. 'With *Intaglio*, his new collection of short stories, Jonathan Speedwell once again demonstrates triumphantly that he is among our most potent younger voices writing today. In luminous silverpoint prose, he deftly renders the struggle of men and women desperate to maintain their purchase on life . . .'"

Deftly, Peter thought. With Jonathan it was always "deftly."

"'. . . But if there is one quality that truly marks Mr. Speedwell as a writer of distinction,'" Charlotte continued, "'it is his deep compassion for his characters.'"

Christ. Again, the compassion-for-his-characters thing. Peter could not understand why it was such a big deal for a writer to have compassion for his characters, as opposed to, say, real people.

"'In perhaps his most finely wrought tale, "The Copse . . ."'" Well, I won't read you the whole thing. But isn't it terrific?"

"Yes."

"He must be very pleased. Will you congratulate him for me?"

"Of course." Charlotte was an earnest person whose demeanor generally was almost grave. Peter imagined what she would be like as she congratulated Jonathan — winsome, crinkling her eyes and grinning.

"He's still pleased about being best man, isn't he?"

"Sure. I told you, the only problem is, he wants to give me away."

"Oh." Charlotte's mind snagged momentarily on the word "problem." Then she got it. "Oh! Yes. You said that. How funny."

"Charlotte —"

"Uh-oh, that's my other line. Sorry, I'd better take that. Thanks for your help. Have fun tonight. Call me."

"Sure, right, okay. Bye."

Throughout this conversation, Peter's other phone lines had quietly burbled again and again. The black diamond seemed to become denser and denser and heavier and heavier with the weight of added messages. Staring at his screens, he saw more e-mails arrive and numbers blip and charts jitter. As usual, the clock in the upper right-hand corner barely seemed to change when he was staring at it, but then when he looked away and checked it again, he was shocked to see how far it had advanced. Still, Peter didn't begrudge Charlotte this expenditure of his time at a pressing moment of his day. Those were the phone calls that brides made two weeks before the wedding, and they were ones a decent bridegroom would tolerate. It was part of life. And, he supposed, it was part of life to be screwed over in your job once in a while. It was part of life to see your best friend have undeserved success. It was part of life, also, not to get the girl.

Just in time, he reached Frankfurt.

~

Why was Peter marrying Charlotte? Why was Charlotte marrying Peter? Charlotte worked in the New York office of L'Alliance
Générale et Spécifique des Pays Francophones. The AGSPF fos-
tered economic and cultural exchange among the French-speaking
peoples of the world and tried to promote the French language
and Francophone civilization in all places sadly suffering from their
lack. Dogged and intelligent, Charlotte had mastered the politics
of Chad (Djamous, the finance minister, was on the rise, though
not supported by the Quay d'Orsay) and the diplomacy of Laos.
She was, it seemed, always writing a report on intra-Francophone
trade. There were lots of tables. In addition to this intellectual
work, Charlotte also participated in the AGSPF's busy social life:
no minor Algerian poet could pass through New York without a
reception. That's what was happening tonight. Charlotte had to attend a dinner for a Belgian economist, who had appeared in town
unexpectedly.

For a time, Charlotte's father had worked in the Paris office of a
New York law firm and the family had moved there when Charlotte
was seven. With this credential, she could legitimately make France
her thing, which she proceeded to do. After her parents divorced,
when she was sixteen, Charlotte's father and her stepmother bought
a small property in the countryside, where they went every summer
and where Charlotte would visit. Charlotte majored in French and
she spent two years in Paris after college.

There she had had the requisite love affair with a Frenchman,
with lots of tears. Maximilien-François-Marie-Isidore had been
thirty-seven, an incredibly ancient and sophisticated age for Charlotte, then twenty-two. He was always lurking in the background,
supposedly poised to swoop in and carry Charlotte back to Paris

forever. That never seemed to happen, but on a regular basis, heavy-smoking, black-whiskered French friends — Héli, Valéry, Claude, Hilaire-Germain, Alexandre-César-Léopold, Gilles — would pass through New York. They would take Charlotte and Peter to obscure rock clubs and talk endlessly about American bands and films and writers whom Peter had never heard of. Of course, they all spoke English perfectly, and from time to time one or the other would engage Peter in conversation, while making it evident that he was merely doing so out of politeness.

One requirement for Charlotte's job was that she speak the language well, and she did, using all sorts of slang. Nevertheless, whenever she spoke it with a Frenchman, there was always the air that she was performing, an amateur-hour talent, rather than simply talking to someone. Whenever they went to a French restaurant, she engaged the staff in long conversations, and they were delighted. Peter — who had taken AP French! — sat there smiling uncomprehendingly for the most part. Eventually his existence would edge into the consciousness of the captain, and he would turn to Peter with an expectant smile.

"Er . . ." Peter would say. *"Pour commencer, je voudrais prendre aussi les moules."* As soon as he heard Peter's accent, the captain's smile would disappear and he would adopt a manner of cold courtesy while Peter, losing his way grammatically, would give the rest of his order.

"Very good, monsieur, and for the wine, shall I give you a moment to decide?" Okay, so he answered in English. Big deal. In fact, that suited Peter just fine, for somewhere deep in his Celtic-Anglo-Saxon bones, he believed that it was improper for any real man to speak French.

Another requirement of Charlotte's job was that she dress well despite her low pay. Charlotte did dress well, if by "well" one meant fairly expensively. Her clothes were fashionable and of good quality. Yet she did not dress well, really. There always seemed to be too many flaps or folds or layers or lappets or something. She always seemed to be reaching for an effect, an effect that was neither achieved nor worth achieving and one that, even if those conditions were met, would not show Charlotte off to her best advantage. When Peter thought about Charlotte's clothes, her stepmother, Julia, always came to mind. She was ten years older than Charlotte and was naturally chic, but as far as Peter could tell she mostly wore a skirt, cardigan, and pearls. Charlotte had always cast Julia in the role of her guide in the ways of the world. Why not simply copy Julia's clothes? But Charlotte, with no intuitive sense of these things, was blind to the example her mentor set for her.

As with Charlotte's clothes, so with her grooming. It was always, somehow, just a bit off. The haircut was either too severe or too full, and, in either case, had a life of its own, regardless of how determinedly brushed; the lipstick was one shade too fauvist; the nails were ragged (Julia wore clear polish on her nails and kept them shaped liked torpedoes). These superficial flaws bothered Peter much more than he thought they should. For reasons that are mysterious, some people — men and women — are always able to look well put together, stylish, suitable, whereas others, to a greater or lesser degree, fail in this. Well, so what? Some people can wiggle their ears, and other people can't. If someone has a good heart, how can that sort of thing possibly matter? Irksomely, it did seem to matter. In a way that was more than irksome, so did Charlotte's looks. It wasn't a question of whether she was good-looking: she was. She had a long, rather concave face, large eyes, and a prominent nose and chin; indeed, it would not be inaccurate, and it would not be at all displeasing to Charlotte, to say that her face was "Pre-Raphaelite." She was pretty.

And yet. When they were at her apartment for the evening and had been reading for a while, and Peter raised his eyes from his laptop and looked at her, that action did not release the spring of delight that he hoped for. He could look at certain paintings over and over again, or certain views or buildings or other people or children, and he would always feel an aesthetic and emotional shiver. Looking at Charlotte after a half hour of reading, he had a rather dull reaction. He had known women who, strictly speaking, were less good-looking than she but whose faces charmed him. The nose might be wrong, but there was some alluring interplay between the eyes and the lips; or everything was too small, but taken together with that big smile that came out of nowhere, it made you swoon. He did not swoon when he looked at Charlotte.

In truth he never had. They had met two years earlier at a party given by married friends, the kind who see matches everywhere. It was more or less a setup. They talked about how terrible the Dutch side of St. Martin was, especially as compared with the French side. They talked, inevitably, about France. They talked about their friends. They got along pretty well. Charlotte liked him, Peter could tell. He liked her, and as he got to know her better, something about her moved him. She had a good heart, and beneath her determination lay a touching vulnerability.

So they got along, there was some kind of emotional connection, and, also, they made sense together. In this day and age, when marriages were no longer arranged and no father would dare forbid his daughter to marry anyone, the notion of suitable matches was supposedly archaic. Yet even when there were no overt social conventions to keep lovers apart (and to inspire novels), it struck Peter how often people still married within a fairly narrow social range. Within that range, there were further delimitations; the mates tended to come out with the same overall score on a gender-adjusted index of talent, money, expectations, polish, personality, intellect. The process of weighting and calculation was far less cynical than that employed by mothers during the London Season of the nineteenth century, but it seemed to Peter that it bore a resemblance. There were still rules, and lots of people still married the people they were supposed to marry, despite all this talk of marrying for love that one has heard for the last several hundred years or so.

Peter was an attractive fellow with a good job and a suitable background. He was presentable. Charlotte, meanwhile, was also attractive. She had the kind of job that the kind of woman whom Peter would marry would have. She had the kind of parents and friends that a woman whom Peter would marry would have. They got along. They were good, decent people. The numbers went into their supercomputers time and again, and time and again the results came out: marriage. He knew he was not in love with Charlotte, and he accepted that. But this was not because he was indifferent to love. Indeed, the opposite was the case. The reason he accepted his lack of passionate love for Charlotte was not that he did not feel love strongly but rather that he felt love much too strongly. He was capable of being deeply, passionately, heartbreakingly, searingly in love with someone. Indeed, at this very moment he was deeply, passionately, heartbreakingly, searingly in love with someone. That person just didn't happen to be Charlotte. And that person was unavailable to him. So he had given up on love altogether.

It had taken him some time to come to that position. Peter happened to be in love with Jonathan's wife. Before Jonathan and she were married, Peter watched intently, looking for any break. Yet day by day, month by month, year by year, they moved steadily closer. Had there ever been a sign of trouble? Had Jonathan failed to call? But Jonathan had never been the type who failed to call, and his wife had never been the type to be upset if he had. Had Jonathan offended her family? No. Had the magic simply disappeared? No.

Jonathan's wife was very pretty, she was kind, she was smart, she was funny, and she was much too good for Jonathan, who was a fairly despicable character. She and Peter particularly liked each other. That had been true before she married Jonathan, but there were rules about how you conduct yourself around your best friend's protowife. If they broke up and a decent interval passed, you could then make an approach. But the honorable friend would do nothing to drive the two apart. Really, honor alone had not inhibited him. So had the fear of rejection, and he considered the odds of rejection high. Whatever affection Jonathan's wife may have felt for him back then, and felt for him now, he knew that, romantically, it meant nothing — to the contrary. They had established the kind of fraternal relationship, perhaps a bit closer than the typical one, that often arises between a man's girlfriend or wife and his best friend. She took an interest in Peter and in his love life in the way married women, or virtually married women, do with the single friends of their mates, the ones they like. Their "intimacy" had been possible for the very reason that it had no sexual or romantic overtones. If Peter tried to convert intimacy of this type into sexual currency, he knew, he would be met with shock, disgust, pity, laughter, and derision. He would lose his friend, his friendship with his friend's wife, and his pride. He would have to kill himself.

Peter had been the best man at the wedding, and after that he had given up on ever marrying someone with whom he was deeply, passionately, heartbreakingly, searingly in love. Then he met Charlotte. They got along. Over time he became attached to her. She moved him. Charlotte was attractive to him, periodically. Charlotte was the kind of person a person like him married, and she wanted to marry him. Love — come on. How many people are really in love when they get married? And if they are at that moment, how many remain so two years later?

Having allowed matters to proceed as far as he had, Peter would have found it very difficult to break things off. Charlotte had something in her, that fearful look in her eye, that made it hard, very hard, for Peter to hurt her. True, her panic about getting married may have been premature, but in her circle, there seemed to be an unstated agreement that if you let your early thirties go by without settling on someone, then it was a very fast shoot to forty, when you really would be desperate. Peter did not think so well of himself or so little of Charlotte to assume that if he didn't marry her, she would never be able to find any happiness. Still, she was counting on him. Charlotte had wanted to get married so badly. Steadily applying herself and moving at a pace that was faster than what was natural, she had begun to treat him more and more like a presumptive husband, taking him to events with her family or friends or related to her work to which one would take only one's fiancé or spouse or the person one had been living with for ages. She would ask him to perform spousal tasks, like picking her mother up at the airport. She used the first-person plural pronoun. Soon enough, Peter found himself in a different country without the right papers to get back over the border. Then, too, like all young people nowadays, they had had a conversation initiated by the woman about whether their relationship was moving forward; they had been seeing each other for about a year at that point, and they'd agreed that it was.

Over and over and over, Peter asked himself if it was really fair for him to marry Charlotte if he wasn't truly in love with her. An advice columnist would say it was not, without question, and he sometimes wished he could agree. But this was the real world. Of course the chances of Charlotte's being happy were better if Peter married her. Or maybe this argument was just a rationalization for his cowardice. But no, it was surely the more loving thing to marry Charlotte. And as for Peter himself? Married to Charlotte or not, he was out of luck. He was due to marry, and he and Charlotte had a pretty good chance of being pretty happy. It would be fine.

And Charlotte, why did she want to marry Peter? She liked to present herself as being very worldly, always collecting interesting people, scoffing at the bourgeoisie, but she was, in fact, deeply cautious and conventional. Although she would never have admitted it, she was terrified of being either unmarried or married to someone who was odd or ugly or impoverished or who required her parents and grandmothers to make an uncomfortable social stretch. Peter saved her from those fates. Also, she did love him. She liked the feel of his arms around her. He had a comforting, dry smell, like cork. He was kind, and her father, though charming and well dressed, had never been. Once when she was thirteen, she was going to a dance in what was really her first grown-up dress, and she ran into the living room to show it to him and her mother. "Ah," he had said, drink in hand, *"voici la coquette!"* She felt as if he had slapped her, but she couldn't explain precisely why. When she got older, she learned enough from her therapists and her friends and her friends' therapists to understand that there was a danger that, replicating the relationship with her father, she would marry someone cruel. She had tried to avoid that. Maybe — maybe she had to force it a little bit; maybe she wasn't "in love" in love with Peter and had to fashion a notion that she was. This she managed to do. In any case, she had already filled in the Passionate, Crisis-Filled, Tempestuous Love bubble on her answer sheet of life. Deep down, she suspected that, probably, Peter was not "in love" in love with her either, but this was a condition she could live with. The marriage problem would be solved, and she knew she could trust him and that he would treat her with kindness.

So it had come to be that, on an evening in early spring, Peter had arrived at Charlotte's door with the intention of asking her to marry him. She lived in a one-bedroom apartment in a brownstone on a handsome block uptown between Park and Madison avenues. Peter had come from work and, leaving the subway, he had passed a Korean market, where it had occurred to him to buy some flowers. He decided on daisies; they seemed winningly simple. The daisies smelled of earth and grass; water had dripped from their green stalks onto Peter's hand when he took them out of their bucket. Daylight saving time had just returned, and the light at that hour, still so surprising, made Charlotte's street look as if a lid had been lifted from it. The brownstone seemed softer, and the air, a little warm now, seemed to buoy him up gently.

No young man carrying flowers on an evening in early spring down a handsome street with the intention of asking a woman to marry him can be entirely immune to the romance of the occasion. And indeed Peter did feel romantic, nervous and eager. His jacket pocket held a small velvet box that contained a diamond ring whose stone was not ostentatious but still sizable.

He greeted Charlotte. She was wearing lighter clothes than she had worn in recent days. She had had her hair cut that day and looked especially young. She had known telepathically that something was up and greeted him with a longer and more than usually tender kiss. "How pretty. Let me put these in water," she said, taking the flowers from him. "Lots of chances for me to play 'He loves me, he loves me not.'"

They sat down on the love seat and chatted awhile. For the thousandth time, Peter looked at the framed engravings taken from an eighteenth-century French instruction book on dancing, at the painting above the fireplace that had been a gift from her father and her stepmother when Charlotte turned twenty-one.

Peter decided to be gay, as the occasion warranted. "Let's have a glass of champagne," he said. Charlotte usually kept a bottle in her tiny refrigerator. She looked at him, and their eyes met for a second. "Champagne? What are we celebrating?"

"Oh, I don't know. Daylight saving time? Your haircut?" She gave a little hmm and went to the kitchen. As she walked away from him, she seemed self-conscious, as if she were thinking that he was looking at her, which he was, and he was reminded, with a trickle of lust, that the back of her neck was a good feature. She returned with the bottle and two wineglasses (champagne flutes were something you got as a wedding present). "Here," she said, "you know how to do it."

It was a little joke between them how her father had once pedantically demonstrated to Peter the best way to open a bottle of champagne. He gently prodded the cork with his thumbs while turning the bottle, as he had been taught, and the cork fell out, rather than rocketing, with a faint, hollow report and a wisp of smoke. The ceremony complete, he filled their glasses halfway; the bubbles tossed up their tiny hats.

Charlotte and Peter talked a little bit more.

"We have Moroccan agriculture people coming next week," Charlotte said. "They're going to meet with these Quebecois researchers who have done some interesting work on barley, which is about three percent of Morocco's exports." Charlotte's expression became quizzical. "It's odd that the Moroccans have asked for so much information about golf courses in the area. I don't think that anyone is coming from the tourism ministry."

A breeze entered through the window, bringing a tarry smell from the street. There was a pause in the conversation. Peter refilled their glasses. As he did so, the image of Jonathan's wife came into his mind, and he felt as if a trapdoor had opened under him. He tried to keep his hand steady as he poured. There she was. Well, never mind. What was not to be was not to be. He glanced over at Charlotte. Her eyes were pretty. The silence lasted a few seconds longer than a normal conversational gap. Peter sipped his champagne and looked over his glass at Charlotte. She looked away. She was nervous, and that made Peter feel warmly toward her.

"Charlotte." Peter's voice had an unusual resonance as he took her hands in his. "I have something I want to say, or to ask, actually. Um . . ." He swallowed. "You know, we've been talking about this. And so I was wondering . . . I mean I'd like to ask . . . I wanted to ask . . ." Here Peter paused. "Will you marry me?"

Charlotte had never received a marriage proposal before, not from her French lover and not even during free-play time at nursery school. In this instance, the man making the proposal was one whom Charlotte would quite like to marry. So she immediately began to cry and let out a large sob. She was reacting out of joy, and also from a release of tension, tension that it seemed had been building in her from the time of her birth.

"I know this is all rather sudden," Peter said.

Charlotte laughed and gulped air. "Yes, why . . . sorry . . . just a second." She dabbed her eyes with a handkerchief and tried to catch her breath. When she finished she looked at Peter and in her gray eyes there was the glow of love, an effect enhanced by their moistness.

"Well." She cleared her throat. "Well, the answer to your question is yes."

"Yes?"

"Yes. Yes. Completely, totally yes."

They embraced. The kiss lasted a long time. Peter's first emotion was faint irritation with the way Charlotte kissed. She didn't push her lips out enough, or something. Then he immediately began to think that he had made a tremendous mistake, and he wanted desperately to take back the words he had said a few moments before. Then he thought: It'll be okay. It'll be fine. I do love Charlotte, really. He felt the back of her hand press against the back of his neck, which produced a stirring of affection and desire within him. And then — and then he thought about Jonathan's wife, Mrs. Speedwell. Since the wedding, he often addressed her that way. "Hello, Mrs. Speedwell." "By all means, Mrs. Speedwell." The bottom fell out of his stomach. And then, again, he recovered and thought: It'll be fine. Charlotte will be happy enough and I will be happy enough. Parallel to his fundamental disappointment, he also felt a thrill. He had just made a marriage proposal, and he had held this woman unclothed in his arms countless times. He knew the flaws in her body, her bony hips. This accumulation of intimacy had its effect. Smiling, Peter pulled back from their embrace.

"Hey, wait a minute," he said, reaching into his pocket, "there's something that goes along with this."

~

Peter finished his conversation with Frankfurt. Already, the departing tide of his day had taken him far from his betrothed and any thoughts of her. As usual, though, from time to time throughout the day's voyage he saw in the distance the most beautiful mermaid, sunning herself on a rock, plashing into the sea and rising up again. Against the sun her smoothed head looked like a paper silhouette. It must be said that the creature did not resemble Charlotte, nor, however, was she mythical in her appearance. Even at a distance, Peter recognized her. He would be seeing her that evening, along with his despicable best friend, the writer Jonathan Speedwell.

2

Peter arrived at the bookstore late. It was larger and more commercial than the venues where Jonathan had read in the past.
The crowd was larger too, although its composition was the same:
mostly postgraduate women who were mostly willowy, mostly with
their dark hair loosely pulled back. One or two of them may have
primped for this evening, which meant wearing new sandals and
a discreet application of paint. It was June, so they were wearing
filmy skirts or short skirts with tops that showed off their slender,
downy arms; those who wore jeans looked really good in jeans and
wore the same kinds of tops. There were also some older women
in modish clothes but with heads of gray hair, coloring it being
anathema to them. They kept up with the new books. A smattering of skinny, unkempt, unshaven young men lurked in the back,
their sullen faces registering both envy and disgust. Later, at the bar
downtown, they would snigger about how Speedwell truly did suck.
There were no older males. Only Peter was wearing a suit.

At first glance, Jonathan himself might have seemed not very
distinguishable from his rivals. His dark brown curls fell to his collar without discipline. He too had stubble. He wore a checked shirt

over a T-shirt, just as they did. But there were differences. While Jonathan was on the tall side and certainly remained romantically thin, his outline was drawn with a thicker nib than that used for the others, for, unlike them, he had both been partaking of lobster ravioli at restaurants and spending hours each week at the gym. Jonathan's hair, while tousled, was clean. His jeans were clean. He had clean hands and clean, trimmed fingernails. Indeed, he was certainly the only person in the room who ever received a manicure at the Waldorf-Astoria barbershop. His black shoes, seemingly unremarkable, were custom-made five-hole derbies, which of course he never wore two days in a row.

More than anything, though, what set Jonathan apart from the other young men in the room was his glorious beauty and the sweet light that surrounded him. Standing before the audience, Jonathan seemed like the most innocent creature of heaven, favoring this base world with a sojourn. His untended curls and blue eyes and fair skin with hints of pink all suggested a person of pure goodness. No snigger passed those delicate, crimson lips. What was most beautiful was that although he possessed such physical charms he appeared to have no knowledge of them. Artless and free! How painful it was then, considering all this, to realize that his work registered so acutely the harshness with which we so often repay love, the cruel deceptions that greet those who trust. Jonathan Speedwell, his readers knew, must feel all that very deeply. And yet, and yet, how much humor and strength were in his work! And in the man himself!

As Peter arrived, Jonathan was just finishing a story. Here is what he read:

It was cold. The sky was clear. Dogs growled and barked. The man next door kept three, tied up. A breeze, out of the south now, carried a faint, acrid odor from the plant. The rusty frame of a swing set, with no swings, stood near the fence. Typical Jake, to scavenge the frame and never find swings. At this time of year it was hard to believe that in a few months wildflowers would grow up around it. Dana tried to picture them, and to remember their names: pussytoes, Venus's looking-glass, cocklebur. The sun rose higher in the bright azure sky. All of a sudden, Dana saw the crystals of frost on the grass glitter with reds and purples and yellows. It was if the entire yard had been scattered with gemstones.

Dana shivered. She lit a cigarette. On the sofa in the double-wide, Jen was still asleep. Dana should wake her. Jen would say, "Mom, you've been smoking!" Dana would wait. She would finish her cigarette and she would wait awhile. This was something Jen didn't have to know. There were so many things that she did.

Here Jonathan fell silent. He kept his head down, still staring at the book on the lectern. He tightened his lips. Then he looked up with a distracted, vulnerable expression. The inside tips of his eyebrows were raised, creating an ankh-shaped wrinkle in his brow. When the audience began to applaud, Jonathan lowered and raised his head again. Startled, pleased, humbled, embarrassed. Then he nodded his thanks, as a gray-haired woman stepped up to the lectern.

"Thank you, Jonathan. Thank you. That was just marvelous." After a new crescendo, the applause died down. The woman spoke. "I'm sure many of you have questions for Jonathan. And goodness, the hour is drawing nigh, isn't it? So I think, now, if Jonathan wouldn't mind, we'll open up the floor."

"Certainly, Martha, thank you," said Jonathan. A willowy young woman, but they were all willowy young women, raised her hand.

"Yes, right there," said Jonathan.

"Hi, Jonathan," she said. "Thanks. I'd just like to ask, what do you think about the environment?"

A question like this, both very heavy and inane, didn't faze Jonathan for a second. "It's incredibly important," he replied in a solemn tone. "I get so angry when I think about what we're doing to it. I wish my publisher would use recycled paper. There's no reason that a tree should die for this." He held up his book, prompting gentle, sympathetic laughter. "Well, they say that trees are one thing that are renewable. I try to do what I can. What I think is very important is . . . mindfulness . . . to have mindfulness about how we are treating our world. You know, there are poets who are known as nature poets, but to my mind, all writers are nature poets, and so have a special interest in protecting nature, and a special duty." Applause.

There were a few more questions. "In your first novel, when Sam drowns in the drinking game, did that really happen?" "Where do you get the names for your characters?"

Jonathan called on another young woman. "Hi," she said. She was dark-skinned and slight, and she wore a thin, peasanty blouse. "I just wanted to ask, you seem to be able to write about women so well, from their point of view. I wonder if you would tell us something about that?"

"Oh, that's kind of you, very kind." Jonathan smiled thoughtfully. "Let me think. I don't really know what to say." In truth, Jonathan had been asked this question at every reading he had ever given and in every interview. "If I'm able to get into the heads of women I guess it's because women have always seemed so much more interesting to me than men, frankly. Women are more powerful, and I'm interested in power. So maybe I've watched women more carefully." Jonathan paused. He looked down and swallowed. He seemed to be collecting himself. Then he spoke.

"But . . . but I guess there's a simple explanation. It's not something I usually mention, but something about tonight . . ." The heads of loosely gathered hair canted forward. "You see . . . my mother died when I was quite young." Jonathan paused again, remembering. "In the last memory I have of her, we were at the shore and we were playing in the waves, and she was holding me." He fell silent. The room was silent. The salt water, the sun, the smell of his mother's suntan lotion, the feel of her body against his, the thrilling surf — everyone in the room believed that they were sharing Jonathan's recollected sensations. "So of course I've spent my whole life trying to get her back and a lot of time trying to get close to women, studying them, trying to figure them out." He laughed. "Trying to get them to love me!" The audience laughed, then sighed, then applauded.

Jonathan signed books for a while, chatting with members of his public. They said things to him that they had obviously been rehearsing in their minds. "Thank you for telling the truth." Bashful Jonathan would reply, "Please — no. Well . . . thanks." Peter hovered outside the eddy of admirers. Finally Jonathan had given his last humble smile, the smile of a servant unworthy of his mistress's praise, and turned so that his eyes lit upon Peter, which prompted a different kind of smile. He signaled Peter over with a nod. Jonathan stood up and they shook hands.

"Hello, my friend," he said. "Thanks for coming."

Peter looked at him for a second.

"When did you get so green?"

"Me?" Jonathan said. "Why, I've always been that way! You remember — I drove that guy's hybrid once." Then he began to chuckle. His eyes narrowed and he grinned, pleased with himself.

"How did you like the thing about my mother?"

"I thought it was asinine."

Jonathan chuckled.

"Your mother lives on a golf course in South Carolina."

"Oh, come on," Jonathan said, "nobody's going to write an exposé. Anyway, if I ever became famous enough for anyone to care, it would just cause a fuss about how I mythologized my past. That's always good copy." He laughed and shook his head. "Maybe I'll try a dead little sister next time, 'the bravest person I've ever known' . . . Oh, Christ! Hold on a second."

Two women were approaching, one in her forties, the other in her twenties, and Jonathan moved to greet them.

"Sasha! Allison!" Jonathan said. He embraced them both. "Thanks for being here. It makes it so much easier to get through these things."

You were terrific, it went great, they told him. Jonathan made the introductions.

"Sasha Petrof, Allison Meeker, this is Russell Peters, one of my good friends. Russ, Sasha is my editor, the person who has almost convinced me to share her delusion that I can write. And Allison's her assistant, and she's — well, she's the person I depend on for everything."

Both women were very good-looking. Sasha was lean and tall, chicly dressed; Allison was shorter and more voluptuous, a quality that seemed to embarrass her, and dressed more like a kid, but expensively. They both carried the same costly bag (Sasha was married to a Wall Street guy and Allison was the daughter of a Wall Street guy). Peter shook hands with them. Sasha's fingers were narrow and he could feel the bones and knuckles. The skin was moisturized, but a little rough nevertheless. Shaking Allison's hand, in contrast, was more like grasping a ripe plum. Peter noticed how in chatting with Jonathan they both had the same coded look, a look that was intended to be understood by Jonathan but not the other person standing there.

Sasha addressed Peter. "Allison and I were talking before. We hadn't known that Jonathan's mother had died when he was so young. Is that something he's ever really talked about?"

"No," Peter said. "No, he never has."

"Did you know?"

"If you had asked me, I would have told you Jonathan's mother was living."

"Really? Jonathan, you're so private, not even your friends . . . ?"

Jonathan glanced at Peter. "No, I don't talk about it . . . well, the cancer. I'll tell you about it sometime, Sasha. I'm not sure what came over me tonight."

They chatted a little bit more about Jonathan's publicity schedule. Then Sasha made a whoop. How could she have forgotten! The review in the paper! She had called Jonathan but hadn't reached him.

"Oh, that," Jonathan said bashfully. "I guess it was okay."

"It was just terrific!" said Sasha. "Some wonderful things. Really insightful."

"Just so long as there's a money quote," said Jonathan, skillfully making the cynical crack of a noncynic.

"Oh, there was! There was!" said Sasha, laughing. Allison, her lips moist, glowed with awe.

After some more talk, Jonathan said, "Well, we need to get downtown for dinner. I guess we should get going."

"Yes, I'd better run home," said Sasha. "You were great, Jonathan. Really great. We'll talk." She embraced him and gave him an all but undetectable extra squeeze.

"Bye, Jonathan," said Allison. "You were great." She embraced him and gave him an all but undetectable extra squeeze.

~

In the cab downtown, Jonathan leaned his head against the seat and let out a sigh of exhaustion. He started talking. "Do you have any idea how hard it is to be screwing both your editor and her assistant? Christ, it's complicated. Allison . . . God . . . Allison. She has this way of lifting her legs up and putting her heels on your back and sort of massaging it with them. The thing about Allison — God. She's young and not that experienced, but it's the enthusiasm. The zest. She just loves it. Though, of course, in the hands of the master . . . She's such a kid, unsure, and I so dig that, you know?"

Peter, actually, didn't know.

"But then when Sasha is tough and businesslike it's also one of the most exciting things. 'No, Tom, I will not give him a two-book contract!' I remember once we were, uh, in conference and she was running late. She had herself completely put back together in about two minutes and was all business. I just wanted to grab her and start all over again. I love the way her hands feel, sort of corrugated."

The cab proceeded down Park Avenue South, with its disturbingly narrow "parks."

"But, you know, there have been some real close calls, with both of them. And it's not only that. I have to remember which one I've said what to, and when all three of us are together, there's the chance that somebody is going to make a slip. I mean, usually it's only two people out of three, but here it's all of us! Then when I call for Sasha I get Allison, and of course I've got to give her some of the old okeydoke. 'Oh God, Allison, you are so beautiful.' And then she switches me to Sasha, and immediately I've got to go through it with her. 'Oh, God, Sasha, I just can't stop thinking about you, I think it's the backs of your knees . . .'" Jonathan looked over at Peter with a leer. "All true by the way," he said before continuing. "Then back to Allison to make the appointment, and I have to hope she won't be mooning when Sasha brings her something to type or some damn thing." He shook his head wearily. "Yep, it's hard. Especially with Mags, too, you know, that chick from the fancy soup place? Old Maggie Mae. Catholic girls. Jesus. There's nothing like seeing the crucifix bouncing around their collarbone. Sometimes she clenches it in her teeth."

All the while that Jonathan spoke, Peter had been staring at a tear in the back of the taxi's front seat. It was vaguely K-shaped and had been covered with dark red tape, a shade lighter than the rubbery purplish seat back itself. The edges of the tape were gummy and dirty. The cab, making the usual sudden starts and stops, jounced Peter around, but he kept staring at this cicatrix. His brow and lips and nose and chin were all shut up like a drawstring pouch. He really had no thoughts about what he was hearing, or rather his many thoughts formed an undifferentiated, scowling black cloud in his mind. It was all disgusting and infuriating. This was not because, in general, Peter was puritanical about such activities as Jonathan described. Over the years, he had listened to his friend's accounts again and again, and while they were often repellent, Peter could not help but find it fun and exciting to hear them, and to admire Jonathan in the way that all men, in truth, admire another's promiscuity.

For some time, though, Peter's reaction had been more judgmental when Jonathan talked like this. "I don't suppose," he said finally, "that the fact that you're married makes it any more complicated."

Jonathan said nothing for a moment and then looked over at Peter with a kind, condescending expression. "Ah, Peter," he said. "When you're older, you'll understand these things better."

Peter continued to study the ill-repaired gash.

"Don't sweat it, old sport," Jonathan said, putting his hand on Peter's shoulder. "Nothing's going to happen. Nobody's going to get hurt." He laughed. "I'm going to be sent to hell, is all."

~

Peter and Jonathan entered the restaurant. It was small and crowded, with stark décor and very large windows.

"You are the first to arrive," the maître d' said. "Would you like to sit at the bar, or shall I escort you to your table?"

They went to the table and ordered drinks, a martini for Jonathan and a beer for Peter. Jonathan asked for the wine list, and as he studied it he made a running commentary. Sipping his beer, Peter began to undergo the physiological changes that he always experienced when he was anticipating the appearance of Jonathan's wife: his heart began to pound, his arteries throbbed, he felt pressure in the hollows of his hands, he swallowed several times, his stomach did flips. He imagined that he would feel the same way just before his first skydiving lesson. What was ridiculous was that he had been in this situation a thousand times, so it made no sense to still have these reactions.

"Incredible," Jonathan was muttering, "two hundred bucks for that piece of crap." In restaurants like this, he always ordered the cheapest wine, and it gave him a nice feeling of satisfaction to see what the suckers were buying. As Jonathan spoke, Peter was looking toward the door. He could see the maître d's back, partially obscured, and the top quarter of the door. The door opened, and Peter caught a glimpse of blond hair. His heart leapt into his throat. She had arrived. He could see the maître d' lean forward to talk to her, and nod, and then turn and lead her toward the table. As she walked behind the maître d', Peter saw a part of her face, her shoulder, her arm.

"Here you are, miss," the maître d' said, stepping aside. "Gentlemen, the other member of your party has arrived."

She was wearing a pale green sundress; the color brought out her green eyes. Her long brown arms were bare, and she had her hair pinned up, exposing all of her long brown neck. She was not necessarily the most stunning woman in the restaurant; she was not someone who would cause a stir just by walking in. But she was so pretty. Her reddish blond hair was thick and sleek, although exhibiting a little frizz on this muggy June night. The green eyes were large and set far apart and her jawbone made a beautiful curve from her ear to her chin; her nose had a delicate little knob at the tip. She was on the tall side and nicely formed, slender without noticeable hips (unless one made a point of noticing them), with fine shoulders, wide, level, smooth, rounded. Her collarbones looked like arrow shafts.

She was smiling and she looked flushed and bright-eyed from having hurried to arrive without being too late, and from the pleasure of seeing them both.

"Hello, boys," she said.

Jonathan and Peter stood up.

"Hello, luv," said Jonathan. They hugged and kissed, more than just a token public peck.

"Hi, Holly!"

She gave Peter a kiss on the cheek, and in returning it Peter had to put his hands on her bare shoulders.

As they settled into their seats, Holly apologized for being late ("It took me longer to get ready than I expected"; she and Jonathan exchanged conjugal looks, mock sheepishness on her part, mock exasperation on his), and she told Peter that it was so nice to see him but that she was so sorry Charlotte couldn't come.

"She was really sorry to miss you both," Peter said.

"Well, say hello to her for me, will you?" said Holly. She ordered a glass of wine. "Oh, Peter, weren't you supposed to be giving some kind of presentation today?"

"Did I mention that?"

"Yes, I think so, when we were arranging dinner. I think you said that tonight would be good because you'd be done with that, or something."

"Oh."

"So how did it go?"

"I killed," Peter said.

"Really! That's great!"

"It wasn't a big deal at all."

"I'm glad it went so well," Holly said. "Jonathan, did you hear? Peter killed."

"Yes, I heard. Congratulations, Peter. What was it all about? Debentures?" Jonathan thought it was funny just to say the word "debentures."

"Oh, it was nothing worth talking about." Peter shook his head dismissively.

"Okay," said Holly, looking at Peter with a tiny frown.

"And how was the play?" Peter asked. Holly taught eighth- and ninth-grade Classics at a private girls' school, and she had helped with the eighth-grade play, which had been performed that night.

"It was wonderful!" Holly said. "The girls were great. They were so funny! The boys too. And boy, let me tell you, there is nothing quite as intense as a thirteen-year-old Hermia who really is in love with her Lysander."

The girls had performed *A Midsummer Night's Dream* with students from an all-boys' school. As the rehearsals progressed, complicated romantic dramas had, of course, arisen among members of the cast.

"Well," said Holly, nodding at Jonathan, "and how about Anton Pavlovich here? Did you see the review?"

"Oh God," Peter said. "Charlotte read only part of it to me. Don't tell me it made that comparison."

"It did. And I have to live with him."

"Please," said Jonathan, "you know me. Unworthy as I am to receive such praise, I accept it with the deepest humility and gratitude."

Holly asked about the reading. It went well, they told her.

"So we all have something to celebrate," she said, and they talked some more. Then the waiter came over and started describing the specials, ingredient by ingredient, and at about the third appetizer ("fava beans . . .") Peter's mind began to wander. It drifted back . . . back . . . back to that fateful night three years before . . .

~

After he graduated from college, Jonathan lived in a one-bedroom apartment far downtown, but then his stepfather died (as Jonathan's father had before him) and his mother inherited an apartment in a hotel on the Upper East Side. She and her husband had used it only on visits to the city, but she decided to keep it — more accurately, Jonathan convinced her to keep it — as an investment. While it appreciated, it only made sense for someone to live there — Jonathan, say. He could not afford the monthly maintenance, so she handled that as well as the room service charges, which the hotel simply sent her as a matter of course. The apartment consisted of a bedroom, a library, a dining room, a sitting room, and a kitchen (which saw little use). Meanwhile, Jonathan kept his old place to use as an office (and it didn't hurt his social life to have some geographical diversity). It was from these precincts that his tales of human struggle issued forth.

One day Jonathan called Peter and said that he was having a few people over that night and that Peter should come. It was an invitation Peter readily accepted, for the people Jonathan had over were usually women whom Peter found very attractive; of course they were pretty, but they were also either smart or a little tragic or rich or minor geniuses at something or other — or all of these. Beautiful, taken-seriously painters who came into a vast fortune as infants when their parents were murdered, these were Jonathan's specialty. Moreover, at Jonathan's, a fume of amorousness always hung in the air, and, so, well, who knows?

"Sure," Peter said. "What time?"

"Around ten or whenever."

"What can I bring?"

"Just your fascinating self, that'll be fine."

Peter asked who was going to be there and Jonathan mentioned a few names. "Oh, yeah," he said, "and this girl I met at a campus thing." A prestigious university had invited Jonathan to spend a term in residence. "We've kind of been hanging out a lot together up there."

"Uh-huh."

Jonathan paused for a moment before continuing. "I've got to say, she's, well, she's kind of fantastic, actually."

"She is."

"Yeah, she is."

"So what's her name?"

"Holly."

Holly.

Peter reacted with a start. His heart began to pound and he flushed. Four years before he had sat next to a girl named Holly on a long airline flight and had fallen deeply in love with her; he had lost her phone number and had never seen her again, but he had thought about her hourly ever since. But what were the chances that Jonathan's Holly and Peter's Holly were the same person? He wanted to ask Jonathan more about her. But it was crazy. There were a million Hollys in the world.

Jonathan's apartment was already crowded when Peter arrived. How glossy everyone always looked at parties there, how loud and vibrant was the cacophonous talk. Peter got a drink and chatted with some people, and then he looked around for Jonathan. He found him easily, for he was sitting on the sofa in the living room. A young woman sat next to him, and she and Jonathan were holding hands. It was the young woman whom Peter had met on the plane. She looked almost exactly the same, except that her hair was shorter. The sight of her stunned Peter, knocking the wind out of him.

He needed a moment to recover, but Jonathan had seen him and waved him over. The introduction. Exclamations. We've met before! You have? Yes, years ago on a plane. How amazing! Holly was excited and very friendly, but Peter felt nothing but despair, for she gave no indication that she had spent every waking moment since their parting thinking about him. She was wearing a rather low-cut silk blouse and extremely narrow black pants with a faint chalk stripe. She looked fantastic.

Peter and Holly told Jonathan their story. They had bonded over Thomas Mann, of all things! Then their narrative petered out.

"Well, so," Jonathan asked, "you never saw each other after that?"

Peter took Jonathan's question to be a challenge. Of course, any halfway competent male who flew across the continent sitting next to a young woman like Holly would have managed to get her phone number. Peter felt compelled to stake his own claim to Holly, to show Jonathan that he had not failed in this respect, and to make sure Holly knew what had happened, whether she cared or not. True, in achieving these aims, he would make himself look idiotic, but that was not too high a price to pay.

"Actually," he said, "we were going to see each other again. Holly wrote her number on a piece of paper, and we were going to have dinner." To identify the piece of paper would be to give Jonathan too intimate a detail, Peter thought. "But . . . uh . . . well . . ." He paused, turning red. "Well, I actually lost the piece of paper."

"You lost it!" said Holly. She put her hand on Peter's arm. "You *lost* it! I always assumed that you just blew me off!"

"Oh no!" Peter said. In his solipsism, it had never occurred to him that Holly might have been hurt. "I lost the number. I know, it was a fairly idiotic thing to do. I was at my hotel, and it was gone. I looked everywhere," Peter said, "but somehow or other, the thing just disappeared."

"How kind of too bad," Holly said. Her tone and expression reflected a touch of spontaneous warmth toward him that had thus far been lacking.

"I sure thought so!" said Peter.

"I bet you did!" said Jonathan.

They all laughed a little.

Jonathan had been observing the others closely. Now he smiled at both with affection. "What a close call for me!" he said. "If it had been different, then, well, who knows what might have happened? And maybe we would all be sitting here together, but it would all be . . . different." His tone was mild, sweet, humorous, even a wee bit vulnerable. "I'm pretty lucky that Peter chose that moment to be fairly idiotic. It might be hard to believe, Holly, but that was actually out of character for him."

Holly laughed and squeezed Jonathan's hand. No spoilsport, Peter laughed too. He and Holly exchanged a glance, and then some other guests approached, and the party's momentum swept them all away. For the rest of the night, Peter sought out Holly, trying to have a private moment with her, but for some reason this opportunity was always denied him.

One evening shortly after Peter had met Holly again, he received some further information about her attitude toward the Lost Phone Number. Holly was out and Peter was having a drink in Jonathan's apartment before going to dinner. Waiting for a call from some other friends, Peter watched a hockey game and Jonathan corrected a proof.

"Hey," Jonathan said, without looking up from the page, "did you know that Holly really got a crush on you that time when you sat next to each other on the plane?"

Trying to remain as cool as possible, Peter took a sip of his beer and continued to watch the Devils' power play. "Really?" he said.

"Yeah," said Jonathan. He scrawled a couple of words in the margin and continued to work as he talked. "Yeah. We were talking about it, and that's what she told me. So naturally it got me concerned and I said, 'So what about now?' She laughed. She said, 'You're jealous over somebody I sat next to on a plane years ago? Are you crazy?' I guess it did sound pretty silly. Oh hell!" Jonathan drummed his pencil on the paper and then made an erasure. "Anyway, she told me not to worry. 'You know how those things go,' she said, 'you meet somebody someplace with some kind of forced intimacy and you think there's been some magic, and then two days later you've forgotten all about them.' It's interesting. That's really true, don't you think?" He whispered aloud a few words of his text and made a change. "Well, also she said that, you know, you're such a nice guy that she bet you felt bad about not calling, but actually it was a relief that you didn't. She had gotten so wrapped up in the baby, you can imagine, and there was the whole scene with her father and her sister, and then her mother coming. She didn't know what she would have done if you had." He crossed out a couple of words. "So anyway, phew. I wouldn't want to have had to shoot you." He teethed on his pencil, reclined in his chair, and held the proof up, frowning at it.

This account had the unmistakable ring of truth, although Peter wished desperately that he could convince himself Jonathan was making it all up. But why would he bother? He had Holly. Also, Peter couldn't remember a time when Jonathan had lied to him. Indeed, Jonathan had his own code of honor and rarely outright *lied* to any of his friends, not even to the women he was involved with; it was almost a principle, and it was part of the game, to juggle them without resorting to sheer mendacity.

She laughed. Really nothing Jonathan had said had surprised Peter. Still, he felt heartsick. The Devils' pusillanimous line had barely managed to get off a shot before the two sides evened up. Peter drank again from his beer and continued staring at the TV. "Oh, yeah," he said, "we had a lot of fun talking on that flight. Holly's great."

~

Peter saw very little of Jonathan and Holly over the following several weeks. She was getting a master's degree in Classics at the university where Jonathan had his fellowship, and he virtually moved in with her as she finished. When they came to the city, Jonathan did not include Peter in their activities. Uncharacteristically, Jonathan rarely came to the city by himself, and he seemed to be devoting all his attention (within reason) to Holly alone. This time, it seemed to be serious. Holly had a thesis topic she was quite excited about (Horace, "authority"), but did she really want to be an academic? Jonathan was urging her to move to New York, and when Holly learned about a last-minute opening at an excellent girls' school she applied and was hired. After a summer of travel, she and Jonathan established themselves in his apartment. Having seen Holly so rarely, Peter had not had much chance to return to the subject of their first meeting, and as time passed it felt more and more as if it would be awkward and strange to bring it up.

The thing between Jonathan and Holly was serious. After living together for a while, they were married. Peter and Holly had become quite good friends, but they never discussed their first meeting again. Peter had watched and waited — foolishly, he knew — and then he'd given up.

~

Peter had eaten his appetizer without taking any notice of it; he could not have told anyone what it was. Holly was saying something to him, but he hadn't answered.

"Peter?"

"Oh sorry. What was it you said?"

"You seem to be a million miles away. Thinking about the big day?" Holly said this with the smile of a female friend who is indulgent of a man's dread of his own wedding.

"Oh, no, actually. But I should be. There's a crisis about the cheese."

"Oh God!" Holly cried. "How horrible! I suppose Charlotte and her mother are treating it like the Algerian civil war."

"Basically, yeah. Torture, assassination, the whole bit."

"I guess I was lucky. My mother sat back and sort of vaguely watched everything happen. 'That sounds lovely, dear' was all she ever said. The only problem was that she easily could have forgotten the date and set off that day to buy a butterfly collection, or something else she had suddenly decided was a necessity."

"She certainly looked beautiful," Peter said.

"Well, she couldn't help that." Holly looked at Peter sympathetically. "I hope your nerves hold out for the next couple of weeks."

"Me, too."

Holly turned to Jonathan. "And as for you, you know your job, right? You do for Peter what he did for you: make sure he shows up."

"Don't worry about that," said Jonathan. "He'll show up. Even if it's at gunpoint."

~

The following morning Mac McClernand's secretary called Peter to say that Mr. McClernand would like to see him "ay-sap." After hanging up Peter stared at the phone. Maybe he should just resign right then and there. He could have a new job in a day! But . . . but . . . Beeche was where he wanted to work and he had come pretty far, and if he quit, Thropp would win. Peter had told his father about the situation, and he had laughed. "A boss who's a son-of-a-bitch, a real son-of-a-bitch!" he had said. "Welcome to the club." Peter's father had begun his career working for an industrial pipe manufacturer, and he had risen fairly high in the company that had bought the company that had bought that one. He was canny and levelheaded about these things, and he advised Peter not to quit or to go at Thropp directly, but to figure out whose team he wanted to be on and do everything he could to convince that person that he was indispensable to him or her and that he or she had to steal him away from Thropp. Otherwise, he should sit tight. Some employers value loyalty, and this trial would pass. That was all very sound, but didn't it reflect an old-fashioned corporate mentality that ill suited today's buccaneering, fast-paced securities industry, where patience and loyalty lasted only as long as it took for the bonus check to clear? Actually, at Beeche patience and loyalty were often well rewarded, and the culture discouraged self-serving intrigue, although the firm still had its Thropps. It was a class operation, as people liked to say. So, okay, he'd overcome other challenges, it was just a matter of bearing down, enduring this one and learning as much from it as he could.

Okay! All right! Let's do it! With his confidence and optimism renewed by this self-administered pregame pep talk, Peter set off to find McClernand's office. This was more difficult than he'd expected, even taking into account the size of the Beeche Building. He went up and down and up again in a couple of elevator banks until he finally reached the wing and floor that he thought were the right ones. Stepping out of the elevator, Peter found that there was no security desk or departmental receptionist, just a pair of glass doors at one end of a vestibule. He approached them and saw that the device that read identification cards had a yellowing, handwritten sign over it: OUT OF ORDER PLEAS CALL SECURITY. He noticed that one door was open a crack, and he tried it; it swung open easily — its lock and latch were broken. He walked along a corridor and in one office saw desks and chairs stacked up. In another, computer monitors lay strewn on the floor.

Peter followed the office numbers until he found the right one. The door was open, and he peered inside and saw a woman with her head bent over her desk; he knocked, and the woman looked up, saying, "Oh! It's you! We've been expecting you! Please come in!"

Peter entered and the woman quickly rose to greet him. She was full-figured and in her fifties, with brassy red hair, black eyebrows, and one discolored front tooth. She made every utterance with great enthusiasm.

"You're Mr. Russell, aren't you?!"

"That's right."

"I'm Sheila, Mr. McClernand's secretary!"

"How do you do, Sheila?"

They shook hands.

"Very nice to meet you! I'm so glad you're here! Now, just have a seat, and I'll tell Mr. McClernand!"

Peter sat. He had noticed that she had been working on a crossword puzzle and now he saw that well-worn books of crosswords and brainteasers were piled on her desk.

"Mr. McClernand?! Mr. Russell is here to see you!" A pause. "Yes, sir! I'll tell him!" Sheila hung up the phone. "He'll be with you in just a few minutes!" She smiled brightly at Peter, as if she had delivered the most exciting news. And then she returned to her crossword.

Peter waited. The only sounds came from the occasional scratch of Sheila's pencil and the white hum of the air handlers. Time passed. No one popped his head in the door to have a word with Mac. The phone did not ring, and no lights shone to indicate that any lines were engaged. Sheila's pencil made a skittering noise, like a small reptile running across the sand. After what seemed like a long time, the door to the inner office did suddenly open, very loudly, and, preceded by a waft of "masculine" scent, there appeared Mac McClernand.

"Well, well!" he said, smiling broadly and holding out his hand. "Peter Russell! Sorry to keep you waiting. Got hung up on a couple of things." He cocked his head toward the ceiling with a smirk. "Sixty-eight. You know how it is." Sixty-eight was a floor where some of the biggest big shots had their offices.

Peter rose and shook McClernand's hand.

"How do you do?" he said.

"Fine, fine. I'll just be one more minute." McClernand spoke sharply to Sheila. "Sheila, did we get that packet out?"

Sheila had not been listening.

"Sheila, did we get that packet out?"

Sheila heard this time and looked up with an expression of shock and bewilderment. "The packet . . . ?" she said. "The pack — ? Oh! The packet! Yes, sir! It's being messengered!"

"Good," McClernand said. "And you've moved my breakfast with Erlanger to Wednesday, right?"

"Yes, sir! All taken care of!"

"Okay! Well, Peter, please, come on in."

McClernand put his hand on Peter's back and guided him through the door, then turned to Sheila. "Move my five o'clock back to five-thirty," he said. "Oh — and hold my calls."

Mac McClernand was in his sixties. He had an egg-shaped body, and his pants, held up by suspenders, rode at the latitude of greatest circumference. Freckles covered his hands and face, and his flesh tone was taupe. His furzelike hair seemed to hover above his scalp, and Peter could not determine whether that was because of its natural buoyancy, or because it was a comb-over, or because it was fake.

They had sat, and McClernand was leaning far back in his desk chair and looking at Peter so that his chin and jaw disappeared in folds of flesh. His hands were clasped, except for his index fingers, which were extended together; studying Peter, he tapped his mouth with their tips.

"So. Peter," he said finally. "I guess we're going to do a little work together."

"Yes, sir."

"I hear good things about you. You've made quite a name for yourself."

"Thank you, sir."

"Of course, they only send me the best." McClernand laughed, baring his grayish teeth. Presently his laugh turned into a phlegmy, wheezing, racking cough. He covered his mouth with a handkerchief and bent over, coughing so long and hard that his face turned red and his eyes teared.

Peter half rose from his seat. "Are you okay?"

"Fine, fine," McClernand said in a stage whisper. After a moment or two he brought the eruptions under control, took a gulp from a glass of water, and wiped his brow and eyes.

"Harrumm. Harrumrummrum. Damn allergies. So where were we? Oh yes. Yes, I've been told damn good things about you."

"I'm certainly glad to hear that."

McClernand smiled a bit devilishly.

"But," he said, "but . . . I guess maybe you took a knock with that new idea of yours."

"It was very preliminary."

Holding up his hand, McClernand knit his brow and pursed his lips and nodded. "Oh, I know, I know. It was very preliminary, just something to kick around. Of course." He chuckled and shook his head. "But still, I guess they figured it wouldn't do you any harm to buddy up with an old bastard who's seen a thing or two in his time, eh?"

"Yes."

As he looked at Peter, McClernand's expression softened, becoming almost paternal. He nodded his head slowly. "You know," he said, "you remind me of myself when I was just coming along."

Oh God! Peter almost blurted out. "Really?"

"Yes, yes indeed," McClernand said. He beamed at Peter. He made a mumbly-grumbly noise. Then he clapped his hands, rubbed them together, and said, "Okay, then. Let's get to work."

He swiveled in his chair and lifted an object off a shelf. Then, holding it with care between his hands, he gently set it down on his desk. He adjusted it fussily so that it was parallel to the desk's edge. Then he took his hands away slowly, as if it were carefully balanced. He had been mumbly-grumbling throughout this operation, but now, leaning back in his chair, he stopped and sighed. He gestured to the object with an open hand, smiling. "Peter," he said, "what do you see in front of you?"

It was a breakfast-cereal box.

Peter was unsure of what to say. There didn't seem to be many alternatives. "A breakfast-cereal box?"

"Ha!" McClernand said. "Not a wrong answer. But not the right one either. Look again. Tell me what you see."

What Peter saw was a breakfast-cereal box.

"I . . . I don't know," he said. He smiled. He was a good sport! "I give up!" he said brightly.

McClernand nodded. "I'll tell you what that is," he said. And then he leaned forward, fixed his eyes on Peter, and said in a low voice, "It's money." Then he leaned back in his chair again, still looking at Peter but now with his former devilish grin.

Money. Right. Yet there was nothing to do but carry on. "Money?" Peter asked. "How so?"

"Pick up the box and tell me what it says on the top flap."

Peter picked up the box. "'May fight heart disease.'"

"No! Not that! Further over on the side."

"Well, there's a thing here. It says that the company will give your school ten cents for every one of these coupons you send in."

"Very good," said McClernand. He stood up and began to pace behind his desk. "I suppose I would be correct in saying that in many cases you can send the cereal manufacturer some box tops and receive a toy in return, wouldn't I?"

"Yes."

"Excellent. Peter, let's think a little about that coupon. It's just a piece of paper, isn't it? Now, what —"

"Cardboard, actually."

"All right, cardboard," McClernand said with a look of annoyance. "Now, what happens when you send this piece of cardboard to the cereal manufacturer? The manufacturer gives something of value to you, or rather, in certain cases, to a third party as directed by you. Are you with me so far?"

"Yes."

"Good. Tell me, the piece of paper — or rather, cardboard — does it have any intrinsic value?"

"No."

"But it represents a claim on an asset, doesn't it?"

"Yes."

"Well, what does that sound like?" McClernand, still pacing, was taking great pleasure in this use of the Socratic method.

"A stock certificate, a bond, any security, really."

"Bingo!" McClernand said. "Just think, Peter, there are millions upon millions of boxes of cereal sitting in kitchen cupboards or closets or on kitchen counters at this very moment, each one with a top — a top that is not doing anything for anybody. People don't want to bother to redeem their box tops. They don't want the toy, or they don't care enough about their school.

"What if those very same box tops could be sold for cash? Eh? Do you see where I'm going? If someone could sell a ten-cent box top for five cents, and a school could buy it for five cents and redeem it for ten cents, wouldn't everyone come out ahead? Or if you needed twelve box tops for a toy, you could buy them for cash, rather than spending the money to buy the extra cereal boxes. You see, don't you?

"But first, there has to be a box-top market. To create that market somebody has to act as an intermediary. And do you know who that's going to be? Beeche and Company. And then, once the market is launched and flourishing, the paper will begin to trade on its own, as an investment or speculation. Think of the volume! With the firm taking a little bit on either side, the profits will be phenomenal!

"Of course, there are all sorts of challenges and uncertainties — the Internet auction people; taxes; regs; there's an option aspect, since most cereal box tops expire; and so forth. But that's where you come in, laddie." McClernand smiled at Peter with pride and affection. Then his expression slowly changed to one of mystical transport.

"So," he said quietly, "that's the idea. But we aren't stopping there. No. No. We aren't stopping there."

Peter had had a feeling that they weren't stopping there. The worst thing about all this, he thought, was that he must have sounded just like McClernand to everyone at Thropp's meeting. Maybe they did belong together.

"It won't be long," McClernand was saying, "before banks start to accept cereal box tops for deposit and to make loans accordingly. Securities firms will allow you to write checks based on your holdings. The same way people used discounted paper in the past as money, they'll start using box tops. You know what will happen, don't you?" He didn't wait for a reply. "The Fed isn't going to stand back and lose control of the money supply. So they'll want to step in." McClernand smiled quiveringly at Peter and continued in almost a whisper.

"It's only a matter of time before the dollar goes completely in the tank. Everybody knows that the euro is a piece of crap. So you see? You see? The world is going to need a new reserve currency. Gold?" He let out a braying laugh and exclaimed, "*Gold?* Pathetic! No. No! The cereal box top!"

Then his voice grew soft again and even more intense. "All this time, while we are making a market in them, we are slowly accumulating and accumulating and accumulating, so when it all comes together, who will have amassed holdings of cereal box tops that are greater than even those of the United States government? Us, Peter, us! Beeche and Company!" McClernand closed his eyes for a moment of silent meditation, then popped them open with a big grin. "Quite a play, isn't it?"

"Yes, sir," said Peter.

3

*H*aving depressed the appropriate keys and pedals with all his strength, the organist suddenly removed, respectively, his fingers and his feet from them, and his instrument fell mute. The last fortissimo chord of the prelude expanded and refracted in every direction, overlapping itself, shifting its shape and color, until it finally decayed into silence, a silence so deep that it seemed as if the mighty blast had permanently driven all sound from the church. Yet, to Peter, at least, standing in the transept, that silence itself reverberated with one low tone, the sound of one's own existence, of a windless wood, of the Marabar Caves.

Within seconds, the organ would begin to play again, and the bridesmaids and ushers, and then the flower girls, and finally the bride and her father, would begin their slow march, out of time and out of step, and approach Peter more and more closely. Then they would arrange themselves on either side, and her father would hand Charlotte off. Then they would have the ceremony. And then it would be over. Peter was about to take the most important action of his life. Staring down the aisle, with Charlotte's and his families and all their friends fuzzily crowding his peripheral vision, he tried to smile, as he thought he ought to do.

The ceremony was taking place on the North Shore of Long Island. The day was muggy; the church was hot. Peter felt uncomfortable in his rented cutaway, pants, waistcoat, tie, and shoes. His discomfort was both physical and mental. The costume was silly, he thought. Rented, it was by definition a contrivance. Rented shoes! He was participating in this most personally profound event while wearing rented shoes? Meanwhile, the shirtsleeves were too short. In dignity and dress, Peter believed he compared quite unfavorably to the officiant, who stood to his right. Reverend Mickle-thwaite looked awfully good in his surplice and gold-embroidered stole. He was a handsome, robust man in his sixties with a full head of steel gray hair and weathered hands. From what Peter had gathered during premarital counseling, it was pretty clear that Reverend Micklethwaite had spent a good deal more time thinking about the gauge of his spinnaker sheets than about the doctrine of the Real Presence. He stood there beaming, aglow with vitality and optimism.

Then, on Peter's other side, stood Jonathan. He wore his own morning coat and almost gaudy waistcoat, bought, he had explained, because he had been going to so many weddings in England. If Peter had worn that waistcoat, he would have looked moronic, but on Jonathan it had flair. The coat hung beautifully on Jonathan's long frame, and it was very smart. Jonathan managed to look both more trig and less stiff than Peter. So attired and with his long brown curls brushed but still giving the hint of disorder, Jonathan might have been the hero of a nineteenth-century romance.

As Peter stared down the aisle, he was aware of one blurry dot on his left, but he was determined not to look over there. Earlier, he had noted Holly's place, three rows back on the groom's side. He had studied her while pretending to aimlessly survey the congregation. But he would not look again. He would not! Especially at this of all moments. Of course, his effort at self-control failed. He could not help himself, and he slid his eyes over for one last glance. She was looking at him and smiling. A thousand suns. In her smile there was affection and a tiny mock suggestion of pity. Peter could not help but think that of all the people in the church, including the members of the Holy Trinity, the two who were in closest communion were Holly and he. Today, with her hair up and wearing more makeup than usual — her red lipstick was a darker shade and more thickly laid on, as was appropriate for a formal, "lipsticky" occasion — and with the added color induced by the drama of a wedding and in the handsome setting, which became her, she looked especially beautiful. Yet this was as nothing compared with the beauty of her soul. Balanced, graceful, funny, and kind. If there was a Holy Trinity, Peter was quite sure that as they looked down on her they sighed with approbation. He loved her. He loved her. But she would never be his. But she would never be his.

The organ sounded. Peter felt Jonathan's hand on his back.

"Here we go," Jonathan whispered. "Whatever you do, don't laugh." Hearing this, Peter laughed.

The bridesmaids and ushers began their approach, the former galumphing and the latter shambling like hungover zombies. Here were the flower girls, dropping petals with solemn care. They made Peter smile. After them, the bride herself, on her father's arm. She was beaming and her face was flushed. She wore a simple dress; it had some kind of beads on it. She was very, very happy. A woman on her wedding day. Peter thought she really did look wonderful. Her father released her and stepped back. She looked at Peter with excitement, joy, love, and . . . what? Trust: she was safe. He smiled at her, and there was love in that smile. It would be fine.

"We are gathered here in the sight of God," Reverend Mickle-thwaite proclaimed in his luscious baritone.

It would be fine.

~

As he led his daughter down the aisle, Dick Montague had reason to feel well pleased with himself, not that he ever really needed a reason. He had had a new morning coat built for the occasion, and he did look very fine. He was about six feet tall, and he had a face that was ruddy with health and prosperity and thick light brown hair that he held aloft like a pennon. He was paying for the wedding and everything was being done just right, without ostentation but with evident expense. In fact, he had had nothing to do with the planning — his former wife handled all that — except to upgrade the wines, but the effect would redound to him.

It would be a better dinner than the one the night before, given by the groom's parents. They had hired out at a restaurant, quite a nice restaurant, but the waiters were a little too evangelistic with the water pitchers and they scraped food onto plates as they were clearing. Indifferent food, and as for wine, borderline plonk. Of course, the Russells were at a disadvantage, as parents of the groom always are when they are from a different town. They were nice, nondescript people. The father was an executive with a big company, Dick could not remember which one. While not particularly old, he had thinned-out white hair and a face with lots of lines going in different directions. The wife was very pleasant; today she wore a coral suit. Dick's toast had gone off well, rather better than anyone else's, in fact (somehow, in thanking the Russells for the dinner, Dick had managed to work in his own ancestors). He and his wife, Julia, had gone back to the city for the night and returned this afternoon.

That had caused some friction with Charlotte's mother, Janet, who was annoyed that he would not be "on hand." As he looked up the aisle, he could see Janet sitting thirty inches away from his current wife. In her pale blue dress, Janet looked thick around the shoulder blades, but it thrilled Dick to see the back of Julia's neck. Julia never gave any trouble over this sort of thing, and Janet had too much pride to make a fuss, so there had been immediate agreement on where the stepmother would sit, but Dick knew that sharing the pew with Julia, as was customary, would make Janet livid. Of course, it was often difficult dealing with his ex-wife, and an occasion like this wedding — the first of any of their children — meant they had to reconstitute the family like some ersatz beef product. There was tension. The divorce had all been very painful for everyone. Or anyway, that's what Dick said to himself. He had simply not been able to feel too bad about it either at the time or later. Julia had played an instrumental part in the breakup.

As awkward as it sometimes was, when Dick had to talk to his former wife or see her or hear about her, it usually gave him satisfaction. Every time that she tried to get the better of him or hold her own or stand on her dignity, he secretly gloated. The same was true when he heard about her divorcée life, the interior decorating and trips with friends (the fjords, St. Petersburg). She had thick, green, leaf-shaped objects in her divorcée house. How did these things appear, like mushrooms after a thunderstorm? There were occasional "boyfriends." How basically pathetic to be a grown-up woman and to have to have "boyfriends" and worry about the phone ringing. She made some false starts at marrying again, and each one ended in a mild humiliation. It was quite simple: Dick had won.

As for his children, he had vanquished them, too. In addition to Charlotte, there were two others, both younger, David and Deirdre. David was a groomsman, and Charlotte had dutifully made Deirdre her maid of honor. Dick had not crushed them completely, but it was understood that he could. Each one felt like a mouse caught in his fist. At bottom, he liked that too. Charlotte was a bit tiresome. In fact, she bored him to tears. She was the kind of person who wanted to win over her stepmother, instead of saying, "That harlot destroyed my family (such as it was), I despise her, if I see her I will spit upon her." No, Charlotte thought she should be worldly about it all and that she and Julia should be "friends." So she would invite Julia to lunch. Julia was a good sport and had lunch with her now and then, and they were "friends." They would talk about clothes — Charlotte went through phases at overreaching to be chic — and Julia liked clothes, but Charlotte would talk about them in such a charmless, methodical way that, as Julia put it, she sounded as if she were preparing for her A levels.

There was the son, David. Drugs. The terror and work associated with this fell almost entirely to Janet. The worry about the call in the middle of the night was hers, the visits to the emergency room, all the lies. The scenes in the kitchen — the smell of sautéed garlic (Janet was something of a cook) and Janet's screaming, "How could you do this?!" Oh, how she loved her son, though, and how he could make her laugh, and how much better company he was than her daughters. She had seen the scabs, bruises, and thick purple lines running down his arms. This was on the hairless inner side of the arms, the soft pale paths her fingers had walked up when he was a little boy. What could she do? How could she stop him? What did they say in those meetings? She couldn't stop him. It was his self-esteem, and the divorce . . . But to Dick, in an odd way, David seemed most vital in his pursuit of his drug avocation. He had never been particularly focused or accomplished, had never had very much drive; he was a bookish, indolent, dreamy, nervous boy who drew girls to him but who was unfit and a poor athlete.

He certainly had drive now. Still, the fact remained that David was a fairly pointless piece of protoplasm. This gave Dick subconscious satisfaction: he had won. It was all very well for men to talk about how eager they were for their sons to make a success of themselves, how much more it meant than their own success, how tickled they were by the idea of a son entering the firm. Bullshit. Wives and sons: they were the ones who would plot against you, either separately or in treacherous alliance, and if they did, they must be put down, ruthlessly if necessary, all the villages burnt.

Finally, Deirdre. She had freckles and a round face, but she was quite pretty (of all the siblings, David was the best-looking). Deirdre had always had trouble in school. She was dyslexic, and even though they were always reassured that dyslexia has nothing to do with intelligence and that lots of kids who suffer from it are superbright, Dick was always amazed at her ignorance and primitive methods of analysis. Her mind seemed like a map with vast areas left blank. "Pearl Harbor — that was World War I, right?" She loved animals and had a knack for working with horses and dogs, which her parents hoped would turn into something. Dick liked her more than his other children, quite a bit more. She wasn't like Charlotte, bringing her tiresome friends from Paris to his house in the countryside, speaking her pedantic idiomatic French and always trying to act so grown-up; or like David, with his problems and sarcasm. "Hi, Dad," Deirdre would say, whereas Charlotte called him "Father" or "Papa" with the accent on the second syllable and David didn't call him anything.

Dick was now married to a woman nineteen years younger than he. She was much prettier than his first wife had ever been, and she was very clever about — about everything, really, but particularly about clothes and furniture and silver and so on. His wife made him happy. That morning they had almost made love, but there hadn't been enough time. Then they had had a good early lunch in town with some friends. Dick could still taste the wine and the crispy artichokes. In the afternoon, when they arrived in their suite at the club where the reception would be held, he suddenly became ravenous and ordered a grilled ham and cheese sandwich, some coffee, and chocolates. In his dressing gown, he ate his sandwich, which was delicious (the frizzled crusty corners tucked up in just the right nooks of his belly), and drank the coffee; he ate some chocolate. His wife drank coffee and nibbled on a piece of chocolate. She was wearing a slip, and Dick thought how nice it would be to work his fingers up her inner thigh. Grasping her slender forearm, he drew her to him; but once again there was no time; she had to attend to her hair.

Here is what Dick Montague was thinking as he escorted his elder daughter down the aisle. He was thinking about the poppies in a painting he was working on and about a young woman in London whose lips had within recent weeks found themselves girdling his copulatory organ. He was thinking about Julia's best friend, Anna, who was blond, big-boned, and athletic, not a dark, fine-featured chic type like his wife, and who was beautiful and neurotic about men. One of Dick's greatest pleasures was to sit on the terrace of their house in France drinking the last wine of lunch and watching Julia and Anna talking intimately; with her loose, open-necked blouse settled against her freckled chest, Anna licked olive brine off her lips (she flirted with Dick and teased him, calling him *"cher maître"*). A possible weakness in a very complicated contract that was near completion kept nagging at him. The damn windows in the apartment. Also, there was a money thing, an awkward situation.

Then — of course — he was thinking about the event unfolding before him and his surroundings. He was happy for Charlotte. She looked good and she was excited. The night before, as the dinner was breaking up (and while Julia stood patiently off to one side), he had taken Charlotte's hands and looked at her and said, "So tomorrow is the big day. My little girl isn't going to be mine anymore. It doesn't seem so long ago that you were running around with that little pony of yours, Chestnut —"

"Peanut."

"Peanut. And now here you are. I know you are going to look beautiful tomorrow. Peter is a very fine man. I'm so proud of you. You seem very happy. That's all I've ever wanted. And I know that you and Peter will always be happy."

"Oh, Papa," Charlotte said. She threw her arms around him and pressed against his chest, wetting his tie with tears.

Dick held her; her body was shuddering.

"Oh, Papa, I am happy. Thank you so much for everything." Throughout this scene Dick thought he should say "I love you," but there didn't seem to be a good moment for that. And although Julia was standing nearby with perfect patience, he was conscious of keeping her waiting, so he thought he should conclude with Charlotte. That's what he wanted to do anyway. He put his hands on her shoulders and kissed her head. Then, almost imperceptibly, he shifted his pressure in the other direction, pushed her away gently, and took her hands. "Let's have another look at you." She wore an expectant expression that he could not bear to meet, so he smiled and looked at her in an unfocused way. "Beautiful girl," he said. They remained in this pose for a moment, as long as Dick believed was sufficient. Then he gave her another quick hug, and, with a minimum of violence, released her.

"Well!" he said. "Big day tomorrow! Good night, my dear."

"Good night, Papa."

"Try to get some rest."

He turned, and, with too quick a step, betraying that he felt he was making an escape, joined his wife.

Walking down the aisle with her now, Dick brimmed with pride. This was a mixture of fatherly pride and self-regard, for as he saw all the smiling people look at them, he had the impression that they were admiring him as much as Charlotte. He was looking well, although it was true that his middle had grown a shade thicker than he liked. He had to watch that and take some more exercise. Still, he thought about the silky claret and the fried artichokes at lunch and the grilled ham and cheese sandwich, the chocolate, and almost purred. He thought about his wife wearing her satiny slip, which revealed her shoulders and the smooth inside of her breast. He glanced up the aisle: in her suit she looked chic and shipshape. She had pinned her hair up so that it was as neat and tight as a flower bud (Janet had had her hair "done," balloon-style). There was something both orderly and vibrant about it all that made Julia particularly desirable; he wanted to tear off those clothes like the paper and ribbons of a crisply wrapped birthday present. Later that night, when all this was over and they were in their room, he would order some brandy . . .

Dick and Charlotte were approaching their destination. She was smiling broadly and crying a bit and trembling on his arm. Ahead of them stood Peter Russell, the man Charlotte would marry. He seemed like a decent fellow. By Dick's lights, indeed, he was ideal. The only real danger that daughters posed, in Dick's view, was that they might marry some fantastically successful young guy who would show him no respect. All he needed was to have some aggressive kid who was making a fortune ironically calling him "sir" all the time. And with a second serve like a bullet. At the same time, it mattered to Dick that his sons-in-law be suitable. Given these considerations, Charlotte had made an exemplary choice. This young man, Peter, was perfectly presentable. He worked for Beeche, the financial outfit, doing . . . in fact, Dick didn't exactly know what he did there. But he had a good well-paid professional job at a place everyone recognized. Peter was deferential. There had been a much older Frenchman with whom Charlotte had become involved, a dark, dramatic know-it-all bohemian from an ancient family. He would dominate the whole house with his restlessness, and, correcting Dick on some point of history or politics, he would be downright rude. Thank God he was gone. Peter was far from being that way. When he called Dick "sir," it was with unqualified courtesy.

Dick saw the row of bridesmaids, some of whom he vaguely recognized. One was a true knockout. Deirdre looked overweight in her dress; Dick had never seen her face so made up. It didn't suit her. Then the smiling minister. Dick had known these virile, confident churchmen, impossibly self-assured. The groom, looking quite nervous and sallow but smiling bravely. Ah, well. Poor bastard. He'd be moderately miserable for the next forty years, but he'd be okay. Next to Peter was his best man. A writer. Julia had sat next to him the previous night and had said he was "very interesting." He looked like a fruit. Then, stretching to Dick's right, the line of ushers, who, overall, were not too grotesque a sampling of youths. There was David, looking skeletal. At least he had cleaned up, even shaving, albeit patchily.

Now it was time to hand Charlotte off. He pressed one of her hands in both of his and gave her a smile, which she returned tremulously. Then he took a couple of steps back and awaited his cue to say, "Her mother and I do," after which he would withdraw to the front pew and sit between his wives. Janet would smile at him, as if to say, patronizingly, "Good job." But mixed with that smile would be detestation. As the mother of the bride, as the hostess of the big party to follow, as his ex-wife, she would be surrounded, despite her outward composure, by an invisible, agitated cloud of female anxiety, nostalgia, sentiment, bitterness, joy, envy. For the next forty-five minutes, he would be subject to all these emanations, and every time she moved, the scratchy noises made by the tulle or some damn thing she was wearing would irritate him. He would try to take solace in the calm, erect presence of Julia on his left. She would look perfect and act perfectly, he knew, throughout this whole — ordeal. He could not wait until it was all over and they were alone, and he would dishevel her. How satisfying that she belonged to him.

~

"Oh, Peter, you looked so handsome up there, and she is such a lovely girl. We're so happy for you."

"Thank you, Mrs. Matthews. Charlotte and I are so happy you could come."

"Well, Peter, so it's life without parole, is it?"

"Oh, Dan!"

"It's not so bad, son. Food's decent, and sometimes they let you out for an hour, you know, have a walk around the prison yard."

"Oh, Dan!"

Peter laughed appropriately. "Great to see you, Mr. Matthews. Thanks for coming." They were friends of his parents. The wife was short and thin; the husband was short and stout, with a red face. He had gripped Peter's hand so hard as to cause him pain. They had a son whom Peter used to smoke pot with; he now ran a landscaping business.

Everything had gone well. They had heard a reading from Colossians. Reverend Micklethwaite had given a brief sermon ("I always tell the bride and groom not even to bother listening, because they'll never remember a word of it anyway"). They had said their vows. Charlotte had had a catch in her voice. Jonathan had proffered the ring at the right moment and Peter had slipped it on Charlotte's finger. They had kissed. They had gone down the aisle while the organ blared out an anthem. Flushed with excitement, they had been driven to the reception. Some long kisses in the back of the limousine. "I love you, Peter." "Oh, Charlotte, I love you." The photographer, a dark little man of foreign aspect, had behaved like a vicious dancing master and the picture taking was over quickly. And now they were in the receiving line.

He did love Charlotte. She looked very pretty today. He did love her. She was laughing, giggling! She had given him a passionate kiss in the car, and her thin lips seemed engorged. He could not think of a single reason not to have married her. They had some fun talks. She was bright. She was a good person, without excessive neuroses (sure, her family, but everybody had a family). He liked her friends, and they had some in common. He did love her.

Everything had gone well. The family members and friends from both sides were meshing easily. Charlotte's and Peter's parents were behaving as well-socialized grown-ups do. Peter's were interchangeable with all the other members in their set, a set that entirely lacked the éclat of the guests from Charlotte's side, but the Russells could hold their own, and these distinctions didn't bother anyone very much. So it was all going well. As for protocol, the only slight lapse was that Isabella, the one truly stunning bridesmaid, had practically joined the receiving line. The maid of honor and the best man were supposed to be there, but not any of the other attendants. But Jonathan had been talking to the girl and they kept talking as he took his post, so that guests would try to shake her hand too. She was Chilean and very tall, with black hair but fair skin. When she laughed at something Jonathan said, she lowered her head and looked up at him through her long lashes. Her forearm was a slender shoot. In time, she wandered off, with a glance back at Jonathan, who attended more faithfully to his duties.

Later, Peter heard Jonathan saying to Charlotte's jolly, round great-aunt, "Now, you know, Mrs. LeMenthe, it's really not fair of you to upstage the bride this way, looking so beautiful!" Then Jonathan looked over again at the Chilean, who was talking to someone. She noticed this and slid her eyes toward him. Peter sighed. Who knew where this would lead? Jonathan worked fast. Then Peter supposed that they had book festivals in Santiago, in February, when it was summer down there. First-class ticket. The girl was drinking champagne, and Peter was thinking about how the tall, slender, delicate flute resembled her. These considerations abstracted him so much that he did not notice the guest who was now before him, having already chatted with Charlotte.

"Oh! Holly! Hello!"

"Hi!"

"I saw you in the church."

"I saw you there, too."

"Everything okay? Have you gotten a glass of champagne? Some hors d'oeuvres? They have these little puffy ham things —"

"Yes, I have everything I could want, and it's all perfect."

"Good, good. So — I was okay?"

"You were perfect."

"And how about Jonathan? The way he handled the ring? Outstanding."

"Not bad. I like to see a sharper attack on the pocket. But not bad."

Peter and Holly stood there looking at each other, and all of his urges flooded back. This was the moment to seize her and run off.

Holly pressed his hand with both of hers. "I hope so much that you will be happy, Peter," she said. "I know you will. To see you happy makes me very happy." She began to cry. "Oh, how silly!" she said. She dabbed her eyes with a handkerchief, then crumpled it up. "I get to kiss the groom, don't I?"

"Of course."

They kissed on the cheek.

"Have a great trip," Holly said. "Send a postcard and call us as soon as you get back."

Us.

So it was all over. Peter had to put aside his hope or dream or fantasy, or whatever it was. He had married Charlotte, putting the final barrier between them. Holly could not be his and now he could not be hers. He had watched and waited to see if her bond to Jonathan would crack. Three years. Three years of dinners with the two of them, of watching her cook while they waited for Jonathan. ("Of course you can help! Let's see — how about making some lemon zest?") Three years of abashed answers to her discreet inquiries about his romantic life. Three years of going with them to the beach, and seeing her remove, to take one example, the short white denim skirt she had worn over her bathing suit, so coarse against her smooth thigh; and the flecks of blond hair against her tan forearm, slivered, golden glints. Three years of hearing her say things like "I was reading that new book the other day, you know, *Europe in the High Middle Ages*? And you know what's really funny?" Three years of hearing her tell the truth when it would have been easier to lie, of seeing her help out friends, of watching her save a pupil from some ghastly situation or other, in addition to teaching her the ablative absolute. Even now, at this moment, while one of Charlotte's cousins was telling him how much she loved their China pattern, Peter could feel the pressure of Holly's hands. And he thought about the three years of seeing her overtip.

Well, forget it. After three years, it seemed clear that Holly was not going to break Jonathan's heart and throw herself at Peter. How many millions of times Peter had considered taking some action of his own. He could have declared his true feelings. After all, she had once had a crush on him, if only for two minutes! And how many millions of times had he imagined her response, assuring him with utmost kindness that they were friends and that that was how she wished them to remain. Peter, such a nice guy. He could have told her the truth about Jonathan. You just didn't do that to one of your mates, though. And he just couldn't do it to her. In any event, the effect would have been so destructive to her that the messenger would hardly have been a candidate for Jonathan's successor. In fact, Jonathan would probably have found a way to turn it all to his advantage ("I'm *afraid* of how much I love you"), and then the whole tearful drama of the second chance would have brought them even closer, as would their mutual disgust for the weasely busybody who had interfered. So Peter had simply lurked and waited, to no purpose. Holly would never be free. Never. So it was time for Peter to give up. To put her away from him. He felt a little like someone who had joined the French Foreign Legion to get away from a married woman with whom he had fallen in love. Farewell, dear friend (*chère amie* — *amie* was such an ambiguous word). Dear friend, farewell.

"Hello!" "Great to see you!" "Thanks for coming!" "Oh! So you're Uncle Robert! I've heard so much about you!" "Yes, it is a beautiful spot. We'll be there for a week and then drive down the coast. Oh, you did? Two years ago?" "I sure hope I said them as if I meant them!" "No, we haven't begun to look for a place." "Hello!" "Yes!" "Thanks so much for coming!" "Thanks!" "Yes!" "Yes, very happy!"

~

The clubhouse where Charlotte and Peter held their reception was a large clapboard building that dated from about 1900. French doors gave out from the ballroom onto a wide, deep grass terrace that overlooked lawns, a former polo field, and a golf course. The course was beautifully maintained but not challenging. The first hole, in particular, was straight and short, to give players an optimistic beginning. On this night, which had no stars and no moon and was muggy, the grass looked black; the white sand in the traps, which sometimes glowed at night, resembled gray ash. To reach the first tee, one walked to the far side of the terrace and then went down a short path; the path continued through some rough that extended down a bank for about thirty yards beyond the ladies' tee, and then the fairway began. The grass here was closely cut, well watered, and soft.

Someone entering the fairway on this evening and then walking about a hundred yards would have been confused to see a gray, rounded form that was moving in an odd way. He would have heard the sound of the grass being torn and a kind of grumbling. It might at first appear that a bear was inexplicably rooting in the turf. If, dismissing that possibility, the observer drew closer he would have seen a creature with a baffling number and arrangement of limbs, and possibly two, or three, heads. Then, when his mental eye suddenly made the image coherent, he would have stopped in his tracks. Before withdrawing, however, he would have stood there watching for a minute or two, his embarrassment overmatched by his prurience.

~

Jonathan and his companion were lying on their backs. Then she turned on her side and kissed him and with one hand held him at the root. "Poor little guy," she said. "He's so teeny —"

"Now! *Now* he's so teeny is what you mean."

"Of course." She giggled and kissed him. "Now." She lightly scratched him in that place. "But I wonder why they do that. It's like a snail shrinking back into his shell."

"Just gathering strength." Jonathan smiled and turned on his side and regarded the grisaille figure next to him: her shoulders a darker gray than her light gray breasts; her stomach a darker gray than her light gray pelvis (except for the black thatch). When he had first seen her that day and noted how a creamy blouse veiled her, he had almost been unable to restrain himself. Now here she was before him, unclad. He caressed the curve of the woman's torso. He was as convinced as any religious zealot that he knew the purpose of life: to make love with Julia Montague.

They had met the night before. During cocktails, Julia had at one point found herself alone and unsure what to do next. Nearby, Jonathan was standing with a couple of older women. He had turned to Julia and, with a beautiful smile, said, "We're talking about whether Peter and Charlotte will stay in the city or move out of town." His tone had had a conspiratorial subtext: Save me from these old ladies! Julia had joined the group, introductions were made, and they were still canvassing the question when they were called for dinner.

Julia and Jonathan, it turned out, were seated next to each other. Jonathan was scrupulously proper about how he divided his conversation between Julia and the woman on his other side (it was the minister's wife; she was fit and had startling blue eyes and white hair like whipped cream, and she had, in fact, set Jonathan's mind going — a great-looking woman in her sixties?), but when he did talk to Julia, he was attentive.

"Let's see: Julia Montague," he had said, furrowing his brow. "I didn't know that Charlotte had another sister, besides Deirdre."

This was obvious flattery, intended to amuse Julia — and flatter her. She laughed.

"You're very kind," she said. "But no, I'm not Charlotte's sister. I'm her stepmother."

"Oh! Of course! Of course, I know your name." He gave a little nod. "How do you do, Mrs. Montague?"

"Oh, please! Call me Julia."

"Charlotte has always spoken so highly of you! Peter, too."

"That's so kind of Charlotte. Not everybody says nice things about their stepmother."

"She does," Jonathan continued. "Actually, to be honest, I think that Charlotte sort of hero-worships you. Heroine-worships?"

"Well, I can't believe that. But I am very fond of Charlotte."

"It's true. And Peter — I probably shouldn't be saying this, but I've always thought Peter was a little bit in love with you."

Julia laughed. "Really, now!" she said. "That's ridiculous!"

"Not at all. You can tell." Jonathan looked at her and smiled and shrugged. "And after all," he said mildly, "why shouldn't he be in love with you?"

A waiter interrupted them. They ate and spoke to their other tablemates for a while. When their conversation resumed they had both drunk a little more wine, and they found themselves looking into each other's eyes.

"I've read one of your books, you know," Julia said.

"Which one?"

"Longer Light's Delay."

When she said this, Jonathan buried his head in his hands. "I've written exactly two novels, and you had to choose the one that's terrible."

Julia reflexively touched his arm. "Oh no! No. I thought it was terrific. Really."

Jonathan was shaking his head.

"It was very moving," Julia said. "That scene where they discover the mother has run off, and the little girl runs into the kitchen to see if she has taken her pictures, and of course she hasn't. I mean, I was in tears."

"I stole that, actually, from someone's real life."

"Well, okay, but still. And isn't that allowed?"

"I guess," Jonathan said. "Anyway, thanks."

They talked about books, which was something Julia didn't have a chance to do very often. Julia liked to read and she pushed herself to read new fiction; every week she read the short story in one of the magazines she got. But new fiction bored Dick to tears, and her friends weren't readers, either. Jonathan's book really had stayed with her. She had found herself staring with interest at the author's photo.

Jonathan mentioned that these family things can be so tense and asked Julia how it was all going. He asked her about her childhood, her parents, how and where she grew up. Julia found herself becoming uncharacteristically voluble. It turned out that Jonathan knew the younger brothers and sisters of people she knew. It turned out that there were a couple of amazing small-world coincidences. Julia was a passionate skier and so was Jonathan, and he amazed her with the accounts of his daring. "Now, I'm not saying this to impress you!" he had protested.

Jonathan confided in Julia that he had felt a lot of pressure preparing his toast and that he was pretty nervous about it. Julia reassured him that it would go over well. And it did: it was funny, dear, heartfelt, an arabesque in which the lines were at the end touchingly and wittily tied together. All its praise was directed at Charlotte, and the crowd clapped and cheered and stood when he finally asked its members to drink to her.

"Was that okay?" Jonathan asked Julia after he sat down.

Julia was laughing and her eyes were glistening with tears. She took his hand and kissed him on the cheek. "Oh, Jonathan! It was wonderful!" She was looking into his eyes.

He put his free hand on top of hers. "Thanks," he said quietly, looking back into her eyes. "Thanks."

The dinner was breaking up. Jonathan found Julia standing near the door, waiting patiently while Dick spoke to Charlotte.

"Good night, Julia," he said. "I hope you had a nice time."

"Yes, I had a very nice time, thank you. I am so happy for Charlotte. What a fun dinner. I'll have to thank Charlotte and Janet for putting me at such a good table. The man on my other side, Peter's uncle, he was fascinating. Did you know that he and his wife recently took a trip to Africa? You must ask him about it sometime." She paused and looked at Jonathan with a smile. "And of course I enjoyed getting to know you a little."

"I'm glad we were able to talk for a bit."

"Yes, that was nice."

They glanced into each other's eyes again in a final, contractual way, then stood silent for a moment, looking at Dick and Charlotte and the crowd beyond them.

"Well," Jonathan said, "I should probably be fetching something for someone. Good night."

They shook hands.

"Good night, Jonathan," said Julia. "See you tomorrow!"

"Oh yes! See you tomorrow!"

The following day Jonathan and Julia had not spoken until the reception was well under way. They did see each other. Standing at the front of the church just before the ceremony started, Jonathan saw her arrive and got goose bumps. He had to make an effort not to stare at her during the ceremony. For much of the reception, their paths had not crossed. Then he had seen her through the French doors giving onto the terrace. She was smoking a cigarette with her right elbow resting in her left hand. At that moment, she turned and saw him. She held her look at him for two seconds.

He joined her. Getting some air. They chatted. Jonathan mimed the exchange he hoped anyone watching would think they were having. *Oh, you'd like to walk around a bit? Of course, I'd be happy to join you. Do you know the club? No? Then you haven't seen the giant cedar?* They walked off slowly. Jonathan gesticulated, and Julia nodded her head, as if she were charitably listening to a country-club bore who was about to tell her its history.

They walked down the path to the first tee and then to the fairway. Here they had their first kiss. Then they continued farther for about a hundred yards.

Jonathan laid his coat on the ground, and Julia removed her clothes carefully and put them on it. Jonathan was less scrupulous. He had developed a system whereby if he removed only one shoe he could free one leg from his pants and shorts, and so achieve the necessary freedom of movement without taking the time to completely disrobe. They were both extremely attracted to each other, they were very accomplished at giving pleasure, and they enjoyed themselves immensely.

Now, afterward, they lay talking. They were not cold, for it was a hot, muggy night. The grass was soft and weedless. Julia lay on her back, Jonathan was on his side, propping himself up on one elbow. He softly held his hand flat against one side of her face, his palm covering her cheek and his fingertips at her temple. He knew better than to touch her hair.

"Julia," he said, gazing into her eyes, "run away with me. Tonight! We'll go someplace where people know how to live, and we can be together, always."

Julia laughed. It was a joke, but there was an undercurrent in which Jonathan actually sounded sincere, as, in part, he was. Julia stroked his back with one hand and with the other ran her fingers through the hair on the back of his head. She pulled his head down to her chest and continued to hold it. Her left arm lay across his back and she held the hand against his right side. She didn't speak.

"Well," Jonathan said eventually, "if you won't abandon everything and come away to live with me forever in someplace far, far from all this, can we at least have lunch?"

Julia thought for a moment. "All right," she said.

"Good. How about Monday at Poquelin's?"

"But won't it be closed on Monday?"

"You're just putting up obstacles!"

"I think I'm right."

"Okay. Tuesday, then, at one?"

"Yes," she said.

Jonathan paused as he looked at her. "Thank you," he said softly. Then he added, "It's convenient for me because I have my study nearby."

"I see," said Julia. She was glad. She would not at all mind repeating this experience in more comfortable surroundings. She would look forward to Tuesday; she would have a hard time waiting.

They kissed and caressed each other, then lay back again.

"I never know what to feel at weddings," Julia said after a moment. "Happiness for the couple, or dread. I like Peter a lot. And Charlotte, I'm fond of Charlotte, even though . . . even though . . ."

"She can be quite a drag?"

Julia laughed. "Yeah." She thought for a minute. "It's just that, well, I know that no man completely wants to get married. So maybe it was just that, and nervousness. But Peter, he seemed pretty subdued, really."

"Poor old Peter," Jonathan said.

"Why do you say that?"

Jonathan raised himself up and stroked Julia's cheek with the back of his hand.

"It's a secret," he said.

"Oh, come on! I think that, you know, under the circumstances, you can't exactly keep any secrets from me."

"What do I get for telling you?"

"I suppose we can think of something."

"Okay, I'll trust you," Jonathan said. He paused for effect. "Peter isn't in love with Charlotte."

"Oh no. I had a feeling, actually. It's too bad."

"That's not all, though," said Jonathan. "The real truth is that he *is* in love with somebody else."

"Really? Who?"

Jonathan paused before answering. "Peter is in love with my wife, Holly."

"Your wife?"

"Yes."

"Really? How long has that been going on?"

"Years and years."

Julia thought about this. "Wow," she said. "Poor Peter. In love with his best friend's girl. I guess it happens all the time."

"Yes." Jonathan let that thought hang in the air and moved his hand lightly along Julia's neck, over her shoulder, and down part of her arm. "But do you want to know something even more amazing?"

"Okay. What?"

"Holly is in love with him."

"What?!"

Jonathan shrugged. "Yes, it's true. Of course, neither of them knows how the other feels."

"But you do?"

"The human heart, baby — that's what I'm all about."

"But — but — did you know this before you and Holly got married?"

"Yes, I did."

"And you married her anyway?"

Jonathan kissed Julia's nose. "Yes," he said. "You see, Holly, she's pretty great. They really don't come much better. So, I thought,

Well, who should have her, Peter or me? And it's a funny thing, but the answer I came up with was me."

"But if you knew she was in love with Peter, what about her happiness?"

"I guess I lack imagination," Jonathan said, "but it's hard for me to see how any woman would be happier with Peter than with me. I mean, I love the guy. But really. I have no doubt that Holly's better off as Mrs. Speedwell. You see, I was looking out for her."

"And Peter?"

"Oh, well, aside from the fact that I totally screwed over my best friend, I don't feel so bad about him." Jonathan sighed. "You see, I'm really not a very nice person."

Julia now stroked his hair and curled some behind his ear. "Oh well," she said. "Neither am I." Then a thought occurred to her. She raised her eyebrows and tilted her head. "I know about Peter and I know about Holly, but I don't know about you. Are you in love with Holly?"

Jonathan's eyes darted away for a second and then he looked back into Julia's, meltingly. He spoke in a soft, purring voice. "The truly astounding thing," he said, "is that I am so deeply, passionately, ecstatically in love with you."

~

Jonathan and Julia were conscious that it was past time that they both got back to the party. Also, in the last few minutes the wind had come up in cold gusts. They noticed now that dark clouds were hurtling toward them like a black avalanche in the sky. A few drops of rain fell, then it began to rain harder, and thunder rumbled.

"Oh hell!" said Jonathan. "Christ!" Julia was now partially dressed and had carefully gathered the rest of her clothing. "Come on," said Jonathan, "over there." A band of rough ran alongside the fairway and beyond it were some woods; a shed with a projecting roof stood at the edge of the woods. Half-dressed and carrying their remaining clothes, Jonathan and Julia hurried over to it; the rough hurt Julia's bare feet. Just as they got under the roof, lightning flashed, there was a loud crack of thunder, and the rain began to beat down heavily. Nervous and excited, they dressed, pausing for a moment to hold hands and watch the sheets of rain move across the open ground of the course. The air felt cool and smooth. So much rain was now running off the edge of the shed's roof that they felt as if they were standing behind a waterfall. They kissed, wetly, and looked into each other's eyes through their wet lashes. Then they returned to their buttons and zippers.

Jonathan had pretty well put himself back together. Then he started looking around on the ground. "Oh, Christ!" he said. "God. Dammit."

"What is it?" asked Julia.

"My shoe. Damn. I must have left it out there."

It was true. They could not see it, but his right shoe was lying on its side in the fairway.

"I better go get it," he said.

"But you'll get soaked."

"I know. But I guess explaining that will be easier than explaining why I'm wearing only one shoe. Anyway, it's letting up a little, isn't it?"

He took her in his arms. "You go on back," he said. They kissed. "See you Tuesday."

"Yes. Tuesday. One o'clock."

They had a long passionate kiss.

Then, having turned up the collar of his coat and hesitated a moment, Jonathan plunged into the rain and dashed away.

Julia did not think it was letting up. She remained standing in the shelter. Who would miss her, after all? She could say she had been bored and decided to walk around the club and had gotten caught in the rain. Watching Jonathan, she almost had to laugh. With one bare foot and trying to hold his coat closed, he ran lopsidedly, and his tails flapped behind him. He looked like someone in a silent comedy. The rain was falling harder than ever. The poor guy, she thought, what a thorough soaking his hair and clothes were getting. He was now skipping around near the spot where they had lain, trying to find his shoe, and looking even more ridiculous. Finally, he picked something up, examined it, and shook water out of it.

At that moment, a bolt of lightning forked the sky. It struck Jonathan and he fell. Julia gasped. She jumped back. The boom of thunder hurt her ears. Her mind retained the image of the lightning strike. The grass and trees had looked like ghostly figures in a negative or an X-ray. She kept staring ahead. Jonathan did not move. He looked like a crumpled wet tarp. The rain beat steadily. Julia was paralyzed, not knowing what to do. Then she heard some calls and cries in Spanish, and a pair of kitchen workers in white coats ran down from the clubhouse. Reaching Jonathan, one of them knelt over him and then called to the other, who ran part of the way back up the fairway and yelled up to people standing outside. Then there was more calling and yelling and more commotion. A group of people, some from the wedding, some members of the club staff, ran to Jonathan. A moment later Julia saw a young man, an usher, running a few feet in front of someone plumper and shorter, whose running was labored.

"Please!" "Move away!" "He's a doctor!" Julia heard. By now a crowd had gathered on the terrace. Floodlights had been turned on. A larger group headed down from above to join the advance parties. Rooted in place, Julia watched it all through the sheet of rain running off the shed's roof.

~

When Peter first learned that there had been some kind of disturbance, he was standing at the edge of the dance floor talking to two of his mother's friends.

"Now, I think the bank where I have my checking account was bought by them," one of the women was saying. "I've had that account for the longest time. Why, years ago they would call Mother when she was overdrawn. I don't suppose you could do that for me, Peter?"

"Unfortunately, Mrs. Whelan, I don't think it could have been the company I work for."

"What is it that you do there?" asked the other woman.

"Right now, I'm in a division where we, well, we devise products —" He always found this part difficult. "We help companies hedge, that is, lessen the risk of, when they own something or do something, by owning, although not necessarily owning exactly, other things, that are negatively correlated."

"Oh?" said the first woman dimly. "And is that interesting work?"

"Yes, very." Peter was about to deliver the enthusiastic speech that the occasion demanded when he heard some loud talk coming from the far side of the ballroom. Peter turned and saw that people seemed to be moving toward the terrace. Someone cried out, "Oh no!" The dancers stopped and turned, and the band stopped playing. An even louder, more agitated murmur flowed through the crowd.

"Goodness," said Mrs. Whelan. "I wonder what the commotion is?"

"I better see," said Peter. He trotted over and asked a guest what was going on.

"I think they said someone was hit by lightning."

"Oh no!" said Peter. "A man or woman?"

"A man, I think."

"Is he badly hurt?"

"I don't know. I think they've called for help."

Peter now pushed through the crowd and went outside. There were lots of people milling around the terrace. They were wet and their shoes sank into the spongy ground. One of his ushers raced up.

"Peter! Peter!"

"What's happened?"

"Somebody was hit. Out there." The friend pointed. The floodlights from the clubhouse allowed Peter to see a knot of people on the fairway. Those on the terrace were gabbling. "What happened?" "Who is it?" "Isn't it terrible?" "Lightning!" "Out on the course!" "How awful for Charlotte!"

Peter began to run across the terrace. An ambulance had appeared. Cube-shaped and painted pea green and white, lashed by rain, it was making its way down a narrow road that led from the parking lot to the first tee with its red lights flashing and white lights burning blindingly in all directions. Peter ran toward it and then trotted alongside as it drove over the tees. Bouncing and caroming in an alarming way, it went down the bank that was in rough. Once on the fairway, the ambulance gained speed, tearing up the grass as it went. The driver sounded the siren to urge people to move out of the way, and then the medical technicians jumped out and ran to the victim. Peter caught up just as they reached him. The ambulance's red lights continued to flash and the white ones were so bright and so numerous that it was hard to see, and they gave everything they fell on a flat, bled-out cast. The technicians, a man and a woman, wore latex gloves and their belts were laden with gear. A guest was kneeling down beside the victim; he was one of Janet's friends, Dr. Smythe. As the technicians knelt, tearing open packets and Velcro patches, the doctor spoke to them loudly but indistinctly and then stood aside to let them do their work. Moving in an organized frenzy, they shouted jargon at each other while static and voices came out of their radios. One of the technicians yelled to the ambulance, and a second man jumped out of the back. He lifted down a cart that carried a box with cables running out of it, and, at full speed, pushed the cart up to the others. After a pause while her colleagues prepared the victim and the machine, the female technician applied the two paddles to the victim's chest, jolting his body. The crowd gasped and took a step back. The technicians leaned over the victim. Then the woman gave him another charge. After another wait, she did it again, and once again the victim's body leapt up like a flopping fish.

The technicians huddled, taking readings again. Then their shoulders seemed to sag and their bodies to lose tension. They rose unhurriedly. The crowd was utterly silent. One of the technicians called over the doctor. They spoke and the doctor nodded; he knelt down and examined the victim for a moment, then rose and nodded again. Businesslike, but without urgency, the technicians drew the stretcher out of the ambulance. They rearranged the limbs and carefully lifted the victim onto the stretcher, covered him with blankets, and strapped him securely. They covered his face. Seeing this, people in the crowd let out moans and cries. The technicians popped open the undercarriage of the stretcher so that it was waist-high and wheeled it to the back of the ambulance, where they stowed it, after first popping it closed again. They approached the doctor. In the bright white light and flashing red lights they spoke for a moment, and the doctor scanned the crowd. His eyes lit on Peter and he pointed toward him.

"Peter!" he called, and beckoned with his hand.

Peter joined him and the paramedic in the field of the bright white and flashing red lights.

"Peter," said the doctor, "I'm so sorry. It's the best man."

Peter had thought that he recognized Jonathan's waistcoat. Still the doctor's words stunned him, and he stared back blankly.

The doctor tried again. "I don't know his name," he said. "I'm sorry. He was your best man. Your best man."

"Jonathan?" Peter managed to say. "You mean it was Jonathan?" The voice that came out of Peter didn't seem like his own.

"I'm sorry," the doctor said.

"Uh . . . oh God. Jonathan."

The doctor allowed some time for the news to sink in, then said, "I'll go to the hospital, of course. Is there anyone else . . . ?"

Peter swallowed and took a couple of breaths. "Yes," he said, "there is somebody. His wife is here."

"I see." The doctor thought for a moment. "Peter, someone should ride in the ambulance. If you do that, I'll find his wife and . . . explain. Then we can follow you."

This sounded like a wise plan to Peter. "All right," he said. "But you don't know her. Her name is Holly. She's kind of tall and has reddish blond hair —"

"Oh, her? I know who you mean," said the doctor. Peter looked at him. He was stocky and his face was dented all over and creased with a hundred varieties of fine and thick wrinkles. His suit and shirt were wet and soiled. Peter could hardly think of anything specific about him. He was one of those anonymous figures who fell into the category of people who parents believed must be invited to weddings as a matter of course. Peter remembered that earlier he had been bouncing on the dance floor: a slightly soused doctor friend of his mother-in-law's. At this moment, he seemed to have the noblest face in all of humanity.

Peter hoisted himself into the back of the ambulance. The female technician was already inside and one of the men got in after Peter and closed the thick doors behind him. The stretcher sat in a bay in the middle of the enclosure. There were benches on either side. The place had a green glow to it and lots of equipment — dangling plastic face masks, tubes, tanks, monitors with dials. With a jolt the truck started moving and swung around in a wide turn and then slowly made its way back up the fairway.

After a few minutes, Peter asked, "Was he . . . was there —"

"We found no vitals when we arrived," said the woman. "We did what we could." She paused. "I'm sorry about your friend."

"Yes, sir," said the man.

So, dressed in his cutaway, with mud on his rented patent leather shoes and his silver tie blotched with water, having just married Charlotte, Peter rode off in an ambulance with Jonathan, who was dead.

The ambulance arrived at the emergency room and the technicians told Peter to go into the waiting area. It was a clean place. The molded-plastic chairs (bright blue) and the linoleum floor (white, flecked with green, red, and blue) glowed with good upkeep. Despite the storm and the fact that it was Saturday night, the cases were few and didn't seem very serious. Among the half-dozen people he saw, Peter couldn't even distinguish between the patients and their companions. A TV was on. All of this contrasted sharply, and confusingly, with the turmoil within Peter. Where were the sirens and the blood and the paramedics bursting through doors with people on stretchers? These would have corresponded better with Peter's emotions.

An orderly or someone like that walked by and said to him,

"They'll take care of you over there," and motioned to a counter with an opened glass partition. The woman sitting behind it gave Peter a ballpoint pen and clipboard with a form on it. Some interest, but not much, came into her face when she noticed Peter's clothes. "Please have a seat and fill that out," she said. Peter sat and looked at the form. It asked for the patient's name and address and date of birth, your name if you were not the patient, relationship to patient, insurance, nature of injury, previous hospitalizations, current medications, allergies. Peter put the clipboard and pen on the seat beside him. Allergies. Peter happened to know that Jonathan had been allergic to shrimp. In college once they had been eating Chinese food with a girl whom Jonathan was pursuing. She was awfully pretty and had the sliest way about her and smoked Marlboros. One of the dishes had shrimp in it, which they didn't know. Jonathan ate some and almost immediately began to turn red and swell up. Peter and the girl had taken him to an emergency room in a taxi. It wasn't like this one; it was filthy and crowded with moaning poor people. Peter had thought about that girl over the years. A thing with Jonathan had developed but not lasted very long. When she and Peter ran into each other from time to time, she acted in a friendly way toward him, but he clearly made her uncomfortable.

Jonathan, Peter also happened to know, had had one hospitalization, to have his appendix removed. He had not smoked, he had not suffered from depression or any nervous disorders. He had never had cancer. He was taking one prescription medication, to control his cholesterol. He had a mild heart murmur.

Peter knew all these things about Jonathan. He probably knew more about Jonathan, in fact, than anyone else did. He knew about the terrifying time when, as a child, Jonathan had been left behind on a train. He knew about the maudlin singer-songwriter whom Jonathan secretly adored. Although Jonathan never talked to anyone about his work, he had even told Peter about an idea he had for another novel: "It's a coming-of-age story," Jonathan had said. "I have it pretty well planned out, and it should be very moving. What it's really about is the sexual awakening of Peter Randall, a boy just coming into manhood. He falls in love with his right hand, and they have this passionate emotional and physical relationship. At first, it's only a sort of innocent playful romance: they walk on the beach, lie together on hot summer nights listening to the whip-poor-wills. Then this lust just overtakes them. It's so intense that it's almost frightening. But they must meet furtively, for theirs is a forbidden love. Oh, it's very painful."

What else did Peter know about Jonathan? He glanced over at the list — heart, lungs, bones. Peter knew that Jonathan's urine was not discolored, or anyway it hadn't been the times he'd seen it. He knew that Jonathan had had a tetanus booster in the last ten years (they had gotten them together before a trip to Guatemala). He knew something about Jonathan's broken foot, the third-degree burn on his hand. He had seen Jonathan's snot, blood, piss, pus, spit, puke, and sweat. He had probably somewhere along the line seen his feces. What did that leave? Tears and semen. Well, those were for the girls. But that's all Jonathan was now, wasn't it? Just some fluids and goop and gristle dripping off his bones. Jonathan's sensitive-looking fingers now lay limp, as did his tongue, as did . . . Cheese puffs and meat and cake and wine sat undigested in his stomach. The electrons racing along the neural pathways had come to a sudden stop and flickered out. The large wrinkly gray mass under Jonathan's skull just sat there and oozed. That was it for Jonathan.

Peter tried to figure out how grief-stricken he was. In his shock, and in the bright, antiseptic waiting room, it was hard to feel anything. Then, too, Jonathan had never seemed solid. He had never seemed like a human being weighted down with organs and worries. It was as if you could pass your hand through him. Flitting from one crowd to another, from one woman to another, Jonathan had not been a person who seemed fixed on earth. Indeed, he had never seemed to become mired in any aspect of life. He hadn't had money worries. He had written easily. He had made friends easily. He had easily maintained a light diet of food, drink, and drugs. In his own way, he did fall in love, but even so, his relations with women never seemed to lead to crisis. He always recovered quickly from disappointments, and, no matter how inconstant he may have been, the women whose hearts he had broken still regarded him with remarkable indulgence and affection, or at least tolerance. There had been no stalkings, no two a.m. phone calls, no tableside appearances with wrists bleeding when Jonathan was dining with someone else. Jonathan had never seemed to meet resistance from the forces — gravity, friction — that others had to work against.

So now this shimmering apparition was gone. Why should its vanishing confound Peter's emotions or his sense of the world? It wasn't as if Jonathan and he had shared some profound intimacy: if Peter were in the hospital with cancer, Jonathan might visit every day, but he would never hug Peter tightly and cry, "I love you, buddy! I love you!" Peter and Jonathan had never had a cross word, but neither had they ever said a word about anything of any importance. There was no hard evidence that they particularly cared about each other, and a claim that they did might not have stood up under cross-examination. In fact, Peter disapproved of Jonathan in so many ways — despised and hated him, really, for his disloyalty to Holly. What he should be thinking, he concluded as he sat in his blue chair, was Good riddance. The bastard got what he deserved.

And yet . . . oh, Christ . . . he wasn't actually going to start to cry, was he? There had been periods when Jonathan would call Peter every day. "Peter, what's up?" Well, actually, Jonathan, I'm working. That's what we do here at the office. "Oh, right. How are you getting along with your supervisees today? Being tough but fair?" I try. "And are you sharpening the saw, Peter? Sometimes I worry about that. I worry that you're not sharpening the saw." Yes, look —. Then Jonathan would ask if Peter had happened to see an item in the paper, or he would tell him some gossip, or he would recall the beautiful day at that girl's parents' beach house when, under the influence of a hallucinogen, she and her friend and they had eaten all those avocados, and the word *avocado* had set them into fits of laughter the rest of the weekend. Whatever the topic, Peter would soon be drawn in and discover that he had spent twenty minutes talking to Jonathan, twenty minutes he certainly could not spare. Finally, Peter would insist that he had to go, and Jonathan would say, "Okay, okay, but what are you doing tonight?" I'm not sure, I have a lot of stuff here. "Oh, come on, you can go out." Jonathan would take Peter to a party at which, depending on the crowd, there would be the prettiest literary girls, or the prettiest art girls, or the prettiest rich girls, or the prettiest bohemian girls, or the prettiest actresses, or the prettiest dancers, or the prettiest musicians.

Peter couldn't think of any particularly self-sacrificing or meaningful thing that Jonathan had ever done for him. Jonathan had only provided him with affection, intelligence, energy, beauty, pleasure — life. Life. The tears began to come. What a selfish bastard he was, really. But still Peter wept.

He heard footsteps and looked up. Here was Holly.

4

Holly's hair was wet and tangled. She was pale — what a beautiful moonlike pallor, Peter thought, so different from her usual sun-warm blush — and her clothes were in disarray. Dr. Smythe accompanied her. His hair was plastered in stripes on his balding head. Peter could see that he had taken Holly in hand in a manner that was caring and professional. Peter began to cry harder as he approached Holly and embraced her. They sobbed together for a moment. "Oh, Peter, he loved you so much," Holly said.

"Holly," Peter said, but he couldn't continue.

After a moment, the doctor said softly, "I'll go see where things stand."

Holly and Peter held on to each other, sobbing and heaving almost in unison. Their bodies were touching along their entire length. With his eyes closed, Peter felt as if he were rapidly falling or rising with Holly in his arms. He couldn't tell which direction it was. They were swirling down, or spiraling up, together somewhere as one, for just as he could not tell where he seemed to be going, he could not tell where his body stopped and Holly's began. Holly stroked the back of his head and said, "It's okay, it's okay, it's okay, it's okay."

Hearing Holly's murmur and smelling her damp hair (wet leaves and wet wool), Peter felt himself even more lost within her. When he opened his eyes, he was shocked to see the clean, mundane waiting room, the blue chairs, the acoustical tile, the framed notices and the prints, a few colorful strokes depicting athletes. With instinctive simultaneity, he and Holly gently separated and held each other's forearms. They looked at each other's face. Holly was pale. Some straggly hairs were stuck to her forehead. Her eyes were red, and her whole face looked drawn. She had never before seemed ethereal, with such a translucent complexion.

"Peter —"

"Holly —"

"Oh, Peter —"

"I'm so sor —"

They waited a moment, smiling a little, to collect themselves. Holly let Peter go ahead.

"Oh God, Holly. I'm so sorry. I'm so sorry. It's terrible. I can't help feeling — if it had been another night — I'm so sorry. He was . . . he was . . . he was . . . he was . . ." No word came to Peter to say what Jonathan was.

"I'm really just in shock," said Holly. "You saw him?"

Peter nodded.

"Oh, how horrible! Will I have to look at him? I want to. I do. I have to. But I'm so scared." She began to cry again.

"Let's sit down," Peter said.

They sat. Holly became a little more composed.

"I was sitting in one of those anterooms talking to Charlotte's great-aunt," she said. "A funny name. Mrs. LeMenthe. She was telling me about her wedding day and how everything went wrong, but they all had so much fun. I talked about my wedding day too, and we were laughing. We both thought our husbands were the best-looking men in the world, and we laughed about that. We could tell something was happening because of the way people were walking by and talking, but we really had no idea. Then Dr. Smythe came in." Holly gulped, and she spoke in a whisper. "He told me what happened." After collecting herself for a moment, Holly went on to say that as Dr. Smythe led her out of the club, Charlotte had fallen upon her, wailing. Charlotte wouldn't let go, and finally her father and brother had to pull her away. Then David Montague had driven Holly and the doctor to the hospital.

"I'm so glad you're here," she said, looking at Peter with her chin trembling.

They sat in silence, holding hands. Then Dr. Smythe came over with a doctor in scrubs. She told Holly that Jonathan had been pronounced dead on arrival and that there was no indication that he had suffered. She then said that it was necessary for someone to identify the body. Peter volunteered, but Holly said she wanted to see Jonathan. The doctor led them to a room with greenish light where a body covered in a sheet lay on a gurney. A woman with repulsive jowls asked Holly her name, address, and relationship to the deceased. Then she nodded at the attendant, and he pulled back the sheet to reveal Jonathan's head and shoulders. He had some burns and his hair was singed; his skin looked like putty.

"Oh God!" Holly cried, turning and burying her face in Peter's chest. But after a moment she stood back. "It's okay," she said. She took a couple of steps toward Jonathan.

"Can you identify this as the body of Jonathan Selway Speedwell of New York County, State of New York?"

"Yes," Holly said softly.

"Thank you. Please sign here. There are several copies so please press down hard."

Holly signed and the woman bustled out of the room. The at-

126

tendant moved to cover Jonathan again, but Holly raised her hand and stopped him.

"Not yet," she said. She walked to Jonathan and tentatively stroked his cheek. She leaned down and kissed his lips.

Although he thought it should, it did not disgust Peter that he was thinking, as he looked at her, about the beauty of her form as she did this, with her wild hair hanging down and covering her face.

Holly rose. She laid her hand on Jonathan's sternum and rested it there for a while as she looked at his face. "Good-bye," she whispered.

Then she turned and looked at Peter. She wasn't crying, although her face was drawn and her body shuddered. Peter realized that she assumed that he would want to take a last look at Jonathan, too. He stepped forward, and Holly and he gave each other a little hug. Then Holly moved back to join Dr. Smythe. Peter was aware that they were both looking at him, and that a gesture was expected. Peter had never touched Jonathan, except maybe to shake hands. Now, with Jonathan stretched out dead before him, singed and cold, he was supposed to? Yes, he felt shocked and bereft, and even on his own account he had the desire to say or do something meaningful. But how could he act in a way that was contrary to the nature of his and Jonathan's friend-ship? Peter couldn't escape the feeling that if he showed too much sentiment, even in this situation, Jonathan would laugh at him. But he felt Holly's eyes and those of the doctor on his back. He didn't want to disappoint Holly. Or the doctor either, for Peter had come to respect him to a degree that was probably excessive.

He pressed Jonathan's shoulder. Then he slowly moved his hand to Jonathan's head and stroked his hair where it had not been singed. It felt surprisingly thick and soft. Then, amid Peter's confused impulses, an action emerged, which was for him to lean down and kiss Jonathan's brow. Just because he did it for an audience didn't mean that it wasn't sincere.

Dr. Smythe insisted that he would arrange for a funeral home to come for Jonathan and that Peter and Holly should go along. Leaving the emergency room, Peter had half expected to find David gone, having figured, with wild inaccuracy, that he could make a run into the city and be back before they needed him. But there he was in the parking lot, leaning against his father's magnificent vehicle and then approaching and trying to find words of comfort. Now he was driving them back to the club, where they would collect some of Holly's clothes and toiletries before they all went on to Janet's house. The rain had stopped and the roads glistened orange from the streetlights. The lights themselves had an orange haze around them; along the dark stretches of road, meanwhile, the black puddles appeared as slick and dense as oil. The trees flapped their leaves and waved their branches senselessly in the wind. David drove. Holly sat in the back seat looking out the window. Peter sat in the back seat looking at her. She had taken his hand again when the car first began to move, and she held it the whole way.

When they arrived at the club, it seemed deserted. Holly and Peter entered the main hall, where the lights were dimmed, and they were surprised to find Charlotte's great-aunt sitting in a chair near the door. Seeing the two young people, she stood up.

"Mrs. LeMenthe!" said Peter. "What — why are you still here? Is there anything I can do for you?"

Mrs. LeMenthe did not acknowledge him but rather walked up to Holly and gave her an embrace. She simply closed her eyes and said nothing.

Then, turning from Holly, Mrs. LeMenthe spoke. "Holly will be coming with me to spend the night at my house. As many nights as she wants, for that matter. I have my car at the curb."

"But, Mrs. LeMenthe," Peter said, "we were planning on taking her to Charlotte's mother's house. Holly can't stay here, of course, and that was where we thought —"

"No," Mrs. LeMenthe said. She had shed her silly-goose, great-aunt demeanor. "Certainly not. I will not have Holly staying in that house with those bothersome women. Charlotte suffered a complete nervous collapse tonight and was still hysterical when they put her in the car. She and her mother are in no condition to give Holly the peace and care she needs. No, that house is the last place on earth Holly will go tonight." Then in a milder tone, Mrs. Le-Menthe said, "She will be much happier with me. My house is not big, but it's comfortable. The guest room is especially pleasant. I've just put in new curtains. I know how to cook and how to make tea and how to be quiet."

Peter and Holly looked at each other, back at Mrs. LeMenthe, and back at each other again. Holly, who had been relatively calm, began to burble. She embraced Mrs. LeMenthe and cried on her shoulders. Mrs. LeMenthe spoke soothingly but without condescension. "There, there, my dear. We'll have some cries together."

Then she asked, "Holly, did you have any particular friends at the wedding? Anyone who would be a comfort to you?"

"No," Holly said. "No. No one." She pointed at Peter, laughing and crying at the same time. "Only the groom!"

"Very well," said Mrs. LeMenthe. "You will come with us too. There is a cot in the basement. Or perhaps you should sleep on the daybed in the guest room. That way Holly won't be alone. It might be a comfort, like having a dog sleep in a room with you."

"But, Mrs. LeMenthe!" Peter said. "I mean . . . Charlotte . . . I should see how she is doing and, well, tonight, be with her . . ."

Mrs. LeMenthe's expression and tone were resolute. "I imagine," she said, "that you and Charlotte had planned to go to a very nice hotel tonight, probably one in town, and then leave tomorrow on your wedding trip, to Italy or some such place."

"Well, yes —"

"Will you be carrying out those plans?"

"Oh no, not now. At least not for a few days, whenever we can reschedule."

"Good. Then you can reschedule your wedding night. At this moment, having exhausted herself crying and moaning, Charlotte is in a deep sleep; you can count on that. Her mother is pacing around, drinking decaffeinated coffee and fretting pointlessly about a thousand things. Deirdre is watching television. There is no point whatsoever in your going there." She took Holly's hand and spoke in a passionate whisper. "This young woman has suffered a grievous blow. A grievous blow. My companionship, the companionship of a stranger, however well intentioned, can only help her so much. She needs a friend to be with her. A close friend, a dear friend. Someone who knows her and cares about her, as I can see that you do."

So that took care of that.

Peter spoke to David about their plans and called Janet, who told him that Charlotte had indeed fallen asleep. After explaining to Janet, as best as he could, what they were doing, Peter went up to Holly and Jonathan's room at the club and gathered up some of her things. Then he rejoined Holly and Mrs. LeMenthe and they drove off in Mrs. LeMenthe's tiny car.

~

Dick had watched the paramedics work and then saw Peter speaking to the doctor before getting into the ambulance. After it drove off, Dick caught up with the doctor, who told him that the victim was the best man and that he seemed to have been killed instantly. Jesus

Christ! Dick went back to the clubhouse to tell Janet and Charlotte. Charlotte went berserk. He and Janet agreed that they should call off the rest of the party, and Dick went off to tell the assistant manager, who was in charge that evening. The news of what had happened spread quickly and the guests were standing around at a loss as to what to do. Dick worked his way among them, explaining quietly that the party wouldn't continue. At one point, as he was trying to find the bandleader, Dick ran across Julia. She was sitting in a corner by herself, drinking a bourbon and smoking a cigarette. Her hair was wet and she looked disheveled. Dick had spoken to her and she had seemed not to hear. "Julia," he said again, and she slowly looked up at him. He had never seen the expression that she wore. It was weird. It was — he'd almost have to say that it was hateful. Clearly she was upset. He asked what had happened to her, where she had been all this time. She told him that she had gotten bored and gone outside to walk around the club a bit and have a smoke and the storm had started. Then people started running around and calling and she had gone over to see what was wrong. She had sat next to the best man the night before and talked with him a fair amount, and now . . . now . . .

"Well, sure, of course it's upsetting," Dick said. "A young guy like that. It's terribly upsetting." She didn't respond, and he asked if she was okay. "Yes, I'm fine," she said. "Sure you're all right now?" "Yes, of course. Please — go see to things."

Well, he had a hell of a time. Everyone asking questions. Despite what Dick told them, it took awhile for the guests to begin to leave. He kept reassuring them, as if he were the captain of a sinking ocean liner. He tried to comfort Charlotte as best he could; she took it very hard, sobbing and carrying on. It was an awful thing. And a girl on her wedding day, there would be a lot of emotion. The thing had been going off perfectly well until the accident had happened, although, in fact, just before then, a great load of boredom had dropped on Dick. It was all people from his days with Janet, and obviously people from the groom's side, and the moment came when you just hit the wall, and thought you could barely stand another second. Then the thought of Julia had popped into his head. Julia was looking particularly fine that day in her silk suit. What great legs she had, those fine ankles, the curve of her calf. Near the base of his spine, Dick had felt a familiar stirring. He had thought about his plan for that night, later on, after this was all finally over, upstairs, when he would run his hand along Julia's cool, smooth, gently concave inner thigh. And then, well, Christ, all hell had broken loose. The best man hit by lightning and killed, everybody running around and Charlotte in hysterics.

After the place finally cleared out and he had agreed to come by Janet's place the next morning, to "help" (what in the world was he going to be able to do to help?), he returned to where Julia had been sitting but didn't find her. So he went up to their suite. There she was, curled up in a chair wearing her bathrobe. She had brushed her hair and taken off her makeup and looked pale. The robe wrapped her tightly from her neck down to her ankles; all Dick could see of her flesh was her face, her hands, and her feet, those long rabbit feet.

"Hello, darling," he said. "So here you are."

"Yes, here I am," she said flatly, glancing at him without meeting his eye. He went over to her and leaned down to give her a kiss. She did not turn toward him, so he kissed her on the brow. He took off his coat and began talking. "Christ, what a night . . ." She didn't say anything, just stared into the cold maw of the fireplace. Dick walked around unbuttoning his waistcoat and undoing his tie and working out his cuff links; he wanted to talk and he wanted to engage her. "So then the bandleader asked me if he should play something. I mean, Christ, what did he think, 'Nearer, My God, to Thee'? You can bet if they had kept playing, Janet's friends would have been out there doing the fox-trot." This was not going right. The evening had overexcited him, and so had seeing Julia. He didn't even sound like himself. He allowed a long pause.

"It's just a tragedy. A tragedy," he said finally. His voice was quiet, grave, the right tone. After a moment, Julia looked over at him. She had that same expression she had had when he had run into her earlier. He was taken aback. Then she turned away. "Yes, it's very sad," she said. There was silence.

Obviously, he shouldn't try anything, that was clear. He should put it out of his mind entirely. But the ashy taste of repudiated desire made him resentful. He had arranged for there to be some brandy in the room and he now poured himself some and sat down in the chair on the other side of the low table from Julia. The table had a small vase with flowers on it. He wanted very badly to take off his shoes but thought that this would be undignified.

He tried another tack. "Are you all right, darling? This all seems to have gotten to you."

She looked over. "Certainly I'm all right. It's very shocking, that's all. I'm very tired."

"I can see that."

She didn't respond. There was a glass of water near her.

"What have you got there? Are you sure you wouldn't like some of this brandy? My nerves are pretty well shot, and it's the best thing."

"No thank you," she said.

Sympathy. Sorrow. That direction. "I'm worried about Charlotte," he said. "She took it very hard. Very hard. Of course, her wedding day, and all the emotions. The joy turned all around to, well, tragedy, really. Of course there's that poor girl, Jonathan's wife, do you know the one?"

"No."

"Oh, well, quite pretty. How she will carry on, I don't know. But I suppose she will. People do. Good God! Do they have children?"

Julia didn't respond.

"Then of course there's Peter. His best friend dead. Terrible." Generous now, bighearted. "I saw him go off in the ambulance. That's got to be tough."

"Peter is a good and capable guy," said Julia. "I'm sure he'll handle himself well."

As far as Dick knew, Julia had never given Peter's character a moment's thought, so he was surprised to hear her express such a firm and respectful opinion of it. Staring at his brandy, he waited for her to say, Oh, but what about you, darling? You were the one in charge of the evening, and no one could have carried off such a difficult situation better. You amaze me in a crisis. To which he would have replied with a wave of his hand, Oh, come on. I just tried to keep things on an even keel. But she didn't say that.

They sat in silence awhile. Dick turned over in his mind the day's events, what would happen tomorrow, his trip to London on Thursday. Notwithstanding all those distractions, the worm of his lust continued to burrow. In Dick's case, the vinegar of resentment, when applied to its tail, gave it a sting but also prodded it. It strained and twisted and wanted to push on. Dick looked over at Julia. He looked at the triangle of white skin below her neck formed by the lapels of her robe; he looked below there; the robe was snug. It was thick and had bunched up on account of the way she was sitting. His eye could find nothing to rest on until he reached those feet again. They were tucked up under her, so that she was sitting on the hem of the robe. No point of entry.

He was analyzing these features when suddenly the whole to-pography shifted. Julia had put her feet on the floor and was now standing up. As she did so, the robe fell open for a moment. She was wearing a thin cotton nightgown, and he could see the shapes and shadows of her body. It occurred to Dick that he had been married to Julia for fourteen years; when he had been married to Janet for fourteen years, such a sight would have slightly disgusted him, and not because Janet was a bad-looking woman at that time. But now, this glimpse — especially after all the crap of the long, awful, expensive day, after his lust had waxed so long, after putting up with this coldness — caused an eruption in his breast. Wouldn't it be sort of right? With all the emotion of the day, the intensity, wouldn't that propel them together?

She gathered the robe up and retied it tightly, saying, "I'm aw-fully tired. I'm going to go to bed." With one hand she collected from the table and compacted some bunched-up tissue, the plastic wrapper of a cigarette pack, foil from the brandy bottle, and the cardboard and plastic container that Dick's new shoelaces had come in. She put those items in the ashtray, picked up both the ashtray and her glass, and began to move away.

"How about a good-night kiss?" said Dick.

Julia stopped. "Oh, of course, darling," she said. "Sorry, you know. Just, so awful —"

"A terrible thing."

He stood and drew her to him, and in the split second available he tempered his eagerness and chose the extra-dose-of-affection hug and kiss, a firm hug and a sweet, soft kiss and a long, firm hug again, rather than the ever-so-slightly-suggestive hug and kiss, the hug a little tighter, one hand a little lower on her back, the kiss a notch or two longer and wetter. During his embrace, Julia's arms were spread out wide as she held the ashtray in one hand and the glass in the other.

When they separated she smiled again and moved off. She emptied the ashtray in a wastebasket and put it and the glass on a sideboard, on a tray with other glasses and an empty water bottle.

"Good night," she said again, and walked into the bedroom.

"Be in soon!" Dick called after her. Seen from behind, the thick, tightly cinched robe exaggerated the curve of her hips.

Ah, well, Christ. Dick settled down in the chair again. He took off his shoes, partially unzipped his fly, and undid the studs in his shirt and pulled out the tails; he was wearing an undershirt. The great thing about Julia — the great thing — was that she understood him and really cared for him. She was very bright, and in some ways they had more fun just talking than doing anything else. That first passion, of course it wasn't the same as it had been, but it was still there. Fourteen years since they had been married. Fourteen years after he had been married to Janet, he had long since begun to dislike her smell; once he had liked it. Funny, Julia didn't seem to have a smell. Well, she was a great girl, and, God knows, he wasn't the easiest person to live with. The house in France, that was really all her doing. Usually she would be there in June, and he would join her for a week. With the wedding, of course, they couldn't do that this year. He should really take her someplace to make up for it. But he had London coming up. Meanwhile, there was whatever the next day was going to bring. He wanted nothing more than to get away from this place, and they had planned to leave first thing in the morning, but now, who knows. He'd promised to appear at Janet's place, dear God. It was a terrible, terrible, tragic thing that had happened, and he felt terrible for Charlotte. But what was he supposed to do? Stand around and be grief-stricken and do the busywork of seeming helpful? That place of Janet's, he couldn't stand it. It never seemed exactly clean. Lying around the kitchen someplace there was always a hairbrush with dead hairs so thick you couldn't see the bristles. Well, there was no alternative.

More pleasantly, his thoughts returned to Julia lying in bed. It had been crazy of him, after what they had all been through, to even think of anything. Of course she would be terribly upset. But he'd go in and lie down next to her, put his arm around her. When they awoke, drowsy . . .

Dick poured himself a bit more brandy and walked over to the sideboard. There had been a chocolate bar, dark chocolate with hazelnuts. Yes, still some left. He loved to crack the hazelnuts with his teeth, then run his tongue along the sharp edges; they contrasted deliciously with the texture of the melting chocolate. He sat down and stretched out his legs. The brandy tasted good, and so did the chocolate bar (and he knew where there was another one).

~

After leaving Dick, Julia had closed the bedroom door and leaned her back against it. She took a deep breath and exhaled. It had been an ordeal to sit in the room with him, but she knew she had to be there to receive him when he returned. Jesus Christ. That man.

She went into the bathroom, hung up the robe, brushed her teeth and tongue vigorously, and drank two full glasses of water. She had drunk much more that night than she usually did. Although she did not feel drunk at all, she noticed that she was unsteady and felt ill. She hadn't smoked so much for a long time, either. Like a layer of dark paint bleeding through a coat of white, the taste of the bourbon and cigarettes emerged underneath the taste of the toothpaste, despite her efforts, and indeed that added ingredient made for an even more disgusting combination. She rinsed and spat again. Then she looked at herself in the mirror.

She knew she was very good-looking, but she was not vain. Nor did she have the terror of losing her looks so typical of beautiful neurotics. Certainly she would have liked to arrest the effects of time, and she sometimes asked herself what cost she would bear to achieve that. A million dollars? Ten million? The loss of a couple of toes? The loss of the sight in one eye? To be beautiful forever? The fact was that she secretly believed she would remain beautiful and, relatively speaking, become even more beautiful as she grew older. She saw herself living in France as a beautiful eighty-year-old. She would be called "extraordinary." That role appealed to her, being one of those extraordinary, beautiful eighty-year-olds. Then, as Julia continued looking at her face, her focus changed. The thought came, as usual: who is this person?

She stared for another minute, then squeezed a dab of moisturizer from a slender tube and worked it into the skin of her hands. She picked up an errant cotton ball she had used when taking off her makeup and tossed it in the wastebasket with the others. She shut off the light, closed the door, and got into bed.

Lying on her back, Julia stared at the ceiling. When she was a teenager, she had read in a magazine that sleeping on your side gave you wrinkles, and she decided then that for the rest of her life she would sleep only on her back. To a remarkable degree, she had succeeded. There was a light on somewhere outside, and on the window shade she could see the shadow of a tree branch and its leaves swell and shrink as they swayed in the wind. She lay for a while with her arms outside the bedclothes, resting at her side. It was unpleasant, having drunk as much as she had, especially when it hadn't even made her drunk. It seemed that at any moment, a gear would become unlocked and the ceiling would begin spinning. At least she had been able to escape from Dick as soon as was decent. She knew that she had to wait for him to come back. He would expect that. She had tried to summon up the initiative to ask him grave questions about the crisis that would allow him to describe his steadying role. She wasn't up to it. And that lecherous glint in his eye, which he had tried to disguise. No doubt he had hoped that the heightened, tragic atmosphere of the evening would have made her emotional, and, after she threw herself into his arms, he would kiss away her tears, and end up getting laid.

She stared at the ceiling for a while. Then a tear trickled out of her eye and ran down her cheek, wetting the pillow; now came one more out of her other eye. Still more followed. She wiped her eyes with her fingers and her face with the back of her hand, then shut her eyes with her hand over them. The image she saw was of Jonathan when he first spoke to her at the bridal dinner.

My God, he was handsome. But it wasn't just that. They had talked at the dinner, and there had been chemistry, a connection. The book had stayed with her. So had a story she had read not so long ago in the magazine she got. It was about a fourteen-year-old girl who was driving around a suburb on a Saturday afternoon with a college friend of her brother's. Nothing much happened. He wore a short-sleeved dress shirt, and the girl was revolted by the hair on his arms, which made her think of nests of spiders.

It was absurd, insane, pathetic. She could not stop herself from thinking that she had fallen in love with him. She had had a few other similar adventures (which was something that Jonathan's sensors had immediately picked up on), and they had been fun. Of course — of course — this was absolutely no different. It was just that this incredible, horrible tragedy had intervened. She had drunk too much and she was extremely emotional. In the morning she would wake up and everything would be back in the right perspective. But oh God! Oh God, to wake up in the morning and find Jonathan next to her. Quietly, she began to weep, and she turned on her side and curled up. To wake up in the morning and find him next to her, to feel his body's smoothness and warmth, and to stay there for most of the day. But dear God, no, no, no, no! He was dead. Dead. Think of it. He was dead and he had been killed right before her eyes and she had been with him and then seen it happen. She burst into heaving sobs, which she tried to suppress, for she did not want Dick to hear and use the sound as an excuse to come to her.

Later, when she was able to think again, she saw that obviously she hadn't fallen in love with Jonathan. Given the danger and excitement and pleasure of what they had just done, and then the violent, terrifying, deadly turn of events, anyone's emotions would go haywire. They could not be trusted, and all she needed to do was ride them out. But what if Jonathan's death was a nightmare, and he called her tomorrow? She would have sold her soul to the devil to make that happen, to touch him, to hear his voice.

No, Jonathan was dead. And then, with a shudder, she realized that he was not entirely dead. Some parts of him were still alive. They were inside her, living and active. It was like the light from a star that still reaches the earth after the star itself has been extinguished. She put her hand on her stomach. If only it were his hand.

~

Mrs. LeMenthe took Holly and Peter along deserted roads lined with large properties, and then up a long, unlit drive to her little brick house. It was snug and cluttered but immaculate. Mrs. LeMenthe made some tea. Holly took a bath. Peter went into a small study to carry out a difficult task: to track down Jonathan's older sister, Emma, and tell her what had happened and ask her to call her mother and the others who should know. Emma became upset and immediately put her husband on the phone. Jonathan had sometimes told stories about Alan's cautious, dull ways: "If you want to know the best route to take to avoid a toll, and you have about an hour to listen, Alan is your man." For his part, Alan received the news with stoicism.

Holly came down from her bath, and they drank tea and talked, cried, and hugged some more. Mrs. LeMenthe said little, but she and the two dogs — old, floppy, and affectionate — filled the room with a mammalian warmth. Finally, Holly wanted to try to get some sleep. It was decided that the cot in the basement was much too distant for anyone's happiness, so Mrs. LeMenthe made up the daybed in the guest room, and there Peter now lay. It hadn't occurred to him to bring any of his own pajamas, so Mrs. Le-Menthe had given him an ancient pair of her late husband's.

Peter lay awake. Here he was spending his wedding night in a bedroom with Holly. How often had he imagined that? Despite his roiling emotions, he tried to think about it all as clearly as he could, to look at the events of the past few hours rationally and analyti-cally and to put them in their broader context.

First of all, there was this salient fact: Jonathan was dead. This was tragic. Peter had wept over the loss of his best friend. Peter's grief aside, however, did not Jonathan's terrible fate have certain im-plications? If Jonathan was dead, there followed axiomatically this conclusion: he was no longer Holly's husband. Further, he was no longer a person, a living person at least, with whom Holly could be in love. Therefore, Holly was free to be in love with someone else. Thus, everything Peter had always wanted was suddenly available to him. The breeze riffling the hairs on his naked arm as he held

Holly to him, the setting sun casting her face in its rosy light, the high curve of her foot nestled in the arch of his own.

To be sure, it wasn't all clear sailing. Holly was not at present in love with him, for one thing. Of course, she "loved" him. But it was best-friend-of-my-boyfriend-then-husband love. Safe eunuch-intimacy love. Once her period of mourning was over and she got on her feet again, she would be pursued by males who would not have the disadvantage of already being classified in her mind as of only platonic interest. Unbearably, she would probably consult Peter about her love life, asking him to interpret some man's baffling behavior. It was so nice to have a friend of the opposite sex!

And yet as the man to whom Holly would turn in her time of grief, Peter did have some advantages. If he bided his time and used subtle encouragements, he might become the object of such an intense attachment on Holly's part that she would awaken one day and realize that she was in love with him. By sly dealings, he could try to maneuver the vulnerable widow into this position. Peter did not know the success rate, on average, of this approach, but he imagined he was working with decent probabilities. There were, however, other factors that came into play. To take one important example, he himself had gotten married that day. He had dressed up in fancy clothes. His bride had worn white. There had been a church full of well-wishers. There had been vows. Afterward, the bride's parents had hosted a big party. If he wished to pursue Holly, it would seem evident that his having got married that day would present an obstacle.

Obstacle? Or opportunity? Nobody stayed married who didn't want to, did they? It wasn't any big deal, was it? Sure, no problem. He could flip Charlotte in a year, and nobody would care. In fact, when seeking your own romantic happiness, causing others pain actually gave you a badge of honor. It showed that you were tough enough to do what was necessary for the higher goal — your own fulfillment. No one respects a war leader who goes all soft over civilian casualties, and no one respects a lover who hesitates to pursue his beloved for fear of hurting someone else. In both cases, ruthlessly doing what has to be done earns you credit. How many people, Peter thought, have really been censured for abandoning their wife or husband for the sake of true love and sex? Soon enough, the formerly aghast friends were inviting them around with their new mates, and their air of danger and passion actually made them attractive, while the spouse left behind seemed a bit pathetic, and his or her presence was dreary.

Peter recalled Charlotte's face when they were saying their vows. Her expression moved him. She was very happy: her wedding day. She looked pretty and she was glowing. She loved Peter. Her expression told him that. But there was that other sentiment, too, that she conveyed: I know you will be kind to me, Peter, and I am counting on you. Peter *was* kind, and all along he had had the sense that Charlotte was proud of herself for choosing someone who was not a destructive, cruel, heartbreaking male.

Peter didn't mind this. Although it was hard, really, to see any advantage to it in life, he thought it was a good thing that he was kind and that it came naturally. If that was a quality that attracted Charlotte to him as a result of her own weaknesses and painful experiences, why should he object, even if it seemed less like "love" than dependence, or whatever word people who talked about these things used? Charlotte had anchored in what she believed to be a tranquil harbor; could he now surprise her with uncharted reefs and exposure to gales? Left for another woman, Charlotte would feel humiliated, degraded; she would become fraught, and in all the ways she always thought she had to try hard, she would try still harder, and she would wind herself around herself like the wire in a cable. This, of course, would make her less attractive, causing her fraughtness to intensify. Peter imagined a divorced Charlotte as she got older: a fussy, nervous woman with her work and her things, "wonderful friends," a penchant for burgundy, good seats for the ballet, travel, special relationships with certain children. She would not experience two relaxed, happy minutes consecutively (except after some of that wine, which would sometimes make her giddy and flirtatious in a way that would set the other dinner guests' teeth on edge). Good old Charlotte. Could Peter condemn her to this fate?

The vows you made at the altar, everyone recognized, were not worth the breath you used to say them. And yet, something in Peter made it difficult for him to imagine breaking them. A plan to run off with Holly? It was hopeless and stupid, but it was not only hopeless and stupid. It was wrong. This fact counted quite heavily with Peter. It was like a timbered door secured with thick iron bands and padlocks the size of purses that stood between him and the thing he wanted. It was wrong. It was just wrong. Peter felt no pride in his virtue (if that was what it was). He couldn't go back on his word, he couldn't betray Charlotte, he couldn't hurt her. He just couldn't.

Earlier that day, Peter had inalterably resolved, for the ten millionth time, to accept the fact that Holly was not free. Now she was, but Peter was not. He really did believe that the universe had been programmed to bring them together. But it hadn't happened, had it? Why, why, why? Some zeros and ones in the wrong place? Typical glitch? He understood that it would be asking a lot of the universe to reboot and start all over. Or maybe there was an entirely different explanation — this free-will business. If so, then it was still in his power to make it all work, and maybe he could find a way? Peter turned the facts over in his mind again and again and again, searching, without success, for an interpretation that would reconcile them with his desire.

After he had been performing this exercise for a few hours, Peter was suddenly overcome with disgust. For God's sake, what had he been thinking? Pitying himself, becoming carried away with absurd schemes, when all this time he should have thinking about *Holly's* suffering. Poor Holly. Poor, poor Holly. How sad, how horrible for her. The horror of Jonathan's death would crush her heart. Peter imagined Holly with her heart crushed, and it was almost unbearable. It didn't matter very much that Jonathan was dead: Jonathan deserved whatever fate handed him. It didn't matter very much that Peter's best friend had died: Peter would get over it. And it didn't matter very much whether Peter and Charlotte would be happy: they would be happy enough. But what about Holly? She would suffer pain. Real, horrible pain, as if she were being slashed by a dull, serrated knife. Tears began rolling onto Peter's cheeks. This was love, he thought ruefully, to be devastated by the unhappiness of the beloved on account of your rival's death. He would have to help her, with no other object but her well-being. He would have to comfort her. He would have to ease her suffering any way he could.

The window shades glowed and a gray light filled the room. Birds twittered, and a puff of warm, humid air foretold the day to come. Peter rose and stepped over to the bed where Holly was sleeping. She lay cushioned by Mrs. LeMenthe's soft pillows and linens. Her color had returned, and the red, raw areas around her eyes and nose had faded. Her serene sleeping expression was that of someone without a single care. Peter softly stroked her hair. He leaned over and kissed her on the forehead.

He lay down on the daybed again. Charlotte had fallen asleep hours before. Janet had fallen asleep, as had David and Deirdre and Dr. Smythe. So, eventually, had Julia, and Dick had lain down beside her and fallen asleep. Mrs. LeMenthe was asleep. Holly was asleep. Now Peter slept too.

~

Jonathan was buried three days later in New York. No one could figure out what he had been doing out on the golf course. If he had just wanted to get some air and stretch his legs, why would he go that way? If Isabella had disappeared, Peter might have had his suspicions, but she had remained in view all evening, so he was baffled too. Then the groundskeeper faced a conundrum when, while repairing the turf that the ambulance had damaged, he found one of Jonathan's patent leather shoes. Even though it had gotten soaked and maybe run over, it didn't sit right with the groundskeeper just to throw it away, so he gave it to the assistant manager to return, and the assistant manager threw it away.

5

With his wedding trip, the arrival of August, which was always slow, and Mac McClernand's own holiday in September, Peter had managed to avoid McClernand for weeks. Meanwhile, Thropp seemed to be ignoring him, having moved on to other victims, and Peter had managed to sneak back onto some of his old projects. He had almost begun to believe that he would escape altogether and that his association with McClernand would go up in smoke. But it was not to be, and there came a day when McClernand called Peter down to his office. "I've got a surprise for you!" he said. When Peter arrived, McClernand was jumping around like an impatient puppy. "Come on! Come on!" he said. "How the hell did you get here? By way of China?" He led Peter into his office and rubbed his hands together. A cloth was covering something that rested on McClernand's desk. "I bet you can't guess what this is!" McClernand said. When Peter said no, McClernand pulled off the cloth with a flourish, revealing an unusual object: two vertical wooden panels, a foot square and marked with grid lines and numbers, had been placed on adjacent sides of a wooden base, also a foot square and so marked, which was oriented diamond-wise; a square sheet of rubber, attached at various points and supported by posts of varying heights, had been slung inside the panels.

McClernand pulled himself erect with pride. "What about that? Go ahead, go ahead, you can come closer." Peter edged forward. "Pick it up," said McClernand. As soon as Peter began to lift, McClernand yelled, "Hold on! Take it by the base! There you go. Attaboy."

Peter turned the piece this way and that, examining it. He had a pretty good idea what it was. "It's a three-dimensional model of the box-tops market!" he said. "How . . . ingenious! And such beautiful workmanship."

McClernand dismissed the praise with a shrug. "Oh, it was really nothing. Four different woods, not a big deal." Then he leaned over Peter and ran his finger down the outside of the corner where the panels met. "But you might take a look at that dovetailing. Not bad, eh?"

"Beautiful."

"And along the base, too."

"Yes, I see that. Well, well, well, quite impressive, I must say."

They both sat and McClernand explained. It emerged that he had spent several nights describing his box-tops vision to Manny, one of the firm's more eccentric physicists. Taken with the idea (and without enough work to fill the twenty-three hours he spent at the firm each day), Manny wrote algorithms and formulas and code that, when entered into a computer, produced a drawing of a three-dimensional surface. McClernand had taken the computer model and spent weeks making his own version in wood and rubber. The panels measured implied volatility and the base showed the box tops' validity term. McClernand was quite happy with the result.

After McClernand discussed his router for a while, he leaned back in his chair and smiled at Peter.

"So," he said. "What have you got?"

"Sir?"

"What have you got? What have you come up with? Let's have it. The projections. The data. The outlook. The firming or softening trends. The market risk, the political risk, the dispersion. Legal."

"Er . . . you mean . . . er . . . you're referring to the box-tops scheme?"

"Yes! Of course."

"Of course . . . of course." Peter cleared his throat. "Well, you see, Mac, without your leadership, I was at a loss to know how to proceed, and since I didn't hear from you, I didn't want to presume to go in any particular direction on my own authority."

"You mean you've done nothing?"

"Nothing? Nothing? No, I wouldn't say nothing. Of course, I've given the whole matter a great deal of thought, and I . . . uh . . . you know, whenever I have bought cereal, it's really very fascinating, I've studied and compared the box-top coupons very carefully —"

McClernand's face was purple, and he exploded. "Goddammit, Russell! Who the hell do you think you're dealing with here? Oh, yeah, I know what you're probably saying, you and the other smart-ass-kid bastards: 'Mac McClernand, don't hear much from him any-more. Mac McClernand, he's all washed up. Mac McClernand, we know about him, he spends all his time making observations of his own fecal matter and carefully recording its color, consistency, and weight.'" McClernand looked at Peter defiantly. "Am I right?"

Peter said nothing and McClernand grunted.

"Okay, sure," he continued, "maybe there's been a bear market in Mac McClernand the past couple of years. Maybe there's been a correction. Maybe there's been a sell-off. Well, let me tell you some-thing, sonny boy. I still know the players, I can pick up that phone and call Lou Budenz or Al Kreymbourg or Stone Blackwell — or even Seth Bernard himself, I taught him a thing or two when he was a smart-ass kid — and have your ass fired like that." He snapped his fingers, although they didn't really snap, and he tried it again two or three times, like someone trying to get a flame from a cigarette lighter. He leaned back in his chair and looked at Peter with disgust. "I guess the picture looks a little different to you now, doesn't it?"

"Yes, sir."

"I guess Mac McClernand isn't exactly the guy you thought he was?"

"No, sir."

Now McClernand had a more benign expression.

"Aw, hell. I know what it's like. You're young and you think that you know about twenty times more than all the old farts in the firm put together, eh? Eh?"

"Yes, sir."

"Well, who knows? You might just get lucky and learn something." He snorted, then continued. "Right. Let's get to work. Harvey O'Connor is our grain analyst. I want you to get on with him right away. Then Charlie Price, leisure comestibles. Talk to them, get an idea of the size, direction, forecasts for their industries. Some preliminary conversations with legal and compliance. Talk to some traders, get an idea of what kind of customers could use our product right away. But don't let on why you're interested.

"Now, what Manny and I did here, it was all theoretical, treating a box top basically like an option. To put some more meat on it, we're going to have the data — get our hands around the size of the market and its flows, the new issues trading right now, if you know what I mean — and then extrapolate to the potential for a secondary market. We need the number of cereal boxes sold domestically and worldwide each year, and the number of box tops that were redeemed, say, for the past fifty years." McClernand went on at length in this vein. "Let's have some regressions, see how box tops stack up with stocks, T-bills, milk-solid forward prices, the EAFE, monthly change in private nonfarm employment . . ."

Finally, he wrapped up with a flourish: "We're gonna do it! We're gonna do it! And this is just the beginning!" After staring off for a moment, transported, he turned sharply to Peter. "Well, go on!" he barked out. "Get your ass in gear!"

"Yes, sir." Peter rose and nodded and stepped toward the door.

"Hold it! Just a second."

Peter turned.

McClernand was wearing a big grin. "Go ahead," he said, motioning. "Take it up to your office. You can keep it for a while."

"Yes, sir." Peter moved to pick up the model.

"By the base!" McClernand cried.

Peter traveled through the corridors and in the elevators of Beeche and Company carrying his unusual trophy, which received stares, and then, when he reached his office, he set it down on his desk. He had stared at it for a few minutes when his phone rang.

It was McClernand. "Say, Pete," he said, "right after you left, I realized that since we've gotten the ball rolling we ought to let Gregg Thropp in on what we're up to. You can't start early enough getting someone like him on board. So I gave him a call and I was just about to tell him all about it, when I thought, Now, wait a minute, here's a chance for Pete to show off for the boss! So I just gave him some hints but said that if he really wanted to know, he should talk to Pete Russell. He was *very* interested. Seemed like he was peeing in his pants, to tell you the truth, he was so eager to hear all about it, especially from you. He wants to see you right away."

Peter had gone into a kind of trance.

"Pete? Pete? You still with me?"

"Uh . . . oh . . . yes, Mac. Right. I'll check in with Gregg."

"Just lookin' out for my boy!"

"Yes, Mac. I appreciate that."

Peter stared at the phone for a moment, then went up to Thropp's office. There he found Thropp stretched out with his feet on his desk and his hands behind his head as if he were sunbathing.

"Ah, it's the Champ," he said. "Please. Have a seat."

Peter sat. Thropp looked at him with a big smile. Then he sighed, stretched, and brought his feet down. He cleared his throat and spoke in a sincere and serious tone.

"Peter," he said, "I owe you an apology."

"You do?"

"Yes, I do. Do you remember some time ago when I promised to utterly destroy you?"

"Vaguely."

"Well," Thropp said, shaking his head in dismay, "I'm ashamed to admit that I haven't followed through. Every Monday, making out my to-do list for the week, I've put down, 'Peter Russell: destruction of.' But I'm afraid that I've still dropped the ball. There's no excuse."

"Please, Gregg," said Peter, "don't go to any extra trouble on my account."

"No, no. A commitment is a commitment." Thropp smiled. "Now, I just got off the phone with Mac McClernand and he mentioned very briefly what you guys were working on, but I don't know if I followed. What is it again?"

Peter fidgeted for a moment, before muttering, "Breakfast-cereal box tops."

Thropp cupped his ear with his hand. "What was that? I couldn't hear you."

"Breakfast-cereal box tops," Peter said more loudly.

"Goodness, I must be going deaf. Speak up, please."

"Breakfast-cereal box tops!"

"Oh yes, that's right!" Thropp said brightly. "Breakfast-cereal box tops. I thought that's what Mac told me, but I wasn't sure." He looked at Peter with eager interest. "What has he got in mind to do with them?"

Peter fidgeted some more and his throat went dry. "He . . . well, he thinks . . . he wants the firm to establish a secondary market for them, where people could trade them. Once they become established as securities, he thinks that they would begin to function as money. The dollar, the yen, the euro are all flawed, and gold is a joke, he says, so eventually he sees box tops becoming the world's reserve currency. All the while Beeche is trading them, we'll also be acquiring them for our own account, so when everyone gives up on the dollar, we'll have the largest holdings anywhere and can, you know, dominate the world, and all that."

While Peter spoke, Thropp gave him sympathetic nods and said, "Mm-hm. Mm-hm. I see." But then he could restrain himself no longer. He began to sputter, then to chuckle, then to laugh, and then suddenly his whole body was shaken by successive waves of huge guffaws. He reached a stage when he heaved but no sound came out of his gaping mouth. His face turned bright red and tears came to his eyes. Partially regaining the power of speech, he was able to say only "B-b-b-box tops!" before becoming convulsed once again. Three or four times, the fit seemed to have passed, and Thropp would wipe his eyes and sigh. "Oh, man. God. Perfect, perfect." But then he'd say "Box tops" and erupt again. Throughout, Peter sat there quietly, trying to maintain as much dignity as possible.

Finally, Thropp had more or less recovered and was able to converse. "Champ, I'm excited for you," he said, "I really am. This is a great opportunity . . . *for you to go down in flames!*" Thropp cackled.

Then he looked at Peter with loathing. "Russell, get this: you're McClernand's rent boy. When he says 'Jump!' you're not going to just say 'How high?' but also 'May I please suck your cock first?' Understand?" He cackled again. "This is wonderful. Not in my wildest dreams! Oh, are you going to suffer. And you're a guy who, when you suffer, I'm happy. You're the Christian that a lion is eating for lunch; I'm the emperor. You're the spy; I'm the guy attaching electrodes to your scrotum. You're the wart; I'm the person who's got the wart and who likes to pick it until it's gone altogether."

"Those would be genital warts."

"Now get out of here."

"All right, Gregg," Peter said as he stood, "I'll leave. But I have just one thing to say."

"Oh yeah? What's that?"

"You. Are. Incredibly. Short."

"Get out!"

~

Peter had returned to his office and was doing a postmortem on his discussion with Thropp. It was always good to try to find the positives you could take away from moments of adversity. Also — lessons. The important thing was to learn something from these experiences. After several minutes, Peter had to admit that the positives remained elusive. Surely, though, with the perspective of a little time, they would emerge! As for the lessons, yes, there was at least one lesson — that his situation was a total, complete, unmitigated, horrendous, epochal disaster.

Okay, so things professionally are a "challenge" right now. You've got to expect that from time to time. Work through it. See it as an opportunity. And, in any case, at least you've got a wonderful home life. Oh, wait . . .

Charlotte. Four months of marriage to Charlotte had been everything he had expected, only slightly worse.

They had gone to Italy for their wedding trip. Peter had enjoyed that. In the evening, they had eaten gelato while walking on streets that looked out on the Mediterranean. The food had been incredible. He liked the way the cypresses, so upright and regular, were the only upright and regular element in the landscape. Charlotte and he had had romantic times showing each other favorite streets in cities that they had visited before they met. Nevertheless, almost instantly Charlotte had begun to drive him crazy. It wasn't just that when she used an Italian word or name with him in conversation, she would pronounce it with a full-strength Italian accent (Pi-AZ-za Sahn MARRRRco); that was no surprise and the kind of thing to which he had become inured. No, what was driving him crazy was that, like so many women with their new husbands, it seemed she had set herself the task of civilizing him. Thus, whenever Peter wanted to do something any tourist would want to do, see the world-famous view or ruin, she would frown a little, and say, "Oh, you don't really want to do that, do you? Didn't you say you'd done that years ago?" To Peter's mind, if you saw the sun set over the Mediterranean from the ideal corniche or walked through a two-thousand-year-old site once a decade, you would not be overdoing it. But Charlotte preferred to visit the old abattoir district, which, beginning a few years earlier when a disused counting house had been renovated by married Dutch architects (identical glasses), was now attracting an interesting mix of people from all over the EU. Of course, Charlotte would never object to anything as being "touristy"; that would have made it too obvious that she was worried about distinguishing herself from the tourists. Rather, she adopted the air of a virtual native, and, as a (virtual) native, of course she never even thought about the main attractions. Peter would not have minded this if it had meant that they stayed in a pleasant residential neighborhood and went to a few museums and churches. But no. She would drag Peter to the old abattoir district or to the "undiscovered" side of the lagoon where, it was true, you didn't see the average tourist, but where you did see tourists a lot like Peter and Charlotte. "You don't really want to go there, do you?" "You don't really want to eat that, do you?" "You don't really want to see those paintings, do you? That period here was so vulgar."

Ah, well. Charlotte was happy, and when she was not being smug, she was sweet. She was slightly giddy, having had the marriage burden lifted from her. Less pinched by anxiety, she also became freer and more passionate in the passionate arena of life. This was a development that Peter had to confess he viewed with mixed feelings. Charlotte would put her hand on his chest in bed; he would feel it through his cotton pajama top. Later, she would rest her hand, a moist pad with short tendrils, on his naked chest. She might then trail the tip of her index finger along the line of his profile. "Oh, what a beautiful boy," she would say. He would return the compliment, and add some others, and he would do so hovering in a no-man's-land of partially believing what he said, wanting to believe it, and utterly disbelieving it. Sometimes when that sat fully clothed in their fully illuminated living room, Charlotte wanted to talk to him in an intimate way, to stroke and pet him. She would place her hand against his cheek and bring her own face so close to his that he could not focus properly and saw two noses and four eyes. "Oh, Peter," she would say. "Baby. I love you so much." Her breath was hot, moist, and musty. "I don't know what I'd do without you. I want you so much as a man and I hope you want me as a woman." This embarrassed Peter, but he blamed himself. How could he be so uptight! So scared of intimacy! Guilt-ridden, stupefied, and self-conscious, he would do the only thing one could do in such a situation — he would embrace Charlotte and kiss her. This would be a long kiss, eyes shut. When it ended, Charlotte would smile and put her forehead on his, then frisk away to the kitchen, with one grinning backward glance. Watching her, Peter could not help but notice how woodenly she moved, yet her earnest desire to be a lithe woman of sensuality was so apparent as to be heartbreaking.

At the moment, though, these were not matters that Peter had to contend with, because Charlotte was intensely preoccupied with her job. The AGSPF was holding an important conference in Paris, and much of the planning had fallen to her. For weeks she had been coming home at night exhausted and tense. She ate little for supper and then sat on the floor in the living room working on her laptop with her papers spread out around her. She drank green tea and tried to decide if she should stay up late enough so that she could call Hanoi. Peter would receive a full report of her troubles that day: "Ibrahim Soulaiyman al Sherif al Muhammad bin al Hashem refuses to come to the convocation breakfast! I just cannot believe it. He was giving one of the addresses! It's because Jacques Becqx is speaking. Apparently, at a conference a few years ago, M. Becqx ordered a dozen pizzas to be delivered to M. Soulaiyman al Sherif's hotel room, or that's what M. Soulaiyman al Sherif said. M. Becqx denied it and threatened an angry démarche from his government. Anyway, it seems they're both still angry about it." A sigh. A moment of thought. "I suppose we could ask Muhammad Ibrahim al Sherif al bin Soulaiyman-Hashem." Then there was the official, male, from Mauritius who wanted a translator, female, to accompany him at the AGSPF's expense. Charlotte had to explain that the AGSPF would balk at paying for a translator to attend a conference of people whose whole purpose for gathering was that they spoke the same language. The official had now submitted new papers in which the same woman was listed as a "hydrologist." Peter was patient and helpful, he hoped. In a way, it was better like this. A swamped Charlotte kept him at a distance. This could work, Peter thought to himself. He could remain supportively at her side. He could listen; he could help. That could be okay. For a lifetime? It depended on your expectations.

Meanwhile — well, meanwhile, Peter had seen Holly regularly. She had come for dinner; she had accompanied Peter and Charlotte to the movies; she had asked them to come along with her to parties. Sometimes, Peter and she took a walk on a Sunday afternoon when Charlotte was working with Frau Schimmelfennig, her German tutor, sometimes following an aimless path through the streets, where they would do research for the coffee-table book they hoped someday to produce, *The Tenement Cornices of Yorkville;* sometimes they went to the museum, where they would also amble without much purpose, from the Etruscans to the South Pacific Islanders to Federal Americans. Holly sometimes said to Peter, "Come on, let's go see your countess, the one with the beautiful gloves." She was referring to a portrait of an Englishwoman that Peter had once mentioned that he particularly admired. Sometimes they just went to the park. Leaving it, all but deserted, at dusk, they made a loud scratchy noise when stepping on the dry leaves; the dim rocks rose from the ground like smooth, oblong whales; Holly's face reflected the fading light and shone in the surrounding gloom. Peter liked these outings.

Sitting in his office, staring at McClernand's contraption, and still smarting from his encounter with Thropp, Peter ruminated about his life. The Holly part, he couldn't help it, made him smile. He would see her on Saturday night, when she came over to make dinner. Charlotte was leaving on Sunday, and the idea was that if Holly cooked, Charlotte could concentrate on her final preparations for her trip. Holly's enthusiasm as a cook exceeded her competence, but it was a meal that Peter looked forward to.

~

Charlotte was sitting in the living room of her, and now Peter's, apartment. After the wedding, Peter had given up his place near the East River and they were living at Charlotte's until they bought something. This had made sense: her apartment was much nicer than his, and he could shed his shell far more easily than she, since his was so much lighter. He had never furnished his apartment with much more than a bed and a sofa and a couple of chairs. Books, CDs, squash racquets, and hockey sticks provided the only decoration. Saying that Peter never allowed her to see his apartment, his mother had once asked Jonathan what it was like, and Jonathan had said, "Ah, well, Mrs. Russell, ah, Peter's apartment is what you might call minimally appointed." She had laughed and said, "I knew he needed things!" Peter's father, who was always one step behind a joke, especially when Jonathan was making Mrs. Russell laugh, had looked from one to the other like someone trying to identify a sound.

Charlotte's case was different. Her apartment was part of her identity. She had the whole parlor floor of a brownstone — it was expensive, but her father helped with the rent — and no first-time visitor left without her docent's account of the pocket doors, the mantel, the extensive molding, and other decorative details. Somewhere along the line, after the part about the social customs of

middle-class New Yorkers of the nineteenth century and the parlor's place in them, Charlotte would say, "And do you know what?"
For some time, the eyeballs of her listener might have been rolling
around on his or her lower lids, but stimulated by a new sharpness
in Charlotte's voice they would dart back into their accustomed
place, as if pulled by a string. "And do you know what?" There
would be a dramatic pause. "I have gargoyles." This, clearly, was
the climax of the performance and always provoked the outburst
"Really!" Or sometimes "No! Really!" and even, from time to time,
"No! Really! I can't believe it!"

"I really do," Charlotte would continue. "Right above both of
those windows there. I don't know what happened on this street, but
they are both certainly very frightened-looking!" Then she would
make a face like that of the gargoyles, with her mouth making an
O and all her features drawn down. It was a mistake for Charlotte
to make this face. While she hoped doing so would seem game
and fun and cute and spontaneous and adorable, she actually made
herself look too weird for comfort.

Charlotte had many acquisitions, and each came with a story. In
London she had come across a French treatise on dance from the
eighteenth century; a friend was studying the history of dance, and
Charlotte bought the book thinking her friend might want it; it
turned out that this was a cheaper, more popular edition of a fairly
rare book that was in the library the friend was using, and so she
didn't have any need of it. Charlotte thought that the engravings
were quite nice and decided to cut some of them out and frame
them (she had a framer she was crazy about) and she really thought
they had turned out well. "This little set of prints is by an Italian
friend. That's a watercolor — isn't it pretty? — that I bought years
ago, when I was on a college program in Devon . . . It's a Ghanaian
mask, really quite ferocious, don't you think? They wore it when

making . . . Oh, come on, now, what is it? Oh, I forget, it's a sort of fermented drink, in gourds . . . The little horse from Spain . . . the figurines, also Spanish . . . the fourth-century bust from Turkey, amazing how cheap . . ." And so it went, until a guest had had the entire catalogue.

Invariably, the tour ended with what was obviously the finest piece in the collection. Over the mantel hung a medium-sized landscape painted in a postimpressionist style — hills, houses, grass, trees, sky, clouds (a couple of very beautiful clouds). The setting was, a viewer could guess, the South of France. The frame would have been old-fashioned when the painting was made. Although the artist was minor, it was a very good painting. Not that this consideration counted much with Charlotte, but it was also worth several tens of thousands of dollars. It was a real painting, by someone who knew what he was doing, who had excellent taste and who had put something precious and indissolubly his own into the work. As it should have been, the painting was Charlotte's pride and joy. She told the story: it was a present from her father and her stepmother for her twenty-first birthday. Her father had first bought a painting by this artist when he was spending a year in Paris before going to law school. It was a tiny still life and it was "far more than I could afford." Then one day a few weeks later a note arrived for him from the artist's daughter asking him to tea: she was very curious to meet this young American who had taken an interest in her father's work. The dealer, it turned out, had mentioned the sale to her and given her the address. Charlotte's father went to see the woman, who was in her sixties, and he found her "utterly charming." She was so cultivated. She had never married, but she had had many lovers. Her house was in a suburb of Paris and they had tea in her garden, which was now almost wild. And the house! It was so very dark and musty and so cluttered, full of paintings by the woman's father and his friends (some of whom were well known). Charlotte's father and the woman got along tremendously well, and he continued to see her and to buy paintings by her father until her death. He had taken Charlotte's mother to see her once; that had not gone well. But she had lived into her nineties, and she and Julia had gotten to know each other and became great friends. Charlotte loved this story. She loved to tell it. She loved her father for having such a connection and providing such a story. Indeed, she loved all this almost more than she loved the painting itself.

On this evening, while Peter was off playing hockey, Charlotte was sitting on the rug in the living room and she had her laptop in front of her. Spread out before her on the rug, in concentric semicircles, were piles of papers. She stretched and looked at the time. Holly would be arriving soon to cook dinner. Charlotte wore a comfortable long skirt and had taken out her contact lenses. She was wearing her glasses, and she wondered if, with Holly coming over, she should put her contacts back in. She decided to do so and to do something about her hair. She would brush it and maybe pull it back? There wasn't time to wash it. That was scheduled for later tonight.

Charlotte liked Holly. She did. But she did not feel at ease with her, and she almost wished that Holly were not coming over. Charlotte and Peter could have just ordered something. She could not have declined Holly's offer, though. She knew that Holly wanted to do something for them and that Holly's grief had made her restless, eager to find ways to dissipate energy, and she knew that Holly was lonely. Finally, she knew that Peter would want to indulge her. So when Holly had called, Charlotte sounded enthusiastic and grateful. Charlotte did appreciate the gesture.

The reasons that Charlotte felt ill at ease with Holly were various. To begin with, they would never have been people who had a natural rapport, regardless of the circumstances in which they knew each other; some ineffable qualities of their natures prevented them from feeling an instant bond, as occasionally happened with people who had friends in common, and in this case, as in others, the explanation was a mystery. But there was more to it than the fact that their keys did not fit each other's locks. To take one aspect of the problem, Holly was very pretty, and this caused Charlotte discomfort. Charlotte was less pretty and, in fact, the degree to which she was pretty at all was, to her mind, a matter of debate. In the presence of a certifiable beauty, Charlotte began to question her own looks, a process that could cascade endlessly. At the same time, she searched for a way in which she could "count," since she believed that in any social setting, a beautiful woman made everything else irrelevant. Beauty was the unavoidable factor. When a beautiful woman joined a group in conversation, the ecology changed, and Charlotte found herself transformed from a bird flying through the air reasonably well into a bird struggling to take off. Once or twice in her life she had had the experience of joining a group and feeling its entire tone shift, the film going from black-and-white to color, once or twice in her life when she was looking her best. She had wondered a billion times what it would be like to be the kind of person for whom that happened every day.

How often had Charlotte studied herself in the bathroom mirror! She moved her chin up, down, to the left, to the right, holding up a hand mirror to show her profile, testing the angles she could test (and it was frustrating that she could not see herself from all possible ones), trying to decide, seeking the definitive answer. Was she pretty, was she pretty, was she pretty? Sometimes she thought that of course she was very pretty, and it was only her insecurities that prevented her from seeing it. But she knew that wasn't true. From a certain angle, her face looked so narrow and her nose and chin stuck out so much; there was a suggestion of witchiness. At best she had one of those faces with character and appeal even if they were not conventionally attractive. But that wasn't true either. She was better-looking than that. The question would never be settled, and she sometimes wished she were frankly ugly so that it would be.

Alone with a beautiful woman, with no one else to carry the conversation, Charlotte always felt that she was alone with a she-leopard: what do you say? Charlotte was a witness, standing there watching the beauty, but she wasn't participating in the same world. When Holly's hand touched the saltcellar, it would be a different saltcellar from what it was when Charlotte touched it. Holly wasn't a pure, absolute beauty, but she was beautiful enough. The natural thing for Charlotte to do would be to fall into the role of the Plain One to the other girl's Pretty One; the Plain One was supposed to be friendly and eager, almost grateful to be in the Pretty One's presence. Well, Charlotte had too much pride for that, and she wasn't that plain.

Then there was something else that made Charlotte uncomfortable in Holly's company: Charlotte felt jealous of Holly romantically. The other party in this triangle was Jonathan. He had turned Charlotte's head from the moment she had met him. She had always known that any involvement with him was impossible; in fact, even if neither of them had been attached to others, she knew that Jonathan was too beautiful and swift a beast for her to manage, or complement, or deserve. When he walked into a room, or she and Peter joined him and Holly at a table, Charlotte felt as if she had lost control of a car. She blushed and her heart beat faster. There were a couple of times when she found herself alone with him and she had suspected he was flirting with her and she had had the fleeting thought — but no, that would have been impossible. This attraction to Jonathan had made Charlotte feel jealous of Holly and uncomfortable with her when Jonathan was alive, and that remained true now.

Then, finally, Jonathan's death had added another layer of awkwardness: it was such a big thing for two people who didn't know each other well to go through and so made it even harder to talk to Holly in a superficial way, but going deep down into the tragedy didn't seem like an option either. Charlotte felt embarrassed by what had happened, that her wedding had been the scene of something so dramatic, and that she had reacted as she had. Jonathan's death had certainly not brought them closer; rather, they were like two acquaintances in a tragedy who, after all the leads had died, had to stay onstage and talk about the weather.

It was just about time for Holly to arrive. Charlotte wondered when Peter would get home. Peter was so good with Holly. She had certainly needed him in the months since Jonathan's death, and, Charlotte was quite sure, Peter had certainly needed Holly. Peter had a good heart, and Charlotte knew he was devastated by the death of his friend. Being with Holly helped. She didn't begrudge them the time they spent together. Soon enough, she expected, Holly would move on to another life. That there should be any attraction between Peter and Holly had never occurred to her: she never imagined that Peter, good, solid Peter, would feel misbegotten passion, or that Holly, beautiful, swift Holly, would tarry for a domestic animal such as he.

Charlotte looked again at the time. She saved her work on the laptop and closed it (she had been tweaking a chart that showed the yearly caloric production per hectare of French Guiana); she would have to leave the papers where they were, because she had a map of her work in her mind and they represented the terrain. It would make the apartment look messy, but Holly wouldn't mind about that. She got up and put in her contacts and brushed her hair and decided to leave it down; assessing her attire, she found it suitable. She spent a moment looking at her face in the mirror. Then the intercom buzzed. Charlotte took another look at herself in the mirror; what she saw did not displease her, but it didn't please her so much, either. She had to answer the buzzer, but she lingered at the mirror for another moment: her heart sank, anxiety and irritation fluttered in her breast; she felt as if it had become occupied by a swarm of dirty flies. She went to the intercom and said, "Holly?" "Yes, it's me!" came the reply. "Great! Come on up!"

Charlotte pressed the buzzer. In the lag before Holly arrived there was plenty of time for a swirling galaxy of thoughts to form. Charlotte stood by the intercom thinking: What, what, what could she claim as an attribute in which she was superior to Holly? Looks? Cleverness? Success? Husband? Grace? Charm? Happiness? Social status? Wealth? Taste? Charlotte ran all these categories through her mind, searching for Holly's weak points; she was like a rock climber desperately searching for a crevice into which she could insert her fingertips. Teaching Latin to private-school girls? That wasn't very major. Charlotte remembered her own teachers and how insignificant they now seemed. Charlotte's work was international in scope. Meanwhile, the gods had ill-favored Holly, as evidenced by the tragedy she had undergone, a tragedy that was so public and odd that it made her an object of unwelcome curiosity. Also, Charlotte was more sophisticated about, well, lots of things. She knew it was small of her, but she felt better.

Holly arrived carrying shopping bags made of thick brown paper and with fat cords for handles. She had gone to one of the fancy food shops nearby. The end of a baguette stuck out of one of the bags, like a phallus.

"Charlotte! Hi!" Holly said.

"Holly! Hello!" They kissed. "Wow, did you buy out the whole store?" Charlotte asked. "Here, let me take one of those." She leaned in to take a bag.

"Thanks," said Holly. "You know, you get into one of those places and can't resist things. I probably overdid it. But I've got the menu all planned."

"Great!"

Holly followed as Charlotte led the way to her kitchen, a small space where there would barely be enough room on the counters for all the viands that Holly had produced.

"All of this looks so good," Charlotte said, unpacking the bags. "It's really nice of you to do this. I'm in a state of near panic." Charlotte had intended to say this with genuine appreciation and friendliness, but it came out singsong and fakey; and, at the same time, that wasn't an effect she altogether regretted. Holly had been studying a jar in her hand. When Charlotte spoke she looked up and smiled at her.

"I'm so happy to do it. And anyway, you know that you are really doing me the favor. I don't know what else I'd be doing tonight. I'm really glad to have the company and to be busy doing something."

Charlotte did not say anything to this.

Holly looked at the jar again. "The problem with these recipes," she said, "is that they always call for two tablespoons of whatever, so you run out and buy a whole bottle of grapeseed oil, which you won't have any reason to use ever again in your life, and so the bottle will stay in your cupboard, and probably move with you several times." She looked over at Charlotte with a smile.

"Yes," Charlotte said. "I find that's true with . . . with . . ." She couldn't think of anything, so she just repeated, "I find that's true."

Holly removed the baguette, butter, olives. "I hope this turns out all right," she said. "You can't ruin loin of pork, can you?"

"We've had delicious dinners at your place!"

Holly rolled her eyes. "That's nice of you to say. I've been trying to learn from my father over the past few years. I usually have to call him when I'm about halfway through."

She removed a bunch of parsley from a bag and unwound the rubber band that bound it. "I think the greatest revelation I have had so far in my not very distinguished career as a cook is that parsley could actually be chopped up and used in a dish. Growing up, I never saw it except when they put it next to a steak in a restaurant."

Charlotte felt she ought to say something in response to this. "That's one thing they didn't do in restaurants in Paris."

Holly laughed. "I don't imagine they did. It was different in Chicago."

Instantly, Charlotte felt bad for having played the Paris-childhood card. "Oh, Holly," she said. "How rude of me! Wouldn't you like a drink?"

"I completely forgot," Holly said. She pulled a bottle out of a bag. "I brought this for you. It's sort of like one of those aperitifs that I know are favorites of yours. I don't know if you know it. It's kind of hard to find, even in France."

Charlotte looked at the label. She was surprised to find that she didn't recognize the name. "I don't think I've ever had this," she said. "Thanks, Holly, that's really thoughtful of you. Why don't we have some right now?"

"I'd love a drink. Maybe a couple, to calm my cooking nerves."

Charlotte put ice in short glasses and poured the drinks; the liquid looked like a more golden version of sherry. Now what? It wasn't very comfortable standing in the tiny kitchen, either physically or psychologically, and Charlotte didn't want to look over

Holly's shoulder while she cooked. Yet the food preparation did provide a distraction and an opportunity for lots of busywork. Still, Holly had not sat down since she arrived. And anyway, what kind of mouse was Charlotte that she couldn't sit and make conversation with Holly for ten minutes? Charlotte determined to be at her ease and to be a good hostess.

"If you've got things organized," she said, "why don't we sit down for a minute if you'd like?"

They took their drinks into the living room and presently they were settled, with Holly in one corner of the love seat, and Charlotte in the chair near its opposite end.

Charlotte sipped her drink. "Mmm. This is delicious," she said. "Isn't it good?"

A moment passed while they savored their drinks. Charlotte realized that she had hardly ever been alone with Holly before. In fact, Charlotte couldn't think of a single substantive conversation the two of them had ever had. She felt a quiver of social panic. What on earth would they talk about?

Just then, Holly spoke. "God, Charlotte, that's such a beautiful painting," she said. She had been looking at the painting above the mantel, which was opposite the love seat.

Charlotte glanced over her shoulder and smiled reflexively. "Oh, yes, thanks."

"I'm not sure I have ever heard the full story of it. I think you said — didn't your father give it to you for your birthday? When you turned twenty-one?"

"That's right. Papa and Julia, my stepmother, gave it to me."

"What a great thing. Didn't you once say that the artist was a friend of your father's? But no, that can't be right."

"Well." Charlotte took another sip of her drink. "Well, I'll tell you. Before law school, my father lived in Paris for a year. He'd studied art in college, and he would wander around galleries and antiques shops." And so Charlotte began to tell the story, as she had so often. What struck her this time, though, was that Holly interrupted to ask questions. Had the old woman painted at all herself, what happened when she met Charlotte's mother, did the painter leave any drawings? It seemed to Charlotte that no one had ever asked her a question when she had told this story before and, in fact, if she were honest with herself, she was always conscious of a chasm opening up between herself and her auditors. On this occasion, the experience was quite different. Holly's questions were very interesting to answer. The painter had been a gifted draftsman, in fact. Charlotte's father had collected many of his drawings.

As they talked, Charlotte asked herself in one part of her mind, Why was Holly being so nice? But suspicions could gain no foothold. Charlotte was enjoying herself. They had another drink.

Holly looked around at the papers that lay on the floor before her.

"Okay, so what exactly is this conference that you're organizing?" she asked.

"Well it's — I'm certainly not organizing the whole thing, I'm just one of the people. It's something that happens just about every year, when people from all over come. This is the first time it's been held in Paris for a pretty long time, so it's an especially big deal. There will be lots of events. For example — are you really interested in this?" It was highly unusual for Charlotte to ask such a question. Typically, once set out on a course of explaining one of her pet subjects, she beat on without stopping, for the contradictory reasons that, on the one hand, she assumed everyone shared her passion, and, on the other, she feared that if she did stop, she would allow the opportunity for the others' boredom to erupt into the open.

But Holly said, "Sure!"

So Charlotte began to tell Holly all about the conference and its various symposia, colloquia, forums, and panels. The *Code Napoléon:* Twenty-First-Century Perspectives. Technical information in French. *Le Jazz de la Francophonie.* Charlotte had worked hard to learn the names for the different styles: makossa, Cameroon; ikalanga, Gabon; bembeya, Guinea Bissau. And there was this star coming from Vietnam, Trahn Vam . . . oh no, she couldn't remember his name! Holly asked questions, and they even had a laugh or two. Eventually, her main remarks having run their course, Charlotte fell silent for a moment and got a bashful look on her face.

"Do you want to know what I'm really excited about?" she asked without looking at Holly.

"Of course."

"Well," said Charlotte, her voice quickening, "this year, it might just happen, we aren't sure and so it would be bad to get our hopes up too much, but it might just happen this year that Maine is granted Observer Status."

"Maine. Our Maine?"

"Oh, yes. Observer Status is the lowest ranking. But wouldn't it be wonderful? You see, there are French-speaking communities in Maine that go back generations, and after decades when the language was suppressed, it's having a real revival. New Brunswick is right next door, and it has become a full member after having been an associate for a while. There have been all sorts of complications and it's failed in other years, but this time it looks as if we have a shot. I've been working really hard on it."

"You mean," Holly said, "you'd have guys from Maine meeting there with people from Paris and Geneva and, you know, Cambodia and, what, the Congo —?"

"Both Congos."

"Both Congos!"

Holly laughed and Charlotte did too.

"Oh, Charlotte," Holly said, "that *would* be fantastic. Oh, I hope it happens! You would feel so proud."

Something in Holly's tone startled Charlotte. Holly sounded sincere. Charlotte spent her entire life looking around the corners of things people said to her. She could let down her guard with Peter, and a couple of really old friends, but practically no one else. Here, though, she found Holly's conversation to have no corners, no other side. The effect on her was far stronger than was sensible, given the straightforward subjects under discussion. Charlotte could not quite account for the feeling of easiness that had come over her. Holly's utterances seemed to arrive along two channels: the words, which were friendly, but nothing out of the ordinary; and the tone of voice, which operated on a wavelength that penetrated Charlotte's armor. No one listening to a recording of what Holly had said would understand what Charlotte felt: there was no extraordinary "delivery" on Holly's part, but there was something solid in her tone, and something gentle about it, which was rare.

And now Charlotte began to feel a little odd. She liked the drink that Holly had brought very much, and she may have begun to be the slightest bit tipsy, but that could not account for the sensation. She looked around the room and it seemed to be bathed in a soft, golden glow. She settled into her chair, and the upholstery plushly bulged around her. The air itself in the room seemed clear and fresh, but with enough warmth to make its gentle presence felt, as if it had been boxed up on a sunny spring day and delivered to Charlotte's apartment. Charlotte looked at Holly. How beautiful she was! How graceful! How melodious her voice was, like the piping of a shepherd boy. That was how Charlotte put it to herself, although she had never heard a shepherd boy pipe. She began to laugh, and Holly asked her what was so funny, to which she replied "Nothing, nothing" before beginning to laugh again. Beautiful, wonderful Holly! Charlotte's hands tingled with the desire to stroke Holly's soft hair, to hold her hand and stroke her arm, to kiss her cheeks. Of course, Charlotte had had crushes on females, and in one case it had come to something, allowing Charlotte to check that experience off her list. Her present feeling was different. True, a low-voltage sexual current ran through it, but what she really felt was — what? Love? She just loved Holly. She felt happy in her presence. It was so strange. Charlotte was always trying. Trying to do something, trying to fulfill some requirement, either of duty or fashion, trying so hard to be good and correct, in ways that no one appreciated, not even Peter. But for the moment, for reasons that she could not discern, she found she did not have to try. To think of how nervous Holly had always made her, and yet in Holly's company right now she felt like a cat who's found a warm spot on the floor, like a sentry relieved of duty.

They talked for a while longer, about all sorts of things — their mothers (Holly's was vague but loving, prompting Charlotte inwardly to give all praise to vague but loving mothers), stepmothers (they had both had one, though Holly's had lasted only a year); the trials of a friend of Charlotte's whose children were monsters. Throughout, Charlotte's sense of placid well-being only deepened; she would have gathered Holly up in her arms and petted her if such a thing had been appropriate. Then Holly looked at her watch and became startled.

"Oh my God!" she said. "Look what time it is! I've got to start cooking or you and Peter will starve before I'm done!"

"Don't worry," Charlotte said. "Peter's playing hockey and he's always late."

"But still!" Holly rose and took a step toward the kitchen. "I haven't even begun!"

The thought of separating from Holly almost panicked Charlotte, a problem that she solved brilliantly, in her own estimation.

"Well," she said, rising herself, "then I'll help. That should make it go faster."

"But what about all the last-minute stuff you have to do?" asked Holly, motioning to the papers and binders and folders on the floor.

Charlotte dismissed the work with a wave of her hand.

"Do you really mean it?" Holly asked.

"Sure, I'd love to."

"Er, okay," Holly said, looking at Charlotte a little dubiously. "That would be great."

Charlotte and Holly went to the kitchen. Holly read out the recipe and assigned Charlotte her tasks. The kitchen was so small that, as they worked, it was unavoidable that their hands and arms would accidentally touch. They stood hip to hip and shoulder to shoulder. Their bodies would graze as one passed the other. Their hands became juicy and oily and they both had some flour on their faces. Charlotte felt so happy! Food and mess; and that bottle, which they had of course brought to the kitchen; her wonderful new friend. They got a Latin music station on the radio and turned it up.

Charlotte was cutting fresh figs in half; the feel of their furry pulp and the juice that ran on her fingers, and the look of their loose, liquid, swollen, purplish, drop-shaped insides, and their sweet smell — you could smell the Mediterranean sun — all of these made Charlotte quiver.

The two gabbled on, and eventually the conversation turned to the subject of men. This was not inevitable, for Charlotte had always been reticent in discussions of romantic matters with her female friends. Except for a period in the seventh grade, she hadn't been one to be on the phone constantly talking about boys. For a while, they discussed this and that person who was hopelessly in love or who had been hopelessly hurt, and then Charlotte took a death-defying leap into the personal.

"And what about you, Holly?" she asked. "How are you? How is it without Jonathan?"

Holly was chopping onions and didn't answer for a moment.

"I'm fine," she said. "In a way, my entire time with Jonathan seems like a dream, and now I have woken up and things are normal. He was like that. And what happened was so sudden. He was just suddenly gone, poof. We didn't have children, and we hadn't really settled down somewhere, living in his bachelor pad. So we hadn't constructed and settled into a whole life that was destroyed, if you know what I mean. Anyway, yes, I miss him." Holly smiled and shook her head. "Jonathan was not the model husband. But I miss him. But basically I'm fine."

They worked a bit in silence. Then it was Holly's turn to ask Charlotte about herself.

"So? You and Peter? The newlyweds? Everything going well?"

"I think so," said Charlotte. "I know I'm happy, and I think Peter is. Although I also know that I am definitely the one who got the better deal."

"Now, Charlotte —"

"Oh, it's true. The thing about Peter, he's just so solid. He's so good, and he is so lacking in any complexes or weirdnesses, really. He's attentive and patient. He's true, you know? I'd say 'normal,' but that makes it sound as if he's dull, and he's not dull. I mean normal but the highest level of normal. Does that make any sense?"

There was a pause, and then Holly spoke. "I think what you mean is 'ideal.'"

"You're right, Holly!" said Charlotte. "You understand." She had been looking down, snapping beans, and with this remark she looked up at Holly and saw that she was teary-eyed. "Holly!" Charlotte said. "You're crying! I'm sorry!" The sight of Holly in pain made Charlotte's heart shudder.

"Please." Holly laughed. "Don't worry. It's the onions." She scraped the chopped onions into a pan where she had heated oil, and they sizzled loudly.

Peter arrived shortly thereafter and leaned into the kitchen to survey the preparations.

"What's for dinner?" he asked. "I guess, from the looks of things, something delivered from the Indian place?"

"Peter!" said Charlotte. "How can you say that! Thanks to Holly, we are going to have an exquisite meal."

"And thanks to my expert sous-chef," said Holly.

"I'm sorry," said Peter. "I didn't mean . . . it was just that, from appearances, it seemed that, you know, the menu hadn't quite gelled."

" 'From appearances'!" Charlotte said. "I guess you aren't aware that when a cook like Holly is really inspired and imaginative, there are certain improvisations and so the kitchen may have an air of creative tumult. It's her process. Right, Holly?"

"Er, right."

"Everything is going to come together beautifully," said Charlotte. "So, Peter, my sweet" — Charlotte pushed him away with her fingertips while giving him a peck on the cheek — "why don't you just go into the living room and make yourself a scotch —"

"We don't have any scotch —"

"Go along now."

Peter went into the living room and read a magazine.

~

The dinner ended up being pretty good. Holly had made a dish of thinly sliced potatoes and cream that qualified as delicious. The conversation flowed along happily, led by an unusually vivacious Charlotte. They drank a fair amount of wine. The three of them were eating a flourless chocolate cake and drinking some more wine when Holly lightly tapped on her glass with a fork.

"I'd like to propose a toast," she said.

Peter and Charlotte looked at Holly and at each other and back at Holly.

"I didn't give a toast at your dinner, so I'd like to do it now. A toast to you and your love for each other." She took a deep breath. "As you may know, various people over the years have spoken and written on the topic of love. Some of the writers whom I would teach to my students if they were advanced enough, which they aren't, wrote of it very eloquently and sometimes very coarsely. So I doubt I will say anything original or profound or even very coherent, but I am inspired by this company to say something.

"Um . . . let's see . . . well — first of all, let me say, I have the utmost respect for the Buddha. I think he thought thoughts in five hundred BCE that were truly excellent. Now, Buddha promulgated the four noble truths, and let me refresh your memory of what they are: all existence is suffering, the cause of all suffering is desire, freedom from suffering is nirvana, and nirvana is attained through the eightfold path of ethical conduct, wisdom, and mental discipline. Not having founded a religion that has had millions upon millions of adherents over the past twenty-five hundred years, I am hardly in a position to criticize, but I personally don't accept the validity of all four of the noble truths. I don't know if all existence is suffering. Most cats aren't suffering, as far as I can tell; people at a movie that they really like aren't suffering. But the second noble truth is definitely true, to my mind. All suffering does come from desire. Definitely. Number three: Absolutely. Totally. The extinction of self, that desiring self, leads to freedom. And as for the last one, yes, sure, the eightfold path, I'm all for it, one hundred percent.

"But — and again, who am I to judge? — I don't think that is the only way. I think you can also escape suffering through . . . love. When you really love someone and they really love you, you have desire, but not in the sense of wanting things that you can't get or shouldn't want in the first place. It's not even that your desire has been satisfied. It's not satiety. You lie in that person's arms and you aren't thinking about what's next or what's wrong or what you want. You aren't trying to get someplace. Rather than doing or proving or striving for something, you just sort of *are,* as a lyric poem or work of art is supposed to be, or like a big boulder that's really just there. And again, it's not that you've gotten what you desire and so are satisfied; it's that there is no doingness or provingness or strivingness. To my mind, this sounds a little like nirvana and I'd say you are emptied of your self. The difference, maybe, is that in my scheme you aren't just emptied, you are also filled — but filled with one big thing that replaces all the ten million nettle-some, egotistical things that are inside you as a rule. And with that one thing comes a feeling of joy — not no feeling. You're like a big boulder that somehow has levitated six feet off the ground. Then there is one more thing, which is wanting to make the person you love happy, to give yourself to him or her, but this wanting is not a feeling external to love or the result of any incompleteness; it is one component of that big single thing. And serving the person you love isn't something you 'do.' It is entirely natural. It's guided by the same part of your brain, whatever it is, that controls your heartbeat and your — oh — kidney function or whatever.

"If you love someone, then you feel about them the way I've described, and if that person shares that feeling and you are together, then that is the highest state of being, and the happiest."

Holly was about to cry. She swallowed, and then laughed a little in embarrassment. She looked at Peter and Charlotte. "So, you two, nice going." She let out a combined laugh and sob. "Here's to you. And remember, neither of you can drink." She raised her glass and drank.

Charlotte looked at the curve of Holly's face, and it seemed like the most beautiful shape in the world. Oh, Holly, she thought, how beautiful you are, how fair. And Peter — Peter was so handsome. It wasn't a showy handsomeness like Jonathan's, but quiet, sound, well made. Handsome rather than beautiful.

~

Charlotte began to clear away the dessert plates. Peter and Holly stirred to help, but she insisted that they stay where they were. She would make coffee, she said. She took the plates into the kitchen and deposited them in the sink. She unscrewed her espresso pot (she had the jumbo size, and it had become stained a deep brown with use) and ran water into the base. A delicious smell of coffee grounds wafted to her when she opened the container. She filled the sieve, screwed on the top, and set the pot on the burner. Over Holly's objections, she had used their wedding-present china for their little dinner party, and the demitasse cups and saucers were rimmed in gold. She set these on a tray with sugar. As she was arranging them she glanced through the kitchen entranceway, which gave her a view of the dining table and Peter and Holly. She saw that they were talking and she smiled to herself and went back to her task. Completing it, she leaned against the counter to wait for the water to boil and now gazed out at the pair. She was very happy. It made her happy to see Holly and Peter talking together. Why was that? There was this odd experience she had been having of love for Holly, and Peter too. Peter was very good.

She watched them. Seen together, Peter and Holly gave her great pleasure. Because of the way the light fell and the composition of the view she had — with the round table-half bowing in her direction and the open curtains behind them — they seemed enclosed in a circle. Rather than mere glints, the silver seemed to give off sparks. Peter laughed at something Holly said. Charlotte never made Peter laugh that way; no one did, other than Holly. Holly looked at Peter with a smile and eyes that were open and eager. They were both leaning forward and they both had an arm stretched out a bit and resting on the table. Their hands were about two feet apart. It was typical of this night that she thought she saw a kind of yellowish white charge pass between these hands. It must have been an effect of the lights on the street.

And then something happened. It was if Charlotte had been stunned by a bright flash. This was what it must have been like for Paul on the road to Damascus. For, all of a sudden, she saw it: Peter and Holly were in love with each other.

Of course! It had always been evident. How foolish and blinkered she had been not to have seen it all along! Whenever Peter was with Holly, his spirits would rise. He would listen to her and watch her closely, and tiny adjustments in his expression would register her every nuance and gesture. He never looked at Charlotte that way. In fairness to herself, she had to say that these signs had been subtle. Peter did not leap around like an overeager headwaiter in Holly's presence; he did not appear wearing an ascot when she came over; he did not blatantly sigh and moon. Nor did he behave coldly or suspiciously scrupulously. He seemed to be very natural around Holly, and when they were going to take a walk together he always told Charlotte in the most relaxed way. Peter's manner toward Holly was respectful and delicate. It was perfect. Too perfect! How many times in history had it happened that a widow fell in love with the man who comforted her and shared her grief, her husband's closest friend, and vice versa? But Charlotte knew that the feelings between Peter and Holly long antedated the current period. Looking back, it all became obvious to her; it was if she had suddenly become equipped with a kind of infrared sight that allowed her to see what had been invisible.

She had never thought about it. When all four of them had been together, her attention had been taken up with her attraction to Jonathan, her jealousy of Holly, and the uneasiness about herself that women like Holly made her feel. After Jonathan's death, as previously stated, she still felt awkward around Holly for all those reasons, plus a couple more. These matters occupied her mind; she never thought to watch Peter and Holly for signs of an attachment that went beyond an affectionate friendship heightened by a shared tragedy.

Charlotte suddenly remembered the coffee. The espresso pot was spitting and hissing as it does when all the water has been boiled out of the base. She quickly turned off the burner, poured coffee into the cups on the tray, and headed toward the table. As she approached, Holly and Peter turned toward her simultaneously, smiling. Charlotte felt like a priestess officiating at some ceremony in which the other two were the principals.

~

Holly insisted on washing up alone.

"That was the whole point," she said. "That I would do everything while you got ready for your trip."

"I'll help, of course," said Peter.

"No," Holly replied. "You keep Charlotte company, or help her. Tonight I am your caterer." After a couple more rounds of this kind of talk — "Oh, but it won't take a minute," said Charlotte — Holly prevailed.

"I guess you have a lot still to do," Peter said to Charlotte.

"It's not so bad, and anyway, half the time we have to redo the stuff. Some delegate or speaker hasn't shown up or something. Anyway, what's the point of it all when people in some of these countries are slaughtering each other? Come on, let's take our wine and sit down." This was not Charlotte's usual manner. More typically she would have immediately returned to her laptop and her sheaves. Instead, she moved over to the love seat and, looking at Peter, patted the cushion to her left. He sat where she indicated. She turned toward him and took his hand; then she rested her head against the back of the love seat and closed her eyes.

"Tired?" Peter said.

"Not really. Maybe. A little." Then, after a moment, Charlotte opened her eyes and said, "It's nice having Holly here, isn't it?"

"Yes, it is."

Charlotte was silent for a moment. Then she said, "Please spend time with her while I'm away. It all must still be very raw, and I'm sure she's lonely."

"I'll try."

Charlotte lifted her hand and touched Peter's hair near his temple and then stroked his cheek. "Good, dear Peter," she said. Then she closed her eyes again.

~

Charlotte's alarm was always set for 6:10, but it never went off, since she woke up automatically at 6:09 every day, even on weekends. She slept much later, however, on the morning after the dinner with Holly. Sitting up in bed, she felt disoriented. Where was she? What day was it? What had happened the night before? She had been in a very deep sleep, and it took a moment or two for her confusion to lift. Of course, she was at home; it was Sunday morning. Peter's blue-striped pajamas (all of Peter's pajamas seemed to have blue stripes) lay draped over a chair. Suddenly Charlotte felt a stab of panic. She was leaving that day and she still had a million things to do! She began running over them in her head (confirm with Agnès, slides, draft to Théophile-Hector, dry cleaning, most recent figures . . .). Why in the world had she wasted all of last night? The whole point of Holly's cooking dinner was to leave Charlotte free to work. Instead, what had happened? Charlotte had had some drinks with Holly and talked to her for ages and had helped her cook, and basically abandoned all the things she had to get done. At this moment, Charlotte was having a hard time making her images and memories of the previous night cohere. She had gotten pretty drunk, she realized; her body ached, and someone had been tossing her brain around, bruising it. A sort of haze illuminated with bright lights enveloped those hours.

Charlotte got up and groggily walked to the kitchen. There was no sign of Peter, who was probably on his run. She poured herself a glass of water, and as she drank it the mist lifted a bit. Holly. Yes, she remembered now, this crazy feeling of affection for Holly. And a smile involuntarily came to her lips; traces of the feeling remained. But what had that been all about? She removed the coffeepot from the drying rack, filled the base, and set the sieve in it. When she opened the coffee container, the smell of the coffee, finely ground, dark, was strong. Charlotte reacted to this stimulus by immediately turning to look through the kitchen doorway at the dining table, which still had its cloth on it. The window behind shone with a dim, clouded glow. Charlotte stared at the table, the tablecloth, the curtains, the chairs, still arranged as they had been the previous night. Oh yes, oh yes, she said to herself, and there was that other thing last night. She closed her eyes; she sighed; she shook her head. She did not feel upset. She felt quite calm. My epiphany, she thought, my epiphany.

~

It was now Sunday afternoon, and Charlotte would be leaving in a few minutes. She was all packed and her suitcase was near the front door. She was dressed and made up, and she looked soignée, Peter thought. Some vestigial instinct led her to dress well for a transatlantic flight. She had put her hair up in what was not quite a chignon, but something close to it, sort of: I am an American and I know that it would be presumptuous of me to wear a chignon, and yet I want to pay tribute to it.

Charlotte was inserting some pages into a binder. For the next week, it would be her most precious possession; using it, she could almost instantly determine where each delegate was supposed to be at any given moment or find a driver's cell-phone number or provide an important statistic. One night she had stayed up until two in the morning redoing the tabs in order to implement a new system of color coding. A few weeks before, in a carefully thought-out act of spontaneity, Peter had bought Charlotte a chic attaché case, thinking it would be especially nice to have for the conference. Unfortunately, the binder was too big to fit into it, and she would have to leave it behind.

Charlotte was sorting and shifting papers at the dining table. Peter stood nearby, leaning against the wall. They had been talking of this and that.

"Is it going to be awkward," Peter asked, "seeing Julia down at the house?"

"I don't think so," Charlotte answered. The marriage of Charlotte's father and stepmother had undergone some recent strain and they were divorcing. "My father is too civilized to be hurt or offended. Or anyway, he'll act as if he is. Part of the shtick." Charlotte paused. "I like Julia and she's a friend. I'm looking forward to seeing her."

"I like her, too. It's kind of a mess."

"It is, but she sounds pretty calm and content."

"Well, that's good. Please give her my best."

"Oh, I will. She's fond of you."

Charlotte closed up the binder.

"There, that's done." She put the binder in a large, satchel-like briefcase which, struggling a little, she zipped closed.

"Say, Peter," she said, "how about a glass of champagne to see me off?"

This had never been part of the routine before.

"Uh . . . sure," said Peter. "Uh . . . let me get it." He hesitated. "Uh . . . not to be a wet blanket, but are you sure you won't feel woozy on the plane and get a headache and everything? Because, usually —"

Charlotte shrugged and smiled. "Oh, I'll live on the edge, just this once."

"Okay, great!" said Peter. He got a bottle of champagne and two flutes (wedding presents). Charlotte had sat on the love seat, and Peter sat beside her. He opened the bottle without allowing the cork to fly anywhere, and he poured them each a glass.

Taking a sip, Charlotte savored it, and then said, "My father. The only time he showed a moment of emotional involvement in our wedding was when he learned what champagne and wines we were serving and ordered that they be upgraded."

Peter nodded. Charlotte rarely spoke disrespectfully of her father.

"And the worst thing about it? Of course he was right, wasn't he?" She looked at Peter.

"Well, yeah, true fact. He was."

"If you ever need someone to tell you what kind of champagne to order or" — she looked at Peter with a smile — "the way to open a bottle —"

"Or," Peter said, "the right way to fold a handkerchief and get it into your breast pocket. The knife — my whole world changed."

"Dick. Dick. Dick." Charlotte sighed.

Peter studied her. She was looking unusually pretty today, and she was acting unusual. Typically when she would go off on a trip like this, she took up the last few minutes before she left with checking and rechecking her carry-on bag to make sure it had slippers, vitamin C, vitamin E, antibacterial hand wipes, moisturizer, and melatonin. Where is my Occitan dictionary?! She was usually in a state of panic. Certainly the day had been full of heaving preparations. But here, at the last minute, she was asking for champagne! She had acted funny the night before. Peter took her hand. Then when he looked at her he saw that she was almost crying.

"Charlotte," he said, "are you okay?"

Charlotte clasped Peter's hand tightly. She looked at him and smiled; her eyes brimmed with tears like a glass of water that would overflow with one more drop.

"Oh, Peter, you're sweet to ask. You are always sweet. The pressure of all this, I guess, maybe my father and Julia —"

"But you're crying —"

"Crying? Crying? I don't see anybody crying."

Peter gave Charlotte a handkerchief, and she dried her eyes as discreetly as she could.

"Of course," she said, "there's also the fact that I'm going to miss you."

"Oh, Charlotte, I'm going to miss you, too. However busy you are, you'll at least be in Paris, and eating in Paris. I'll be sitting here all alone, ordering Thai food —"

"Don't be ridiculous. You'll be at work, and you and your pals will find some way to expense five-course dinners."

"Well, I don't know about that. The firm's been tightening up."

"Okay, maybe not. Really, you should see people and do things. Don't work the whole time. Holly's coming over today, isn't she?"

"Yes, she is, as a matter of fact. We were going to take a walk after you left."

"Well, good. I really like Holly so much. I think the only reason she's gotten through it all is because of you, Peter. You should keep up the good work."

"She has lots of friends, her sister, her mother and father —"

"I know. But she's very lucky to have you."

Peter didn't know what to say to this. He shrugged self-deprecatingly.

"Let me just have half a glass more," Charlotte said, "and then I better go." Peter refilled her glass and his own. "This is extravagant. You'll have to think of some way to use up the rest of the bottle before it goes flat."

"We have that vacuum thing. I'll keep it until you get back."

"Oh good," Charlotte said. She looked down shyly.

Peter suddenly had a premonition. Charlotte was about to say this to him: "Do you remember the last time we sat alone right here drinking champagne?" She would be referring to the evening Peter asked her to marry him. After a moment, she looked up at Peter, shyly. She spoke:

"Do you remember —"

"The last time we sat alone right here drinking champagne? It's funny, I was just thinking about that myself. It was before we went to that Rangers game last winter —"

"Peter, you had two friends here, and it wasn't champagne, it was that weird stout or whatever you bought."

"No it wasn't!" Peter frowned. "Oh, wait a minute. Maybe you're right." He thought for a moment. "I know: Bastille Day."

"We've never done Bastille Day."

"The anniversary of the Battle of Crécy?"

"At Crécy, the English won!"

"Sorry." Peter winced. "Okay, let me think. You and me. Here. Some sort of occasion. Champagne." Peter paused, and his expression grew more sentimental. He and Charlotte looked into each other's eyes. In his, he hoped, Charlotte accurately read nothing but affection.

"It was," Peter said, "when I asked you to marry me."

Charlotte just nodded. Then she moved her face toward Peter's. He reciprocated, and they kissed.

6

*I*n southwestern France in October, the saffron blooms, and the purple of its blossoms matches the purple on the rim of the horizon when the sun has just set. Each evening, Julia watched the sun set from her flagstone terrace, and she loved to see that rim appear. She loved her house, and she loved it in this season, when the trees and grasses were green but on the cusp of their turn to gold. It was still quite warm during the day, although damp and chilly at night, especially if you lived in an old stone house heated only by fireplaces. Previous owners had put in plumbing and electricity, and she and Dick had often vowed to heat at least part of the house, but her heart had not been in it, so this was never done. (The cold bothered Dick quite a lot, and one effect of their failing to modernize was that Julia was able to spend more time here alone.) She loved the house. She loved eating trout and perch and walnuts and plums. She loved the friends she had made; she loved M. and Mme. Gorotiaga, the couple who worked for her. She loved the landscape with its outcroppings of limestone and the rows of erect poplars. She loved the nearby castles, villages, churches, ruins, dolmens, and caves. Layers of civilization had been laid down here over tens of thousands of years, so, sitting on her terrace watching the sun go down, Julia felt she was part of something very ancient. It was a moment not only of pleasure but also of awe and exaltation.

~

When Julia stayed at her house in France in October, her day would typically go something like this: She woke up at about six, when the three knife-edged shafts of light came through gaps in the curtains, and luxuriated for a while in the warmth of her duvet. Almost invariably, since Dick didn't like to come at that time of year, she was alone. Julia, meanwhile, would never even consider spending the night here with someone else. M. and Mme. Gorotiaga would be scandalized. More important, it simply wasn't something she wanted. This was her own queendom (only nominally shared with Dick) and, like Elizabeth I, she did not want to taint or complicate it with the presence of some man to whom she was beholden. She hated the idea of someone feeling he was her equal here and that he had been initiated into the mysteries of the place by virtue of what had transpired between them. The second that a man began to act as if the house were his own — leaving stuff around, giving an order to Mme. Gorotiaga, helping himself to what was in the refrigerator — she would want to have him shot. She didn't want to see dried shaving cream with whiskers in the sink. And she didn't want to experience, here, the emotional instability and vulnerability that would accompany a covert romance. Here she wanted to be Her Most Serene Highness, to be calm, the mistress of herself and her estate. She loved having friends stay, but a man on the sly who'd share her bed? No. And yet every morning, as she stretched and sighed and felt so satisfied in her aloneness, an undercurrent ran in exactly the opposite direction. These thoughts only occasionally rose to the surface, but they were always present. How happy, how happy, how happy she would be if there were someone next to her whom she loved, who loved her, and with whom she would exult in sharing this place. Seeing them through his eyes, her pleasure in every tint of light, every stone, every petal, would be doubled — no, brought to the second power. Who was this man? Oh, right, she would recall, he didn't exist, and love didn't either.

Rousing herself, finally, she leapt out of bed and dressed as quickly as she could; there was always that moment after she had taken off her nightgown when her whole body was covered in goose bumps. And despite the rugs that lay overlapping everywhere, she always put her bare foot down on stone, which felt like a cold puddle. Her toilet consisted of splashing cold water on her face (the water took forever to become hot). Then she ran downstairs and headed for the kitchen and its fiery hearth. Mme. Gorotiaga would already be cooking something. But passing a set of French doors, she hesitated and then stepped outside for a few minutes to see what kind of day it was, breathe the air, and get even colder.

Mme. Gorotiaga made coffee and warmed milk, and Julia poured them into her bowl. She used lots of sugar, and as she drank she ate bread with butter and jam. (At home her breakfast was austere, but she couldn't get bread and butter and jam like this at home.) Sitting at the old kitchen table with its foot-wide planks, Julia ate and listened to Mme. Gorotiaga, a stout, tobacco-colored woman in her sixties, retail the gossip of the town — who was sick, where someone's son had moved, how the newest English couple was regarded, who was paying court to a widow. Mme. Gorotiaga asked about the friends of Julia's who had visited, particularly that very pretty blond mademoiselle who came so often. This was Julia's best friend, Anna. How was her son? Would she ever marry again? "She can't find the right man," Julia would say, and of course Mme.

Gorotiaga would tell her that if every woman waited to find the right man no woman would ever get married. "She once had her heart broken very badly," Julia would answer. "I'm not sure she ever recovered, and I guess she's afraid."

The kitchen was dark usually, but in this season at this time of day, if the sun was out, light did come in from a pair of windows to the right of where Julia generally sat. Julia loved the textures that the light revealed, the old wood, the worn tiles, the rust on the stove and the bristly iron even where there was no rust, Mme. Gorotiaga's hands and woolen scarf, the lumpy wall. The only thing in the whole kitchen that was smooth, Julia noticed one day, was a glazed yellow bowl with a blue stripe that held some Majorcan pears. The brown pears' fur filtered the light, whereas it slid around the yellow glaze. (One morning Julia had suddenly been beset by panic. Oh God, she thought, this looks like a picture in an interior design magazine! But she reassured herself by noting that there were a couple of appliances from the seventies that no design editor would tolerate.)

After breakfast, Julia set out upon her day. She went on long walks with the dogs, she rode, she worked in the garden, she went to the markets, she read, she visited friends. She passed entire days doing she didn't know exactly what. Sooner than seemed possible, evening came. She watched the sunset. Then, after a supper of cassoulet or roast chicken or fish in one of Mme. Gorotiaga's buttery sauces, she got into bed with a novel and a hot water bottle. It might be only nine o'clock. She kept a small fire for a while and lay in bed drinking a last glass of wine and read. Under the covers she felt warm, and the fire created some warmth, but the room had an ambient coldness, and she enjoyed this contrast. Sometimes the side of her face near the fire would be hot and the other side would be cold, and she would turn her face to warm up the latter, feeling it tingle and feeling the other side begin to cool. One window would never close completely, and through it came a plume of damp, cold air with the smell of wet straw. She thought she could smell the cold stone too.

The bed linens carried the scent of the sun and air; after washing them, Mme. Gorotiaga always hung them outside to dry. They were thick, slightly coarse, and extremely costly. Fortunately, Mme. Gorotiaga took great pride in her ironing, so every night, before Julia mussed them, they looked like a rich man's writing paper. Julia did not care very much about luxuries (except clothes, of course), but she had always wanted a life in which she slept on very good sheets every night. It was a pleasure she had enjoyed only sporadically before she married Dick. The stone walls gave her the feeling that she was at once sheltered and also within nature, and with her wine, her bed, her fire, and her novel, and the plume of fresh air, Julia was content. She fell asleep thinking about how cold the room would get when the fire died down completely, and how warm she would be under her duvet.

~

So on a typical day in a typical year when she was staying at her house in France in October, this was Julia's routine. During this particular October, however, it was being varied somewhat. This time, things were a bit different.

For example, Julia's bedroom was not cold when she awoke, for M. Gorotiaga crept in before dawn to lay and light a fire. By the time Julia stirred, the room had warmed up nicely. Also, while she certainly ate her usual breakfast, she did not go down to the kitchen to get it; during this particular October, Mme. Gorotiaga brought it up to her on a tray.

As Julia awaited Mme. Gorotiaga, she sat up in bed and enjoyed the fire. She smiled, for she was happy. In fact, she was in love! She laughed at that thought, but it was true! She moved her hand to her belly and then lightly rubbed it. Her pregnancy was showing clearly now. There would be no dodging questions anymore. In fact, like someone in love, she wanted the world to know, she wanted to cry it from the rooftops. The baby kicked once, twice. "Oooh. Someone else is waking up, is he?" Julia said this in a high, goo-goo-ish voice that also made her laugh. Imagine, her, a woman who spoke perfect French, who for many years had felt far more emotion in buying a handbag than in any human intercourse, imagine her talking the most egregious lisping baby talk. "Good morning, liddle boy, thweet liddle boy. Oooh! Thweet liddle boy ith doing hith Royal Canadian Air Forth calithenicth." She *was* waking up with a man! And she was in love with him.

She was so happy. But, alas, in the very temple of Delight veil'd Melancholy has her sovran shrine. After her ecstatic session of baby talk, Julia usually felt the presence of darker emotions, as when one swims into a cold spot in the ocean. Slowly and then very quickly, her mood changed, and she became utterly depressed and distraught. What had she done? She was bringing a person into the world for no other reason than to make herself happy, to give her life some kind of purpose, to heal the scars from her own childhood. A child who would have no father. And a child whose mother had never had any real attachment to anyone, who was selfish, vain, spoiled — and broke. The egotism. The self-loathing. Whichever. Both. Time and time again she had rationalized that she had known Jonathan when they made love; not only had she talked to him, she had read his books — one book. They had had a connection. Surely that counted for something? Certainly she knew him better than she would a sperm donor. But even a sperm donor, in whatever weird or corrupt way, intends that a baby will result from his donation; and obviously the women who are sperm-bank clients have the same belief. Copulating with Jonathan, the most vagrant act of lust, was less meaningful even than that. She had been insane not to have terminated her pregnancy the instant she had become aware of it, as she had done twice previously.

Terminate her pregnancy? Terminate the darling little boy who was growing inside her? Those other times, she had been so young and had known nothing of the world (whatever she had thought of herself), and she hadn't been capable of love or self-sacrifice. She was capable of them now, wasn't she? She was, oh, she was. They might struggle in some ways, but think of all the advantages they would have compared to so many others in the world, and no matter what, she knew she would love her child. She knew it, and if she gave the child love, nothing else mattered, did it? But would her love last longer and go deeper than any infatuation? How could she be sure it would when she had never bestowed such love before?

Up and down she zoomed, when she did not manage somehow to be up and down simultaneously. The impressions came all jumbled: the baby's sonogram; her childhood; her final encounter with Dick; her one true love (sort of); her first encounter with Dick; her life in New York pre-Dick; money — dear God — money, money, money; her mother, her father; her stepfather, her stepmothers; the past, the future, the present. The baby!

How did I get here? she asked herself. And where am I going to end up? Searching for answers to such questions, she always found that she had to start at the beginning.

~

Julia had been an only child, and she didn't even have any half siblings, despite her parents' several marriages. Her mother, Clare, was a great beauty (one of three beautiful sisters, but she was the most beautiful) who had come east from St. Louis for college, afterward going to New York. There she met Julia's father, Billy Dyer, a dark, taurine stockbroker highly skilled at golf, backgammon, and cards. Julia was lucky, she got all her looks from her mother (and like any copy, she was inferior). Her father had the big head and tough, snub-nosed face that on a man can look dynamic and attractive but are disastrous when inherited by a daughter. As a little girl, Julia was quite scared of him. He was loud and big and always seemed to be baring his teeth either laughing or shouting. When he gave her a piggyback ride or swung her by the arms, he was too rough, too fast, and he hurt her with his grip. He drove fast, too, scaring her.

Julia's parents divorced when she was seven. They had been living in a perfectly nice but quite small apartment in a big building on Park Avenue. A Scottish woman of indeterminate age lived with them, to care for Julia and to cook. Julia spent a great deal of time in Margaret's tiny room in the back of the apartment; when her parents were out, she liked to sit with Margaret and watch TV. Margaret bathed her, picked her up at school, and watched her play in the park. One of Julia's earliest memories was of Margaret giving her spoonfuls of sweet, white tea from her cup. But after the divorce, money was tight, and Julia's mother told Margaret that she would have to let her go and would not listen to her protests that she would rather work for nothing than leave her little girl. Julia's mother had decided not to say anything about Margaret's departure until after she had gone, which she did one morning. Julia was surprised and pleased that afternoon when her mother appeared to pick her up at school. They went to a diner (long since disappeared) nearby and Julia had a milk shake while her mother drank tea. Then they went to a shoe store and bought Julia a new pair of school shoes, a new pair of party shoes, and her first pair of penny loafers, which she wore out of the store. After that they went to a store that sold dollhouse furniture, and Julia's mother bought a canopy bed for Julia's dollhouse! As soon as her mother had opened the front door of the apartment, Julia ran to the kitchen to show Margaret her loafers and the new canopy bed.

Eventually, Julia and her mother went to live in an apartment in a much newer building located farther to the east. In some ways, it seemed fancier than their old one. Instead of needing a man to run it, the elevator had buttons. The lobby had lots of mirrors and gold. Their apartment had lots of windows. The faucets in their bathrooms looked as if they were made out of gold! But Julia missed the feel of the thick spokes on the ceramic handles of the old faucets. Even at her age, Julia sensed that somehow this new place they were living in was not as nice as the old one; she would hesitate to ask friends back, and as she grew older this reluctance would become more and more conscious. Julia's mother always seemed preoccupied. She was impatient with Julia and tried to maintain the same kind of distance that had existed before, when they were physically more separate and there was someone else intervening. Julia's mother did not like disciplining Julia, she did not like it when Julia got out of bed at night. A few years later, she married a heart surgeon, a widower, who was quite a bit older than she. He was a stern, powerful, self-assured person who intimidated Julia, but her mother seemed to draw confidence from these traits. Materially, their lives certainly improved. They lived in another apartment on Park Avenue, but this one was bigger than the one in which they started out, and the building was smaller and Julia could tell it was nicer. Once again, a cook lived with them. Julia's mother could now have people for dinner. She went out for lunch and never had to push to the limit the time between her visits to the hairdresser. As she became more secure, more matronly and serene, and so regarded

Julia from a more august height, she also became more judgmental. By the time Julia had turned thirteen they were having fights, which her stepfather could not abide. Everyone was happy when she went to boarding school.

As for Julia's father, after the divorce he married a woman with two children of her own and moved into her enormous house on Long Island. She was nice to Julia. "I've always wanted a daughter," she said with a smile. Sometimes when Julia was visiting for the weekend, Billy and the sons would watch a football game (Billy had played football in college) in the paneled study, so Julia's stepmother would take her into another room and they would do needlepoint; if Julia had started on something weeks earlier, her stepmother would have saved it. On Sunday evenings Julia's father drove her to the station. In the course of the weekend, he would have played golf, shot skeet, driven miles to see a man about a sports car, invited friends in for a drink, gone to a dinner party, and slept late on Sunday. But as the train pulled in he suddenly became tender. He squatted down so that his head was level with Julia, and he kissed her cheek and hugged her. She felt small and frail clasped in his big arms and pulled to his broad, thick chest.

"Good-bye, Puss," he said. "You be good now. See you in a couple of weeks." Then he hugged her more tightly. "Love you." There were times when Julia felt moistness on her cheek from a tear he had shed.

Her father and first stepmother were eventually divorced, and he married a brassy real estate agent. In marrying Billy she was able to achieve her two greatest ambitions in life: to own a brand-new, full-sized, foreign luxury sedan with her initials on the doors and to become a member of Billy's country club. That marriage lasted ten years. Then, when a friend of his took over one of the firm's branch offices in Florida, Billy moved there. Within six months he had married again. He had met his new wife at a car dealership, where she worked as the receptionist. Lori was thirty-eight, had been married twice, and had three children, one in the service, one living with his father, and one living with her. When Julia first met her it was all she could do to mask her shock at the ampleness of Lori's bosom; it was almost unfair because one tended not to notice Lori's sweet features and pure complexion. "Hey, Julia, this is your stepmom," she would say when she called. Something had gone wrong at the firm, and so Billy retired abruptly. They moved from the lake and were now living in a stucco bungalow in a neighborhood that had been developed during one of the booms early in the century and that hadn't changed. Rust stains beneath the shutters streaked the outside walls. Air conditioners drooped from the windows like sagging rear ends.

When Julia visited, she sat with her father by the pool. There was no wind, and the heavy Florida air seemed to weigh down the palms. Billy lay back on a chaise contentedly, smoking, having a drink. His skin was brown, smooth, and unblemished, and he exposed it to the sun almost as if he were daring it to harm him. Most of the time, but especially when Lori was nearby, he wore an expression very much like that of the cat who ate the canary. For as long as she could remember, Julia's father had flashed his beautiful (and carnivorous) teeth and laughed about some damn thing or other that had happened on the golf course or in the office. This had not changed. He was still as full of stories as ever, and as full of ideas about stocks that were going to double. "That's a seventy-five-dollar stock!" Usually he was excited about a couple of small companies (they'd invented a perpetual motion machine or something). With a certitude that no specialist in these matters would ever claim, Billy could tell you where the dollar would be in a year, why nobody had ever made a dime with the airlines, how scrap steel was going to go through the roof, when rates would rise (or fall), how a vastly complicated new communications bill would benefit the Baby Bells. The backyard of the house on Hibiscus Street was surrounded by hedges, but you could still see the TV dishes on the roofs next door. The cement pool, built in the fifties, cut the size of the yard by a third; yellowing palm leaves floated in it. Here Julia's father reclined; yet from his manner and conversation you would have thought that he was sitting by the pool at his place in Cap Ferrat.

What had happened? Where had it all gone? How well Julia remembered her grandmother's apartment, the one Billy had grown up in. It had two stories and a very big staircase, and Julia and her cousins would run all over it and never seem to master all its hallways and rooms. The big rooms in the front had windows that were twice as tall as any Julia ever saw anywhere else. Julia had been too young to understand much about the vases, the side tables and chairs, and the paintings, all policed vigilantly to protect them from children. She did know they had an aura of preciousness, and she had an innate sense that they were beautiful. Even as a child Julia liked to go to the part of the museum where they had whole rooms set up. It was so mysterious, and no one else was ever there. Some of the furniture was much more fancy-looking than her grandmother's, but being in Gram-Gram's living room felt like climbing over the rope and being in one of those displays. With this difference, though: Gram-Gram owned her furniture and paintings, they were hers in her house, and in this private setting their force was concentrated. At the same time, they were everyday objects, which made Gram-Gram's life seem effortlessly pitched at a certain height.

It did seem effortless. There was a sense of fullness, of amplitude and of plenitude. Gram-Gram's possessions were not pushed on a visitor; they receded, the exact opposite of a façade created to impress someone. It seemed that there must be something very thick and solid behind what you saw. It felt secure; there was more of everything than was necessary, which implied that necessity held no power in Gram-Gram's demesne. Not only were her apartment and her country house big, so was everything in them. The kitchen stove looked like the engine of a steamship. Whenever Julia picked up a knife or fork, she was surprised by its heft. Using it was actually hard for a little girl! The cooks and the maids were big (and there were many of them), the roast beef was big, the napkins were like sails; the blankets and shawls and sheets were big; so were Gram-Gram's pearls and gems. Even the ice cubes were as big and solid as a child's alphabet blocks. The whole of life seemed lush and sturdy.

Then Gram-Gram died. Julia was fifteen years old and she knew that when people died their children inherited their money. She didn't know how exactly, but she expected her life to change, to be resized in a proportionate way to her grandmother's. But nothing happened. Billy had two brothers and two sisters, and they discussed and argued a bit, but fairly quickly decided that it all should be sold (one of the sisters was the impractical holdout, being so attached to "Mother's things"). And it was all sold, except for a few small items that Gram-Gram had left for specific people. Julia got a pair of ruby and diamond earrings, which was her prize possession. Otherwise, it all went: the houses, the furniture, the paintings, the rugs, the vases, the stocks, the large portfolio of Treasury bills. Then there were taxes to pay and the market was way down that year. Everything was. The proceeds were divided five ways. Billy bought a small apartment in the city. Then, a few years later, he sold it.

What had happened? Where had it all gone? Asking herself these questions could make Julia weep. It wasn't just the money, she'd think, it was the lost beauty and the lost dignity. But then she'd recall that it was the money, for there would not have been the beauty and the dignity without it.

And what of Julia's sentimental education? At her school in New York, she was in the popular crowd. She was pretty, and she could be quite mean. In seventh grade she dropped the plain, chubby girl who had been her best friend and confidante since kindergarten. She and her popular friends began smoking cigarettes; they hung around with boys, who provided beer and pot. Julia spent hours on the phone talking to her friends about boys, and she got her first kiss at a young age, and she technically lost her virginity in tenth grade. Her first love appeared that summer: a tall, athletic boy with an upturned nose, prominent lips, and blue eyes. Addison. They spent virtually all their time engaged in some sort of sexual activity. He promised to write her when they went back to school, but he didn't, and still he expected to pick up where they left off the following year, something that Julia, after a few grapples, refused to do.

In college Julia had handsome, confident boyfriends, smart athletes who were headed to good careers. Then, when she had moved to New York, there was a string of handsome and ultraconfident investment bankers and a couple of Euros. For a year she lived with an Englishman named Julian. (Julia, Julian — wasn't that cute?) He did some kind of international PR something or other. She still despised that sponging, lying, short-dicked faggot. A couple of these guys wanted to marry her, but she couldn't go through with it, and then she got on the second-wife track, where every time she went out with someone it was like a job interview.

How, in so many ways, she hated this life. She worked in an advertising firm. She liked some of her colleagues, she liked the secretaries, she liked talking for two minutes each day to the ancient clerk who brought her mail (he had been in the merchant marine), but she despised her boss, an older, senior-executive woman, and her perfect grooming and erect posture and brisk purposeful manner. She hated the tiny, grimy apartment that she lived in by herself, just as she had hated the larger grimy apartment she had previously lived in with roommates, along with hating the roommates. She hated her social life. She was often the pretty single girl asked along by a female friend when a group was going out to dinner at a shockingly expensive restaurant. A repellent man would take care of the bill and then call her the next day. Julia's friend would say to her, "What's the big deal? You can at least have dinner with him. He's sweet. And it doesn't hurt that he's completely loaded." She hated being invited to dinner parties at people's apartments. She would have to rush home after work to get ready and she always felt embittered when she arrived and saw the hostess, who had been dressing and making herself up since noon.

Then Dick had appeared. One weekend she met him at a cocktail party on Long Island, where she was visiting friends. They had talked on the terrace, among flower beds and greensward. The sun gave the humid air a rosy tint. They talked about gardens and Julia's work, about which she was deprecating. Dick told her she shouldn't be and said, "I've always wished I could have done something creative." Julia remembered seeing but not meeting Janet, an attractive large-boned woman. The next day, it happened that Julia and Dick played tennis on neighboring courts; Julia was a very good tennis player, and so was Dick. After their matches, the two groups had a drink together, and Julia and Dick chatted some more. They talked about who had won, how they had played. With her dark coloring, long legs and arms, and her toned figure, Julia looked good in tennis clothes. When they parted, they shook hands, with the most fleeting look into each other's eyes.

The following Wednesday, when she listened to a phone message from Dick asking her if she would like to have lunch, Julia saw the whole story unfold. In an instant, she saw everything that would happen, and everything that did in fact happen. They had lunch. They had lunch again, and once again. They had dinner. On one occasion, Julia asked Dick if he would like to come to her place for a drink before they went out. He did, and soon enough after arriving he was kissing her. The next time he came over, they made love. This continued, most often in the afternoon. Julia was always struck by how incongruous Dick looked getting dressed in her bedroom. It was hardly bigger than her bed. The window was filthy and the walls and ceiling hadn't been painted for decades, it seemed. With his burnished English suits and custom-made shirts, Dick could have been in such a setting only for an illicit purpose.

When she started sleeping with Dick, Julia vowed that she would not be like the typical young woman who is sleeping with a married man. She would not act as if she were desperately hoping that he would leave his family and marry her. She would not extract bogus promises from him that he would tell his wife "after Christmas" or "when Kevin has settled into his new school" or "soon." As it happened, it was Dick who pushed for marriage, and eventually Julia said yes. Dick was good-looking, youthful, well-off, successful, and he seemed crazy about her. They were having a love affair, and it certainly had a love component from Julia's point of view — enough love anyway to suit Julia, who doubted that love really existed. And she liked the idea of their life being done. She just wasn't interested in the sloppy struggles of young marrieds, with their fights and laundry and little children underfoot. She liked the idea that Dick was a finished person and that their life would be finished. It had been okay for a while. Now she couldn't stand him.

It was strange, but out of her whole romantic history, it seemed to Julia as if she could remember only one moment really vividly. A couple of years after college she had become involved with a boy who was different from her other beaux. Joss MacNeill was handsome, but in a delicate way, with the gentlest brown eyes, and he was tall and thin and had beautiful long fingers. More than anyone else, he was someone whom Julia really loved to talk to, and with him she even lost her natural reserve. Joss had many appealing qualities.

He was charming and polite to everyone; he was funny, intelligent, and affectionate. He knew a lot about a lot of things. But despite all these attributes, he was unable to construct a life or career that was well engineered and stable and that took best advantage of his admittedly vague abilities. Eventually he drifted off, and, years later, suffered a couple of crack-ups.

For a time, though, Julia thought she was in love with Joss, really in love with him; he had gotten under her skin as others never had. She remembered one summer evening when she was lying in his arms on his sofa. It had been a hot, muggy, windless day. Now in the early evening, with the day's heat spent, a breeze wafted through the wide-open window. Traffic rumbled, a horn sounded, a loose manhole cover clanked repeatedly. Joss was stroking Julia's hair, and, with her eyes closed, she listened to the thwup-thwup, thwup-thwup of his heart. The tumbling city summer-evening air, tinged with grit and bus fumes, rolled gently over them, lapping last at their feet. Then it was time to go to dinner. It was a Saturday night, so the people out on the street were excited, and it was warm, so they all wore the least clothing possible. After Joss and Julia had walked a few steps down the sidewalk, Joss scratched and tickled her palm with his fingers, then interlaced them with hers and held her hand tightly. She thought then (and sometimes still thought) that this was the happiest moment of her life.

The past! The past! Do we stride before it, trailing it behind? No. It pushes us inexorably forward, like a glacier, into the present.

～

It had not been very far into the summer before Julia suspected that she was pregnant. Years before her doctor had insisted that if she wouldn't give up cigarettes she at least had to stop taking birth-control pills. Complying wasn't too hard. Dick had gotten himself fixed, and as for any non-Dick-related activities, they were pretty infrequent. If anything happened, she'd deal with it. This time a store-bought pregnancy test and a doctor had confirmed her supposition. Of course, Julia had had no doubt about what she would do. And yet she kept putting it off. She had some morning sickness, not too bad, which she tried to hide from Dick until she realized that, despite having had three children, he had no clue what a pregnant woman acted or looked or smelled like. When he finally did ask about her nausea, she said she had some kind of stomach virus she couldn't get rid of.

The point, though, was to keep her head. Nothing — nothing — could be more absurd than the idea of having this child. It would be a huge mess. There would be no money. The child wouldn't even have a father. Moreover, she didn't like babies or children; she had always found the noise and chaos they caused tiresome. She would lose her freedom, for even married to Dick she was quite free (and more freedom was easily attainable). With some indignation, Julia reminded herself of her disdain for these childless women who lost their nerve at the last moment and late in life decided they must have a child, and thought that this would solve all their problems.

But she saw an obstetrician. The doctor told her that everything looked good. "It should be about the size of a coffee bean now," she said with a smile. She explained to Julia their schedule of appointments, the tests, the problems her age might cause. She gave Julia a due date. Julia wrote down the next appointment in her diary, but she had no intention of keeping it. Almost as soon as she left the office and was on the bright sidewalk, where indifferent pedestrians and taxis rushed by, the entire visit vanished from her mind. The doctors' offices on the ground floors of apartment buildings in New York were like caves on the banks of a river, and what happened there was easily forgotten once you left and the current swept you away.

But she did keep the second appointment. She was taking prenatal vitamins and iron, and she had stopped drinking. Dick noticed that. "No wine? Hey, what's this? Have you joined AA?" "I'm having so much trouble sleeping, I'm going to see what it's like without alcohol for a while." Legally, she knew, she could put off a final decision until the twenty-fourth week, but nobody waited beyond the first trimester, and that was her moral and psychological point of no return. The deadline came closer and closer. Terror and joy contended in Julia's breast. She felt both like a prisoner waiting to be executed and like a bride waiting to be married. Three days left, two days left. One day left.

On the last day of her first trimester, Julia rose early, as she usually did. She made coffee and retrieved the papers. When she returned, she heard Dick moving around in his bathroom. He came into the kitchen and sat heavily at the table.

"Good morning, darling," he said as she gave him his cup of coffee. "Thank you. Now, let's see what fresh havoc the politicians have wreaked since yesterday."

Julia had poured out a bowl of Dick's special muesli. "We have blueberries and raspberries. Which would you like?" she asked.

"Would it be too extravagant to have both?"

"Of course not." Julia rinsed the berries, added them to his bowl, and set it down in front of him.

"Merci bien," he said.

"Not a problem," Julia replied with an outer-borough accent.

Dick chortled.

Julia sat down with her own black coffee and a slice of dry, multigrain toast. She broke off a small piece of toast and tugged a section of the paper so it was right side up in front of her. Registering nothing, she looked at the headlines.

After several minutes, Dick muttered without looking up, "New report on abuse by priests . . ."

"The . . . what? I'm sorry —"

"There's a new report on sex abuse by priests. 'Dioceses that had not participated in earlier surveys, et cetera, et cetera. Let's see. Oh, here. Listen to this: 'In thirty-four percent of the cases the priests performed oral sex on their male victims.'" He looked up at Julia with a mischievous grin. "You know the really important number that they don't seem to have?"

"What's that?"

"How often the priests got sucked off by the boys. That's the metric I'd like to see before I went into the priesthood." Dick laughed and Julia smiled wanly, and seeing that this hadn't gone over so well, he adopted a more serious expression, shook his head, and, in a what-is-the-world-coming-to tone, said, "Jesus." He took a sip of coffee and continued reading his paper.

Julia felt sick to her stomach. How disgusting was the male drive for sexual satisfaction; how indiscriminately men spilled their life essence. If she had been born into the right tribe, she could have seen herself worshipping it, the sacred, viscous, life-giving nectar. Body and blood in one convenient serving! But how did men regard it? As no more sacred than the water in a child's squirt gun. Think of their profligacy! Each day men pumped out trillions of spermatozoa, and only a tiny proportion of them were intended to fulfill their actual purpose: the creation of life. These thoughts put Julia into a heavy sea of anxiety whose waves pulled her down, then raised her high before crashing her on the rocks. What about her baby? Her baby was merely the chance by-product of lust; her egg had been fertilized by a sperm of no greater nobility than one that stained a pornographic photo.

It was hard to have these dark, stabbing thoughts, so much darker and sharper on this day than they had ever been before, while sitting across from Dick in their brightly lit kitchen. Dick. His gray stubble, messy hair, and the droopy pads beneath his eyes always made him look old in the morning. The second button of his pajama top was undone, and even his gray chest hairs seemed to have lost their spring. Dick had always been vain about his figure and he kept fairly fit, but he had been less rigorous lately, and he carried the irreducible bulk of late middle age. He liked his food. He was only a little greedy in the morning, but more so at lunch, and by dinnertime he was eager to tuck in. Late at night, he often rooted around the kitchen for cookies, nuts, leftover pie. At breakfast he looked old — unshaven, saggy-faced, overweight, with stained teeth. But somehow after he showered, shaved, and dressed, he was transformed, and without resorting to the corset and powder of an aging matinee idol. Costumed in a suit, tie, shirt, and shoes that all gleamed in their own register, he was as handsome as ever. His hair! His thick head of hair seemed like an extrusion of potency and youth.

The kitchen had strong recessed floodlights, stainless-steel and glossy white surfaces. Julia and Dick sat on hard, highly designed metal kitchen chairs. On this morning, all this made Julia uneasy. She felt vulnerable to scrutiny, and she wished she were in a dark room lying on cushions. All the everyday objects in the room — the toaster, the microwave, the canisters, the breadbox — seemed to be lit as lavishly as a car in a magazine ad, and to Julia they seemed almost alive. From this day forward, her life was going to change irrevocably. How could the breadbox be the same old breadbox? Her state cast a transformative spell on everything around her. Then she refocused her sight, and she could see that of course the breadbox was the same inert object, with a dent in one corner, that it had always been. This was a normal morning in her kitchen. Neither the toaster nor the microwave was responding to her crisis. The hanging spatulas remained insensate and uncaring. Kept in ignorance, so, naturally, did Dick. He had pushed his chair away from the table; his half-glasses had slipped down his nose, giving him an imperious expression as he read his paper. Without taking his eyes off the page, he took sips of his coffee, scratched his ankle.

Then Dick went off to change and emerged in all his gleaming glory.

"Good-bye, darling," Julia said. "Have fun slaying those dragons."

"Ha!" said Dick, smiling. "Those dragons are getting younger and faster, damn them." As he checked himself one more time in the hall mirror, he asked, "What are your plans for today?"

"Ellen wants me to come with her to look at some chairs that she's thinking of buying."

"What's she gotten onto now?"

"Second Empire."

"Really? How odd." Dick patted his tie and turned to Julia. "Well," he continued lightheartedly, but with the edge of giving an order, "don't bring your checkbook."

"No."

"Q3 next year, darling, Q3."

"Yes."

Julia offered her cheek and Dick kissed it. Then, after stepping back, he appraised her.

"You know," he said, "you are looking extraordinarily pretty today."

"Why, thank you."

"In fact, you've been looking extraordinarily pretty for some time now."

"Thanks for waiting so long before telling me."

"Guilty as charged. Anyway, you're beautiful."

"Thanks."

"Well, so long." Dick had already opened the front door when he turned back with an expression of discomfort. "Oh, and you won't forget, tonight —"

"It's in my book." This was a dinner that both acknowledged Julia would find extremely tedious.

"Terrific. Well — bye."

"Bye."

Dick gave a little wave as he closed the door behind him. Julia looked at the door. She closed her eyes for a moment, then she went back to the bedroom and sat on the bed, crying quietly for a few minutes. Then she found her joy and excitement almost unbearable. She bathed. Afterward, as one who believed in grooming, she brushed her hair and applied her makeup with care. She put on a blouse, skirt, shoes, and stockings that she might wear if she were having lunch with a friend. With her watch and her pin and her earrings all in place, she checked herself in a mirror and lightly smoothed her skirt and hair. She went to the kitchen and poured herself a glass of water from the tap. Then she went into the library. Here the lights and colors were muted and the upholstery soft. She sat in the large armchair that she used for reading and put the glass of water down on a coaster on the adjacent side table, next to a couple of books. Where had she left off . . . ? Oh, that terrible Irishman's note had come due. But she didn't pick up a book. Loosely clasped, her hands lay in her lap. She sat, and she watched a shadow move across the opposite bookcase. The hours passed. At about four o'clock, she made herself a cup of tea and drank it back at her place in the library. She sat in dimness for a while. Then it was time to get ready for dinner.

The moment of truth, literally, came three weeks later, when, having put it off as long as she could, she had to tell everyone what was up. She sat Dick down in their living room and told him that she had some news to give him, and that it was going to be a little awkward.

Dick looked at her with narrowed eyes. "Okay," he said. "Let's have it."

Julia took a deep breath and swallowed. "I'm going to have a baby."

Dick looked stunned and didn't say anything. Then he burst out laughing. "Oh, Julia, come on! You're going to have a baby? That's the most ridiculous thing I've ever heard. You can't be serious."

As evenly as she could, Julia said, "I am serious. I'm pregnant, and I want to have the baby."

"My God! You must have gone out of your mind!"

Julia didn't respond.

"It's my understanding," said Dick, "that in these cases there are usually two parties involved. Or did you go with the turkey baster?"

"No."

"Okay. So then would you care to tell me who might the father be?"

"No."

"No? No? You mean it's some kind of secret? Everybody's going to know eventually, aren't they? Doesn't Dad want to be 'involved'" — this word said very sarcastically — "with the child, change its diapers, play peekaboo? Or was this a one-off where you didn't happen to get the fellow's name?"

Julia had vowed, she had sworn, she had taken a mortal oath before God that she would not cry. But now the tears were coming, and her eyes blurred. "He's dead," she said.

Dick threw up his hands. "He's dead! Oh, how convenient."

"I would say it was quite inconvenient for him, and for the people close to him. You don't really think that I would lie about that, do you? The fact is that he's dead. He wasn't anyone you knew, or anyone whom anyone you know knew." Julia could not keep herself from sniffling. "He's dead. He died."

"I guess he died for you," Dick said. "I suppose he died of a broken heart."

"No," Julia said. "He . . . he got sick—"

"And what about you?" Dick asked. "Was he the man of your dreams? Did your feelings run oh so very deep? Did the earth move?"

Julia looked down for a moment. "I —" she said, and then stopped. "Yes." She swallowed. "Yes," she said softly, "I did love him." And now she began to cry outright.

Confronted with that word and with a pregnant woman in tears who has suffered the death of her beloved, Dick could do nothing but remain silent. He got up and fixed himself a bourbon and sipped it while looking at Julia, who was now crying silently. This seemed to go on for a long time. Then Dick came over and sat next to her on the sofa. He put his hand on her shoulder and rested it there for a moment. Then he spoke in a quiet, even gentle, tone.

"Look, Julia," he said, "as you can imagine, this is a difficult piece of information to absorb. I don't know what to say or what to think. I've never . . . well, I've never exactly believed that people should never fall in love again or never act on a desire once they're married. I was going to say 'just because' they're married. That wouldn't accurately reflect my respect for the institution." He gave a breathy, tentative laugh. "Anyway, I can see how something like this happens. Especially with a beautiful woman like you, and especially when she's stuck with some decrepit old guy. The heart is — well, I guess nobody has ever quite figured that out. I know it is very powerful. Look at us when we began. It's very powerful. But the point is, I can understand how something like this happens." He waited a moment before asking a delicate question: "Is it too late to . . . to take care of the problem?"

"I don't want to!" Julia said this forcefully but in a whisper. She would not look at him.

"I understand, I understand," said Dick. He waited a moment before asking, "How far along are you?"

"Almost four months."

"You've seen a doctor and all that?"

"Yes, of course."

"And everything —"

"Everything is fine."

"Good, good," said Dick. "And, do you know . . . have they told you whether it's a —?"

"It's a boy."

"A boy! Well, now, a boy . . ." His voice trailed off. He shook his head and spread open his palms. "I'm sorry. It's just . . . I'm having a hard time. It's hard to believe." He continued shaking his head for a moment and then asked, "What are you planning to do?"

Julia collected herself. "Well, first of all," she said, "I'm going to go to Anna's tonight."

"What?"

"I'm going to stay at Anna's for a little while."

"Anna's! She's barely got space for herself and that psycho kid of hers!"

"It'll be okay. I'll come over sometime in the next few days. Anna and I will come over and get my things. Then in a couple of weeks, I want to go to France before coming back here and having the baby."

There was a pause as Dick regarded her. "I suppose," he said, "you assumed I would throw you out."

"No, no," said Julia. "But I guess I thought it would be awkward, which hardly describes it. So I'd better be prepared to leave here as soon as I told you. People can have funny reactions to the news that their wife is carrying another man's child. I thought it would be best to make some arrangements."

"I see," said Dick. He scowled, stood up, and paced back and forth with his drink for a minute. Then he turned to Julia and spoke softly. "And if that weren't necessary?" he said. "I mean from my point of view?"

Julia was caught off-guard. "I'm sorry, Dick, what did you say?"

"I said what if that weren't necessary, your leaving, from my point of view?"

Julia didn't know how to respond.

Dick started to laugh. "What does it matter? These days people do everything. We can say that you decided you really wanted a baby and I couldn't provide the goods, so you asked your lesbian lover's son." He shook his head. "We can dream up something. Or just tell the truth. People will talk for about five minutes. What do we care? I mean, really?" He stared off into space. "I know we discussed it and it wasn't something we wanted. But it might be kind of fun having a baby around. I missed most of that the first time around, with the kids. I feel bad about it all." He sighed, then smiled. "But having a little baby, a little boy, it could be fun. It could be a lot of fun."

He turned back to Julia and scratched his cheek.

"In any event, that's my proposition. You can stay here and —" He stopped short. "Let me change that. That is my . . . request. I'm asking you to stay."

Julia didn't answer, so Dick spoke again.

"I'd miss you." He paused. "I love you."

Julia had tried to prepare herself for Dick's reaction, but this was one she had not been expecting, and she felt at a loss. Maybe it would work? So many of the problems that she was agonizing over would instantly be solved! They could stay where they were, or move into a bigger place. Her son could go to one of the schools nearby. Dick was right that the "scandal" wouldn't last; if anything, it would give them some cachet, and everyone would make a point of responding with nonjudgmental sophistication. And maybe, maybe having something to do together beyond going out to dinner, especially this thing, would bring out another side of each of them; maybe they would be happier. Maybe Dick would enjoy having a second shot at being a doting father? Think of the alternative! Julia knew she wasn't cut out to be a heroic "single mom," and she couldn't be at all sure how much money she would end up with. By herself, with a child, with no profession — was it realistic to think that she would be content to work as a store clerk or real estate agent and forgo dinners out and new clothes? Anna managed to do it somehow. Anna never had any money and always looked incredible, not chic, but fantastic. But she had that kind of style, and that hippie attitude about comfort. Sitting around with other divorcées complaining about prying money out of their "exes," having the pizza place on speed dial: it would be horrible. Checking a grocery receipt — Julia had never done that in her life! She could always set about landing another rich man, but that prospect was even more horrible. All these things she had been worrying about lately a million times over — and here was a way out.

But what was Dick really up to? Was he making a magnanimous offer he knew she would refuse? He would thereby gain the moral and psychological upper hand. And if he was sincere, would his selflessness last till morning, and would he ever allow the child to exist outside his own self-regard? Julia could see it: he'd be the big hero, having rushed into the burning building and saved the mother and infant. He'd use the kid to gain all this glory as someone with a noble, expansive heart, the great Dick Montague, who accepted his wife's bastard as his own, like some Regency duke. All in great contrast to her perfidy, which he'd never fail to get in a dig about. As soon as he'd achieved that effect, he'd drop the whole thing, except when talking to some friend, whom he'd tell how he'd come to truly love the child, even if it wasn't his. Dick Montague, quite an extraordinary fellow! By making the child his own, he'd save himself from humiliation. Oh, she could see it. At all the important moments, especially the moments when other people were watching, he would swoop in and take over, but the rest of the time he'd ignore the boy. If anything, he would make sure he suffered. Look how his own children had turned out, and in truth he hadn't ever regretted his behavior toward them for more than five minutes running. Well, forget it. He wasn't going to use us — us! us! us! — to serve his vanity!

But when someone ran into a burning building and saved a mother and infant, even if he did it to be a hero, he still saved the mother and the infant.

Julia felt as if she were standing on a precipice in high winds. She knew that if she agreed to stay with Dick, she would never leave. She also knew that if she left, the offer would never come again. With all the emotion of the situation and now this unexpected turn, it was so hard to think.

As she weighed her alternatives, Dick hung fire.

Finally, she spoke. "I am . . . moved . . . by what you've said, Dick, moved by your generosity, and grateful." She looked at him, and even though she was frightened, and even though she was suspicious, she couldn't help but look at him with affection. "But I'm sorry. I think it's best if we go our separate ways."

Dick took a deep breath. He nodded and sipped his drink. He sat down. A long time passed before he spoke again, and when he did so, he adopted his lawyer voice. "Very well, then, if that's your decision, we'll proceed accordingly. Now, you don't imagine that I haven't planned for this eventuality, do you? No prenup. It was so touching, so romantic. Really. My trusting, dewy-eyed bride. I was so very moved. But that didn't prevent me from making my own preparations. And surely you know that law partnerships have ways to protect their partners' interests when greedy ex-wives, and, these days, greedy ex-husbands, start making their demands? Moreover, we don't have no-fault or community property in New York. As I recall quite clearly, the division of property is partly determined by 'marital fault,' adultery being the leading example. Finally, there are no children involved — at least, there are no children involved that are both yours and mine — so you lack leverage there. I can make things very, very difficult for you, so I'd advise you not to come at me with a lot of tricks and threats and ultimatums."

"Oh, Dick," Julia said, "how clever of you. Trying to frighten and bluff me before we've even begun!"

Dick looked at her very steadily. "I'm not bluffing," he said in a stern, hard tone.

Actually, he had succeeded in spooking Julia, but she was determined not to show it.

"You see?" She managed to laugh. "That's what people who are bluffing always say." She looked back at him as coolly as she could.

Dick shrugged. He smelled blood, and he was satisfied. "You say that you and Anna will come by at some point to collect your clothes and so forth?"

"Yes."

"When will that be?"

"I don't know."

"You'd better make it tomorrow. I suggest you take everything you want. What you leave, you will never see again, I assure you."

"But, Dick, that's a lot of stuff —"

"Hire movers. After tomorrow, I'll change the locks and give the people in the building orders not to allow you in."

"All right."

"I assume you have a lawyer?"

"I've talked to someone," Julia said. "I don't know if I would call him my lawyer."

"I know whom I'll use. He'll contact you. Then he and whomever you decide on can take it from there. It should be fairly straight-forward." Dick stared at Julia, coolly evaluating her. "It's none of my business," he said finally, "but I must say, Julia, that I thought better of you. Leaving aside any injury to me, I never would have thought that you would do something so foolish and irresponsible."

Julia wanted to make him understand that she knew that what she was doing was right, that she knew it as well as she knew that water was wet (except when she was beset by her own terrible doubts).

"I've thought a lot about my motivation," she began, but Dick raised his hand.

"No, no. You don't have to justify yourself to me. As I say, it's really none of my business." He looked at her for a moment or two, like someone appraising an object. Then he stood up. "I imagine that you want to be on your way," he said.

Julia stood, too. They looked at each other, and a flare, a flicker of an old feeling of closeness lit up their eyes. Did Julia see some tenderness and hurt behind Dick's peremptory expression? Or was it just wounded pride? Or all of these things?

Dick took a step toward the foyer, and Julia walked with him.

"I'll get my bag," Julia said.

"Please, allow me," said Dick, with sneering chivalrousness.

"All right. Thank you," Julia said. "It's in my dressing room."

Julia took her coat from the closet. She put it on and buttoned it like an automaton. Dick returned, opened the front door, and placed the bag by the elevator, and Julia went to stand by it.

"Good-bye," Dick said.

"Good-bye."

Dick closed the door. Julia pushed the elevator button. One of the odd things about living in an apartment was that you could walk out of someone's life but still have to wait for the elevator.

When Julia and Anna came to the apartment the next day, they found a portly middle-aged man with a red rash on his hands waiting for them. He was somehow associated with the law firm that Dick had already retained. The man politely explained that he was there to provide guidance to Mrs. Montague as to which items she could legitimately remove from the apartment, such as clothing, personal photographs, and memorabilia, and which might be the subject of a dispute and so should remain. He would also make an inventory of everything she was taking and would ask her, if she would be so kind, to sign it.

As she was packing, Julia discovered that her jewelry was gone. With all the other things on her mind, she had not given any thought to it. Nor had it occurred to her that Dick might want to go through her bag before she left. How foolish of her. A woman of the world. A reader of nineteenth-century French novels!

In due course, everyone knew the state of affairs. Julia's mother did not hide her disdain. She had not approved of Julia's marriage, and now Julia had gone and acted like an utter fool. Julia's father was jolly. "So, by hook or by crook, I got me a grandchild," he said. He told Julia that he'd never really liked Dick anyway. As for how the pregnancy had come about, he said, "Well, Puss, if you want this guy's kid, he must have been okay." He hadn't called her Puss in decades.

Julia told each of Dick's children. With great intensity, Charlotte assured her that their relationship would remain the same, whatever occurred between Julia and Charlotte's father. She wanted Julia to know that if she needed to talk to anyone she should call on her anytime, and she wanted to have lunch. Deirdre cried. David was sweet. "You know how when a couple divorces," he said, "the children always think that it's their fault? Well, that wasn't true in my case: when my parents got divorced, I thought it was your fault. Since I couldn't have cared less about either my mother or father, though, not very much anger went along with the blame. Then it got slightly more complicated after I got to know you. I started liking you a whole lot more than I did either of them. Okay! I'll admit it! There was maybe a little bit of a crush, starting when I was about fourteen and lasting until like, oh, say, now." He laughed and harrumphed. "Anyway, I always really did like you a lot, Julia. So I'm going to miss you."

After Dick, the person whose reaction Julia most feared was Mme. Gorotiaga. Julia wondered if she would be horrified, scream maledictions, and leave with her husband immediately. But Mme. Gorotiaga wasn't like that at all. When Julia explained what had happened, she had a look of concern, but all she asked was whether Julia was drinking beer, and when the answer was negative, she tut-tutted, saying, "This is no good." From that point on, Mme. Gorotiaga took complete command of Julia's diet and daily schedule. When Julia protested that the doctor had said one thing or another, Mme. Gorotiaga would ask, Has the doctor had any babies? Julia would reply, Well, in fact, she's a woman and she has. At which point Mme. Gorotiaga would grunt dismissively. Julia also had a good comeback when Mme. Gorotiaga insisted that she was being too active. "I suppose you're right. Didn't you say that when you were having your babies, you would lie on a couch all day long?" "Lie on a couch all day long!" Mme. Gorotiaga said indignantly. "Lie on a couch! No, madame! I was doing the cooking and washing and watching the other children, and I would tend the garden —" That's when she realized that Julia, who looked on smugly, had tricked her. "Bah, I was different from you, you're so skinny." But Julia had made her point. They would also fight about beer (absolutely necessary for a healthy baby, in Mme. Gorotiaga's view) and wine, both of which Julia refused to drink. What did she think women having babies had been drinking for thousands of years, Mme. Gorotiaga asked, Coca-Cola? Julia did appreciate one policy that Mme. Gorotiaga adhered to strictly. She always brought Julia her breakfast in bed. The person who suffered in all this was M. Gorotiaga. Mme. Gorotiaga, who was twice his size, continually berated him for something he had failed to do, inevitably something that the baby's entire life and happiness depended on — fixing a drafty door, laying in an adequate supply of potatoes. When Mme. Gorotiaga turned her attention to Julia after one of her tirades, Julia was always amazed at her instant transformation from harridan to kindly grandmother.

Julia was in her favorite place in the world. She was being cosseted. Her little boy was growing within her. It was all so wonderful. The present, in other words, in and of itself, wasn't so bad. But it wouldn't last, would it? If the past was pushing her inexorably forward, the future sometimes looked like a cliff toward which she was inexorably headed.

Having a baby would be the first thing that Julia had ever done that she could not get out of. This was terrifying. No matter what happened, even if she left the boy on someone's doorstep, she would still be his mother; even if he left home at eighteen and decided never to communicate with her again, she would still be his mother. She would be his mother for the rest of her life, there was no way around it. What commitment had she ever made that even came close in its importance and permanence? Marrying Dick? Ha! She had signed leases on apartments that were more binding than her marriage to Dick had been. With a child, she would have to give of herself over a long period in a way that she never had, and she would have to give consistently every day, even every hour, from the beginning, in a way that she never had. Her life was about to change forever in the most profound and the most trivial ways, and there was no way out. Was she ready, could she change, would she become bored, would she repeat all her own parents' mistakes, would the boy wish he had never been born and would he be right? She didn't know.

Sometimes, trying to find evidence for optimism, she would think about the families she had known throughout her life, but this was exactly the wrong thing to do, for the results were horrifying. So many children hated their parents and vice versa. There was so much strife and unhappiness and disappointment. In fact, if people really looked at the miserable families around them and thought about it, no one would start a family of their own. The odds looked terrible. Why should she be exempt from them? She thought about Anna and her son, Zach, who was now sixteen. To some extent, this was encouraging: as a little boy Zach had been deeply in love with his mother and even now they had an extremely close and intense relationship that seemed enviable. But it was almost too intense, and one reason for their intimacy was that Zach acted more as the parent and Anna as the child, which couldn't be good. Meanwhile, Anna the free spirit had never worried about anything — getting Zach to school on time, his friends — which was probably good in some areas but bordered on neglectful in others. Oh, how Julia would worry, she imagined. She would worry about all the physical and emotional injury that her child might suffer at life's hands; she imagined that she would have her heart in her throat every minute for the next thirty-five years, or longer. Knowing what awaited their children, how could parents endure watching them go through life in all their ignorance and innocence? It was like being a member of the audience who knows the hero is about to walk right into a trap and living in that state for years: wouldn't the tension kill you?

When Julia managed to turn off her brain and simply ride her emotions, she felt only pure love for her baby, and pure happiness and optimism about the little family they would become. There was one subject, however, whose ominousness she could neither ignore nor minimize, no matter what she did. This was the subject of money. Perhaps it was very shallow of her, Julia thought, but she could not shake the conviction that having money was better than not having it. The prospect that she would not have it terrified her, and this terror, unlike the others, had a directness, an immediacy, that made it almost unbearable. As spoiled as she was, and as shallow, she hated the idea of having to live more cheaply, when for the past many years she hadn't thought twice about spending a thousand dollars on a blouse. But she wasn't merely concerned about maintaining her fabulous lifestyle. She really didn't have any idea what her circumstances might end up being, so even though she knew it was probably irrational, she was convinced that she could end up truly broke. She would become consumed with worry that she would be unable to pay the rent or buy her son Christmas presents. A psychological component made her fears still more intense: more than for what it could buy, Julia liked having a superfluity of money for the sense of security it provided, and so the threat of poverty, even if only relative, triggered within her a powerful dread.

Well, she would think, she had a little money of her own (but so little!), and she could probably get some kind of job. She had friends who would help. But the crucial question was how much she would get from Dick. In this regard, Julia had one ace, but she didn't know how or whether to play it.

When Dick's father died, he left each of Dick's children a fairly large amount of money, and Dick was given responsibility for it until the children reached age thirty. In the meantime, the money could be used for the children's education, medical care, and "maintenance." Over the years Dick had gotten into the habit of making purchases and "investments" that stretched the terms to the limit. Wouldn't the children live in the house with the painting or the piece of furniture Dick wanted to buy? And weren't these good investments? Wasn't a country house a good investment, and didn't the children benefit more than anyone from its purchase and up-keep and expansion? Moreover, Dick awarded himself a higher fee than was typical for his administration of the funds, all the while claiming expenses — shooting trips with friends who were money managers, a generously calculated pro-rata share of the maintenance and capital cost of his office in the apartment — that reflected a fairly aggressive posture. Dick had taken loans, too.

Over the years, Julia had slowly figured out what Dick was up to. At first she didn't really understand, then she entered a state of denial, and, finally, having been corrupted herself by having all this lovely extra money, she became passively complicit.

It wasn't really stealing, since the children still owned the things that had been bought, and hadn't their value increased? Everybody charged a fee. Those loans were an asset. And by the time the children were old enough for any of it to matter, it would some-how all have worked out. Of course, as time passed, the imbalance in justified and unjustified spending grew worse and worse, not better, and with corresponding desperation, Julia clung to her rationalizations.

Now she was in a moral, financial, and legal quandary. The worst kind. The children had not been told about this money. Inertia had sustained the argument, well after it had ceased to be valid, that they were too young; fortunately, just as the legal age limit was being reached, another justification had come to hand. It would be dangerous for David to know, given his problem, and so, for the time being, it was probably best not to tell the others, either. All this gave Julia some leverage with Dick. It was clear that he was willing to show some decency where she was concerned if she kept her mouth shut. If she cooperated, if she didn't use "tricks and threats and ultimatums," if she was willing to allow the ruse to go on, maybe she could get a little more money, maybe she could even keep the house. He had almost said as much. In contrast, if she blew the whistle he would have no motivation to restrain himself from fighting Julia to the death, and, indeed, he would have the added incentive of revenge. He had always figured, probably accurately, that his children were too weak to do much if they found that they had been wronged. Still, it could get unpleasant and expensive, and lurking in the background was the attorney general of the state of New York.

As she sat in bed thinking about all this, Julia could become so preoccupied that she consumed the delicious breakfast Mme. Gorotiaga had brought her without paying attention to a single sip or bite. Money, money, money, money, money, money, money, money. Money. The pulsing of that word in her mind paralyzed her.

7

When Charlotte happened to be in Paris and the season was right, she usually went down to her father and stepmother's house, and after her conference she was once again going to pay a visit, a prospect that Julia looked forward to not exactly with dread, but without much enthusiasm. Charlotte had always tended to drive Julia crazy, and now that she was making a special effort to show that she was standing by Julia as her friend, that she was not a narrow-minded prig, this tendency had become more marked. Also, as much as her troubles beset her, Julia had been able at least to forget them occasionally while she was here, so far from the Land of Dick; Charlotte's presence would make them inescapable. But, of course, when Charlotte called, Julia responded with good cheer. Charlotte would stay for two days.

M. Gorotiaga fetched Charlotte from the train station. She was exhausted. In fact, she had never been so exhausted in her life (except for all the other times she had arrived at the house after a conference). Practically before Julia had even led her across the threshold, Charlotte had retailed various crises. The Quebecois delegates had been insulted when they discovered that they had been assigned an all-U.S. TV package at the hotel. *"Comment? Vous croyez que nous sommes venus à Paris pour regarder les sitcoms américains en anglais?"* In Montreal, you see, they are dubbed. At the reception for the jazz symposium and concert, the Andorrans, who hadn't even signed up, ate all the food; the representative from the French government, a Parisian, repeatedly told delegates that he couldn't understand a word they were saying. Charlotte collapsed in a big chair in the sitting room. Julia asked Mme. Gorotiaga to bring some tea, and when she did so, Charlotte told her, "This will do me a world of good," and then roused herself to ask Mme. Gorotiaga lots of questions about herself and M. Gorotiaga and her children, the son in Spain, the daughter with all the babies. This was routine, and Charlotte always spoke in admirably idiomatic French. These conversations made Mme. Gorotiaga uncomfortable, though. She stood stiffly and nodded and said, *"Oui, madame,"* and *"Ça va bien avec lui."* Julia looked over Charlotte's attire, boots that looked like sausages and a sort of gypsy dress with lots of layers. Her hair was dirty.

After tea Charlotte had a rest. Then, at dinner, she was subdued, nervous, and preoccupied. Uncharacteristically quiet, she answered Julia's questions with monosyllables. She tore at the skin on her thumb with the nail of her index finger, and she gulped down wine. Now, after their meal, the two women had moved to the sitting room and were eating cheese and Charlotte was drinking more wine. If she had been alone, Julia would have sat by the fire and allowed herself to melt into a state of sated, pregnant stupefaction. Tonight, though, she was alert, for Charlotte had begun talking about her personal life, and while Julia typically found it difficult to attend very closely to such monologues, this one was of unusual interest.

"Well," Charlotte had said when they were settled, "I guess I've told you just about everything about the conference." Then she chewed a shred of skin off her thumb and drank from her glass. She swallowed and looked up with an agitated expression.

"Julia, there is something I want to talk to you about. You're the only person who I think I really can talk about it with. You understand this kind of thing." Charlotte paused. "You see, something has happened." Charlotte took another drink.

"Do you remember my old French boyfriend, Maximilien-François-Marie-Isidore?"

Julia nodded.

"Well, when I got back to my hotel on the first night of the conference, he was there waiting for me in the lobby. Do you remember how obsessed he was, how possessive? He wanted me to have a drink with him. I told him that it was late and that I had a long day the next day. But he insisted, and he was almost making a scene in the lobby, so I said okay. We went to the hotel bar and had a drink. We had a couple of drinks, actually. After a while, I even started smoking, which I hadn't done in ages. What an awful feeling in my throat the next day." She glanced at Julia, and then seemed to try to gather her thoughts and her strength. "Okay, so then, well . . . uh . . . so then something kind of happened. Well, Maximilien-François-Marie-Isidore came up to my room. And we talked there for a little while, and smoked some more, and drank some things from the fridgie bar. And, well, he spent the night. I mean, we slept together." Charlotte blurted out this information and then began to sob. Using a handkerchief to dab her eyes, she took a moment to compose herself. Then she tried to smile ironically. "So you see," she said, "that I have a little bit of a problem. May I — could I have a little more wine?" Julia replenished her glass and Charlotte drank. She chewed a piece of bread with some cheese, and then continued. "So then the next day I was crazed, as usual, and the dinner lasted until quite late. But even with all that, I spent all day, all day, waiting to see him again. We had agreed that he would come to the hotel again that night." Charlotte's shoulders collapsed and her eyelids and cheeks and mouth drooped down. "Oh, but God, I was so desperate to see him again. And we spent another night together, and the next night, too. And —" Charlotte's lower lip and chin began to tremble. "Oh, Julia!" She began to sob into her handkerchief and then looked up. Bright red patches mottled her face and tears streamed from her eyes. "I love him! I love him! And he loves me!"

I love him, I love him, and he loves me. Julia repeated the words to herself silently. They had a nice rhythm: I LOVE him / I LOVE him / And HE — caesura — loves me. Well done, Charlotte! she thought. To love someone and have him or her love you in return, wasn't that what every person on earth wanted more than anything else?

Charlotte sobbed for a bit and then took a couple of deep breaths, wiped her eyes and nose, and became calmer. "So you see, Julia, that's why I had to talk to you. I knew that you" — Charlotte halfway glanced at Julia's belly — "I knew that you would understand and would give me really good advice on what to do." Charlotte sniffled; she uncrumpled her handkerchief, folded it, and then crumpled it again as she wiped her nose.

After a few moments of silence, Julia spoke. "Why did Maximilien-Mar —, uh, Maximilien-Is —, Maxi —" She stopped short and asked, "Is he ever called anything else?"

Charlotte looked at her blankly. "What do you mean?" she asked.

"You know, does he have a nickname, some sort of affectionate diminutive?"

"No . . ."

"Right," Julia said. "Well, in any case, why did he, your friend, why did he suddenly show up at the hotel? You said it had been years since you'd seen him."

Charlotte began to cry again, almost uncontrollably.

Julia took a sip of mineral water and looked beyond Charlotte to the black windows. They faced east, and she had missed one of her favorite sights of the day, when the rich greens and yellows would emerge on the hillsides in this direction, as the sun set in the other one. The sun, it seemed, bleached the hills so their real colors could be revealed only as it ebbed. The sky would show streaks of yellow, red, and dark blue. There would be black outlines of the land and trees, and black smudges in the sky, and, of course, the rim of purple. But Charlotte had come, and she had missed it.

Studying Charlotte, Julia reflected that some women were quite beautiful when they cried: their high color; the flashing, prismatic tears in their eyes; their swollen lips; their whole body and being vibrating with emotion like a taut, thrummed string. A man could fall for all that pretty hard. In contrast, if crying did not become a woman, and if she seemed to be falling apart rather than ascending to a state of pure feeling, then most men would instantly become irritated and impatient. In the case of patient Peter, though, she thought this likely was not true. That was fortunate, since Charlotte indisputably fell in the latter category. With her long, narrow face, she looked like a "tragedy" mask.

When she regained some composure, Charlotte said, "I was going to get around to that." She had to stop again before continuing. "You see, I called him."

This was interesting news, Julia thought.

"I called him," Charlotte repeated, "as soon as I reached Charles de Gaulle. I didn't know whether the number I had for him was still good or even whether he would be in Paris. Then I heard his voice on the machine. I was actually shaking and wasn't sure I could say anything, but I managed to leave a message. I told him where I was staying and told him to call me. I had thought about it for the whole flight, but I didn't really know what I wanted or what would happen. It was one of those things. I had thought about it for the whole flight, but when I actually made the call, I was doing it on impulse." Charlotte heaved a big sigh. For the moment, all her tears and all her sobs had been wrung out of her.

"Now you're going to wonder why I wanted to see him," Charlotte said. "That's a whole other part of the story. Oh, I don't know what to think." She held her head in her hands, then looked up at Julia, sighed yet again, and yet again wiped her eyes and blew her nose.

"You remember the wedding, of course, and what happened. You remember Peter's friend, Jonathan, the one who died?"

Julia nodded.

"Well, the situation is like this. Did you meet Jonathan's wife, Holly?"

"Yes, at the funeral."

"Okay. The situation is that Peter . . ." She stopped, gathered her strength, and forged ahead. "The situation is that Peter is in love with Holly and she is in love with him." She looked at Julia, clearly expecting a shocked response to her bombshell.

"Oh, Charlotte, you poor girl!" Julia said. "What's happened? Did one of them tell you? Or did you discover . . . did you learn of it some way?"

"No," said Charlotte, "they haven't said anything, and I haven't stumbled across any evidence, and I'm sure that nothing has happened."

"Well, but, Charlotte," Julia asked, "then how do you know? It might not be true at all."

Charlotte was silent. She pulled at her handkerchief and studied her hands as she did so. Finally, she spoke. "This is going to sound crazy to you, Julia, and a crazy thing to base a big decision about your life on. But I'll try to explain.

"The night before I left for Paris, Holly came over to cook dinner for Peter and me. She arrived before Peter had gotten home, and we sat and talked for a little bit. We had never really talked that way before, alone for any amount of time. I had always felt uncomfortable around her, but I found that I liked her very much. I couldn't even tell you one thing we talked about. But I had this feeling of affection and closeness. I felt relaxed, you know? The way you do sometimes with certain people, when your nerves just go slack?"

Julia nodded.

"But the big point is what happened later. We had dinner, right? It was fun, and there wasn't anything big that happened. At the end, Holly started talking about Peter and me, and describing what it meant to be in love, and she gave us a toast. She began to cry. It was the subject and how she talked about it, and also I thought she was crying about Jonathan. But this was no big deal, there wasn't some huge emotional outpouring.

"I went into the kitchen to make the coffee. That took a few minutes. While I was doing that, I happened to turn around and look back at Peter and Holly at the dinner table." She paused and seemed to be reliving that moment. "And that's when it happened. In that instant, I just knew it and it seemed so incredibly obvious that Peter was in love with Holly and she was in love with him. The way they were looking at each other, the way they were talking, I mean it was as plain as day. Anyone with half a brain would have known it all along. They're completely in love. I'm sure of it. And I'm sure the reason she was crying was not because of Jonathan, but because of Peter, who was sitting right there, but married to somebody else.

"So then why did I call Maximilien-François-Marie-Isidore? Because . . . because . . . I don't know! I was confused and I wanted to see him. I guess you could say that having discovered that Peter loved Holly, I wanted to rush into the arms of someone I knew loved me. I'll admit to being insecure enough that that explanation makes sense. But it isn't just that. Looking at Peter and Holly, and thinking about what Holly had said about being in love, I thought, I want that. I had this craving.

"All this must seem totally ridiculous to you, Julia, absurd and crazy. You must think I'm insane to conclude that Peter and Holly are in love, based on no evidence at all, based on an impression. And you must think I'm completely silly to have reacted the way I did, and even more silly to be so upset about what happened. I'm sorry, but my emotions are going in a hundred different directions.

"I feel so sad for Peter and Holly. Jonathan could get anyone to fall in love with him and marry him. But I wonder if all along Holly wasn't actually in love with Peter. There's another thing. Years ago, long before Holly even knew Jonathan, she and Peter sat next to each other on an airplane going to Los Angeles. The couple of times that Peter talked about it, he was very casual and kind of joked about how they had gotten crushes on each other. So — you see — he was so supercasual that I'm sure there was more to it."

"But, Charlotte," Julia said, "if he had made a big deal of it, you would be saying the same thing!"

"I know. Of course you're right. But I'm still convinced. I think about them both being so near the person they love but not being with that person. It's heartbreaking, actually.

"But then I think it's all so ridiculous and all in my head! I think I am in love with Maximilien-François-Marie-Isidore and that I always have been. But is that just some reaction? And maybe I've just managed to create a big emotional whirlpool that is based on nothing, and I should forget about it all and go back home and have my perfectly nice life. That's what I wanted. I didn't want all this kind of muddle and craziness. I had that with Maximilien-François-Marie-

Isidore before. What if I went back to him? If you asked me right now, I'd say that that was what I wanted to do more than anything. The last three nights were the happiest three nights of my life, I think. I know that it wouldn't be like that always, and maybe it was the excitement of the situation and . . . oh, you can find a hundred reasons to dismiss it, but I know, I know . . ." Charlotte began to cry again.

"But what about you and Peter?" Julia asked. "Aren't you in love?"

Charlotte thought for a moment. "Of course I love Peter, and I think he loves me. But, well, you know how it is, Julia, I wanted to marry Peter so badly because of who he is and because of who I am. Peter was safe. It is really hard for me to admit, but I always knew it. I knew that I was always more in love with him than he was with me and that I needed him more. And even for me, it wasn't the same sort of being in love as with Maximilien-François-Marie-Isidore. That's what was good about it, actually.

"Peter is so good. He would never leave me just because he had found somebody else. I'm sure of that. And, anyway, it's obvious that he and Holly don't have any idea how the other feels. If they really *do* feel anything. If he were free, though, which I could make him, then I think about what it would mean for him."

Charlotte looked at Julia with a hapless smile. "I'm so grateful to you for listening to me, Julia. I always thought that we understood each other in a way that others in the family never did."

"Yes," Julia said.

Charlotte sighed and her shoulders slumped. "Oh, I don't know what I'm going to do," she said quietly. She remained silent for a while.

"There are so many problems," she said finally. "What if these feelings Maximilien-François-Marie-Isidore and I have for each other are foolish and temporary, and why would I want to throw

myself back into all that stuff with him? How would I explain it to my parents and the rest of the world? My grandmother. I'll look so foolish. And then, on top of all that, there's something else. I have no idea what we would do for money."

Money. Of course, Julia thought. Of course that would come into it.

"I'm almost ashamed to admit to worrying about that. Money shouldn't matter, should it? We could get by without money. But you can't live only on love, can you? You've got to have *some* money. And maybe I'm a little spoiled, but I'm used to it."

Money. Julia listened closely to what Charlotte was saying.

"Maximilien-François-Marie-Isidore would never, ever live in the States. Right now he rents a room from a family in an apartment in Paris, but when he marries, he has always said he would move to the family seat. His ancestor received it along with the title from Saint Louis for providing boots for a crusade. They keep renouncing the title and then using it again. Maximilien-François-Marie-Isidore's father despised everything about it. Maximilien-François-Marie-Isidore believes in it passionately. He's a royalist. So he'll insist on living in his castle, which is just a pile of stones in the middle of swampland. Nothing has been done to it since someone put in electricity in the 1930s. He says he has to take his place among his ancestors and that his heir must be born there."

Somewhere within her, Charlotte found more tears to shed.

"How are we going to live, though? Nothing happens in that *département.* Nothing. I don't know what kind of job I could get, and right now Maximilien-François-Marie-Isidore lives on a tiny income. He objects to working for wages on principle. A nobleman! But even if he wanted to, there'd be no job he could get that would pay anything. He's writing his poems, of course, which might earn a pittance, if he'd accept payment for them, which he won't. To make

the place habitable and then live there without starving — there's no money for that. Oh, I don't know how we'd do it.

"I've tried to think of everything. There's a town nearby that isn't so small. Maybe I could give English lessons. Maybe there would be something I could do by computer and go to Paris once in a while. Philippe, my boss, he could help. Except that he's hopeless about doing that kind of thing for anybody. And there are some French members of the AGSPF board whom I know. But getting any kind of job in France is impossible, and for me? An American? Even if I am allowed to work here because I'm married . . .

"There's my family, but my mother doesn't have much except what my father sends her, and she wouldn't be inclined to help out anyway, I know that. She'll freak if I go through with this. And my father? God. I wouldn't be surprised if he cut me off without one *sou*. And already he's let drop how much the divorce is going to cost him. Oh! Please, Julia, don't think I'm blaming you, or that I even believe him. I'm just saying that that's his state of mind. So then my grandparents gave us gifts over the years that I've saved. And then I could sell everything I own." She paused. "I've even thought about selling the painting."

"Oh, no! Charlotte, you love that painting."

"I do. But every once in a while I see that one of his things has been sold at auction. It's not exactly Van Gogh prices, but it would be very helpful. It would kill me, but it would be helpful." Charlotte grieved for a bit about losing her painting. Then she looked at Julia with a newly distraught expression. "Even with all that, though? Even with all that? What would it amount to? To improve the place and to live, and to . . . to have children. We want children. In no time we'd be broke." Charlotte shook her head. "It's impossible isn't it?" she said. "It's impossible. It's all crazy, anyway. And it's completely insane when you think about the money." She raised her hands and then let them drop back down. "I give up. I'm going to go back to Peter and keep mum and have a decent life."

Charlotte put her face in her hands. She was spent, and she stayed like that for a long time.

Eventually, Julia rose and touched Charlotte's shoulder. "Come on, now, it's time for bed. You're tired and strung out from everything."

Charlotte nodded. They cleaned up a bit and went upstairs. After some embraces and cries from Charlotte that she wouldn't know what to do were it not for Julia, Charlotte finally lay down and pulled up her covers. Instantly, she fell asleep.

Julia, for her part, stayed up for a little while.

So: money. In order for the four young lovers to be happy, it would require money. Well, guess what? Julia had a way to solve this problem! If she exploded Dick's self-dealing, and thereby made Charlotte aware of her actual financial position, then there would be money. However, there would also be some potentially unpleasant consequences for Julia. Without any reason to placate her, with every reason to be vengeful, Dick would set out to screw her unmercifully. It was even possible, she imagined, that she could be implicated in his wrongdoing. Was this an outcome that Julia was really willing to risk? No.

So it was settled. She would tell Charlotte to stay with her for a few days. (A few days! Had there ever been a greater act of self-sacrifice?) During that time, Julia would soothe and coddle her and quietly counsel her to choose safety and sanity; like a poultice drawing pus from a wound, she would draw out the emotion that had infected Charlotte. Some nights hence, as Charlotte gained perspective on what had happened in Paris, she would have come to her senses. She would look back on those three days of passion as a glorious memory but nothing more. It would all be over, without any mess, and without any added trouble for Julia herself.

Despite Julia's intention at this point to go to sleep, she found it necessary to continue to argue her case.

Regardless of her own self-interest, she thought, the whole business was absurd. To think of Charlotte actually spending the rest of her life with this Maximilien-whatever-his-name-was. It was absurd. It was lunacy. And as for Peter and Holly, who knows? Maybe there was some yearning. Sure. It was very common for men to believe that they were in love with their best friends' wives. Also, their mutual grief had thrown them together under highly emotional circumstances; it would be surprising if some strong feelings had not arisen between them. Of course, she remembered what Jonathan had said about them, and it was hard to doubt his acuity in a matter like that, and there was also this new information about the time they first met, which, sure, did seem to have the characteristics of a love-at-first-sight-type situation, but it was all pretty flimsy, wasn't it?

Julia tried, but she still could not quite make a move toward sleep. She tried hard: she didn't want to think anymore, for she knew that any more thought would only subvert the position she had taken. She didn't want to think about Charlotte; she didn't want to think about Holly; she didn't want to think about Peter. She didn't want to think about whether and how much she cared about them and the duty she owed them (to Charlotte's beau she figured she owed the same consideration that one owed any sentient being). She didn't want to think about their potential happiness, and their pain. She didn't want to think about true love, and the chance that they all might find it. But she couldn't stop herself.

～

Julia had never really been able to care about Charlotte. She had tried over the years, yet she had never quite succeeded. Nevertheless, she could not help feeling some sympathy for her stepdaughter in this situation, because of its nature, because Charlotte had shown more spirit here than usual, and because, after all these years, maybe Charlotte did mean something to her. It was a tough spot: Julia could see that Charlotte really was in love with the Frenchman. Yet pursuing that connection would entail a lot of trouble for her. It would profoundly embarrass Charlotte if a divorce followed her wedding so closely. Charlotte cared about status and about safety, and she would lose both. As for Charlotte's parents, they had long since passed judgment on Maximilien-whatever, finding him impecunious and very, very tiresome. It had been evident to everyone that Charlotte's romance with him was just something that she had to get out of her system, and that she would ultimately come round, as of course she did. For her actually to marry him, though, especially when it would mean tossing away a very good match and a normal life, would cause her parents to react with bewilderment and fury.

Poor old Charlotte. She had been seeking Julia's friendship and asking her advice and sharing her secrets for so long. What was Julia's responsibility now? What was the right thing to do, the thing that, in her heart (if she could find it), she knew that she should do? Charlotte deserved to be happy. If she stayed with Peter, she would spend the rest of her life trying so hard to be interesting, trying so hard to maintain her parents' social and economic position (even as she tried so hard not to care too much about that), trying so hard to have creative, brilliant, French-speaking children who (not that it really mattered) would go to the same schools that Charlotte and her siblings had, despite the orders of ten by which the competition for places in them had risen. But if she threw it all away and ran off with the man she loved and who loved her, she might actually be happy. She might be miserable, but she might actually be happy. Julia knew that passion faded and couldn't be counted on for the long haul. Everyone knew that. Except, deep in her heart, Julia didn't really believe it, if you found the right person.

Oh, hell. Damn. Julia found herself both smiling and beginning to tear up as she imagined Charlotte living in a castle with the man she loved, the heir and perhaps some little sisters scampering around. With or without money, it was a brave thing that Charlotte was contemplating, to throw away her comfortable life and her family's approval for love. That word, that damn word. It could all happen with the help of a fairy godmother, and who might that be?

~

And it wasn't only Charlotte. There was Holly.

When Julia thought of Holly, as of course she often had in the previous months, her heart was filled with tenderness and with excruciating guilt. The second emotion was understandable, but the first less so, since she and Holly had barely spoken. Julia remembered when she had first seen her, without knowing who she was, at the dinner before the wedding. She noticed a young woman who was so pretty that Julia reflexively did a check of her own looks, with an adjustment for age. Even with that handicap, Julia had the unsettling thought that she could not claim to be the prettiest woman in the room. She did not feel too competitive, though, because the young woman neither carried herself in a way that would have declared a challenge nor dressed with the hard-edged chic that also would have done so. She did, however, exhibit a modest elegance in her dress that Julia admired and that she knew required a ton of money to achieve. (Julia remembered the tall, fantastically beautiful South American bridesmaid, but Julia never considered people like that rivals. Rather than being human, a tall, beautiful South American was a phenomenon of nature, and therefore didn't count.)

Julia did not know who the young woman was but felt that she bore some study. There was a sweetness about her looks that Julia was drawn to. When Julia first saw her, the young woman was talking to a short, overweight man. As he spoke, an ill-kempt mustache wiggled like a caterpillar on his upper lip. She was taller than the man and inclined her head toward him, thus extending a neck that Julia found troublingly long. The young woman had piled up her hair on top of her head, which showed her neck to good advantage and revealed her broad, level shoulders. She wore emerald and diamond earrings. These Julia could identify, even at a distance, as some quite fine dead-grandmother jewelry. The young woman nodded at what the man was saying and then laughed, covering her mouth with long, slender fingers. She extended a long, slender arm and rested her hand on the upper arm of the man and said something that caused him to burst into laughter in turn.

What was it about the young woman's appearance, aside from her prettiness (and the dead-grandmother jewelry), that struck Julia so? She was embarrassed even to have the thought that came to her mind, which was that the woman she was looking at seemed . . . good. The fluid, if erect, way she held herself allowed physical *give* in the way she responded to her companion, and the word seemed to describe her overall manner. To the extent detectable, she seemed to be enjoying her conversation with the horrid little man; certainly, she was not behaving in the way that telegraphed that one was miserably bored by the wretch one was talking to and humiliated to be seen in his company. Julia felt a twinge in her conscience: this young woman somehow served as a rebuke to her.

At the ceremony the next day, Julia noticed her again, sitting in the third row on the groom's side. She sat with people who looked like the groom's aunts and uncles, and Julia wondered what relation she had to Peter. Julia, in the first row, made a backward glance or two. She could not take in much, but she saw that the young woman, deep in thought, was looking straight ahead at the altar. Julia became a little curious. To her, and she had a keen eye for this kind of thing, the young woman's expression almost looked like that of someone who had a stake in the proceedings. Poor girl! An afterimage of her — so pretty and good, and possibly wounded — remained with Julia for a moment after she had faced forward again.

During the chaos at the reception, Julia had kept to herself, and in the days following she had spoken to no one but Dick about what had happened, and to him only minimally, so she remained in ignorance of the wife named Holly whom Jonathan had discussed. The name caused Julia dread, since it had for some reason seemed appropriate for many members of the wedding party to reassemble at Jonathan's funeral, whether or not they had known the deceased, and Julia feared that she might have some kind of breakdown when she met the widow. How could she withstand the waves of guilt, grief, and remembered horror that would crash upon her at the moment of that encounter?

Holly. As Julia dressed on the morning of the funeral the name kept running through her mind as dread now mixed with gruesome curiosity. Who was Holly? What was she like? At the church, while she and Dick sought out seats, Julia looked anxiously toward the front pew. A young woman was sitting there, along the aisle, and it seem certain that she was the widow. Julia could not see her face, but the back of her head triggered a spark of recognition. From what Julia could tell, she wore a black suit. Julia stared at her back and broad, level shoulders; then at her reddish blond hair, which was down.

The little girl sitting next to the widow spoke to her, and she tilted her head down to hear. Then she turned her face toward the girl as she made her reply. Julia could see her profile: yes, it was that same young woman, the pretty one she had noticed at the dinner and the wedding service. So she — so pretty and so good, and possibly wounded — was the one whom Julia's degraded and ill-fated acts had so brutally harmed. Then her stomach turned over and she felt faint. The widow, Holly, was now having what looked like a very serious conversation with the little girl. Holly was beautiful; she was good, Julia felt certain. Julia had managed to live through the previous few days with the help of cigarettes, alcohol, a wee pill here and there, but, most important, she had survived because of that well-known phenomenon whereby a horrifying event seems unreal to the participants. "It was like a movie." Now, though, Julia suddenly felt the rough wet grass beneath her feet, she smelled the earth and felt the rain, and she saw the bolt strike Jonathan. In the pew, she almost leapt back as she had at the time. She felt ill. At that moment Holly and the little girl turned around to look down the aisle. Out of the corner of her eye, Holly must have noticed Julia looking at her; she returned the look and gave Julia a smile of recognition ("I remember you from the wedding, too"). Julia attempted to smile back. Holly pointed at something and began to talk to the girl, and Julia looked down at her hands and began to sob.

At the cemetery Julia kept to the rear of the crowd, and she intended to remain elusive during the reception afterward (held at a friend's apartment). But while she was standing near the wall drinking a Bloody Mary, there came the inevitable. Dick appeared by her side. "Here you are," he said. "I thought I'd lost you. We'd better say something to the family; we won't have to stay too much longer after that." He took Julia by the elbow and led her over to where Holly stood among in-laws and her own relatives. Jonathan's mother was plump, with golden hair and red lipstick. Near her stood a tall woman, beautifully dressed, who appeared to be Holly's mother; she had a long, lovely nose. A large, dissipated man with long blond-and-white hair stood with his back to her, talking to someone. He wore a black suit with a ventless jacket; it didn't fit too well and looked a little worse for wear. He, Julia gathered, was Holly's father.

Julia and Dick approached the group and stood by for a moment. Then a guest released Jonathan's mother, and she turned toward Dick. "May I introduce myself?" he said, taking her hand in both of his. "I'm Dick Montague, Charlotte's father."

"Caroline Gould," Jonathan's mother said. "How nice to see you."

"We are all so terribly sad about what happened," said Dick.

"That's so kind of you to say."

Dick removed a hand, put it on Julia's back, and drew her forward. "This is my wife, Julia."

"How do you do?" said Jonathan's mother, shaking hands with Julia, who mumbled a greeting.

"We are so sorry about your loss," Dick said. "We didn't know Jonathan well, but we certainly heard a great deal about him from Charlotte and Peter. I know what a terrific friend he was to Peter."

"Jonny and Peter were such dear friends," Jonathan's mother said. "Peter has been wonderful through all this. He's such a fine person. Jonny was such a fine person, too. I think that's one reason why they were such good friends. I feel terrible that Jonny's accident happened at Peter and your daughter's wedding. It should have been the happiest day of their lives."

"Please, you needn't worry about that," said Dick. "I know all their thoughts are with you and the others who loved Jonathan."

Jonathan's mother wasn't listening. She pulled on the sleeve of a man standing nearby. "Skip, come meet Charlotte's parents. You know, the girl who was getting married."

"Oh! Yes!" said the man, turning around. He had a beautiful head of silver hair and "distinguished" features, although his expression was vacant.

"This is my husband, Skip Gould," said Jonathan's mother. "Skip, this is Dick Montague and — I'm so sorry, it's Ju —?"

"Julia," said Julia.

"Oh, yes. And Julia Montague."

Dick and Julia exchanged greetings with Skip Gould. During the conversation that followed he stood by wearing a charming smile and saying nothing.

"Skip, darling," said Mrs. Gould, "Dick and Julia's daughter was the girl getting married when the accident happened. My goodness, it was quite a shock. We had gone out to dinner at Allie and Ned Barstow's. We've made some wonderful friends since we moved — oh, it must be three years ago now. And the Barstows are so attractive. Allie is such fun. It was such a fun group! Some of Allie's young were there . . ."

Jonathan's mother continued in this vein for some time, smiling and beaming with almost psychotic sociability given the circumstances. Julia did not listen closely, for she was acutely aware that she stood within Holly's conversational sphere of influence. Moreover, she had remained a little behind Dick, and Jonathan's mother did not address her directly, so she was not locked into an alliance with this group. Holly was talking to someone else, but if she made a quarter turn after he left, it would be natural and almost inevitable that she and Julia would speak to each other. Julia could see Holly in her peripheral vision, and she could feel the emanations of Holly's presence almost smother her. Julia was trying to look as if she were rapt in the conversation with Jonathan's mother, but she was actually planning her escape. Then she saw out of the corner of her eye that the man talking to Holly was moving away. Julia froze. She could not just walk off and leave the widow alone, especially since Julia was the person nearest to her and with whom it would be most natural for her to speak, and since, as was evident, the reason Julia and Dick had approached in the first place was to pay their respects.

Julia concentrated on Jonathan's mother. A moment passed, a moment passed, a moment passed. Then Julia heard a pleasing, rather low female voice say to her, "Excuse me, aren't you Julia Montague? Charlotte's stepmother?" With the veins in her head pounding, Julia turned and said in a startled way (or as best as she could imitate one), "Oh! Why, yes!"

"I'm Holly Speedwell."

"Of course. I know," Julia said. She was taken aback by Holly's green eyes: even red-rimmed and bloodshot, or perhaps on account of that, they were striking. They both made hesitant movements with their hands and shoulders, not knowing how to greet each other. Finally, Holly took Julia's hand in both of hers.

"We never got a chance to meet," Holly said. "Thank you so much for coming. Everyone in Charlotte's family has been so kind."

As she heard this, Julia was thinking about her hand and how Holly's enclosed it, with their long fingers and their cool, soft, youngish skin. She recalled how and where her own hand had recently caressed Jonathan, and she felt a shiver.

"I'm . . . we're . . . so very sorry," she said. "I . . . I . . . I . . . I . . . ." Julia felt faint; she was unsure about whether she would be able to utter a sentence. She finally managed it: "I sat next to Jonathan at the dinner."

"Yes, he mentioned that. He enjoyed that very much. You had a great talk, he said."

"Yes," said Julia. Her open mouth quivered and no words came out. "Please," she said finally, "please tell me if there is anything I can do."

Dick loomed up and introduced himself to Holly. Julia stepped back and only half listened as Dick purred his condolences. He tilted his head and knit his brow in the way that he always did when he wanted to convey to a pretty young woman that he took her seriously.

Julia took this opportunity to drift away and go to the bar. Just as the bartender handed her another Bloody Mary, she began to shake, and weep, and to pant so hard that it sounded as if she were hyperventilating. Then she felt a large hand on her shoulder.

"Hey, are you okay?"

Julia looked around and saw Holly's father. She could see some of Holly's features in his big, masculine face — the same green eyes; he was even better-looking.

"I'm . . . yes . . . I'm . . ." Julia now began to break down completely. A couple of people turned around and stared.

"Hey, hey," Holly's father said softly. "Come on. Come on over here."

He put his arm around Julia's shoulders and led her into another room, a library where no lamps were lit. Taking her drink, he eased Julia into a leather chair. In the gray light, she wept. Her tears made black sunbursts on the leather armrest. Holly's father stood a few feet away, watching her and guarding the door.

When Julia had finally gained some control of herself, she spoke. "Thank you. I'm so sorry. I'm not sure what's come over me."

"Graham Edwards." He held out his hand, and she took it and squeezed it.

"Holly's father?"

"Yes."

"I'm Julia Montague, Charlotte's stepmother. The bride —"

"Sure." He handed Julia her drink. She took a big swallow.

"Thanks," she said. She breathed deeply a couple of times. "This has all affected me very much. I don't know why. I didn't know Jonathan, but I sat next to him at the bridal dinner, and we talked quite a bit. You must think I'm a hysterical female."

"Well, yeah, I do. But there's nothing wrong with that," said Graham. He moved his hands dramatically when he talked. "Some of my best friends are hysterical females. And if somebody wanted to get hysterical, this seems like a pretty good time. A young guy you just met, you get to know him, and the next day, this happens? Whew. Anybody'd be hysterical."

Julia tried to smile to thank him for his effort to reassure her. Then she looked as if she would cry again. "Is Holly," she said, "is Holly doing okay?"

Graham didn't answer for a minute. "She's all right." He paused again. "Do you have children?"

"Stepchildren."

Graham stared at the floor, then looked at Julia. "I have two daughters. They're both in their thirties now, and I worry about them just as much as I did when they were little kids. More — I worry about them more because now it's the real thing, real life. When the girls were pretty young, their mother and I split up for some dumb reason that neither of us can even remember. I tried to stay as close to them as I could. I really think I did okay. I just wanted so badly for them to be happy and safe. Their mother too. Well, I don't know if we succeeded. I don't know. This guy, Speedwell." Graham shrugged and tilted his head back and forth. "Anyway . . ." He was lost in thought.

"I'll tell you something," he said, coming to. "I love Alex, the older one. I love her beyond anything. But Holly, you know, just between us, Holly is the apple of my eye. To see her hurt . . ." He winced. "They could do anything to me, any kind of torture, if I could prevent that.

"So I'm just hoping, after all this passes . . . Of course, it's not everything, having the right guy. But maybe there'll be a nice guy she finds." He gave a soft laugh. "Somebody who really deserves her! I guess every father sets that bar impossibly high."

He looked at Julia and tried to grin. His big, masculine, handsome, dissipated face seemed to struggle to light up, like an engine that wouldn't start. He spread out his long arms. "Hey, I was in pictures," he said. "We've got to have a happy ending!"

As he spoke, Julia sat leaning forward in the chair with her knees and ankles together and her hands in her lap. She had stopped crying and listened to Graham with great solemnity.

Dick appeared at the door.

"So this is where you've been hiding," he said. He looked back and forth between Julia and Graham, obviously wondering why in the world they were alone in this twilit room. He and Graham introduced themselves and spoke for a moment about the tragedy. Then Dick said, "Well, darling?" Julia shook Graham's hand and said quietly, "Holly is lucky." "No," he replied. "No, I am."

Recalling all this, thinking about Holly, as she did hourly, Julia wrestled with her responsibility for Jonathan's death. Of course it wasn't her fault, exactly. But if she hadn't been there, if she hadn't agreed to go off with Jonathan . . . It caused her torment. If she struck and killed a pedestrian with her car, even if the fault was entirely the pedestrian's, she knew she would still feel terrible about it. How much worse what had happened with Jonathan! Julia had helped Jonathan betray Holly, which was bad enough in the first place. Then for him to die as a result . . . It was torment. And Holly was her victim.

~

As Julia weighed whether or not to help Charlotte, these thoughts about her and about Holly piled higher on one side of the scales. And it wasn't just Charlotte and Holly, it was also Peter.

～

Julia and Dick were going out to dinner with Charlotte and her new beau. This would be the first time they would meet him, and Julia wasn't looking forward to it. In the presence of her father, Charlotte always tried too hard to seem sophisticated, cosmopolitan, and unbowed by his indifference. Introducing him to a man with whom she was involved, Charlotte would try to act even more self-possessed, confident, knowing. She would tease Dick in an arch, humorless manner. Watching Charlotte in this state was never very enjoyable. In this case, the chances were that Charlotte would likely be especially nervous, for the indications were that the new guy was a serious candidate for husband.

His name was Peter Russell and he did something on Wall Street. He had grown up in a town and gone to schools that Dick and Janet would find entirely unexceptionable. His parents, while not in Dick's social milieu and quite provincial in Dick's view, were solid gentry. (Peter's father had never tried to compose poems in French, as Dick had in his youth, and he bought his suits off the rack, and he had not seduced many women, but he had been a hockey star in college, had run large divisions of a successful company, and had helped materially to improve his state's system of foster care; meanwhile, his wife had raised millions of dollars for different charities, was famous for her rhododendrons, and was a descendant of the founders of Barnstable, Massachusetts; together they had lovingly raised three relatively sane and happy children: it never occurred to Dick that they might look down on him.) As for the lad himself — well, in her time, Julia had met scores of young men who did something on Wall Street. Some were mannerly, others quite loud and coarse. They might be very good-looking with the sleek, strong build of somebody who had lettered in double-scull rowing or something like that, or they might be square-jawed ex-marines. Invariably, they loved golf. She had learned to distinguish easily between those on the sell side and those on the buy side; the former were shorter and louder and drank more, and the latter maintained a more aloof, analytical air. The most courteous and easiest to talk to were the nice young men with smooth complexions and thick heads of chestnut brown hair who worked in the private wealth group at a bank. She wasn't sure where Peter fit in. It probably wouldn't be too bad. She could get him going on his golf game or what he did when a client was looking for a little more yield ("There's usually a corporate out there with a call provision . . ."). If he was interested in Charlotte, though, he might have an "artistic" side, and the thought of this made Julia groan. Little was worse than having to listen to a young man who did something on Wall Street talk about contemporary art or whatever other interest he had cultivated, to show that he had dimensions and contradictions. Why did they always like such junk? You didn't ever hear them say that on their last trip to the museum they had fallen in love with a little tempera of the Annunciation that they had never noticed before. Well — what was two or three hours of her life? Golf, "art," the trip to South America during college, and yield.

They met for a drink at Dick and Julia's. Peter was of medium build and height. He was good-looking in a mild way. He had a pleasant, kind face, with hazel eyes. None of this was unusual, but there was something different about Peter that Julia sensed right away. He had lovely manners and was rather quiet; he let Charlotte take the lead in conversation, and he seemed to have a calming effect on her. What was it about him? A tincture of sadness? Poor boy, for Julia saw it now: his heart had been broken. He obviously wasn't in love with Charlotte, and there was an air of fatalism on his part about their future.

They went to a restaurant and Julia remembered what happened as they were settling in their seats, the women on the banquette and the men opposite them. Charlotte commented on how beautiful the room was and said that it was too bad that Dick and Peter couldn't see it.

"Not at all," Peter said. "Sitting across from two such beautiful women, we have the best view in the house, don't you think so, sir?"

Dick wasn't expecting such "wit" — on an occasion like this, that was his department — so he was momentarily startled. Then he said, "Yes! Yes, indeed!" He put his hand on Peter's shoulder and laughed. "Quite so!"

A moment later, by accident, Peter and Julia caught each other's eye, and Peter reflexively shrugged and grinned, shooting her a look that said, "He bought it."

As the evening progressed Peter continued to surprise Julia. Certainly, it had been revealed that he was a good squash player, that he liked to go hiking, that he had visited Guatemala. Beyond those predictable attributes, however, Julia discovered someone to whom she actually enjoyed talking. By a remarkable coincidence, it turned out that they both had the same favorite Italian song, *"L'alba separa dalla luce l'ombra."* After dessert, Dick had insisted on cognac. Peter hardly could decline, although the women did. Charlotte asked Dick about a recent agricultural ruling handed down by Brussels. Answering, Dick contradicted the whole premise of the question; soon enough he had gained speed and was giving a long explanation of the ruling's effects, while repeatedly referring to one high official by his first name (Jürgen).

Peter and Julia were only half listening. As Dick talked on, Julia leaned forward. "Tell me something," she said to Peter. "We've gotten through this whole evening and you haven't said a word about your career. How come?"

"Oh," Peter said. "Well — I save that for when I am going out to dinner with a woman for the first time. We'll talk about it — that is, I will — for pretty much the entire meal. I mean, not every minute — you've got to order and so forth. Also, when a woman and I are in each other's arms after . . . after . . . you know, I like to tell her about it. It's beautiful."

"I see," said Julia. "But otherwise you don't raise the subject?"

"Not usually."

"What if someone asks you what you do?"

"Well, then you're stuck, aren't you? I've always wanted to sort of draw myself up and say with a withering look, 'I am a gentleman.'"

"Yes, the best answer," said Julia. "But it isn't one you can honestly give, is it — and tell me if I don't have this right — what with the fancy job at the top firm and the big bonus and all?"

"Sadly, no."

Julia liked Peter. Over the months and years, she had always been happy to see him, and, in fact, he had worked his way into her heart.

~

Charlotte had been asleep for two hours or longer, but Julia had gone over all these memories again and again, and by this time she was wide awake. She laughed and cried, thinking about Charlotte, Holly, and Peter. If Charlotte bolted, maybe, probably, they would all end up miserable. Maybe, probably, the love business was completely bogus. But what if it was not? Oh, how she wanted to help all three of them!

Yet a moment came, late into the night, when she hardened herself against all this sentimentality. What had happened to her? Somehow she had fallen under some kind of spell; now the instincts for self-preservation and for the protection of one's child forcefully reasserted themselves. Such mush. No. No, no, no, no. She would not put her own and her baby's well-being at risk for the sake of these others. No. It was too bad, it was tough, but that was life. It is a far, far better thing I do, than I have ever done — this was not Julia's style. She felt sorry for all of them. She really did. What had happened to Jonathan was terrible, of course. But it was an accident, and Julia's role was entirely fortuitous. If Charlotte was so in love, and if she wanted to act accordingly, then she'd have to accept the consequences. As for Holly and Peter — it wasn't any of Julia's business. If they couldn't overcome the obstacles between them, then — it was a harsh judgment, but it was true — it was their own fault, and they didn't deserve to get whatever it was that they wanted. Let Dick and his children hash out their problems in the years to come. Let Peter and Holly figure it out for themselves. Julia's duty was to get money, using any advantage she could.

~

When the sun rose the next day, Julia was awake to watch it. She stood on the terrace in her nightgown, shivering; the cold stone chilled her feet. With no clouds to tint, the sun produced a diffuse red glow. As it rose, Julia saw the sky rinse it of successively lighter shades of red, pink, and yellow, until it was a pure, blinding white. It would be a beautiful day.

Charlotte slept late. Julia wrote letters, read her book, picked apples. When she returned to the house with her basket, she found Charlotte in the kitchen, drinking coffee and chatting with Mme.

Gorotiaga. Charlotte told Julia how wonderfully she had slept. She always slept well here, but she had been in the deepest sleep she had ever known, she thought. This house must be the best place to sleep on earth.

It was decided that for lunch, Julia and Charlotte would walk to a spot with a particularly fine view and have a picnic. Mme. Gorotiaga made them chicken sandwiches with butter and parsley, and they took some water, a third of a bottle of wine, a thermos of coffee, cheese, apples, walnuts, and chocolate. The path was rocky, but it had a gentle slope, and as they walked along it, the valley was slowly revealed. Reaching their destination, Julia and Charlotte could see melon fields, now all astubble, and the vein of silver that was the river. A dozen varieties of shrubs and another dozen of grasses, each its own shade of green, stretched away from them. In the distance, one could see the clustered brown cubes of the village. At this time of day, a little after noon, the sun seemed to brush its light painstakingly on every leaf, twig, and pebble.

Walking had made the women hot and they took off their sweaters. They sat on a blanket and ate their lunch, which was delicious. Why would someone make a sandwich in any other way? Now they were drinking the coffee and eating the chocolate. Charlotte drew up one leg, wrapped her arms around her shin, and rested her chin on her knee. She sighed contentedly.

"I love it here," she said. "What a wonderful spot." She turned her head to the right. "And there's the house. It looks so grand! I love the house, too. It's so beautiful and solid and serene."

She now turned toward Julia; she was smiling eagerly. Julia smiled back and then looked out at the valley. It was hot. The sun seemed to weigh her down, but not in an unpleasant way — more as if it were swaddling her.

They talked about this and that. Charlotte expressed keen, and surely exaggerated, interest in the fate of the espaliered pear trees, which had been faring poorly. Was it really true that one of the Gorotiagas' children intended to go to America? There was a church with a Byzantine-style tower that Charlotte had always wanted to view, and she hoped she would be able to do so on this visit. They didn't talk about the subjects that had occupied them the previous night.

At one point, they fell silent for a while, luxuriating in their full bellies; the sun, whose warmth, with midday well past, had become entirely delicious; the view of valleys and crisscrossing hills. Eventually, Julia spoke.

"Tell me something, Charlotte."

"Yes?"

"Do you really love the house?"

"Oh, yes!"

Julia stared off at a castle that stood on a promontory miles and miles away. This time of year, you could see it so clearly. Charlotte waited for Julia to continue. It seemed like a long time before she did.

"Well, then," she said, still looking off, "if you like it so much, it might interest you to know that you own it."

Charlotte stared at Julia, bewildered. "I'm sorry," Charlotte said. "What do you mean?"

"You own it, with David and Deirdre."

"I still don't understand," said Charlotte. "What do you mean? How can that be?"

Julia turned toward Charlotte. She smiled gently at her and took her hand, something she couldn't remember ever having done before. "Charlotte, I'm going to tell you something that I think will be good news, but that's going to complicate your life and that

257

has some bad news that goes along with it. But it's all things you should know."

Charlotte went pale. "God!" she said. "I have no idea what you're talking about. I'm scared."

"Don't worry," Julia said. "None of it is life-and-death."

So Julia told Charlotte everything. She described the legacy that Charlotte's grandfather had left her and her brother and sister, and how her father had been named the fiduciary responsible for it. Dick, Julia explained, had taken advantage of this position, and she told Charlotte as much as she could about the fees, distributions, loans, purchases, and "investments." The house had been bought with the children's funds, and, technically, it was theirs. This was also true of the country house in Connecticut, various pieces of furniture and works of art, and, probably, some of Dick's cuff links and custom-made shirts. Dick had even used money from Charlotte's share to pay himself for the painting that he had "given" her for her twenty-first birthday. There was a good reason, taxwise, to do it this way, Dick had assured Julia, and he had relied on an appraisal, so no one could question the price. While Charlotte listened, she looked down at a sprig she was twirling in her fingers, but when she heard about the painting she looked up sharply and seemed as if she were about to be ill. Then she went back to studying her sprig.

Like all embezzlers, Julia continued, Dick had probably started small, but as he saw how easy it was, he had begun to think bigger and bigger, and eventually worked himself into a position where all sorts of acts seemed legitimate. You might think that a lawyer would be especially scrupulous, but, well, then you would be wrong about lawyers. Dick had certainly exercised some care, however. Julia understood that it was hard to successfully sue someone in his position, and everything had at least a whiff of plausibility. Moreover, Dick was certain that, even if it occurred to his children that they could sue him, they would be much too afraid to do so. And who could complain? This place, to take just one example, had appreciated far more than the stock market in the same period!

"You know," Julia said, "he was always planning on telling you. But he was going to buy some things back and repay the loans, shape things up, which he never got around to. And he talked about how it would be bad for David to know about the money; and as for you girls, well, he'd say that having money never does a girl any good where men are concerned.

"The point is that whatever your father has done and what you think of it, you have enough money to go live in your castle, if you want; enough to fix it up and support an heir and even a couple of little sisters."

Charlotte kept looking down.

"I know it's a lot to absorb," said Julia. "I'm sorry, Charlotte. I'm sorry for my part in it."

Two or three minutes passed before Charlotte spoke. "It's the painting that really gets me. That was the one thing, the *one* thing that I thought he really cared about and really wanted to be mine, something precious and also, to be honest, pretty valuable, that he wanted to give to me." She tossed the sprig away.

They sat in silence. The sun cooled as it descended from its peak, and now the grasses glowed and cast long shadows. A breeze came up, as it usually did in the afternoon, swirling around Charlotte and Julia. They collected their crusts, plates, silverware, napkins, and cups, folded the blanket, and walked back to the house.

Both Charlotte and Julia took naps. Julia slept deeply and for a long time, having gotten so little sleep the night before. Awaking, she read for a while in bed. She felt oddly serene. Telling Charlotte had turned out to be very easy, for at one point just before dawn it had become inarguable that it was the right — the only — thing to do. She wondered if she had been suckered by her conscience, and by Cupid. After a day or two, she would probably think so. But right now, she felt serene. In this state, it was easy for her to decide to perform another beau geste, which followed logically from the first; for weeks this radical idea had been swimming around, like a large sea monster, just below the surface of her consciousness. In for a penny, in for a pound.

She heard a soft knock and called *"Entrez!"* It was Charlotte, who let in one of the cats when she opened the door. One of the dogs, sleeping on the floor, barked, and the cat jumped on the bed; the dog went back to sleep.

Charlotte looked very solemn.

"Hello," said Julia.

"Hi. I'm not disturbing you, am I?"

"Of course not."

"Are you feeling all right? You had a long nap."

"I'm fine," said Julia. "I get very tired in the afternoon, and there are certain things that are uncomfortable, but mostly I'm having it easy."

"Oh. Good." Charlotte sat on the bed and stroked the cat.

"I'm not sure I did the right thing, telling you what I did," said Julia.

"No. You were right. Definitely right," Charlotte said. "It just has to sink in."

"Yes."

Charlotte lay on her side on the thick duvet; the cat purred as she scratched it behind the ears.

"One thing I don't understand," she said after a minute. "Well, there are a lot of things I don't understand. But he must be making loads of money. Why did he have to do any of this?"

"Ah, my poor child," Julia said, "'loads of money' is relative. Sure, a lawyer like your father makes a nice salary, but it isn't as if he has huge chunks of capital dropping in his lap. You know, lawyers — when the big dealmakers have gone off to drink their three-thousand-dollar bottles of Bordeaux, the lawyers stay behind tidying up the documents. Then, what with taxes, an ex-wife, a very expensive younger wife, a couple of houses and apartments, children, it all adds up. We probably spend seventy-five thousand dollars a year just on going out to dinner, which means making a hundred and fifty thousand. We've never had any staff. 'Staff is what kills you,' Dick always said. So he liked to save money there, but then he'd spend those savings three times over."

Charlotte considered this. "A hundred and fifty thousand dollars a year," she said. "Maximilien-François-Marie-Isidore and I could live in luxury on that."

"Well," Julia said, "you've got it, and more."

"It's a lot to think about."

"Yes."

Charlotte sighed. The cat had curled up and fallen asleep against her stomach.

"Tell me something, Julia."

"Yes?"

"Obviously my father didn't want anyone to know about the money for essentially as long as possible, right?"

"That's right."

"Won't he be pretty angry when he finds out you told me?"

"Yeah, that's a safe bet."

"Won't that make the divorce even harder?"

"Maybe. As long as I kept his secret, he was more likely to be a little more flexible. I guess you'd call it blackmail."

"Well, then," Charlotte said, brightening, "what if I just don't say anything until you have it all settled! See? You get your stuff straightened out, and then I talk to him."

Charlotte was looking at Julia with an expression of anxious hope. She reminded Julia of a little girl afraid for the endangered puppy in a story she was being read. She was really worried that Julia would not take enough money from her own father. Strain lines ran down Charlotte's face. Her concern was completely genuine. Good old Charlotte. For someone who sliced any event into its thinnest contingencies, someone whose worries about herself branched and rebranched like a nervous system, she was remarkably simpleminded in her affections. She thought it was obvious that she and Julia were good friends, and there were no qualifications or cynical crosscurrents to her interest in Julia's well-being.

"But you shouldn't delay what you want to do in your life," Julia said. "And these things are never 'settled,' anyway. So many ex-wives I know spend God knows how much time every month trying to get the money out of their ex-husbands that they agreed to, no matter how rich their husbands are. They and the new wives resent every penny. They can still screw you after the contract. Some guys make a point of doing that in business, and it's no different in divorces. But thank you, Charlotte, I appreciate the thought."

Julia paused and cast her eyes down. It was a long time before she spoke again, and when she did, it was almost in a whisper. "In any case, it doesn't matter," she said. "I've decided I'm not going to take anything from him anyway."

Charlotte sat up with a start, disturbing the cat. "What?!"

Julia shrugged. "I just don't want to take any money from him."

Charlotte was speechless, and it took her several seconds before she could sputter out, "Julia! What are you talking about? Are you out of your mind?"

"First of all," Julia said, "I don't want to go through the bloodletting that these things always require, especially since I don't know how much Dick really has got to give or how much I could get. You see these ex-husbands and ex-wives massacre each other, but no one is ever satisfied. I've been agonizing over how I'll make out, and his lawyer says this and my lawyer says that and if we try this angle — they are all such sleazeballs. So you know what? Screw it. I'd rather just walk away. Secondly, look, if it's anybody's money, it's all of yours. I didn't do anything to deserve it. To the contrary."

Charlotte looked truly shocked. "But Julia, this is crazy! Maybe it would be to our disadvantage, but really, be practical, be sensible. Everyone in this situation gets what they can!"

Julia laughed and gestured to her stomach. "Well, I know, but I don't think I have to be a martyr to acknowledge that, in this situation, the fault lies on my side. I can hardly demand child support. By any system of fairness, other than that under which 'fair' and 'legal' are synonymous, it would be unfair for me to take your father to the cleaners."

It was funny. Here was earnest Charlotte arguing for the most pragmatic, cynical course. Julia the cynic, meanwhile, seemed to have suddenly become an idealist. Had she? It wasn't that she wanted to show Dick that she didn't need him, that she was better than he and wouldn't deign to touch his money. Those would be pleasant side effects. She just wanted to be rid of him. She knew that if she got a settlement, she would always be thinking about whether it had been big enough, and every time she wrote a check she would feel Dick's presence hovering over her. Every object in her house, every taxi ride, every diaper and container of powdered formula and, later on, her son's first blazer and baseball mitt, would be the excrescences of Dick's money. It wasn't her pride, it wasn't a desire to throw his money back at him; it was just that if she took his money, she would never, in her own mind, be free of him. She would be his subject living in internal exile.

Julia tried to explain all this to Charlotte. Finally, she said, "What would you do if you were in my position? What would the Charlotte I know do?"

Charlotte opened and closed her mouth several times as she tried, and failed, to answer.

"I have a little money of my own," Julia said. "I haven't worked in quite a while, and I'm probably too old to do the things I can do and too inexperienced to do the things I'm the right age for, but I still know people and I have friends. Someone will come up with something. They may even offer to lend or give me money, which I won't refuse. One of my rich friends says that she and her husband have a floor — a floor — in their apartment that they 'never use,' and she's offered it to me. I'll be okay."

~

Charlotte stayed on a few days beyond the stated term of her visit. She and Julia spent their time talking about their futures.

"It's all just so much, Julia," Charlotte said at one point. "First, this realization about Peter and Holly, and then getting back involved with Maximilien-François-Marie-Isidore this way. It was like the feelings were all dammed up and suddenly rushed out. Then your news. My head is spinning. And on top of it all, there was the conference, which I think went really well this year, especially the colloquium on penal systems. Did you know that the reason Alexis de Tocqueville came to America was to study the penal system? He admired Albany . . ."

Julia urged Charlotte to make the dangerous leap she was considering. She owed it to herself, to Peter and Holly, to Maximilien-

François-Marie-Isidore (Julia finally got his name right). Of course, Charlotte could play it safe, and they could all lead moderately unhappy lives, and, true, by not playing it safe, it could all become a disaster. But Charlotte was too young to give up!

Charlotte fretted and cried, and swung back and forth from ecstatic bravery to crumpled fear. There was one thing she was sure about: Peter had to believe that her departure was entirely motivated by her own desire. Otherwise he would try to be noble. But what if six months later she realized that she missed him? Or that he and Holly really didn't care for each other? Or that Maximilien-François-Marie-Isidore was emotionally unavailable?

"Do you think," she asked one night, "do you think it's possible for all four of us to end up with the person that he or she is in love with, and who loves him or her, and for all of us to be happy?"

Julia paused long enough so that her answer would sound considered and unqualified. "Yes," she said.

~

The morning that Charlotte left, she and Julia squeezed each other in a tight embrace; they wet each other with their tears. Later in the day, Julia discovered that she was feeling something she never had before and had never imagined that she would: she missed Charlotte.

8

*P*eter met Charlotte at the airport. She had told him that it wasn't necessary, but he insisted. When she finally emerged from customs, Peter saw that she did not seem as shattered as was typical on these occasions. Usually, her face was the color of wet tissue paper, she looked as if she had received two black eyes, and her hair was a nest. She would immediately begin to relate all the vexations of her trip, her problems and how her stratagems for solving them had been thwarted. She would go into quite a lot of detail. All the way back in the cab, Peter would hear exactly what she had said to someone, what the other person had said, what she reported to a third person, how he responded, when the fax arrived, what route the car took, along with analysis of her decisions, justifications thereof, criticisms of others, allowances for them, renewed criticism and digressions about this or that event that really did go quite well. The monologue usually lasted the entire cab ride and continued through supper and until Charlotte collapsed into bed. Today, though, she was well groomed and looked rested and pushed her luggage cart with a calm air. Peter thought that the time she had spent with Julia must have made a big difference.

"Hello, Peter," she said, kissing him and giving him a hug. He took over the cart, and they followed the GROUND TRANSPORTATION signs, a lengthy journey that was rarely undertaken without error.

"Thanks for meeting me," Charlotte said. "I'm glad you did. I always forget what a long trip it is coming this way, and the last leg can be pretty long and lonely without company — forty minutes in a cab. So, anyway, it's sweet of you and thanks."

"Oh, well, sure," he said. "You've been gone for ages! Of course I wanted to see you as soon as possible." Charlotte looked at Peter and smiled; she put her hand on his and pressed it for a moment. They spoke little for the rest of the way home, except that Peter asked how Julia was and Charlotte gave him a brief account.

The next couple of weeks were odd, in Peter's view. Charlotte continued to be unlike herself. She was relaxed, unharried. She never called Peter at work to review a plan ("So you'll come by in a cab at seven-fifteen") that had been settled five or six times already. She cooked some good dinners that required a fair amount of time to prepare, she put her hands on Peter's shoulders in a way that was unfamiliar, and she did not bring any work home. She even looked at the television schedule one night and suggested that they watch a bad crime show.

Something important happened to Peter shortly after Charlotte's return. He went into his office one morning, and on his desk he found a large square envelope with "Mr. Peter Russell" written by hand on it. Peter opened the envelope — not easy, since the paper was so heavy — and withdrew a thick card: "Mr. Arthur Beeche requests the pleasure of your company . . ." So it had come: his first invitation to one of Beeche's dinners. Peter tried to be blasé about it, but he had to admit to himself that he was excited, especially considering the difficulties he had been facing at work. He was excited that he would be in Beeche's house, and he was excited about what it meant for his career.

Try as he might to tell himself that winning these particular corporate brownie points didn't amount to anything, that everybody was invited eventually, that only a philistine would care about getting ahead at the firm anyway — try as he might to tell himself these things, he was still excited. He imagined the low-key way he would drop in a mention of it during chats with his colleagues. Thropp would know. Peter felt certified by his invitation. He was honored. He was proud.

He was also quite nervous. He was worried about whether he would add piquancy and wit to the conversation at his table; he was worried about whether he would step on the hem of some important woman's long dress; he was worried about whether he would knock over his wineglass. Then, as if the need simply to comport himself well didn't create enough pressure, his anxiety was soon fed by an additional source.

One day Peter was just leaving his office when he encountered Mac McClernand. McClernand grabbed Peter's arm and asked if he had a moment to discuss something. McClernand's eyes looked like Rasputin's, and he gripped Peter so hard that he feared his arm might snap. He had heard that in certain extreme situations such as a car accident, so much adrenaline flows that people can acquire almost superhuman strength; McClernand seemed to be in such a state. Peter wondered how long his fingers could survive without blood.

"I want to talk to you about something," McClernand said.

The pain in Peter's arm made it impossible for him to speak, so he merely nodded.

"I know that you are going to Beeche's for dinner in a couple of weeks."

Peter nodded.

"Now, listen. This is very important."

Peter nodded.

"Beeche always has his top people at these dinners. Arnie Goldberg, Ellen Sutphen, Joe Moressi. You know who I'm talking about."

Peter nodded.

"Okay," McClernand continued. "Now, another person who is always there is Seth Bernard." A childhood friend of Arthur Beeche's, Seth Bernard ran the firm with him essentially as an equal.

Peter nodded. Ominously, he no longer felt pain shooting down his arm; he could not feel his arm at all.

"Now, what you don't know is that a couple of weeks ago I talked to Bernard about what we're up to. And by the way, I do mean we. I made a point of mentioning your name. It's a team effort; I've always said that.

"Anyway, when I met with Bernard, well, it wasn't a meeting exactly, we came out of elevators at the same time and I walked with him to his car. But he seemed very, very interested. 'That could be something,' he said." McClernand seemed to enter a trance as he repeated, in a whisper, "That could be something." For a moment, he was a million miles away. "And listen to this: after Bernard got into the car and the driver shut the door, he gave me a thumbs-up sign." McClernand raised his eyebrows and grinned. "Mm-hmm. How about them apples?" He leaned back to observe, and savor, the effect of this news on Peter.

Peter nodded.

Then that intense look returned to McClernand's face. "This is a very important opportunity for us," he said. "This dinner, I mean. I can't emphasize that enough. Seth Bernard is the key, Peter. He's the key. If we get him on board, then we can go straight to Beeche. Do you see? Do you see what this means?"

Peter nodded.

"We've got to sell Bernard, though. And if we want a meeting with him, we've got to get him excited, pique his interest, get it registered on his peter meter. So at that dinner it is very important, it . . . is . . . very . . . important . . . that you handle Bernard just right. I've got him all teed up for you, so it should be easy."

Peter nodded.

"You find him during cocktails. You work your way into the group he's talking to."

Peter nodded.

"Then you get him alone. Five, ten minutes. You've got to sell him on you."

Peter nodded.

"But don't sell him hard."

Peter shook his head.

"Be engaging."

Peter nodded.

"But don't be overly familiar."

Peter shook his head.

"Keep up your end."

Peter nodded.

"But don't talk too much."

Peter shook his head.

"You've got to talk to Bernard and you've got to connect with him. You start with something that has nothing to do with the firm. So you're talking along and you're charming the guy's jock-strap off. He thinks you're just terrific, what a fine young man, smart as a whip. Now, here's when you think it's time to slide into a discussion of our little baby. Eh? Am I right?"

Peter nodded.

"BUT THAT'S EXACTLY WHAT YOU DON'T DO!" McClernand barked.

Startled, Peter just stared at McClernand for a moment. With an effort, McClernand regained his composure. He took a deep breath and spoke as calmly as he could.

"That's exactly what you don't do," he repeated, this time in a whisper. "Here is the crucial thing: You . . . let . . . *him* . . . bring . . . it . . . up. Your job is to get him to the *point* where he will bring it up."

Peter ran over this last direction in his mind: My job is to get him to the *point* where he will bring it up. Okay.

"Everything is riding on this. Everything. Including your future at this firm."

McClernand looked at Peter as if he were trying to bore through him with secret laser vision. Then he gave Peter's arm an extra squeeze and let it go. Peter wanted to collapse in relief. McClernand smiled paternally.

"Look at me," he said, "spoiling the party for you! The important thing is that you relax and have some fun. Right?"

"Yes, sir," Peter managed to say. Feeling began to return to his arm, in particular the feeling of pain.

McClernand looked off in the distance and began to reminisce about the last time he had been at Beeche's, many years before. "Of course," he said, "there were only about thirty of us. It wasn't one of those mob scenes like the one you're going to. Now, this goes back a ways. Let's see, what was it? Beeche was saying something about working in this business. 'Arthur,' I said, 'I've always told people that they have just three things to worry about — their upside, their downside, and their backside!' He got a kick out of that."

"Ah-ha-ha. Ha-ha-ha," Peter said, articulating these sounds rather than actually laughing.

McClernand looked at him and grinned. "Go get 'em, tiger," he said, giving Peter's arm another squeeze.

Peter nodded.

Needless to say, Peter had no intention whatsoever of engaging Seth Bernard in the conversation that McClernand described. If by doing so he could save a large city from destruction by a madman in possession of a nuclear device, maybe. But a medium-sized city? No way.

~

Beeche's dinner was on a Thursday. On the afternoon of the preceding Sunday, Peter was reading the paper and Charlotte was preparing for her lesson with Frau Schimmelfennig. In a little while, Peter was going for a walk with Holly. Charlotte closed her German grammar with a thud, sat up straight, and stretched her arms and neck.

"What time are you meeting Holly?" she asked.

"Around four," Peter said.

"Is it going to stay light long enough?"

"Oh, I think so," Peter said. "Anyway, we like the gloaming."

Charlotte smiled at Peter's remark. " 'We like the gloaming,' " she repeated. "I'm glad to hear it."

Absorbed in the paper, Peter had not paid much attention to Charlotte, and he was embarrassed by his reply. He looked at her and saw — affection? amusement? indulgence? — flicker in her expression. He found her manner odd. Then he noticed that her eyes were moist and that her hands seemed to be shaking.

"Charlotte, what's the matter?" he asked.

"Nothing!" Charlotte said. "Nothing." She sniffled and wiped her cheek with the back of her hand. "I was just thinking what a good person you are, Peter. What a fine person. And I was thinking about how much I care for you. I care for you very much."

Bewildered, Peter said, "I care for you, too, Charlotte, very much."

"I know you do," said Charlotte. Her chin trembled.

"Charlotte —"

"Ssh," she said. "I'm fine, really." She stood. "Now, I think I'll make tea. Would you like some?"

"Yes, please," said Peter, "that would be great."

Charlotte smiled at him again and walked to the kitchen. Peter watched her; she wore a dark gray cardigan and a tweed skirt, a look that was becoming to her. Her hair was pulled back in a ponytail and he could see two white triangles of neck.

Tea was sacred to Charlotte, and so she took its preparation even more seriously than she did that of coffee. Peter heard her put the kettle on; heard her take down the tea canister, the pot, the cups and saucers. Charlotte would have welcomed plague in her kitchen sooner than a tea bag, and she would have gladly died of plague rather than serve tea in a mug. Her teacups were made of china that was so thin as to be translucent. The ratio of leaves to water, the temperature of the water, the steeping time — Charlotte had determined the optimal values for all these variables. Yet to Charlotte, the perfection of materials and techniques would amount to nothing if a person preparing the tea failed to perform the one crucial operation: scalding the pot. "Scald the pot!" she would call to Peter whenever she subcontracted the tea making to him.

Charlotte now appeared with the tea tray and set it down on the table.

"We should wait a moment while it steeps," she said as she sat. This was part of the order of service. They sat in silence as the tea leaves released their essence to the water. It felt like a peaceful ellipsis in time itself. The tea steeped. It was a cloudy day, so the window cast a soft, diffuse light. The plump silver sugar bowl reflected the window with bowed-out squares. The blue, red, and green of the china pattern were matte, but the white background glowed. The milk was a matte white, but the white china of the pitcher also glowed. Charlotte had brought a plate with shortbread cookies arranged in a circle like a dial; even before taking one, Peter could taste them; they were like crumbly butter, and he could feel the crumbs on his fingertips.

Charlotte sat facing the window. Light settled gently and evenly on her face, smoothing its angles and irregularities. How pretty she was, really. Peter put his hand on hers.

The tea steeped. Steam rose from the spouts of both the teapot and the hot-water pot. The plumes curled upward like two quivering wisps of light and shadow, two genies escaping their lamps. Peter left his hand on Charlotte's until the tea had brewed.

~

Peter and Charlotte had drunk their tea and cleaned up. The buzzer from downstairs rang. "That must be Holly," Peter said. "I'll tell her I'm coming down."

"Oh, please ask Holly to come up," Charlotte said. "I'd like to say hi."

Peter conveyed the message, and Holly appeared presently.

"Hi, Peter! Hi, Charlotte!" She and Peter exchanged kisses on the cheek. Charlotte gave her a hug, holding on longer and more tightly than was routine.

"Thanks for coming up," Charlotte said. "As I told Peter, I just wanted to say hi."

"I'm so glad you did, Charlotte," said Holly. "I've hardly seen you since you got back. The trip sounded so draining. Have you recovered?"

"Oh, yes," said Charlotte.

"You're sure looking well," said Holly.

"Thank you," Charlotte said. "So are you."

"Thanks," said Holly.

Then came a moment when no one said anything. Filling in the gap just before the silence would have grown uncomfortable, Holly said, "And your family, they are well?"

"Yes," said Charlotte. "Very well."

"Peter told me that you stayed with your stepmother for a little while. How is all that going?"

"Oh, not so badly," Charlotte said. "As you can imagine, it's difficult."

"God, I'm sure," said Holly. "I got to speak to her for just a second at . . . at the funeral. She was nice."

"Yes," said Charlotte.

Once again, the conversation flagged.

Charlotte swallowed. "Well," she said. "Well, I just wanted to see you, Holly, before you both . . . went on your way. It makes me so happy that you and Peter are such good friends." Her mouth twitched and she had trouble maintaining her smile. She looked back and forth from one to the other. "Enjoy your walk," she said. She laughed nervously. "Enjoy your gloaming!"

Momentarily bemused, neither Peter nor Holly spoke. They eyed each other.

"Thanks, Charlotte," Peter said finally. He gave her a kiss. "We will."

"Yes, thanks, Charlotte," said Holly. "I'm so glad to have seen you for at least a minute."

Charlotte nodded.

"See you in a bit," said Peter. "Hope your lesson goes well. "

"Good-bye, Holly," Charlotte said. "Good-bye, Peter."

Peter and Holly went down the stairs and out the door. They had been walking for a minute before either said anything.

"So," Holly asked, "that was about, like — what?"

Peter shrugged. "Beats me," he said. "Actually, she's been acting kind of weird ever since she got back."

It was cold, and a thick, seamless, static mass of clouds hung overhead. It looked as if a gray woolen blanket covered the entire city. That gray ranged from dull silver to tarnished silver, but within those limits its shades showed infinite variations, and if one stared long enough, one saw a tint of purple. On this cloudy day, the black, wrought-iron railings on the stoops, which in bright sun looked as lithe and slick as snakes, had the iron coldness and hardness of medieval weaponry. The few touches of white on the block — the painted lintels on a couple of houses, the lines on the asphalt — popped to the foreground. It was cold. The cars moved heavily, then with surprising quickness, like bears.

Holly and Peter entered the park and strolled aimlessly. They passed some people walking their dogs and a couple of especially dedicated joggers. A boy and girl sat on a bench kissing, and the boy was rubbing the girl's rear; seeing them, Holly and Peter exchanged a bashful glance. Two men, one short, one tall, both wearing leather jackets, approached. They seemed to be deep in a conversation that was verging on an argument. All Peter and Holly could hear as they passed was the short one saying, "But he rejoined the band in the fall of sixty-six! So of course he was on that album!" A woman fed pigeons.

Peter and Holly walked alongside a high outcropping of rock scored with deep lines. They walked under a bridge and heard the echo of their footsteps. On the wall someone had scratched out "I love you Jessica!" in huge letters.

"What do you think is up with Charlotte?" Holly asked.

"I really have no idea," said Peter.

"There's no . . . trouble between you two?"

"I don't think so," said Peter.

"Has Charlotte found a bill for a mink stole, but not received a mink stole?"

"No."

"Have you been bringing your low-life friends around?"

"No."

"Leaving wet towels on the bathroom floor?"

"No."

"Huh," said Holly. "Then it's sort of a mystery. Oh, well. In the first year of marriage it's typical to have these little periods of estrangement when you both seem to have lost your bearings, as you wonder who this person you have married really is. There'll be rough patches. You just get through it, and the beautiful part is that when you work it out you're closer. I'm sure it's nothing serious. Or at least I doubt that it's a *permanent* problem. I wouldn't worry about it. I wouldn't give it a second thought."

"This is so very helpful," said Peter. "Thank you."

The grass had turned brown and the cold earth had no smell. The trees were tall and grand. They were mature and stood well apart from one another. Bare of leaves, naked and muscular, their turning trunks and outstretched limbs seemed posed to show off their strength, yet when one looked upward, one saw, against the gray sky, the fragile, disordered netting of their topmost twigs. Peter and Holly reached a walk lined with statues of notable literary figures and others. Set on high pedestals, they were larger than life-sized and portrayed their subjects seated in a dignified pose, with frock coats and massive squared-off boots. As they moved from one looming statue to another, Peter and Holly looked like children.

"You know, I think about Julia," Holly said. "At the funeral, she looked distraught. She sat with Jonathan at the dinner, so it must have been pretty shocking, in a way, for her, having just gotten to know him."

"Yes. She certainly seemed upset."

"My father, actually, told me that he had a conversation with her. He liked her. 'Doesn't belong with that self-important creep,' he said. Later, when I mentioned to him that they'd split up and reminded him of that observation, he said, 'See? Casting. That was always something I could do.'"

They strolled along silently.

"What are you thinking about?" Peter asked.

Holly looked over at him and gave him a small smile, with her lips pressed together. "Oh, I don't know," she said. "I was just trying to think about what I would do if I were in Julia's position. I don't know. I just don't think I could go through with it. I wouldn't want to raise a child all by myself, without any father. I guess half the time people end up getting divorced anyway, so the father isn't around that much, or he is around but it's painful. Or look at Alex's situation. The Creep pays attention to Clemmie intensely for a little while and is very demanding, then he's gone for ages. I wish he'd fall off a cliff. So maybe it's not such a problem, there not being a father."

She thought for a moment.

"I was three when my parents broke up, and depending on the year, they lived fifteen hundred or three thousand or eight thousand miles apart; but even still, my father was really in touch with us, and I feel as if we saw a lot of him. I can't imagine life without him. To bring somebody into the world without any father at all, I don't think I could do that, and if I were going to be really honest, I'm not even sure it's right or that I don't think it's kind of self-indulgent. The stakes seem so high, especially considering the uncertainty of the payoff. You're gambling a whole life in order to satisfy some need, some feeling of emptiness, that might only be temporary."

She paused again.

"If I were Julia's age, though — when I'm Julia's age — and if this had happened and it were my last shot, and if the guy, whoever he was, was somebody who I wouldn't mind contributing half my child's genes, then could I stop it? My brain would give me all the reasons that I should, and I'd tell myself, Look, fate or whatever determined that the parent thing simply isn't going to happen for you, and an accidental pregnancy resulting from your adulterous affair doesn't count. But would I want to go ahead anyway? Almost undoubtedly, yes. The desire would probably be so strong that I wouldn't even think that I really had a choice."

"The surprising thing," Peter said, "is that Julia never had any interest in children. I always had the impression that she thought they were boring and demanding and caused too much chaos."

"I guess that's one way we're different," said Holly. "I've always loved the idea of having children."

"Were you and Jonathan, er, working to that end?" Peter asked.

Holly laughed a little. "Actually, no."

"I wanted to give the marriage a chance to — what? — to settle. But Jonathan really wanted children. He would have loved it if I had gotten pregnant immediately and stayed that way for about ten years. He would have been happy if at the wedding I'd been about to deliver."

They both gave Jonathan some silent contemplation.

"Does anybody know anything about the father of Julia's child?" Holly asked.

"Not really," said Peter. In fact, having recalled the seating arrangements at the bridal dinner and counted months and having considered this evidence with regard to Jonathan's mysterious presence on the first fairway, Peter had made a wild speculation about the child's paternity, but he certainly wasn't going to share it. "Nobody even knows how long they were involved. She says that he discovered he was sick right after she got pregnant and went very fast. I guess it must have been something like lung cancer or liver cancer."

"Wow. How horrible," Holly said.

They walked along for a bit, lost in thought. Having passed by all the great men, they had reached a different kind of sculpture: two eagles attacking a ram. The ram twisted in pain as the eagles, their wings spread, ripped into its flesh with their talons and beaks. Holly and Peter stared at it.

"I would like a child, though. Children," Holly said. Peter looked at her profile; a tear was forming in the corner of her eye. "But it's so hard, finding the right person. I'd really want to be in love."

With that last remark, Holly involuntarily, it seemed, glanced at Peter. It took less than a second, a quarter turn of her head, her moist eyes widening and darting over. Holly instantly looked away. She studied the sculpture. "What a strange statue," she said. "I wonder if it's based on some myth or legend."

~

Holly's aunt, her mother's sister, owned a large apartment on Central Park West where Holly had stayed from time to time over the years, and she moved in after Jonathan's death. Her aunt lived there for only part of the year, but she stayed with Holly for several weeks, and Holly's father, mother, sister, and friends visited. At the moment, though, she was staying in the apartment by herself.

Standing outside the building at the conclusion of their walk, Peter put his hands lightly on Holly's shoulders and touched her cheek with his dry, pursed lips. Holly returned this peck, twisting her mouth around and looking beyond Peter's ear at the charcoal clouds above. They said good-bye, and the huge, ferocious-looking doorman let Holly in. He smiled and crinkled his eyes. "Goot eve-en-ink, Miss Owly," he said. "Hello, Josip," she returned. As she walked through the large, high-ceilinged, and gloomy lobby — despite intensive efforts, no one had ever found a way to fully remove decades-old grime from the elaborate plasterwork scrolls and medallions — and rode up in the elevator, Holly's shoulders retained the feeling of Peter's hands, and her cheek, his lips. She saw an afterimage of his ear (out of focus) and the clouds.

She opened the front door of her aunt's apartment. The foyer was large and high-ceilinged — and gloomy. It suffered from some of the same conditions as the lobby. The plasterwork had been painted over so many times that the details seemed to have melted together, and ineradicable grime had silted up in it. Holly tossed her coat, scarf, and keys on a chair. She stood for a moment, lost in thought, then she stepped into the library. This was a room decorated in soft, crimson fabrics; it was plush, cushioned, and dark. Holly went over to the window, lifted it, and leaned out. The wind whipped her hair; she heard the loud wheeze of a bus starting. The streetlamps and scattered windows were lit. Looking down, she experienced mild vertigo; the park seemed to tilt toward her. Looking up at the sky, she was still more disoriented. Her only reference was the side of the building, faced with pale gray limestone. Seen from such a low angle, it raced upward before disappearing. Holly felt as if she were on one of the minor thrill rides at an amusement park.

Leaning out the window on the twelfth floor of a building across from the park, it was easy to imagine that the whole city was being funneled into you. That was interesting and exciting. But if the entire city was being funneled into Holly, she wanted to put it through a sieve — a very, very fine one, so it might take a while — for all she really wanted from the entire city was one morsel. A trained eye could identify the gaps between the buildings on the other side of the park that indicated a side street. An expert could count those gaps and find the side street she wanted. Holly found that street, and then followed it, as if she could look through the buildings, down to an avenue, then across that avenue, and then about half-way down the next block. Here her eye followed a path up a stoop, through heavy wrought-iron doors, up a flight of stairs, and into an apartment. She "stared" at that apartment quite intently. What she really saw was a water tower.

Holly closed the window. She stood there for a moment staring out and sighed shallowly. Then she went back to her bedroom, where she undressed, tossing her clothes on the bed; lying there they looked like burst balloons. Stepping into the bathroom, she found some pins and put up her hair, and then sat down on the edge of the bathtub. She ran a bath and, after testing the water's temperature with her hand, turned off the spigots. The water became calm. Holly looked through it at the crazy porcelain on the bottom of the tub. Then her eyes refocused on the water's surface, where she saw her own wobbly image. A jar of salts sat nearby, and Holly took it. She scattered a handful of the rough crystals in the water and, looking down again, saw her features fragment and collide in a hundred ripples.

Holly lowered herself into the bath. She began to soap herself with a sponge. She lifted a leg and ran the sponge up and down it, and she washed around her stomach and chest and the back of her neck. But then she threw the sponge to the other end of the bath and put her fingers up to her eyes. Her face was hot and damp, so when the tears came, she did not notice for a moment. Now they were flowing freely, dribbling off her jaw and into the tub, and her chest was heaving. Eventually, she wiped her nose with the back of a hand, took a couple of deep breaths, and submerged her shoulders in the warm water. There, that was better. She had stopped crying. Then her shoulders shuddered, and began to heave, and the tears flowed once again.

Peter has been great, she thought, he's been a good friend. When has he ever done anything that would indicate that he wanted to be something other than friends? Never, not once ever. No looks, not even any flirting. Nothing.

She would never forget the conversation she had had with Jonathan shortly after she had met Peter again. They were at Jonathan's apartment and he was correcting a proof, talking idly.

"You know," he said, "Peter really got a crush on you during that plane trip when you sat next to each other."

"Really?" Holly said.

"Yeah," said Jonathan. He scrawled a couple of words in the margin and continued to work on the proof as he talked. "Yeah. We were talking about it, and that's what he told me. So, naturally, I got concerned and I said, 'So what about now?' He laughed. He said, 'You're jealous over somebody I sat next to on a plane years ago? Are you crazy?' I guess it did sound pretty silly. Oh hell!" He drummed his pencil on the paper and then made an erasure. "Anyway, he told me not to worry. 'You know how those things go,' he said, 'you meet somebody someplace with some kind of forced intimacy and you think there's been some magic, and then two days later you've forgotten all about them.' It's interesting. That's really true, don't you think?" He whispered aloud a few words of his text and made a change. "Well, also, he said, you know, he's such a nice guy that he felt really bad about not calling. He had gotten so wrapped up in his business stuff. You can imagine." He crossed out a couple of words. "So anyway, phew. I wouldn't want to have to shoot him." He teethed his pencil, slumped down in his chair, and held the proof up, frowning at it.

"I thought he said he lost the number," Holly said.

Jonathan looked up. "He said he . . . ? He lost the . . . ? Uh-oh. Oops. Well, um, I guess not exactly. I guess he felt so bad, he said that."

So Peter had had a little crush on her — for a minute.

The water had cooled. Holly lifted her foot and with her long toes turned the fat porcelain handle of the hot-water spigot. The water ran for a minute, and then she shut it using the same method. How loud and tumultuous the roiling waters had been! And with what utter quiet had they been followed. The bathroom was as quiet as the moon, Holly thought. This was in contrast to her mind, where her woes reverberated.

How Peter had hurt her! That was the bizarre thing. It can often be particularly painful for women when someone with whom they have been physically intimate fails to call them, despite the promise he made with his parting words. Inexplicably, Holly's experience with Peter had been much more hurtful even than that. She had thought . . . Well, what had she thought? When she left Peter at the baggage claim carousel, she was thinking about Fate, and how eons before it had been determined that Peter and she were to be mates and so were brought together in a manner that seemed completely random — seat assignments — but was in fact part of a sequence set at the dawn of time. Hurray for Fate! she had thought, laughing.

Riding from the airport to her father's house, she had tried to figure out the appeal of her seatmate. He was so sweet and funny. He was obviously intelligent. He had just the faintest air of melancholy. And he was so good-looking. His face was very easy to "read" visually. Holly supposed that some people would say his looks were conventional or even bland. But he had the softest hazel eyes, and his lips appeared to be extremely kissable. His hands were strong-looking, manly hands, and it seemed to Holly he must be some kind of athlete. Oh, who knows? The amazing thing was that they had just started talking and the next five hours had been nothing but fun.

When she arrived at her father's, she was in a very good mood. She was excited about her niece, and she was still feeling the intoxicating effects of the guy she had met on the plane. When Holly first saw Clementine, she was wrapped up in her blanket like a burrito. After washing her hands, Holly picked her up. The baby was perfectly healthy and of normal weight, but Holly could hardly believe how light she was. A whole human being, and she felt as light as a cantaloupe. Meanwhile, her head looked like a tortoise's, wrinkly and hairless. Holly made a hammock of her forearms, held Clementine with them, and gently rocked her back and forth. Holly had rarely held a baby, and this time the sensation was electrifying. A whole life right there in her arms; a whole life, but right now a being that was completely helpless and defenseless. All of Clementine's eggs were inside her, Holly thought, so she was holding more than one life. Also, Clementine had the most adorable flat little nose. Suddenly she awoke and began to scream and cry; her face turned purple. Holly handed her off to Alex and watched as she nursed her daughter and stared at her blissfully. The rest of the evening was taken up with changing Clementine (which, with great enthusiasm, Holly learned how to do), listening out for Clementine's cry, nursing her, rocking her, burping her, checking on her, and just watching her.

Throughout all this, Peter wasn't in the forefront of Holly's mind, but he was in the back of it. When the phone rang, she listened anxiously for her father to summon her, but the only calls were from Holly's mother and Michael, Clementine's father. Michael had been there every day, Alex told Holly, and he was coming over tomorrow. Ugh, thought Holly. That creep. Thumb rings, and sharks' teeth hanging from his neck, and wide leather wrist gear with lots of silver. Spirituality. "Michael says that my being with him now isn't part of his practice," Alex had explained. Holly held her tongue, but she wanted to say, "But screwing Inge is, I suppose?" Inge was Michael's girlfriend, a sloe-eyed Swedish-Hispanic masseuse. He wanted to bring her around: "She's part of my life now. She's the woman I'm with." Michael was one of those people who could not only have his cake and eat it too, but who could, by eating his cake, actually end up with more.

That night Holly told her sister about the guy on the plane. She tried to be nonchalant about it, but anyone could tell by her animation and the glow in her eyes that she had given her heart to this "Peter." Alex reacted with lots of enthusiasm and lots of questions. "Is he in a relationship?" "Does he eat meat?" Peter still hadn't called when Holly went to bed, and she was bothered, but not panicked.

Alex had begun listening intently for the phone, too. Late in the afternoon the next day, Holly's father asked Holly to go to the post office before it closed since he had something that had to be postmarked that day.

"No!" Alex cried. "Holly can't go."

"She can't go? But why —?"

"I need her here."

"You need her here . . . ?"

"Yes." Alex allowed her body to droop and said in a quavering voice. "I'm feeling very weak. Very weak . . ." She trailed off.

"Oh . . . uh . . ."

"So you'll have to go," Alex said.

"But I can't go! I'm making lemon buttercream icing!"

"All right," said Alex, miraculously reviving. "Then I'll go."

"You're nursing!"

"I'll bring the baby. I'll drive with one hand."

"Alex!" Graham said. Then he paused. "Wait a minute. What's going on here?"

"It's nothing, Pop," Holly said. "What do you —"

Alex interrupted with a rapid stream of words: "Holly met someone on the plane who she really likes and she's waiting for him to call, which he's supposed to do, so she has to be here when he does call!"

There was a moment of silence. Then Graham said very mildly, "Oh . . . uh . . . oh . . . I see. Well, then. Well . . ." He looked around, at a bit of a loss.

"Pop —" said Holly.

"No, no-no," said Graham. "It's fine. You sit tight. Um. I'll just run down there myself. You couldn't, with the mixer . . . ? Or Alex . . . ?" They gave him the blank stares of two young women whose mother had taught them only one thing about cooking: how to shirr an egg. "No, I guess not."

With the heavy heart of someone who knew his butter was going to get too warm and that the lemon would curdle it, Graham began to shamble off. Seeing his dejection, Holly insisted on doing the errand and, after making sure she really meant it, he gratefully agreed.

Peter never did call. Holly had proceeded with her life. After the Dominican Republic, she lived in Los Angeles for a while, working for a production company, mostly reading scripts. She went out with a television writer, a brilliant young man whose willful philistinism Holly eventually tired of. Then she moved back east. For a year she lived with a boatbuilder near the resort where her mother had always spent summers; she had been convinced that she could transform herself from a summer person — the men with their bald heads like baby birds and the women dressed to look like hard candies — into a real person, but she had failed. After that, it was graduate school and then Jonathan. The thought of him made Holly smile. It would be difficult for any woman to forget what it was like when he turned to her at a party and she saw his blue eyes, creamy white skin, tousled curly hair, ruby lips, and heard him say, "I don't believe we've met. I'm Jonathan Speedwell." The absolute naturalness of it! And yet with a hint of flirtatiousness. Jonathan set his mind to making her fall in love with him, and it had been impossible to resist. Over time, of course, she learned that he was an almost complete phony. But he was one of those phonies whom you want to let get away with it. He was always kind, fun, thoughtful, and sensitive with her, not least in *la phase érotique* department. He never once treated her badly. He was fun! And he was so encouraging and supportive; along with his vanity came such confidence in his choice of a friend that it didn't occur to him to have any doubts about the person, and this seemed especially true of Holly, with whom he had chosen to fall in love. Now, Holly wasn't entirely naïve, and while Jonathan always was exactly where he said he would be, and while Holly was convinced that he never actually told her any untruths, she had gotten an inkling that perhaps he had strayed. Well, they might have had to have a little chat about that at some point. Meanwhile, she had had no evidence, and strangely, her whiffs of suspicion hadn't bothered her so much. Jonathan hadn't seemed quite real, and while she had loved him she wasn't sure she had felt attached to him — there hadn't been anything solid to attach to — so his possible liaisons had not felt so threatening. Contrariwise, she imagined that if she were with Peter and then discovered that he had slept with another woman, she would toss them both in a wood chipper.

The bathwater had cooled once again. After rinsing herself one last time, Holly got out of the tub and opened the drain. She took a towel and without unfolding it patted her body in a couple of places, but she stopped, and with both hands held the towel up to her chest and rested her chin on it. She stared at the ebbing water. At first only a dimple on the surface above the drain, the whirlpool grew wider and wider until it collapsed and the drain drank down the bath's dregs with a loud slurp.

Holly made a resolution. Peter was very kind, and it was clear that he sincerely cared about her. Nor did she doubt that he and she had an unusual and precious rapport. Nevertheless, it was time for her to put Peter out of her mind as an object of romantic interest. Time? It was long past time. Indeed, she should never have regarded him in that light in the first place. How often had she imagined sitting on the sofa in her aunt's library, telling him her feelings, and having him take her into his arms saying he felt exactly the same way. They would kiss and caress each other for a long time, listening to a certain CD set on repeat: Lee Wiley's *Night in Manhattan* with Joe Bushkin, a collection of ballads recorded in the fifties. It was so silly. The player's tray could hold six CDs and she always left that one in it on the billion-to-one chance all this would actually happen.

Let us face facts, she said to herself. If you meet a male person on a plane and instantly fall in love with him, you and he can have a great love affair, *but not if he doesn't call you.* That first meeting was very nice, fun, exciting, but its epochal significance was entirely vitiated by the fact that the male person never called. With regard to that first meeting, at which you fell in love at first sight, you have been told directly that he did not view it as anything more meaningful than a pleasant jetliner interlude. Further, he has never taken any action since then that would suggest he has romantic feelings toward you; he has never made that suggestion verbally; you have established a friendship whose depth in and of itself suggests that his feelings for you run along that channel, not a romantic one; he is married, quite happily, by all appearances, to someone who is not yourself. What conclusion can be drawn from this evidence?

This conclusion: forget it.

Holly had been very upset by something, and now she wondered, although she knew it was irrational, whether the cosmos was trying to give her a message: she couldn't find the book she had been reading on the plane when she had met Peter, a paperback copy of *The Magic Mountain* by Thomas Mann. They had talked about it, and she had torn out a page from it in order to write down her father's number for Peter. Holly had always kept it with some other precious books, but now it had disappeared. The only explanation she could think of was that it had gotten misplaced when she and Jonathan were shifting their books around after she moved in, and they discovered they had far too many to fit in his apartment. Anyway, it was gone, and maybe this was a sign that she really should give up Peter for good.

Holly felt a chill. She finished drying herself, then took an old cotton nightgown off a peg and slipped it on. She did the same with her bathrobe (toile) and tied it snugly. She cleaned up around the soap dish and wiped the ring off the tub; she squeezed out the sponge and tightened the spigots one last time; she draped the wet towel over a rack. She felt pink and clean, which was a good feeling, but she had papers to correct, and she had a difficult couple of days coming up. It was a lonely Sunday evening. Then it occurred to her that she could give her father a call. Not to talk to him about Peter or anything important, just to talk to him.

At the phone she saw that there was a message. It was from Peter.

"Hi, Holly, it's Peter. It was great seeing you today. Look, do you remember, I think I mentioned that Charlotte and I were going to this big dinner party at Arthur Beeche's, you know, the guy who owns the firm? Well, it's on Thursday, and, um, it turns out, I just found out, that Charlotte is going to be out of town for it, and I was wondering, if I can arrange it, if you'd like to come with me instead? I know it's kind of short notice, so I wanted to call you right away. He has this incredible house and he invites all sorts of people, and these things are supposed to be pretty fun. I'll have to see if it's okay, but it would be great if you could come. So give me a call tonight or at the office or whatever. Okay, so we'll talk. Bye!"

Typical Peter, Holly thought. Giving her some fun. How kind. Dear, sweet Peter. Holly shivered. She had to start thinking about him differently. She had to. She shook her head as if to shake her old thoughts out of it. Calling him back could wait till tomorrow. She didn't have the strength to do that now. She called her father instead.

~

After Holly left him, Peter stood for a moment under the awning of her aunt's apartment building. He held his left elbow in his right hand, pressed his left fist against his mouth, and looked down at the sidewalk. Peter had often noticed that the concrete used on sidewalks in New York varied considerably. Sometimes it was beige and had white and black and brown pebbly bits; sometimes it was just a striated beige. This one must have been quite new, he thought. It was a sleek, smooth gray; there were no cracks or blemishes, and the expansion lines, one wide deep one between two that were shallow and thin, resembled a design element, a border. Yes, it was a handsome sidewalk.

Peter sensed that the doorman was staring at him. He looked up and met the latter's scowl with a nice smile, which had no effect. Then Peter started to walk uptown.

He should have said something. Or should he have? It was all over so fast, and what words could he have found to say — what? It was just the tiniest glance. Did it mean something? Jonathan could have pulled it off. Jonathan would have instinctively expressed the perfect sentiment in the perfect tone, even, low, melting around the edges. Peter was not that kind of person. But what did the glance mean, anyway? It was exactly the kind of thing that Peter knew he could wildly overinterpret by projecting his own feelings.

He hailed a taxi and held on to the leather strap desperately as it raced through the transverse, jolted by potholes. At Charlotte's brownstone Peter got out, climbed the stoop, and opened the heavy wrought-iron door of the vestibule. He unlocked the inner door, which opened onto a small hall with a dirty carpet. After passing through this space, he mounted the stairs; he put his hand on the thick, elaborately carved banister, which, leading from that mean little hall, always seemed so out of place. He reached the door of the apartment, unlocked the big bolt and the latch. Stepping in, Peter noticed that the apartment seemed very quiet. That should not have been surprising. Charlotte wouldn't be back from her German lesson yet. But for some reason this silence had a different quality from the typical one. Peter walked into the living room. There was certainly nothing out of the ordinary there: the paperback he had left open on a chair had not moved; a book of photographs that Charlotte had been examining lay on the love seat; the little pile of clippings, opened mail, scribbled-upon notepad paper, credit-card receipts, and superannuated invitations lay on a side table as it had for days. Peter stepped into the kitchen. The tea things had all been put away and there was nothing out of the ordinary. Peter found nothing amiss in either the bedroom or the bathroom. In a way Peter could not precisely define, though, they both did seem different: lightened of their cargo, in some fashion. Still, Peter could not for the life of him say what the missing objects might be. He returned to the living room. There *was* something about the apartment. It had the air of a place that had been abandoned rather than of a place to which someone had not yet returned.

Peter at this time noticed an envelope propped against one of the candlesticks on the dining table. He approached the table. On the envelope was written "Peter" in Charlotte's semicalligraphic script. She had used her Rapidograph, Peter could tell, and her thick, creamy

Italian writing paper. Peter looked at the envelope for a moment. All the signs suggested that she had written this note in order to say something more significant than that she would be late, so please start cooking the rice since (after soaking for two days) it was ready.

Peter picked up the envelope, carefully tore it open, removed and unfolded the single sheet inside, and held it before him. It felt like cashmere.

Here is what Charlotte had written:

Dear Peter —
   — My darling —
   — By the time you read this — I shall be preparing to board a flight to Charles de Gaulle —
   — I am deeply in love with Maximilien-François-Marie-Isidore — I saw him — I know that now —
   — He is deeply in love with me —
   — Dear, darling Peter —
   — Please forgive me —
   — Farewell —

                                       Charlotte

Peter read the words over several times, then refolded the sheet and dropped it on the table. For a few moments, he stood there thinking nothing. He stared ahead, seeing nothing. So Charlotte had bolted. Peter found this impossible to believe, so he picked up the letter and read it over once again. It yielded to no other interpretation. "Farewell." Farewell was pretty definitive.

Now more thoughts and emotions emerged, like photographs developing. His primary response was happiness for Charlotte. He must have been more of a romantic at heart than he realized because he was proud of her. She had thrown off all the supports of her conventional life in order to be with the man she loved. Good for her, Peter thought. *Bien fait,* Charlotte! And then he felt ashamed: despite all her complexes, Charlotte had shown a lot more nerve than he. Peter found himself tearing up, the sentimental old fool. He cared about Charlotte, the poor kid, and here she was setting off to grab all the love and happiness she could get. He hoped she would succeed. Whenever good people who were weak and timid showed strength and got the things that bad, arrogant people always had handed to them, Peter was moved, and this was especially true in a case like this one, when the heroine of the story was someone he loved.

He had met Maximilien-François-Marie-Isidore (he had to look at the note again to get the name right) and remembered that his soles were suspended by threads from the uppers of his boots, that nicotine had stained his teeth and fingers the same shade of yellow, and that his thick, black, unwashed hair rose up in several multidirectional arcs like a curvilinear modern museum. His appearance aside, it was clear that he was quite mad. He spoke very rapidly and urgently, no matter what the subject, but especially when he was describing his current literary endeavor (he was taking poems by Baudelaire and rewriting them, using exactly the same words and punctuation marks). Nevertheless, Peter could see his appeal. Part of it was his intensity. The rays emanating from him were very strong. Living with him would mean living in the final act of an opera, day in and day out. He suited Charlotte very well, if you thought about it. However much she may have once believed she did, Charlotte didn't like being calm and settled. Her temperament was too jumpy, and it was probably better to be living amid real drama than to be making dramas out of things that weren't. Max-etc.'s utter (mad) assurance might help take away her fear, and maybe her caution would temper his unruliness; the two of them took everything very seriously and were almost tone-deaf to pleasure. And if any of her parents' society friends were disparaging, well, he had one of the most ancient titles in France!

Peter had to ask himself if he didn't really feel hurt or angry or embarrassed. The event didn't touch his amour propre because Peter felt no vulnerabilities or jealousy with respect to his rival. Then Peter laughed, thinking about how he should behave. Of course, he would adopt a very civilized attitude. As a man of the world, he understood these things. He imagined the manly, openhanded talk he would have with Max-etc. "See here, my dear fellow, there's nothing to explain. The vagaries of the heart, you know. Of course I understand. Now, shall we have a glass of port?"

These considerations related to his ego, Peter thought. But what about his feelings? Was there no grief? In truth, not really. This made Peter worry about himself. It seemed so inhuman. He assumed that sorrow and disappointment would come later, as he came fully to accept what had happened. Charlotte had been his companion for almost three years; surely he would miss her; surely her removal would sadden him as he went about his daily life and slept alone. He would miss the little things about their life together, yes? Surely he would regret the waste of all the time they had devoted to courtship and marriage, the efforts to become intimate, the blending of their lives, even the trauma that was their wedding. Wouldn't Peter feel lonely and sad?

Peter picked up Charlotte's note once again. She had centered the text perfectly, and she had made no deletions or corrections. Charlotte was good at that kind of thing. Her descenders curled gracefully and the F in "Farewell" looked like a colophon. The ink had been etched into the paper, not merely applied to the surface. Charlotte's letter was an impressive object; even, or especially, under these circumstances she followed certain instinctive principles of aesthetics.

Charlotte. Peter wished her well. And now he felt as if he had been carrying a tremendous weight without acknowledging it to himself; suddenly it had been lifted from him, and both his body and his mind went limp with fatigue. He had been standing as he ruminated, but now he sat down in one of the dining chairs and rested his chin on his hand. He thought about nothing, it seemed. But in time a single word did enter his consciousness: Holly. He found that he could not move off the single thought of the name itself. Then, very slowly, the gears began to turn. Charlotte is out of the picture. If Charlotte is out of the picture, then I am free to become romantically involved with someone else. If that someone else is unmarried and otherwise unattached, then she is free to become romantically involved with me. Holly is unmarried and otherwise unattached. Therefore, Holly and I are free to become romantically involved with each other.

Peter nodded thoughtfully. If only his mind were not so dull! He felt the way you do in the early evening when you have sobered up after having gotten drunk during the day. He grasped that there was reason to be happy, but that was not his emotion. It was all too momentous. He was going to have his chance with Holly, after all. What should his next step be? What should he tell Holly? He didn't want to cry on her shoulder and receive comfort from her. He wanted to use the power of the revelation to vault them from one kind of love to another, the more exciting kind. When should he tell her? Where?

Then he had an idea: the dinner at Arthur Beeche's was on Thursday. Charlotte was to have accompanied him, but apparently she had made other plans. He would ask Holly. He would just say that Charlotte had to go out of town unexpectedly. Wouldn't that be something? To be at Arthur Beeche's house, the most beautiful house in the city, all dressed up, and to be escorting Holly?

Peter was electrified and now shook off his torpor. He wouldn't tell Holly anything about Charlotte until that night, when, on their way to the party, he would say that he had to talk to her about something and would ask if they could go back to her aunt's afterward. Once there they would go over the party with great animation. It had been thrilling! But then they would grow quiet, and she would ask him what was on his mind, and he would tell her about Charlotte. And then — Uh . . . Then . . . Peter suddenly lost his momentum. What did come next? He wasn't strong on this sort of thing. Should he declare his love for her? Should he enfold her hand in both of his as a calyx enfolds a flower — and then declare his love? Holding her chin as one holds a tennis ball when serving, should he guide it toward him and simply kiss her, and let that say everything? He'd work all of this out later.

Impelled by excitement over his plan, Peter bounded to the telephone, picked it up, and was about to dial Holly's number. Then he gulped and hung up. He was in no condition to have this conversation. He had to calm down. Maybe it would be better if he waited and called her tomorrow, when he could be more coolheaded. But what if between now and the next morning Holly accepted another invitation for Thursday? Or committed herself to something at the school? Or scheduled elective surgery? He had to call her now. He took a couple of deep breaths. Okay. Here goes. He got Holly's voice mail and, with as much composure as possible, left a message.

~

On his own voice mail at work the next day, Peter heard Holly say that she would love to come to Arthur Beeche's party. Now Peter had to inform Miss Harrison, in Beeche's office, about the change. He was worried that she would want to replace Charlotte with someone else, and he toyed with the idea of not telling her at all; that was discourteous, though, and could cause embarrassment. So he wrote Miss Harrison the most polite note he possibly could and sent it through interoffice mail; later in the day he received a call from her. She had a low, purring voice, as if she were talking from a soundproof room. It was fine to take Mrs. Speedwell, she just wanted to ask a couple of questions, for seating, you know, trying to balance the tables. What was her background? Was she an easygoing, congenial type of person, enjoyable to talk to? Oh, yes! said Peter. Very! And if he didn't mind, would he say what her marital status was? A widow. Oh, I am sorry. She asked for a photograph — security. Fortunately, Peter had one he could e-mail her.

Then Miss Harrison mentioned something surprising. She understood that Peter knew a Miss Isabella Echevarria de Sena. Yes, actually, she had been a bridesmaid at his wedding. Miss Harrison explained that Miss Echevarria de Sena was going to be a guest at the dinner and would be seated with a table of some important people; she could certainly hold her own, but it might be nice for her to see a familiar face, so would he mind if she seated them together? Not at all! Peter answered. After he got off the phone, Peter wondered who had invited Isabella. Probably some big shot with whom she was involved, his wife notwithstanding, who wanted both to show her off and to impress her.

Peter organized his evening clothes; he consulted with Holly on what she should wear and was not very helpful; he ordered a car; he checked the time and address on the invitation hourly. He did not tell anyone about Charlotte, nor did he hear from her. He was grateful for that, since talking to her would probably have complicated his thoughts, tangling the simple line he intended his actions, arrowlike, to follow. He waited.

9

*T*hursday evening finally arrived. Peter was in his office, changing his clothes. He felt excited, nervous, hopeful. Holly and he would have dinner in a house that, by all accounts, contained objects of fantastic beauty and that was itself an example of the highest expression of human art; the dinner and the wines would be exquisite, as, by all accounts, they always were; the guests would be powerful, rich, good-looking, beautifully dressed; Holly and Peter themselves would be beautifully dressed. The artwork, the setting, the food, the wine, the crowd, their own and the others' costumes: the combined stimuli from all these sources would engorge them, causing a giddy delirium and putting Holly into the same state of heightened sensation that the heroine of a novel always experiences after a ball. So then, when they returned to her aunt's apartment, and Peter told Holly his news about Charlotte, and then his feelings for her, their sentiments, their hearts, their very souls, would be primed for a climactic fusion.

Maybe. Conceivably. Anyway, it was worth a shot.

There was a full moon. Peter noticed it walking to the car: a full moon, shining like chrome on this cold, clear night. Cold orb, passive and chaste, how have you earned the worship of lovers? You are the sun of the lover's day, which is the night. It was a good omen.

The driver opened the door for Peter and he got in the car, a black Lincoln. Having settled himself in his own seat, the driver looked at his clipboard.

"You are Mr. Russell?" His accent and appearance indicated that he was Indian.

"Yes."

"Good evening, to you, Mr. Russell." The radio was playing. "Do you mind, sir, if I listen to the game?"

"Oh, no, that's fine," Peter said.

After a moment, Peter realized that it was the Devils game. When the other team scored, the driver cursed unintelligibly. The announcer gave the goalie's statistics for the season, which were terrible.

"This Marcotte, he is no good," the driver said to himself. "Son-of-a-bitch."

"Especially since they traded Bjornlund."

The driver looked at Peter in the rearview mirror. "Exactly, sir! You are exactly right!"

The driver and Peter began chatting and continued their conversation during the whole trip uptown. As they talked, Peter found that they were establishing a deep spiritual bond of the type that sometimes does inexplicably arise between oneself and a driver, or teller, or cashier, or waiter. On these occasions, Peter sometimes imagined that sprites had been sent out into the world to occupy unassuming positions where they could observe and protect him. Here was another good omen.

Holly was waiting downstairs at her aunt's building. The driver leapt out of the car and opened the door for her. She got in and she and Peter kissed, chastely.

"You look beautiful," he said.

"Thank you. But I have my overcoat on. How do you know?"

"Uh, well, you know, the from-the-neck-up part."

It was true. Holly had her hair gathered up in a way that made it look especially sleek, and she wore more makeup than usual and had applied it differently, so her cheekbones looked higher, her eyes bigger, her lashes longer, her lips more full. She wore no earrings, and given the beauty of her soft, pendent lobes, they would have been an unwelcome distraction.

"I borrowed some things — well, everything — from my aunt," Holly said. "She was the clotheshorse. I hope my dress will be okay."

"It'll be great."

"What a beautiful lady," the driver said, looking in the rearview mirror. "You are a lucky man, sir, to be with such a beautiful lady. You are married, yes? Or she is your girlfriend?" Peter and Holly exchanged amused, mildly abashed looks, and Peter said, in what he hoped was a friendly and confident way, "Neither, I'm afraid. We're just friends." The driver pulled down the corners of his mouth and nodded slowly. "Aha. Friends."

Believing, as one so often does when one is self-conscious, that he owed this complete stranger a fuller explanation, Peter offered it: "My wife was unexpectedly called out of town, and we were going to this big party, so this lady, who is a friend of both of ours, has kindly agreed to accompany me."

The driver nodded. "Aha. That is nice." Peter could see his eyes moving back and forth in the rearview mirror as he looked at each of them. The driver watched the road for a moment and then looked back into the mirror to address Peter. "Your wife, she knows about this, yes?"

This question caught Peter off-guard, and it was only after a suspicious delay that he managed to force out a laugh and the answer "Of course!"

"Well, I will tell you something," said the driver. "You are a lucky man. My wife never lets me go out with a beautiful lady like this lady when she goes away. To tell it as the truth, my wife never goes away!"

They all laughed at this. For the remainder of the ride, they had an engaging conversation with the driver about his youth, his immigration, his children. Two were in college and another was studying to be a pharmacist.

When they were nearing Beeche's house, Peter turned to Holly and said, "Um, Holly, there's something I wanted to talk to you about."

"Of course, Peter. Is it something important?"

Peter smiled drolly. "I guess you could say it's pretty important. I thought that if the dinner doesn't run too late, when I drop you off I could come up and tell you about it."

"Of course," Holly said, her eyes searching Peter's for some clue as to what this was all about.

They arrived, and the driver scrambled to open the door on the sidewalk side. Peter spoke to him about what time he should pick them up. "No problem, my friend," the driver said. "I will be waiting around the corner for anytime when you want to leave." He had soulful eyes and a huge smile. "You and the lady, your friend, you have a good time."

"Thanks!" said Peter.

When Peter turned toward Holly after this exchange, he saw that she was gazing at the full moon. She quickly turned her head and looked at him with a sheepish smile. A dozen couples were shuffling toward the door of Beeche's house in a formless queue. Holly and Peter joined them. After a moment of staring at the backs of heads and overcoats, Holly gave a nod to the rear.

"Full moon," she said.

"I noticed."

"It's silly," Holly said. "You know, how many full moons have I seen in my life? But whenever I do see one, it makes my heart race a little."

"I know what you mean."

"It always makes me think," Holly said, "that something is going to happen." She looked over at Peter with another sheepish smile. "Do you know what I mean?"

"I know what you mean."

Arthur Beeche's house stretched across an entire block of the avenue and looked as if it might have been built three hundred years earlier. It was three stories high and nine bays across. The central section formed a faux portico, with a pediment and four decorative Corinthian columns. Carvings of vines, flowers, snakes, dolphins, stags, and other plant life and beasts stood in relief around the central windows, along the architrave, and within the pediment. With some effort, one could discern that the arabesques on the keystone of each window depicted two Bs, back to back. Light burst from all the windows as if they were the apertures of a roaring furnace.

Two servants patrolled the sidewalk, helping guests out of their cars and instructing the drivers where to move. Another two stood on either side of the doors, which one reached by a short flight of steps. More servants met the guests inside. They were dressed in several different types of livery: tails and fancy waistcoats on a couple of them, tunics, simple black dresses. A man took Peter's coat and Holly relinquished hers to a maid.

When Peter saw Holly without her coat, he almost jumped backward. She was wearing a gray silk dress with a long, flowing skirt. The bodice was held up by the thinnest possible straps and had been sewn with tiny pearls. She wore no adornments whatsoever, creating a thrilling line, interrupted only by those thin straps, from the fingertips of one hand to those of the other.

"Wow," Peter said. "You really do look beautiful."

"This old thing?" said Holly. "I think my aunt got it forty years ago. But thank you."

"Good evening, Mrs. Speedwell. Good evening, Mr. Russell," one of the senior servants said. "If you will kindly mount the stairs and go to your right, you will find that drinks are being served in the Hall."

Holly and Peter thanked him and were suitably impressed by his ability to recognize them. The entrance hall was a large cube, with fireplaces on either side and, on the ceiling, an enormous painting of Zeus visiting Danae as a shower of gold (this had apparently been an earlier Beeche's idea of a mercenary joke). Holly and Peter went up two flights of marble steps and, as instructed, turned right. Here they found a corridor with a floor inlaid with marble of different colors and lined with paintings, a few busts, and two rows of V-backed gilded chairs. Looking at the chairs with awe, Holly whispered to Peter (whispering seemed appropriate), "Venetian."

At the end of the corridor there stood another servant, who raised his right arm and said, "This way, if you please." They stepped through an archway and then stopped simultaneously. They were on the landing of another marble staircase, which led down to a vast, two-story room — the Hall, evidently. Holly and Peter could look down on the guests, survey the room as a whole. A painting or fresco containing innumerable gods and putti, all twisting and turning dramatically, covered the ceiling. More epic scenes filled the upper halves of the walls. Piers, moldings, and any other spare surface were all carved. Medieval and Renaissance religious paintings lined the lower half of the walls. Spaced along the walls at regular intervals, busts sat on pedestals.

They walked down the staircase and entered the crowd. One servant asked them what they would like to drink, and another appeared with their order almost immediately (wine for Holly, scotch for Peter). They strolled a bit. Trying not to crane his neck too conspicuously, Peter studied the noble marble heads, the muscular bodies of the gods, the putti hurtling toward him from the ceiling. He tried not to stare at the guests, among whom he saw celebrated financiers, dancers, blue bloods, movie stars, and tycoons; legendary members of the firm; and also people of both sexes whom he did not recognize but who were young and incredibly good-looking. Then, about twenty feet away, at the end of a gap that had opened in the crowd, he noted a person of particular interest. There stood Arthur Beeche in a group of three or four others. Peter recognized him immediately, although he had never seen Beeche before in person and his likeness only rarely appeared in the press or company publications. He was unmistakable. Peter was surprised by the strength of his physical presence. He was taller than Peter had thought and had broad shoulders and a commensurately wide, solid-looking torso. But the most striking thing about him was his head, a large oblong block. It looked like a medium-sized stereo speaker.

Beeche was wearing a double-breasted dinner jacket, black pants with a line of satin down the sides, and black patent leather pumps. There was nothing at all out of the ordinary about any of this. Nevertheless, Peter found the clothes arresting. They not only fit perfectly, they fit as if they were Beeche's pelt. Further, the material seemed different from that used to make Peter's own evening clothes and those of the other guests. The black was both deeper and more vivid. The fabric seemed only to absorb light, reflecting none; it had a kind of glow of blackness. Meanwhile, the stripes down the legs and the lapels, also satin, resembled the smoother, glossier passages in an all-black painting.

Peter nudged Holly and nodded in Beeche's direction. "Our host," he said.

Holly looked at Beeche for a moment. "He's different from what I would have expected," she said.

"What did you expect?" asked Peter.

"Oh, I don't know," Holly said. "I thought that after so many generations of having so much money, families were supposed to decline and produce weak, effete, coupon-clipping, zillionth-copy epigones of the founding titan. But Mr. Beeche there seems pretty robust."

"Yes, I guess he is," said Peter. "He runs the firm, he's absolutely the boss, so he's not rising at noon and playing snooker all day."

"What do you know about him?" Holly asked.

Peter shrugged. "I've never met him or talked to him," he said. "Everyone says he's very smart, and the firm is certainly doing well. He's never been interested in creating a financial supermarket and all that stuff. He doesn't hire a lot of people during a boom or fire a lot during a bust. He got into bond futures early. Over the years he's done just about everything, and he will still go down to the trading floor and talk to those guys. He's famous for glancing at somebody's screen and telling him that he's got a great trade going, or a terrible one, or is missing the one he should be doing. With the bankers, he'll call on clients or potential ones, and once in a while he likes to be right in there as part of the team doing a deal, even if it's a fairly small one, staying up until all hours, complaining about the lawyers, all that. People say that he's a really nice guy but always quite formal. He'll laugh and all, but he's a real square.

"What else? He has six or seven or eight houses around the world. He might not visit one for a few years, but they are always kept fully staffed, of course. He likes shooting, he rides, he collects just about everything, but what he seems to like even more is having people make stuff for him, like custom cars. Then there are all the charities; he's very discreet about it, never his name on anything, but everybody knows that he gives away millions, tens of millions.

"Oh, and finally, from what I understand he was married to someone he really loved. She died years ago, and he's never stopped mourning her and will never marry again. Or that's what people say."

"Did they have any children?" Holly asked.

"No, I'm pretty sure they didn't," said Peter.

"But then what about an heir?"

"Well, that's a problem, especially since he's an only child. You know, the Beeches believe in primogeniture, not strictly but pretty close. Arthur owns the firm, and all the houses and so forth that his father owned. Over the years of course there have been settlements on siblings and cousins, and they are all just fine. But Arthur himself owns basically everything."

"That's amazing," said Holly.

"Yes," said Peter, "isn't it?"

"Well, I don't want to hold you back in your career. Aren't you supposed to be going up to him and making him like the cut of your jib or something?"

"I probably should," said Peter. "Uh-oh, wait. There he goes." Beeche shook hands with a couple of the people he had been talking to and then began to walk away. At the same time, the crowd filled in behind him. "I'm not sure that it would be a good idea to push through people and run after him," said Peter.

"No."

"They say he goes around after dinner and makes sure he's had a word with everyone," Peter said. "So I guess I'll have my chance to make an impression."

They moved along slowly through the crowd and headed toward a predella mounted on the wall. After they had undertaken some further sightseeing, a couple of colleagues stopped to talk to Peter, and he introduced Holly, and after a while he did detach himself from her in order to mingle, joking with one colleague about his — Peter's — lack of competence at golf, with another about the lousy performance of a competitor's product, with a third about an office romance. Eventually, stewards (or whoever) appeared to say that dinner was served. Waiters unburdened the guests of their drinks and the crowd was brought through an enormous doorway. Tables had been set in two adjoining rooms (neither the actual dining room), and these, though smaller and with lower ceilings, were in their own ways even more remarkable than the Hall. The first was light, feminine. On the walls hung eighteenth-century panels that showed rose-cheeked girls and boys in pursuit of each other through flamboyant gardens. The second room was dark, masculine, with wood paneling and life-sized carvings of fish, birds, game, and flora on the walls and chimneypiece.

Peter accompanied Holly to her table in the first room. Two guests were already there. On the far side stood a tall young man wearing a shawl-collared dinner jacket; he had a dense head of straight black hair and an aquiline nose. This was the English rock star who was reputed to be so cultivated and literate, everyone's favorite guest for a country-house weekend. A woman in her seventies was sitting down. Her face looked as if it had been fixed for decades in an expression of utter boredom, and she wore a diamond necklace, diamond earrings, a diamond bracelet, and, on her left ring finger, a diamond the size of an ice cube. Holly whispered to Peter, "The Principessa Elisabetta Foscari."

"How do you know that?"

"She was from Chicago. Betty Jones. My grandmother knew her."

Peter pulled Holly's seat out for her.

"So," Holly said, "this is dinner with the boss?"

"Yep."

"Well, it should be interesting."

"I hope so," said Peter.

Most of the guests throughout the room seemed now to be sitting down; Peter went off to seek his own place. Before he had gone too far, he looked back. Holly looked beautiful. The man seated to her right had arrived, and Peter recognized him as a senior member of the legal staff at Beeche, a man reputed to be one of the smartest but most approachable in the firm, and who, Peter had heard, read Virgil in the bathtub. So that should be enjoyable for her. He was probably in his seventies and was quite short and had one of those faces that, while semirepulsive, also had a certain sex appeal. He was the type of man whom Holly liked talking to perhaps more than any other and whom she had a knack for charming.

A servant guided Peter to his own table, which was in the second room. As he walked toward it, he found he had a little spring in his step; he even discovered himself to be humming. You couldn't help but be exhilarated by the surroundings and the people. This was good. And then there was the blessing of the driver-sprite. And the full moon.

Peter was the last to arrive at his table. As he sat down, he first greeted Isabella, who was seated on his left. She exclaimed her hello. "I thought I might be sitting with you!" she said. They kissed on the cheek and caught up for a minute. "How is Charlotte? I have been meaning to call you guys." "Have you been back home recently?" Peter, to be frank, had a difficult time carrying on his side of the conversation. Isabella had jet black hair and silky white skin, not a cold, translucent white, not like porcelain, but warmer — alabaster. Peter's eyes followed her long neck up to her chin and then traced its sharp turn and those of her lips and the tip of her nose. Looking down, Peter saw that the straps of her dress held two narrow panels of fabric that simply hung down from them, concealing very little. All of this was quite distracting.

Peter and Isabella's brief chitchat drew to an end, and the man on her left, to whom she had been speaking before Peter arrived, leaned in to introduce himself.

"Hello. Seth Bernard," said the man, reaching his hand over to shake Peter's. Seth Bernard. Seth Bernard!

"Peter Russell. How do you do?"

"Very well, thank you." Bernard spoke to the woman next to him, a lean, elderly woman. "Mrs. Beeche, do you know Peter Russell?"

"I don't believe I do," she said. "How nice to see you, Mr. Russell."

"How do you do, Mrs. Beeche?" Peter said.

The other guests introduced themselves with a nod or a wave: Otis Bell, Athina Kakouilli, Jack Thorndale, Lisa Eisler. Peter nodded and repeated, "Peter Russell. How do you do?"

With Bernard and Isabella talking on Peter's left, and Lisa Eisler and Jack Thorndale on his right, Peter had a moment to pretend to study his menu card (old-fashioned: *homard aux aromates, gigot de pré-salé braisé*). In fact, he needed time to collect himself. His heart was pounding and his head throbbing; he was so astounded by the identities of his tablemates that he thought he might faint. Seth Bernard was Seth Bernard, Arthur Beeche's alter ego. Mrs. Arthur Beeche was Mrs. Arthur Beeche, Arthur's mother. Otis Bell had recently been appointed chairman of the Federal Reserve Board. Athina Kakouilli, a poet, had won the Nobel Prize for Literature a couple of years back. Jack Thorndale was a legend as a sportsman and adventurer who had known everyone, slept with everyone, been everywhere, and done everything. Finally, Lisa Eisler. Now, who was Lisa Eisler? Peter knew that he recognized the name and had seen pictures of her somewhere. Oh, yes! Lisa Eisler ran an organization that had just completed one of the largest and most successful relief missions in history. There had been stories about her in the papers and magazines. Tens of thousands of lives had been saved.

Which, except for the astoundingly beautiful Isabella, left: Peter. Good old Peter. Peter, who worked up on the fifty-eighth floor of the Beeche Building, and, it was true, had done a couple of decent things in his job. Peter, who had started on the JV hockey team in college. Peter, who was perfectly nice-looking in a boring sort of way. Now, how did this stack up against the people whom he was supposed to impress for the rest of the evening?

Seth Bernard (Seth Bernard!) was a little above medium height and had a smooth oval face that was becoming heavy in the cheeks and an oval build. He was bald, and the top of his head looked polished, as indeed did his entire appearance. His very clothes might have been buffed. The slight downturn of his eyes and the corners of his mouth gave him a mournful air. Bernard's influence upon and closeness to Arthur put him in a category entirely separate from all other executives. According to the stories Peter had heard, the two had grown up a block from each other and had attended the same nursery school, all-boys elementary school, boarding school, and college. Arthur then had his *Wanderjahr* before joining the firm, whereas Bernard studied in England for a couple of years and attended law school. From there he went to Beeche, hired by Arthur's father, who made him superior to Arthur, and soon began giving him firm-wide responsibilities. The elder Beeche came to rely heavily on Bernard, moving him to a nearby office soon after his arrival. Arthur actually rose toward Bernard in the firm's hierarchy, but by the time Arthur took over for his father at forty, he and Bernard had worked closely together for years. Throughout, they remained extremely close friends. After Maria died, Arthur lived with Bernard and his wife and three children for months.

Bernard was famous for his startling competence. Ten minutes after someone had mentioned a problem to him, he would call back, having arranged a solution. He disparaged political maneuvering within the firm, but he was highly competitive and tough: if he had been allowed to mutilate all the antagonists he had vanquished, he could have lined his walls with scrotums, like shrunken heads. Except for Beeche himself, there was no one in the firm who could help, or hinder, a young man more than Seth Bernard.

Mrs. Beeche must have been in her eighties. She was slender and had bright blue eyes and carefully tended white hair. Charlotte often liked to go on and on about how stunning some shriveled old woman was, and while Peter always tried to respond with the appropriate sensitivity, he tended to discount Charlotte's comments as claptrap intended to demonstrate her own appreciation of true beauty. She's just a wrinkly old lady, he would think, who would kill to be eighteen again. But in this case, Peter found himself outdoing what would have been Charlotte's likely estimation. Mrs. Beeche's skin hung loosely around her jaw, it was true, and age spots marked it in an all-over pattern, but one hardly noticed these imperfections. She did not wear much in the way of jewelry: wedding and engagement rings; a brooch in the shape of an elephant, encrusted with various small stones.

For decades Mrs. Beeche had been on the board of the opera. Peter remembered a conversation that he and Charlotte had had with her father and stepmother when for some reason the opera had come up. Charlotte's father had always had a subscription. He asked if Charlotte and Peter would like to use his tickets for the upcoming performance of a particular work by a French composer.

Charlotte leapt at the opportunity. A moment or two later, out of her hearing, Dick said to Peter, "Sorry, son, you've just signed up for one of the most tedious operas on record. Better you than me! Say — do you know, the only reason they perform it is because of your boss's mother. She loves French opera. There isn't much they won't do to please her." It was the kind of thing Dick knew. When Mrs. Beeche had first attended the opera, Peter thought, all the families in the other boxes were probably known to her own; what had been a herd at this watering hole had by now dwindled to a few individuals. Mrs. Beeche, however, gave no impression of having dwindled. Everything about her — her hair, her dress, her adornments — was neat, fresh, bright, gleaming. Only her face and hands, in fact, showed any sign of wear, giving the impression of a portrait in which the drapery had been cleaned and restored but not the subject herself. She had a glint in her eye, a look of wisdom — and of authority, the authority of one who has the backing of great wealth and an entire social system, even if she were the last representative of it.

Good old Peter was sitting across from good old Otis Bell, whose importance in the world of finance was to Peter's as the sun's light was to a match. A lanky black man in his sixties, he had short hair that looked as if it had been dusted by snow. Everyone knew Bell's story: he had grown up in some godforsaken, gnat-infested county with bad soil in the Deep South. When he enlisted in the air force, he was given an intelligence test, and on the quantitative section he received one of the highest scores ever recorded. The air force sent him to college and graduate school, and after he finished his tour he went into academia, with periodic jobs in Washington. Previously, he had been head of the New York Federal Reserve Bank, and even when he had held that position, Peter, of course, would have been unworthy to touch the hem of his garment.

As he would also be in the case of Athina Kakouilli. A slim woman in her fifties with dark circles under her eyes, she carried her large nose with regal dignity. What did Peter remember about her? From a middle-class family in Greece. She had come to the United States to live with relatives in her teens. She wrote poems of every variety, and — this had stuck in Peter's mind — her favorite modern poet writing in English was Robert Frost. Under the dictatorship, her family had been forced to leave the country.

Then came ruddy, big-boned Jack Thorndale. He was probably over seventy, and he had thick white hair that was unkempt. His evening clothes seemed to have been thrown on and to be too small; Peter noticed that he gave the impression of bursting out of them on account of his strength, not flab, and that this effect was not entirely undesirable. Dick Montague knew Thorndale and had talked about him once in a while. He had married a couple of heiresses, and he was a hard drinker, a Don Juan, a fine horseman, a crack shot. Wherever there was game to kill or a fox to chase he could be found. He had big, horny hands that looked as if they had worked an infinite number of snaps, cleats, hinges, buckles, clasps, bolts, winches, ropes, and toggles. He was famous for his molasses-voiced seductiveness, as he played against his rough type to lure countless women of all stripes (including, of course, the wives of his friends) into his bed. In fact, he probably spent less time tracking in the bush than he did going to parties in London and cruising on someone's yacht and visiting rich bohemians in Marrakech. Behind his back, people called him "Papa," but he had the last laugh, since he was the one waking in the arms of a nineteen-year-old beauty. As Thorndale looked over at Isabella, Peter could see him lick his chops.

Finally, to Peter's immediate right sat Lisa Eisler. She had a dark complexion and long, graying, curly hair, which she had worked into a thick braid. Her face had some wrinkles and sags, but she was attractive. She must have been in her fifties and she looked like one of those older models who are sometimes used in fashion advertising. She wore a simple black dress, hardly any makeup, and no jewelry. Her hands were weather-beaten, with prominent veins that looked like the roots of a tree. As Peter remembered, Eisler had grown up in New Jersey, the daughter of an optometrist. She had been smart enough to get into a very good university, and from there she had planned to be a lawyer, but she got married young. She had a couple of children and did volunteer work. One day after her divorce and when her children were grown, she was reading about the victims of famine and war and had the overpowering conviction that she had to do more. So her life took that path. She now spent months at a time in places that were dangerous, diseased, and impoverished. She did not eat meat; she refused to take any but the smallest salary; she liked old-fashioned rock and roll. Peter often wrung his hands about whether the work he did had any real value. Now he was sitting next to someone whose example made him feel depraved.

So here we have a portrait of everyone at the table — oh, but let's not forget Isabella, the leanest, lithest, most silky-skinned, most revealingly dressed, most beautiful (in her way, which was not Holly's), sexiest, most frankly available-seeming woman Peter had ever sat next to in his life. Isabella always cast a spell on him, but tonight the effect was overpowering. Here was a young woman for whom any man would gladly toss away an empire.

And then there was: Peter. Peter knew, of course, that it was pretty pointless and immature to compare yourself to other people. What mattered was whether you believed that you were using your *own* capabilities to the fullest. He also knew that it was of no importance whatsoever what other people thought of you. As long as you were comfortable with yourself and believed in yourself, then you could just throw out all that nonsense of worrying about your status and "success" and other people's opinions. Peter was a valuable, worthwhile human being in his own right! There was no reason whatsoever for him to feel inferior to anyone else at this table. Except that he was inferior to all of them.

Peter had studied the menu card long enough to memorize it. Pretty soon he was going to have to say something to someone, or someone was going to say something to him. He looked over to his left, where Isabella and Bernard were talking. Peter smiled and leaned in their direction, but he hoped his manner conveyed the message Don't worry about me! I am just parking myself here on the edge of your conversation. He couldn't quite understand what they were saying, and he found his attention drawn to the smooth channel between Isabella's breasts.

Then, from his other side, he heard a voice say: "It looks as if you're going to have to settle for talking to me."

Peter did not understand. He turned to his right and saw Lisa Eisler looking at him with a friendly smile.

"I'm sorry," he said. "I'm afraid I didn't —"

"It wasn't anything important," Eisler said. "I only said, 'It looks as if you're going to have to settle for talking to me,'" and she nodded toward Isabella.

Peter glanced to his left and then looked back at Eisler. "Oh, uh, she — Isabella — actually, we're friends. She was a bridesmaid at my wedding."

"I see."

"It was last June. We haven't seen each other since then."

"I understand," said Eisler. "But please, even if you'd never met I'd think there was definitely something wrong with you, a young man your age, if you would rather talk to me than to her!"

"Well," Peter said, "I hope you're also willing to make allowances for Mr. Bernard and Mr. Bell and Mr. Thorndale. They probably think of themselves as being my age, or younger."

"Hmmm," Eisler said, glancing around at the other men. "Okay." She shrugged. "High-status male primates. What can you do?"

There was a pause. Peter swallowed. He figured he might as well just plunge right in. "Ms. Eisler," he said, "I . . . that is . . . when you tell people you admire them, I've usually found that they don't take it too well. They usually look down their nose at you as if to say, Why do you imagine I could care less whether you admire me? So I hope you don't mind if I say that it is really an honor for me to be sitting next to you. I've been reading about all your work, and, well, with what you are doing and the people you are helping, it seems ridiculous of me to think that whatever I said would mean a thing, but, anyway, it is an honor."

"Please call me Lisa," Eisler said. "Thank you. I do appreciate what you have said very much."

Peter thought for a moment. "You know, I feel like kind of a hypocrite saying that. I don't actually do anything that reflects the beliefs that I've just implied that I have. I mean, I give a few hundred dollars, or, okay, even a couple of thousand, to something here and there, but really . . ." He switched gears. "Does it often happen that people you've just met start justifying their lives to you?"

Eisler laughed. "I have never thought about it quite like that, but yes. I suppose I do have that effect on some people."

"Because, boy, I have to be honest, it seems very important for me to convince you that I'm not a bad person. Really, I'm not!"

She laughed again. "Peter, you shouldn't feel that way. You don't need to prove something to me."

"Yes! Yes, I do!"

"No, really. It's true that when you're in my position, you can make people feel guilty just by saying hello. It's as if the rabbi or the minister showed up. 'It's Lisa! What if she sees our SUV?!' I get very, very angry when I'm in the States and I see all the waste and the overconsumption. Going into a supermarket, seeing the fruit they throw out because it has one little blemish. It makes me mad because of all the people who could be helped if the waste were used properly, and it just disgusts me, on principle, and even aesthetically, if that's the right word. It's not so bad for me now, coming back. But the kids I work with, after they've been doing something overseas for a couple of years in a really poor country and they return, it can be really hard.

"But with individuals I'm not that judgmental. The point is, Peter, if you are giving money and doing what you can and living a good life, that's all anybody can expect — although you probably could give more money!" She smiled at him.

"You know, I'm not against pleasure. In my own way I'm not even against luxury." She motioned with her hand around the room. "Take all this. Look at that painting." It was a painting of Mars and Venus, both naked except for a robe draped across her lap; with their arms spread out, they held each other's hands. Venus was plump, and she wore a pearl choker, pearls in her blond hair, and two ruby, pearl, and gold bracelets; she was in profile and had a straight nose and delicate lips and chin. Mars's muscles in his shoulders and arms bunched up as he leaned toward Venus. You wanted to finger the blue robe, to touch their rosy flesh.

"You could sell that painting for a few million dollars and provide food and medicine to thousands of people," Eisler said. "But do I want to hector Arthur to sell it? No. Why? Well, there's a place in the world for beautiful things and people who own them, protect them, and enjoy them. I haven't gotten it all sorted out, but in the great scheme of things, I figure that somebody should lead the life

Arthur does. He almost has an obligation to the rest of humanity to do that. It's not the Arthurs who bother me; it's the millions of people who waste money and resources on crap. So you see, I'm really quite a snob.

"But the other thing is, I've managed to soak Arthur for a lot, a whole lot. I sure don't want to get rid of the Arthurs and kill the golden goose."

"Yes," Peter said. "I suppose that if you want to take from the rich and give to the poor, you've got to have the rich."

Eisler laughed. "Yes, I guess that's true," she said. Peter had not even intended for his remark to be funny, but a booming laugh came from across the table. It was Otis Bell.

"Now what was that?" he said. "'If you want to take from the rich and give to the poor, you've got to have the rich'? I hope you don't mind if I steal that, young man. I know several people whom I can use that with." He laughed again loudly. The others asked what it was all about, and Bell told them, and there was a murmur of amusement and approval.

"Well, Otis," said Seth Bernard, "I'm glad to learn that you see your job as preserving the rich."

"Oh, no," said Bell. "But I don't see it as eliminating them either."

Thorndale piped up. "It seems to me," he said, "that rich people are a necessary evil."

"It's a dirty job, but somebody's got to do it," said Eisler. "You guys don't get enough credit."

"Well," said Peter, "that's really up to Mr. Bell, isn't it, how much credit we get?"

Ha ha! Otis Bell laughed at this heartily.

The conversation eddied among two or three people, flowed crosswise, split into branches, then formed pools that included everyone. As it did so, Peter emerged as sort of a mascot of the table.

Two people would be discussing something — a movie, a political issue, the economy, the human condition — and then they would turn to him and ask him his opinion. Peter found himself able to talk with perfect ease on any subject at all.

Mrs. Beeche and Otis Bell, for example, got onto China. What did Peter think, Mrs. Beeche wondered. "I really don't know much about it," he said, "but it's a country that has several thousand riots a year, that has a seriously aging population, that is an environmental disaster, that suffers from massive corruption, that has a completely screwed-up banking system, that is seeing speculation run wild, and that is tyrannical. Rather than seeing it as a threat, I worry that it will all fall to pieces." "Exactly," Bernard chimed in. Or, at another point, Thorndale and Isabella were trying to figure out the domestic arrangements of a movie-star couple and became hopelessly confused. They appealed to Peter, who lucidly catalogued the relevant pregnancies, adoptions, marriages, out-of-wedlock births, third parties, divorces, and box office. "The judge said he wanted to give custody to a screenwriter, since that way, with two stars and a director already attached, the kid would have a package." Having gone shooting once in his life, he was able to discuss with Thorndale the tricks of working setters and retrievers together; he made an apposite comment when Bernard, a philatelist, mentioned that he had just acquired a misprint from the Kingdom of Naples.

Later on Bernard and Bell were talking. Bernard asked Bell about measuring the effect of Federal Reserve policy statements on markets. "How'm I going to fool you if I tell you that?" Bell said. "Why don't you ask your colleague here? Or, I'm sorry, Peter, maybe you're off-duty?"

"Never!" said Bernard.

Peter took a sip of wine. "I guess," he said, "you could start by using a Cholesky decomposition to construct some indicators of how policy expectations change." He carried on for a bit, describing the indicators he might use. "You could follow Kohn and Sack, maybe, and regress the squared values of each of the factors on several dummy variables. You'd get into some equations."

"Gurkaynak, Sack, and Swanson," Bell said.

"Yes, sir," said Peter.

"Jesus Christ!" Thorndale cried from the other side of the table. "If you guys are going to keep this up, you can take your damn slide rules someplace else." He and Kakouilli began conversing in Greek. They knew each other, it turned out, because both were friends with an American poet who had lived in Greece much of the time. They were talking about him and switched to English. What was that very early poem, something about learning Greek? How did it start — smelling the sun? They both turned to Peter. Miraculously, Peter remembered this work and was able to recite it.

"You mean 'Beginner's Greek'? Let's see . . .

To one
　Who smells the sun,
　　Eyes shut, and tastes that rain is sweet;
Who hears
　Music, but fears
　　Its presence in empty gardens; or, discreet,
Only observes
　The nerves
　　And fibers of a painting — shade, technique;
What is
　Beyond analysis
　　Is perilous: we must not wish to seek
And cry
　'This is what I

Love, what I cherish!" Instead, be wary of such
Intensity
That we
May never be hurt or happy or anything too
much.*"

Isabella had been listening intently. "Oh, Peter, that's so beautiful," she said in a whisper.

"He was twenty," Peter said.

Kakouilli and Thorndale just stared at him.

Filling himself with good wine and food, laughing with his new
friends, hearing the burbling of the other conversations in the room
(not a cacophony, more like the sound when all of a city's churches
ring their bells), seeing the carved birds and hares on the wall seem
to grow fatter and fatter, Peter felt as if he had lowered himself into
a warm bath of well-being. Responding to such global delicious-
ness, all his senses had become more acute. To his touch, the table
linen had an unusual density and thickness. Isabella's scent almost
made him swoon, as if he were in a hothouse filled with orchids.
Although silver, the forks and knives had the heft of solid gold.
Looking at the painting nearby, he could see the colors pulsate.
Beautiful and rare, all the objects in the room seemed to hum.

What a wonderful world it was!

By the time dessert (*reine de saba*) was served, Peter had decided
that he loved everyone at the table, that they all loved one another,
and that they all loved him. This feeling was enhanced by the
knowledge that they had various overlapping connections, and so
they were friends meeting over dinner, not just posturing guests at
a party. Peter felt he had been welcomed into an intimate circle and
loved them all the more for that: unlikely as it might have seemed,
Thorndale and Eisler knew each other well; he was close to an older

man who had been her mentor. "Sure, Ben would let me come out now and then, and even though I wasn't good for much I'd try to help." "Not good for much!" Eisler said. "You saved his life!" "Rubbish! Nonsense!" Thorndale wouldn't let Eisler tell the story to the table, but she whispered to Peter that Thorndale and the other man had been captured by members of a particularly brutal rebel army and Thorndale had killed two men in order to effect their escape. Thorndale had known Bernard for decades and he knew Bell because he knew everyone. Meanwhile, Bell had taught Arthur Beeche and Bernard and had known Arthur's father. Bell knew Mrs. Beeche because he was also on the board of the opera; he had become a fan as a boy because his mother took him along on Saturdays when she worked at the house of a white lady who unfailingly listened to the opera broadcast. Then Athina Kakouilli and Lisa Eisler had been college friends of Arthur's late wife, Maria.

The mention of Maria's name put everyone at the table in a wistful mood, even Isabella and Peter, for the others' response was contagious. Everyone wore a bittersweet smile.

"What was she like?" Isabella asked.

The others glanced around at one another.

Thorndale spoke first. "I'll tell you what," he said. "She was the only woman who ever really broke my heart."

Rather than joshing him for this comment, the others took it seriously.

"She was so kind," said Kakouilli. "Who would pay attention to a Greek girl? I had my aunt and uncle, but I knew nobody in America, much less at the college, and my English was poor. She befriended me; I stayed with her family. I never would have lasted without her."

"I remember so many things about her," said Bernard. "But she was so funny the way she was so patient with Arthur, but then made fun of him too, in just the way he needed to be made fun of. Do you know what I mean, Mrs. Beeche?"

"I certainly do!" Mrs. Beeche said, laughing. "She would say, 'Well, Arthur, when those nice people told you about their country house, and you said, "And where are your other houses?" Well, you see, darling, not everyone has seven houses. Some don't even have one.' 'Oh. Yes. I suppose you're right,' says Arthur." She laughed again. "Hopeless."

"She certainly was crazy about him," said Eisler, "and he cared for her so much. What do you think, Mrs. Beeche — not to pry, but we're among friends here — do you think he'll ever marry again?"

Mrs. Beeche sighed. "I hope so." She thought for a moment. "You know, I think he may be ready. I do. They certainly were in love. But I think he's ready to fall in love again."

"I wish I knew what love was," said Eisler.

"Who does know?" said Thorndale. "I don't, and it's not for lack of effort to find out."

"Mr. Russell," said Kakouilli, "why do you not enlighten us?"

Everyone looked at Peter with indulgent, eager smiles.

He surveyed the group in one direction and then the other, and then back again. He had thought of a response. "When two people are in love," he said solemnly, "they are parallel lines. That intersect."

The others received this with a hush, then burst out laughing.

Peter raised his hands and shrugged. "I tried! You put a guy on the spot like that . . ."

"You did very well," said Kakouilli. "I like it. I think it's marvelous. Together but separate. Infinity."

"If I'm parallel to a girl," Thorndale said under his breath, "I bloody well hope we'll intersect before infinity."

"Oh, Jack," said Eisler, laughing, and the conversation took off again.

10

The waiters were removing the dessert plates. Coffee, brandy, and cigars were to be offered in rooms beyond the Sculpture Gallery.

"Peter?" said Mrs. Beeche. "Do you by any chance have an interest in opera?"

"Well, as a matter of fact, I do."

"I thought you might." She smiled. "I have a box, which I so often can't fill, and it's such a waste. I hate to say it, but at my age my cronies are not as eager — or able! — to join me as they once were. If you wouldn't mind, perhaps I'll track you down through Arthur sometime and ask if you would like to come along. You can bring your girl, or perhaps you're married?"

"Yes, yes, I am," said Peter, thinking he'd have to work out this part later. "That sounds wonderful! Of course, I'd be thrilled." Peter could not help himself. He mentioned that there was a new production of a French opera that he was eager to see.

Mrs. Beeche's eyes widened. "You are? Now, that surprises me. One doesn't usually find young people who have much interest in that kind of thing. It so happens that it's one of my favorites. It's a date. You and your bride will join me for the first night, if that suits you both. I'll put a call in to Arthur's office first thing in the morning, and you both look at your books, and we'll try to arrange it. Oh, I am so pleased!"

"But, Mrs. Beeche, I'm sure that there are others, I mean, for a premiere, you must have friends —"

"Don't give it a thought, my dear. My friends are quite familiar with my taste, and whenever I call to invite them to an evening like that, I find that they already have plans to be on another continent."

"Well, then, thank you, thank you very much! I'll look forward to it."

"Oh, what fun!"

Otis Bell had risen and was saying a few words to each of the others before leaving the table. As he approached, Peter started to stand.

"No, no, don't get up," Bell said. "A pleasure, Peter, a pleasure."

Peter stood anyway. They shook hands.

"Thank you, sir. It's been an honor, sir."

Bell tapped him on the arm. "If you find you're down in DC, give us a holler."

"Yes, sir, thank you, sir."

Before she left, Athina Kakouilli asked Peter if he knew Greek. No, he said, neither modern nor ancient. That was a shame. She had an appointment for the second semester at a local university. Would he be interested in taking some lessons from her?

Jack Thorndale told him that in a few weeks he and others would be going after late-season pheasant in North Dakota and that he should consider coming along. "Of course," Thorndale said, "you'll want to bring your heavier gun."

Lisa Eisler looked him over. "Well, Peter, I think maybe your soul can be saved. If you want to get involved somehow, call the office here." She touched his arm and kissed him on the cheek.

Mrs. Beeche stood up. Bernard, who had already risen, helped her.

"Thank you, Seth," she said. "I forgot to ask. How was the dollar today?"

"Quite strong again, Mrs. Beeche. It's opened higher in Asia, too."

"Oh, dear, and I'm short. Well, I'm not ready to fold my cards just yet. Now I must go find Arthur. Good night, Peter. I'll be coming after you, and don't think you can hide!"

"Oh no! I wouldn't want to do that! Good night, Mrs. Beeche."

They shook hands. Her palm was soft and creased.

"Oh, Seth! How is your mother?"

"She's doing better, Mrs. Beeche."

"I am glad. Please give her my love. I've been very bad and haven't written to her."

"She would like that, but please don't go to any trouble. I'll tell her that you asked after her."

"Lovely woman. Thank you. Well, good night!"

"Good night!"

"Good night!"

Mrs. Beeche turned and slowly walked off. Her thin frame wavered, yet she nevertheless achieved a stately effect.

"She's taking you to the opera?" Bernard said. "That should be fun." He thought for a moment. "The first time she took me to the opera I was seven years old. Arthur misbehaved and had to be sent home after Act I. I got to stay, although 'got to' may not be the right way to put it. But something about Mrs. Beeche always made me want her to think well of me. That's still true. She's someone whose good opinion matters to you. You'll be very lucky if you become her friend."

Then he turned to Isabella. "Isabella," he said, "I hope you don't mind if Peter and I talk about business for a moment?"

"No, of course not."

Bernard motioned for Peter to sit down and he took the chair on Peter's right.

"Now, Peter," Bernard said, "I ran into Mac McClernand a while back, and he was telling me about some project of his. I have to admit I wasn't paying too much attention. But I recall that he mentioned your name. What has he got you doing?"

Peter's entire body was trembling. So this was the end. All the good of the evening would come crashing down. Ah, well, it had been fun while it lasted. He gulped and tried to sound nonidiotic. "It's this idea of Mac's," he said. "This cereal thing —"

Bernard looked surprised and interrupted him.

"You've been working on that?" he said.

"Yes, sir."

"Really? How interesting," Bernard said, furrowing his brow. "I thought it was Paul Fry's shop. Paul Fry is quite a dum-dum, frankly. But McClernand?" He shook his head. "Well, how far along are you?"

What could Peter say? "Pretty far."

"This is something that Arthur is quite interested in. Anybody who can figure out how to do it right will certainly be noticed and rewarded. I want to set up a presentation with Arthur. He won't have an opening on his schedule for a month. I'll send you the details."

"Yes, sir. Thank you, sir."

"Very good. I think that's all I need to know for the moment. Yes, Peter, this could be a very interesting opportunity for you." Bernard smiled broadly. "And now I think it's about time you relieved Arthur of some cognac and one of his cigars."

"Yes, sir," said Peter.

"The cigars won't actually kill you, I can say that for them," Bernard said. "I, on the other hand, have a video conference in half an hour. What a wonderful world, isn't it? It'll be breakfast time for the clients. I'm going to have to change back into a suit. Maybe I should have a cup of coffee and a couple of Danishes on the table." He chuckled ruefully. "Good night, Peter. It's been a pleasure. I'll be back to you."

"Good night, Mr. Bernard. I've enjoyed it very much!"

They stood up again and shook hands. Bernard said good-bye to Isabella and moved off, and Peter sat. He found himself staring at Mars and Venus and trying to think through calmly what he had just heard. He could hardly believe his ears. Had Bernard really said that Arthur Beeche knew about and took an interest in the cereal project? That it would be a good opportunity? Yes, Bernard had said those things. So rather than a wretched, pointless suicide mission, the cereal project was a path to glory (potentially)? Peter didn't believe it was possible. But could it be that Mac McClernand was one of those eccentric geniuses who gets put in the far corner of the lab and then comes up with the revolutionary compound and that, therefore, there was at least *something* to his insane idea? Add that to his triumph with his fellow diners, and Peter found himself almost overwhelmed by self-confidence, happiness, and vitality. It had all come together, more satisfyingly than he could have dreamt. And then — he wanted to hold off thinking about it, delaying the pleasure — he was going to see Holly shortly, and "something would happen"! Yes, the moon had foretold it, something would happen.

Peter was completely absorbed in all these thoughts so it was some time before he realized that his inner left thigh felt strange. He thought about it for a moment, and then recognized the sensation of a hand stroking him there. He knew that the hand was a female one, for even through his trousers he could feel the fineness of its digits. He looked down and to the left, and then his gaze traveled from a bare wrist to a bare forearm, around a bare elbow, up a bare upper arm, over a bare shoulder, over a thin strap, up a long neck, around an ear (hung with sapphires), along a jawline, then following the undulant contours of a chin and mouth and nose until he was looking into two huge, liquid, glittering, chocolatey eyes.

"Penny for your thoughts," Isabella said in a breathy whisper.

"I . . . uh . . . I . . . that is . . . uh—"

"I'll give you mine for free." She moved her hand from Peter's thigh, put her arm around his shoulders, and pulled him toward her. She began to whisper to him, and as she did so, the tip of her tongue tickled his ear. "Peter," she said, rolling her r's and lisping slightly, "let's go somewhere and make love right now. There are so many rooms. We can find one where we will be alone. I've been going crazy all night waiting to get my hands on you and I can't stand it any longer."

Isabella had slipped the fingers of her free hand into the front of his shirt and was stroking one of his nipples through his undershirt. "If you don't take me away now," she said, "I'll start tearing off your clothes right here."

"Isabella," Peter said, "you know how much I like you, and you are extremely attractive. But what about Charlotte?"

Isabella blew out her lips dismissively. "Charlotte. I love Charlotte! What does she have to do with it? How are we hurting her? I'm here with someone, but that won't stop me. Why deny ourselves what we want?"

"Isabella, your argument is very convincing, and yes, I find you extremely attractive and I do really like you. I am incredibly flattered. But it's complicated. Charlotte isn't here, and I brought a friend, and I have to make sure she's okay."

Isabella pulled away from him and smiled conspiratorially. "Ah, I see. The friend is here. I understand."

"No, Isabella, it's not —"

Isabella furrowed her brow and pursed her lips delectably. "No, no. Of course not. It's not anything. She is a friend." She put both

her hands on top of Peter's. Then she picked up her evening bag and smiled at him, revealing teeth as even and white as tiles. "Oh, well, and it would have been so much fun."

Isabella stood up and so did Peter. She rested one wrist on his shoulder and looked to her left and right.

"Let me have one kiss," she whispered, then pulled Peter toward her. They kissed. *Well, actually, Isabella, on second thought, maybe you do have a point . . .*

"Good night, Peter."

"Good night."

Isabella gave his hand a squeeze. As she walked off, her progress was halted by a jam of people. While she waited for it to clear, Peter saw that her dress revealed all of her back; sharpness (her shoulder blades) contrasted with, or, rather, complemented softness (the curve of her waist), and her sleek, glossy black hair, tightly pinned behind her head, created an onyx oval that punctuated the whole structure. Now she was able to move on, but just before she did so she turned and smiled leeringly at Peter and gave him a little wave. He waved back.

There are times in life, all too rare, when one suddenly experiences such good fortune that one can almost fancy oneself a god. Not a top god, maybe — maybe the one who holds the portfolio for well-lit public areas rather than that for poetry or wisdom — but a god nevertheless. Taking mortal form, in the manner so beloved of the Olympians, one walks among members of humankind. This is fun. One stands apart from all the trials that man suffers, one carries none of his burdens, one occupies a realm where, indeed, death itself has no power, and, viewed from such a remove, man's doings are quite satisfying to observe, since one knows that his wretchedness will be forever foreign to one. At the same time, one looks upon the mortals with great affection. One sees their basic

goodness and courage, despite all their foibles. One views them with expansive benevolence.

It was in such a mood that, after his conversation with Isabella, Peter set off to obtain a drink and a cigar, and to find Holly. The guests were gathering in the Library and the Antelibrary, in the Blue Drawing Room, the Yellow Drawing Room and, grandest of all, the State Drawing Room. Grinning superiorly, Peter strolled toward them through the Sculpture Gallery, glancing at the marble nudes. A waiter appeared bearing a tray of glasses with brandy; Peter took one and had a gulp. The taste was delicious and the drink sent out little emissaries of warmth to his every nerve ending. Immediately thereafter, another servant proffered a box of cigars. Assuming a look of great concentration, Peter picked one, drew it under his nose, rolled it between his fingers next to his ear, and returned it to the box. He repeated this operation twice before he found a cigar that was acceptable to him. Of course, the cigars were all exactly the same as far as he could tell, but he enjoyed putting on this display, and it seemed to satisfy the expectation of the cigar bearer, who smiled broadly when Peter finally made his selection. He was a short, slight man with a dark olive complexion, and when he smiled, Peter wanted to embrace him. He wanted to reward him with untold riches for his hospitality (big test for mortals, how hospitable they are to gods in mortal guise). And that was before the man clipped the end of the cigar Peter had chosen and gave him a light. Peter drew in the smoke and let it billow in his mouth for a moment before expelling it. It tasted of the leaves' entire history, green and gold and seasoned brown.

He entered the State Drawing Room. Huge mirrors in gilded frames hung on the walls. They alternated with paintings of earlier Arthur Beeches, shown with dogs or horses, or holding a book into which they had inserted an index finger, or resting their hand on a

globe, or standing with all the members of their family and a dog or two. Peter looked at the people in the room: he was with them, but he was not of them; he was observing as if from afar; they little knew that he, Peter Russell, as he appeared, supped on ambrosia and could, if he wanted, turn any one of them into a tree. He wandered around and studied the gabbling clutches of men and women. With one hand in his pants pocket and the other holding the snifter and cigar, he swaggered. The brandy and cigar had settled him into an almost perfect equipoise of warmth, good cheer, and alertness.

How well he felt! Echoes of the meal and the wine chimed within him. He had made a great success. He had even enjoyed it. He was smoking by far the finest cigar that he had ever held. And the house was beautiful, astonishing. One's eye met a sublime object every-where one turned. Arthur was interested in the cereal thing! How amazing! What deliverance! Peter would take Holly with him to the opera in Mrs. Beeche's box. Holly would love Mrs. Beeche, and Mrs. Beeche would love Holly. Then there had been Isabella, the thought of whom made him shiver; to be desired by her was absolute proof of Peter's irresistible sexual magnetism, was it not? In all respects, what glory he had won for himself! And now, to the ultimate ascension: Holly.

An incident from a couple of years before came to Peter's mind.

~

Holly and Jonathan and Charlotte and Peter had driven together to visit a friend of Charlotte's who lived several hours north of New York. The trip, partially through a snowstorm, had been very dif-ficult. They had gotten lost and members of the group had held sharply divergent opinions as to where to lay the blame for this problem and the best way to remedy it. Likewise, when a tire went flat, those changing it, as snow fell, expressed the view that the comments being made by the others were not helpful.

When they arrived, they were frustrated, tired, cross, and very hungry. The assumption that a good dinner would be waiting for them had kept them going, but as it turned out their hosts had eaten some cheese and crackers for dinner and that was all that they could offer the travelers. At the mention of cheese and crackers, Peter had almost begun to cry. They had been brought into the dining room, and Peter could still see the friend's boyfriend, who had not greeted them or helped with their luggage, sitting at the table. He had a thin face with sunken eyes and a beard, and he wore a big, cream-colored cable-knit sweater. Cracker crumbs fanned out from his place. Charlotte's friend herself, Margo, was cylinder-shaped and wore a down vest over a couple of layers of fleece and flannel. Peter realized the place was freezing.

Oh, why had they come! Margo was an old elementary-school classmate of Charlotte's who was from a family of high rank but who had moved up here and gone native. Holding a master's in social work, she was employed by the state, for which she labored tirelessly. She had a dozen bumper stickers on her car urging care for the planet and votes for liberals. Her boyfriend, Lester, made mandolins or some such goddamned thing. Peter had noticed the various pairs of boots and bootlets and Muck shoes by the door. His feeling of loathing for this footwear was indescribable; he despised it.

The visitors said they were really starved and asked if they could make an omelette, but there were no eggs. No restaurants would be open except the fast-food places back out toward the highway. There was a supermarket open twenty-four hours a day, though, and it was decided that Holly and Peter would drive there and pick up a few things.

Peter could not have been in a fouler mood. The supermarket was a run-down place, one of the last outposts of a once great chain. Holly asked Peter to get a couple of items while she headed in another direction. Mustard? Heavy cream? What in the world? Peter asked himself. Why can't we just get hamburger meat and rolls and get out of here? He carried out his mission, and Holly sent him on another, then another. "Spinach. Frozen is okay." Finally, when Holly wanted him to look for cilantro, he could stand it no longer.

"Cilantro? Cilantro?! Jesus Christ, Holly! What are you talking about? Are you crazy? Are you actually saying that you want me to hunt around for *cilantro* in this place? Holly, this is the kind of place where the peanut butter is past its sell date! Nobody's going to find cilantro here! We might as well try to find truffles! Or eel? Yeah, I think I'll just go over to the seafood department and ask how their eel is today. Come on! I'm getting a couple of frozen pizzas and we're getting out of here."

Holly looked at him with fury. Her face was red, except where she had scrunched up her brow, making white bulges. "I bet they do have cilantro," Holly said, "because every goddamned grocery store in the country has cilantro nowadays. I was going to make a chicken thing, which is really good and takes about half an hour and that I thought would be a nice thing for me to make — me — after this goddamned trip so we would have a good meal, especially since it looks like for the rest of the weekend we won't be eating anything."

Her voice dripped with sarcasm. "But forgive me. Please forgive me for presuming that you would like to eat anything halfway decent. I do apologize. Please, you go off and buy whatever the fuck you want."

She turned and started pushing the cart away. Only a few people were in the store and they all seemed to have been watching the argument. An obese teenaged checkout clerk, with a black smudge of nascent mustache on his upper lip, stared at Holly and Peter. Peter took a couple of steps toward her, then stopped and watched her move off with an indignant stomp. Screw it, he thought, and went off to find the pizzas. When he actually saw them, though, he couldn't go through with it. They looked like props for a school play that someone had painted to look like pizza, and he knew they would taste like it too. So he skulked around until Holly appeared at the checkout. She had put her hair up in what seemed a frosty gesture, and she silently refused his offer to help with the bags. Neither said anything on the trip back.

Jonathan had brought some very good wine as a house present. When Peter and Holly returned, they found him drinking a glass of it. Red wine gave Margo a headache; Lester was a recovering alcoholic and drug addict, as he informed them all; only Charlotte had joined Jonathan, and she was nursing half a glass. Jonathan had obviously already had a glass or two. He was asking Lester about the latter's time on a shrimp boat, while Charlotte listened patiently to Margo. Margo was the kind of person who had one and only one topic of conversation, her workplace. In no time she was telling Charlotte about all her crises there and presenting them in such a way that only someone intimately familiar with the individuals involved and their duties could possibly understand what she was talking about ("So when I took over Patty's unit . . .").

"Oh, hi, you guys," Jonathan said when Holly and Peter came in the door. "How did it go? Here, let me help." He leapt up and took a couple of bags.

"It went fine," said Holly. They bustled into the kitchen, Margo following. Holly made many apologies to her for taking over her kitchen and asked if it was okay and explained that they were all just so starved they really needed a meal, and of course she and

Lester would never have expected them to be so late or, if they were to arrive so late, that they wouldn't have eaten on the road.

"That's fine," Margo said dully, turning to leave.

"Oh, Margo?" Jonathan said.

"Yes?"

"I was wondering if there was any more of that toast with cheese. It was so good."

The fluorescent kitchen light made Margo's round face shine like a waxed apple. "That was all the cheese," she said, and went on her way.

"Margo made us — well, Charlotte didn't have any — some little toast points with melted cheese," Jonathan explained. "It's too bad there's no cheese left because it was delicious. Oh, well. Now, what can I do?"

Holly set him about a task and went to work herself. Peter was leaning against the opposite counter and watched them from behind. Holly had not addressed him since she had stormed off at the store, and she did not now request his assistance. After a few moments of feeling uncomfortable, he finally said, "Well, guys . . ." and strolled out of the kitchen as casually as he could. He felt the sting of Holly's glare on the back of his neck, like a poisoned dart. Half an hour later, dinner was ready. It was very good. Peter could taste an especially delicious ingredient. Cilantro.

Later that night, when everyone was going to bed, Peter looked around for Holly. She was brushing her teeth at the sink in the bathroom the guests were sharing; the door was open.

"Oh, Holly, hi," Peter said.

"Hrgl," said Holly, still brushing.

Her hair was down and had been brushed. She wore flannel pajamas.

"Look," said Peter, "I'm really sorry I got so pissed off back there. I'm really sorry. I was so cold and tired and hungry — and so frustrated." He tilted his head and rolled his eyes to take in the whole household. "I thought we were going to get some micro-wavable cheeseburgers or something that would be ready in three minutes, so when there was a recipe involved . . . But it was really good, and you were completely right, it was much better to actually eat something."

Holly looked at Peter while he spoke but continued to brush her teeth. Peter noticed a hardness in her eyes, and he became frankly alarmed when he reached the end of his speech and saw that they had not softened whatsoever.

Holly spat. She rinsed her brush, and then used it once again. She looked at Peter with cold contempt. Again, she spat. Again, she rinsed her brush. Taking her time, she put it in a holder above the basin. She filled a cup of water, swished some water around in her mouth, spat, and repeated the sequence. Finally, she returned the cup to the shelf and patted her mouth with a face towel. She looked at Peter with those hard eyes and spoke evenly. "I think we both know that this fight wasn't really about cilantro."

Peter gulped. Uh-oh. Had he stumbled into some intense conflict with Holly? Then he intuited the truth.

"No," he said. "Uh . . . it was really about cumin?"

"Shoot!" Holly said with a laugh. "I had you going."

They stood there for moment.

"Anyway," Peter said, "I am sorry."

"Me too," said Holly.

"Well — good night."

"Good night, Peter."

They embraced. Peter held Holly with a polite tentativeness that he believed was suitable given her state of dishabille. Holly kissed him on the cheek.

~

The image from that night that came to Peter now was Holly's face when she had finally smiled at him. She had had a little crescent of toothpaste under her lip. She had left some of it on his cheek when she kissed him, and later he had had to wipe it off. He couldn't say that he had enjoyed it when Holly was yelling at him in the store, but, at the same time, he wasn't completely averse to repeating the experience. Charlotte had never yelled at him; she had sulked, or become arch. Being married to Holly and having a life in which every so often they had a huge fight about some ridiculously trivial matter, this appealed to Peter. It meant that their lives really would be mixed up together; he liked the domesticity and married-ness of it. What better proof could there be that he really loved Holly?

That ultimately was where his thoughts led him: to the fact that he loved Holly, really, actually did love her. It wasn't only that he was *in* love with her. He couldn't put "in love" and "love" in separate categories, for the sexual, romantic, and affective aspects of his feelings for her all partook of and reinforced one another in an incomprehensibly multifarious way as part of one organic system, but he loved her. He *really* loved her. No matter what happened, what he really cared about was her happiness. He knew this. He loved her.

Peter had a very clear idea of what would happen when they returned to her aunt's apartment — up to a certain point. Watching her from behind as they entered; tossing aside his coat; making a drink; settling on the soft sofa of her aunt's cushioned, pillowy library; talking about the party. What a spectacular house! Holly would say. Did you see the paintings in the Music Room! Then the moment when they would fall silent, and Peter would stare at his drink, feeling Holly's tender, expectant gaze on his profile. She would have taken off her shoes and her legs would be curled up under her. What's up? she would ask.

Then he would tell her what had happened with Charlotte. He would speak of it with the underlying tone of seriousness that one ought to use in a case like this, out of respect for the emotions, persons, and customs involved. Holly would think him heartless if he appeared to view Charlotte's departure with no sense of loss. But he would also add touches of self-deprecating humor. Then, bringing Holly down with him into a deeper zone of intimacy, Peter would confide that while there was of course a feeling of sorrow, he had to acknowledge, as hard as it was to admit, that the marriage had been a mistake and that he didn't doubt that Charlotte would be happier. Good for her, in fact, for having the courage finally to join the man of her dreams. A soft laugh. True, not necessarily the man of everyone's dreams . . .

Yes, Holly would say, almost to herself, good for her.

Then there would be a pause. Peter would look into Holly's eyes. He would take her hand. "Holly," he would say, "there's something else . . ."

From this point, Peter couldn't predict how things would go. He knew what he hoped for: Holly would cry and embrace him. "Oh, Peter, I love you, too!" For a long time they would kiss, pet, and caress each other, murmuring the sweetest endearments. Peter happened to know that a collection of ballads recorded in the fifties, Lee Wiley's *Night in Manhattan* with Joe Bushkin, was in the CD player, and they would listen to it over and over, set on repeat.

Would this happen? Yes, Peter thought now, yes it would. In his current mood, he was sure that this ultimate triumph awaited him. He had never before allowed himself to be so certain of it. He closed his eyes and imagined her lips on his, her hand stroking his hair. His heart was pounding as hard as a blacksmith hammering on an anvil. He had to find her and bring her home.

Peter first sought Holly in the State Drawing Room, but she wasn't there. She wasn't in the Yellow or Blue Drawing Room either. A smattering of people were lounging around the Library; some were playing cards. But there was no Holly. Peter found three men in the Antelibrary who were huddled together whispering. When Peter entered, they looked at him and scowled. Now, this was strange: Holly should have been in one of these rooms. Peter returned to the State Drawing Room. It had thinned out a bit as people had begun to go home. He walked around twice. No Holly. He rechecked the other drawing rooms without success. When he returned to the Library the group was smaller, and as for the Antelibrary, the three men had vanished.

Peter was at a loss. It was inconceivable that Holly had left. There simply had to be some out-of-the-way place that he hadn't found, where she had become engrossed in a conversation. He shed his brandy and cigar as he set out on a more intensive search. The Orangery? He hadn't been there, but it was completely empty when he arrived. The Music Room? Empty. Likewise the West Hall. In the Studiolo, a man and woman were admiring the fantastic trompe l'oeil marquetry representing books and musical instruments on shelves; but the woman was not Holly. He returned to the Sculpture Gallery. No one. Then Peter thought he heard voices. He stopped to listen. While the words were indistinct, it seemed to be a man and a woman. There was laughter. The sound bounced around, making it difficult to figure out where it was coming from, but as best Peter could tell it originated from somewhere farther along in the direction he was headed. The room where Peter had eaten dinner was on the far side of the Sculpture Gallery, and the other room, the feminine one, was beyond that. Peter walked through the gallery and came to the first room. White tableclothes still covered the tables, but they had been cleared of everything but their flowers. He could hear a man's voice easily now. It was coming from the farther room. Weaving between tables, Peter headed toward it. Before reaching the door, he stopped. He heard a woman's laughter. Peter walked a little ways and then passed through the doorway to the other room, the one with the panels depicting amorous children of the ancien régime. He had taken only one step inside when he came to a sudden halt. To his left, catty-corner from him, at a table about forty feet away, seated side by side, in chairs facing out, leaning their heads close together, speaking in a very confidential fashion, then breaking apart in laughter, were a man and a woman. The woman was Holly. The man was Arthur Beeche. Peter saw flowers and two champagne glasses on the table. Nearby, a stand held an ice bucket. A bottle protruded from the bucket with its neck covered in gold foil, like an Egyptian queen's necklace.

As Peter took in this sight, all the blood in his head and body seemed to rush to his feet, as if someone had pulled a plug. His stomach seemed to fall several stories, as if someone had opened a trapdoor beneath it. It is interesting how powerful the effect of an entire gestalt can be even when its discrete elements, in and of themselves, are of little importance. No doubt early man, in adapting to life on the savanna of southeastern Africa, developed the skill of meshing the information he received from his different senses and then comparing the result with similar combinations stored in memory. A movement in the grass, the cry of a bird. But like so many of our mental adaptations to our original environment, this one could produce the effect of instinct overruling reason, and, as a result of our primitive fears, we can draw unwarranted conclusions. For, taken individually, what would each datum confronting Peter really signify? There was a man. There was a woman. There was a table. There were flowers. There were glasses of champagne. There was a bottle of champagne. The man and woman were inclining their heads so close to each other that they almost touched. Why, without knowing more, one could interpret these details in a thousand different ways!

Holly saw him. She turned to Arthur and said something, and then Arthur also looked over at Peter, smiling broadly. Holly smiled broadly, too. "Peter!" she called. In a gesture worthy of a ballerina known especially for her graceful arms, she raised her hand to beckon him. "Peter!"

"Hello!" Peter cried with a wave and a smile.

Locking his eyes on the pair and maintaining his smile as if rigor mortis had set in, Peter barely avoided walking into tables and tripping on chairs as he approached his destination. Arriving there, he found an Arthur and a Holly who slid their eyes over to look at each other even as they greeted him.

Arthur rose; he had a powerful presence, and his movement created a heavy wake in the ether. "So! This is our Mr. Russell!" he said cheerily, holding out his hand.

"Hello!" said Peter. He and Arthur shook hands vigorously. Arthur had a big, powerful hand.

"Hi, Peter," said Holly.

"Holly! Hello!" said Peter.

"Please, sit down," Arthur said. "Join us. Would you like a glass of champagne?"

Peter looked at their half-full glasses. The idea of drinking champagne on top of the cognac and the cigar was disgusting. "Thank you!" he said. "Yes, that would be lovely." Lovely? Lovely? Where in God's name had that word come from?

Peter sat. A servant appeared with a glass and poured champagne for him. He drank some down and almost retched.

"Well, well," said Arthur. "I've been neglecting my duties. Haven't made my rounds. So I'm glad that we have a chance to meet."

"Yes, sir."

"You know, Holly, your friend here probably doesn't talk to you about reinsurance very often."

"No," Holly said, laughing, "not really."

"Well, he did a fine job, a fine job on a deal that was in trouble."

"Thank you, sir."

"And just now, Seth Bernard came by and met Holly and we mentioned you, and he told me that you're working on something that we take quite an interest in."

"I . . . yes, sir. That's what he told me."

"Well, that's fine, fine. I look forward to hearing more about it. But we are committing a terrible sin, talking like this. It must be very boring for Holly."

They looked over at her. Peter saw that she was beaming at him. He was making a good impression with the boss! Out of the corner of his eye, Peter could see Beeche studying Holly closely.

They chatted for a bit about nothing consequential. Peter could hardly manage to say more than three words in a row. He noticed that whenever either Arthur or Holly spoke to him, the other one did not look at him but at the speaker. Meanwhile, whenever Peter was speaking, their eyes tended to drift away from him and toward each other. They were like two people sharing a private joke.

After a few minutes, they heard a voice calling from behind them.

"Arthur, my dear!"

They turned and saw Mrs. Beeche approaching.

"Arthur, my dear," she said again. "Here you are! I've looked all over for you." Arthur, Peter, and Holly all stood up. "Oh, please, don't get up," she said.

"I'm so sorry, Mother. I was . . . detained here at my table." He made the slightest nod toward Holly.

"Oh, I see," said Mrs. Beeche.

"Mother, I'd like to introduce you to Holly Speedwell."

"How do you do?" said Holly.

"Very well, thank you," said Mrs. Beeche. "How very nice to see you." As she looked at Holly, Mrs. Beeche's face had the expression of someone who has been dragged around to dozens of houses by a Realtor and then walks into one that she instantly knows is perfect.

"And, Mother, this is Mr. Russell."

"Oh," said Mrs. Beeche, "I know Peter. Peter and I are old friends, aren't we?"

"Yes, Mrs. Beeche," Peter said. "Nice to see you again."

"We were at the same table," Mrs. Beeche explained.

"I see," said Arthur. "Well, Peter brought Holly to the dinner tonight. Unfortunately, Mrs. Russell was unable to come."

"That is unfortunate," Mrs. Beeche said. "She wasn't taken ill, I hope?"

"Oh no," said Peter. "At the last minute, she was called out of the country. My parents always told me that death is the only proper excuse for missing a dinner party you have accepted, but this was something of a crisis."

"Of course, I understand," said Arthur. "I certainly hope that I do meet her someday."

"You would like Charlotte," said Holly.

"I'm sure I would," Arthur said.

"Yes," said Mrs. Beeche, "I look forward to seeing her on our opera date."

Peter nodded politely.

"You and Peter are going to the opera?" Arthur asked.

"Yes, Arthur," said Mrs. Beeche. "It will be a pleasure to be with a young person who appreciates what he's hearing rather than one who fidgets the whole time and reminds everyone over and over that in Russian novels, when people go to the opera, they stay for only one act."

"Mother and I," Arthur said to Holly and Peter, "have different tastes in these things."

"It isn't a matter of different tastes," Mrs. Beeche corrected him. "It's a matter of having taste or having none."

"Mother," said Arthur with mock gravity, "let's not have a family argument in front of our guests."

"No, of course not," Mrs. Beeche said. She bowed her head slightly to Holly and Peter. "Forgive me.

"Well, Arthur," she continued, "I wanted to say good night. I had a wonderful time. You know how much I always enjoy talking to these bright people. And tonight I sat next to Seth, and that is always a treat. But, Arthur, he seemed to be a little thin. Is there anything wrong?"

"Not at all, Mother," said Arthur. "I imagine he's on a diet. He usually is."

"He is such a dear person. I suppose he's worried about his mother. Terrible." Her eyes cast down, Mrs. Beeche shook her head and remained silent a moment. Then she looked up and said brightly, "Well, I shall wish you all a good night. Good night, Peter. We will check our calendars, won't we?" Then she turned to Holly. "Good night. Any friend of Peter's is a friend of mine."

"Good night!" Holly said.

Here Mrs. Beeche took the briefest pause and tilted her head one degree more toward Holly. "You must call on me sometime, too, my dear." She said this in an offhand way, with a simple, friendly smile, but also with purpose and deadly aim.

She took both of Arthur's hands in hers and held her cheek out for a kiss. "Good night, darling," she said. "Do get some sleep, will you?"

"Yes, Mother. Good night."

"Oh, and Arthur, you might want to check Roger's book. Just a notion I have from what I've picked up. Your father . . . well, but times change."

"Thanks, Mother. I'll do that."

"Good night, all!" Mrs. Beeche said.

She toddled away and the others watched her.

"Arthur, I'm so glad to have had a chance to meet your mother," Holly said. "She seems wonderful."

"Yes," said Peter. "I enjoyed being at her table very much."

"Thank you," Arthur said. "I'm pretty fond of her myself."

Thoughts of Mrs. Beeche hung in the air for a moment.

Then Holly spoke. "Well, now," she asked, "what time is it?"

Peter told her.

"Oh no!" Holly said. "I had no idea it was so late! Poor Peter! I'm sure you were coming to fetch me! We really ought to be going."

"Not at all!" said Arthur. "The night is still young."

"You're very kind, but really, it's time we were off. Don't you think, Peter?"

"If that's what you'd like, Holly."

"Very well," Arthur said. "If you insist. I'll see you out." He spread his arms, inviting them to walk ahead of him. "Do you need a car?" he asked.

"No, thank you," said Holly. "We came in one. Peter told the driver to wait."

"I see," said Arthur. "That's fine, that's fine. If for any reason there is a problem, please just let me know. I'll have someone take you."

"That's so nice of you, Arthur," said Holly. "Thank you!"

"Yes, thank you," Peter said as brightly as he could.

"But," Holly continued, "I'm sure that won't be necessary."

During the next few minutes, as they walked toward the entrance hall, Holly and Arthur talked about a couple of people at their table; Holly asked Arthur about the predella she and Peter had admired earlier, and he said that it was funny she should have noticed it because it had always been one of his favorite pieces. Peter watched the other two; he smiled; he nodded; and by his general demeanor he tried to act as if he were actually a participant in the conversation. In the entrance hall, other departing guests approached Arthur to say good-bye. Servants appeared with Holly's and Peter's overcoats. Other servants held open the doors, and Arthur accompanied Holly and Peter outside. Arthur and Holly stood on the landing of the flight of steps down to the sidewalk; Peter stood one step below them. The night had become gusty; coats flapped and women put a hand to their hair. Gunning their engines loudly, limousines and black sedans pulled away from the front of Beeche's house, and others replaced them. Their doors opened and shut, drivers called to their passengers and vice versa; guests called and waved good-bye to Arthur; other guests rushed up the steps to retrieve a thing or person that had been forgotten; while still others rushed down to meet those they had kept waiting. Cars on the avenue raced by.

Arthur held out his hand to Peter. "Good night, Peter. We must have you around again sometime. Can't let Mother keep you to herself!"

"It was a terrific dinner, Mr. Beeche. Thanks very much."

"Arthur!" Arthur said.

"Arthur. Thank you."

Arthur now turned to Holly. They looked at each other bashfully. There was a pause before either spoke.

"Good night, Holly," Arthur said. "It's been a pleasure. It's too bad Mrs. Russell couldn't come, but if Peter had to bring a substitute, he did very well in making his choice, in my opinion."

"I had a wonderful time," said Holly. "Thank you. It was so much fun, and the food was so delicious. Everything was perfect. I'm glad, too, that Peter needed someone to fill in."

"Well, good night," said Arthur.

"Good night."

They shook hands and then stuttered with their bodies for a moment before awkwardly giving each other a kiss on the cheek. Having retreated from this, they continued to hold hands and fleetingly looked into each other's eyes. Finally, they released their hands, and Holly stepped down to join Peter.

"Good night!" Arthur called.

"Good night!"

"Thank you!"

As they walked down the steps, Peter looked over at Holly, about to say something, but he could see that she was smiling, that her eyes were bright, and that her mind was dwelling somewhere pleasant. Peter chose not to break this spell. They reached the sidewalk and Peter muttered that he would look for the driver. He took some steps this way and that, surveying, and then returned to her.

"I don't see him," he said. "He's probably waiting around the corner. I'll go check."

On his way, Peter walked by several drivers, some in their cars, some standing. Every morphological type, and every shade of complexion from jet black to paste, was represented. But he did not see his driver even though the lane in front of the house was not too crowded at this point, so he could have brought the car around. Peter turned the corner and was disheartened, but not altogether surprised, to see not a single black sedan parked along the side street. It was a very fine street, lined with handsome town houses; the orange light from the streetlamps reflected off the ironwork and the asphalt, which had that dark, soft look indicating that it was new. Despite these virtues, the street nevertheless lacked one thing: an idling black sedan.

Peter shut his eyes, took a deep breath, and let it out. He would look again in front of the house; he would even go around the other corner (pointless, since the one-way side street ran in the wrong direction). He walked back as he had come; the cars were fewer now. The last guests were leaving. Holly stood there hugging herself against the chill of the wind.

When Peter reached her, he said, "Oh, Holly, he wasn't there!"

"I'm sorry — what?" Holly answered.

"The driver wasn't there. Waiting around the corner. He wasn't there."

"Oh no!" said Holly. "You're kidding!"

"He hasn't shown up out front here, either. I'll check the other side street, just in case."

"Okay."

He walked to the other corner and saw a street as handsome as the other; this one featured a fine row of four Georgian houses built by a developer in 1886. But no idling black sedan.

Turning and retracing his steps, Peter had half a block during which to observe Holly as the wind whipped around her and she retrieved and attempted to secure the locks of hair that it set flying. She was completely alone now. A servant tripped down the steps and spoke to her. She shook her head and pointed to Peter. With a little bow the servant withdrew.

"Well," Peter said, opening his arms and shrugging, "I can't find him. He must have gone cruising for fares and hasn't made it back."

"How irritating!" Holly's tone betrayed no irritation whatsoever, and she had obviously said this for Peter's benefit. As she knew, men set great store by showing mastery over drivers, train conductors, airline-ticket-counter attendants, and other such-like transport personnel, and so, since the driver's treachery surely distressed Peter, she wanted to show that she took it as seriously as he did.

"What should we do?" she cried plaintively.

Peter steeled himself and then asked as matter-of-factly as he could, "Would you like me to ask Beeche if we could take him up on his offer?"

"No!" said Holly, laughing. "Of course not."

"Well, then," said Peter, "I guess we'll just have to find a cab."

Peter said this in the manner of a cowboy telling the womenfolk that, because of the avalanche, they were going to have to take the pass through Indian country. In fact, as Holly and Peter both knew, nothing could have been easier than finding a free cab, for at this hour they flowed steadily down the avenue. But if Peter were to regain some face by wrangling one, the fiction had to be kept up that this would be a challenging task.

"Will you try?" Holly asked.

"Sure," said Peter. He stepped off the curb, raised his hand, and a taxi pulled up in front of them about five seconds later.

"Thank goodness!" Holly said.

Peter opened the passenger door.

"Now, let's see," said Holly. "How should we do this?"

"I'll take you home," said Peter.

"Oh, Peter, that's so sweet of you," Holly said, "but it's really not necessary. I live twice as far away as you! Here, we'll both go uptown, and then —"

"No," said Peter. "That means you have to backtrack to get across the park. I'll take you home."

"But, Peter! That's just silly. Really. I'm sure the night has already been long enough for you."

"No, I insist." Peter had an edge in his voice. "Come on, now, get in and I'll see you get back safely, like a proper escort."

Holly put her hand on Peter's forearm and kissed him on the cheek.

"Oh, Peter. You're sweet. I really can't let you go to all that trouble."

The driver, a chubby man with a complexion the color of wet sand, listened to this conversation through his open window. He sat impassively, as one who, possessing the wisdom of eternity, never suffered impatience, and who also knew that this was a fare and he could cruise for another twenty minutes without finding another one.

"No!" Peter cried. "Holly —"

Peter stopped himself and looked at Holly's face. He read there that the "ball" had indeed transported her; she had been lifted up to a higher plane of feeling and being; all her senses were atingle. It was a brilliant plan, and it had worked perfectly! The only problem was that, having drunk the magic potion, Holly had opened her eyes and seen the wrong man. Given Holly's current state, Peter realized, it would be not only pointless but perhaps even a bit counterproductive to force upon her the talk that he had proposed earlier and that clearly was now the furthest thing from her mind. He smiled at her affectionately.

"Okay," he said. "All right. I'll let you go on by yourself. But you go straight home, now. No stopping off anyplace where you could get into trouble. "

"I promise," Holly said. "Can't I drop you?"

"Oh, no, that makes no sense. Anyway, I think I might just walk home."

"Sure?"

Peter nodded.

"Okay, then." Holly gave him a hug and kissed him again on the cheek. "Thank you so much, Peter. I did have a wonderful time. What a place."

"It's pretty incredible, isn't it?" Peter said.

"And he's a nice guy."

"Yes."

"Well, good night!" Holly got into the cab and Peter closed the door behind her. He saw her lean forward to speak to the driver, placing a hand on her sternum. Loose hair floated around her as if she were underwater. She sat back; the driver shifted, and then, with a lurch, took off at high speed.

Peter now stood by himself on the sidewalk. There were no other pedestrians. The wind shook the trees and rattled a parking sign and rolled a plastic bag down the road like tumbleweed. Shut up tight, the doors to Beeche's house looked as if they never had been nor ever could be opened. The windows were as dark as ink pads. Peter remembered that when he had seen Holly standing at this spot a few hours earlier, she had been gazing at the sky. He looked up over the park and saw a featureless black expanse, without even the fuzzy orange tinge that the streetlights produced elsewhere. The moon had set. Peter hiked up his shoulders and pulled his coat tighter, and began his walk home.

11

As soon as he arrived at the office the next day, Peter received a call from Mac McClernand. When Peter told him about his encounter with Seth Bernard and that, after hearing what Peter was working on, Bernard had said that he wanted to set up a presentation with Arthur Beeche, McClernand remained silent for several moments, then whimpered, then exclaimed, "Straight to Arthur Beeche! You see, didn't I tell you to do some selling? Didn't I tell you to let him bring it up? But, my God, Pete, I knew you were good, but not that good!" Peter said he couldn't understand how Bernard knew all about their project, and Mc-Clernand responded patronizingly to his evident naïveté. "Peter, Peter," he said. "Do you think that anything goes on around here that Beeche and Bernard don't know about? And when they get a line on something terrific, they hustle. It's that kind of thing that has kept Beeche so agile even as it has grown." McClernand then launched into an increasingly hysterical recitation of all the tasks they had to complete before their presentation. "We have to be ready for anything they throw at us: what about the trade-in credit card points?"

All morning Peter kept staring at his phone, trying to will a call from Holly. Why, he didn't exactly know. He couldn't imagine what she might say that would please him, except possibly that Arthur Beeche had called her at four a.m. completely drunk and made several obscene suggestions. He guessed that he just wanted some indication that she still knew he was alive.

She did call eventually, but not when Peter was in his office. She left this message: "Hi, Peter, it's Holly. I know you're really busy, but I was hoping I'd get you. I have to take off in a minute. I had such a great time last night. Thank you so much for taking me. I'd love to go over the whole thing with you. That house! Incredible. And it really is so beautifully put together — you don't just feel pounded by collector mojo, do you know what I mean? Oh, and my table was so much fun. The princess speaks English as if she's lived in Naples her entire life, and Gerald Hoffheimer and I had a funny conversation about Epode VIII.

"So here is something sort of funny, and it's why I have to leave pretty soon. Your boss has asked me to go away for the weekend. It turns out that I am able to get away, so I said yes. He's taking a bunch of people — well, I'm still not sure where exactly. It involves a helicopter ride, and I am in a panic, because I have no idea what one wears on a helicopter. Anyway — um — that's what's happening. It should be interesting.

"But also — I remembered that you wanted to talk to me about something, which I got the feeling was important. I'm so sorry! I forgot all about it last night. You can actually call me on my cell if you want. It works basically anywhere in the world.

"Okay! I'm really sorry I missed you! Call me. Bye!"

Pistol? Razor blade? Poison? Barbiturates? Jumping off a building? Peter weighed each of these options. They all had something to be said for them.

Listening to the message that followed Holly's, Peter was startled to hear a cool, clear, low voice. Miss Harrison's.

"Mr. Russell, this is Miss Harrison in Arthur Beeche's office. Would you be kind enough to phone me as soon as possible? Mr. Beeche would like to see you right away. He is leaving shortly. It is nine forty-eight. Thank you very much."

Miss Harrison was informing him that Arthur Beeche wanted to see him. Most employees of Beeche would go through their entire careers without anything like that ever happening. However, under the circumstances, Peter could feel little pride. He doubted that Beeche was calling him in to inquire about his views on the structural imbalances in the economy. By reflecting on the call for even a few seconds, Peter had already let too much time go before returning it, for of course his response to such a message from such a source should have been instantaneous. He called Miss Harrison's extension and reached a secretary, who immediately put him through.

"Hello, Mr. Russell. Thank you for calling back."

"Of course," Peter said.

"Fortunately, we still have some time. May I trouble you to come to the sixty-third floor? You'll have to use the south elevators. I'll meet you there and take you up to Mr. Beeche's office."

"Yes, of course. I'll leave right now."

"We'll see you in few minutes then. Thank you so much."

"Thank *you*, Miss Harrison," Peter said, inanely.

Stepping out of the elevator on the sixty-third floor, Peter was greeted by a woman who seemed to be in her late thirties. She wore a gray skirt that ended just above the knee, a cream-colored silk blouse, and pearls. She was flawlessly groomed, but in such a way as to make this condition seem perfectly natural rather than effortfully wrought. Smooth, straight, and full, her dark hair fell to her shoulders. Miss Harrison had such regular features that her face would have almost been dull had it not been animated by her purposefulness and intelligence.

"Hello, Mr. Russell. I'm Miss Harrison." In her speech, she rounded off every sound, producing no harsh notes or reverberations; it reminded Peter of the sound made by a rap on a hollow wooden box.

"Hello, Miss Harrison," said Peter. "Very nice to see you."

"We go this way."

She led Peter over to an elevator in the corner, whose doors were already open. This must be the elevator, Peter thought, that goes straight from the ground floor up to seventy-seven, where Arthur had his office. Miss Harrison put a card in a slot, and they began to move. The elevator had elaborate wood paneling and the fittings — the little lamp over the buttons, the ceiling light, the grilles — were all in brass and seemed not to belong in an elevator, but Peter could not identify their likely origin. Miss Harrison noticed his perplexity.

"This was all taken from one of the Beeches' old private railcars. They don't get much use now, but Mr. Beeche remembered them from his childhood, and when the new building went up, it occurred to him that he could use some elements here."

The doors of the elevator opened directly onto a large room with an enormous floral rug. Two women sat at desks on one side, a woman and a man sat at desks on the other. They murmured into the mouthpieces of their headsets. Miss Harrison nodded as she passed by, executing a more pointed tilt to one of the women, who nodded back crisply and pushed a button. Miss Harrison opened one of a pair of double doors, and they entered a room that had been decorated as if by an extremely rich person who has sought an "informal" look for his or her apartment — American antiques and furniture covered in fantastically expensive chintzes and plaids.

Not a single thread of upholstery showed any sign that a person had ever sat on or against it.

They came to a door on the far side of this room. Miss Harrison knocked.

"Come," they heard Arthur say.

They entered and took a few steps. Miss Harrison stopped and raised her hand slightly to indicate that Peter should also stop and remain silent.

Beeche sat at a large desk at the far end of the room. Behind him, Peter saw only blue sky and a shallow, streaky cloud. His desk held no computer screen. No papers sat on it, only a lamp, a telephone, and a small picture frame. Highly polished and reflecting the sky behind it, the desk looked like a lake on a windless day. With his chair pushed a couple of feet back, Beeche sat staring straight ahead. His hands lay folded in his lap. His face and body were impassive, an immobile yet vital mass.

Miss Harrison and Peter stood by for a full minute. Finally, Beeche said in a matter-of-fact tone, "Please tell them, 'No, thank you.' Of course, you'll want to call them motherfucking cocksuckers and say they can go fuck themselves and so on."

"Got it," said a voice.

"They'll be back," Beeche said.

"Okay, chief."

For a moment Beeche stayed in the same attitude. Then he broke out of it. "Sorry about that, you two!" he called. "Was just finishing up." Beeche rose out of his chair and came around his desk with his hand out, a hand that looked like a two-by-six.

"Hello, Mr. Beeche," Peter said.

"Arthur!"

"Arthur."

They shook hands and Beeche put his left hand on Peter's shoulder.

"Have you ever been up here to our . . . ah . . . aerie before?"

This was one of those questions that people like Arthur always asked. Of course Peter had never been there before.

"No, I haven't," Peter said.

"Then I would love to show you around," said Beeche. "There are some things that would interest you. In the gallery, next door, we've just installed the Beeche Venus. Do you follow Upper Paleolithic art at all?"

"No, I'm afraid I don't."

"Oh, you should! It's fascinating. The Venus is extraordinary. There are also some English drawings I'd like you to see." Arthur frowned. "The thing of it is, I'm in an awful rush. We'll plan a tour for another day, when we can spend some time."

"Certainly. I'll look forward to it."

Arthur guided Peter to a chair.

"Please, have a seat," he said. Peter sat, and Arthur settled himself at the end of a sofa. Miss Harrison had dematerialized, and now a wizened old woman in a maid's uniform appeared with a coffee service.

"Hello, Noreen," Arthur said. "Perfect timing, as usual."

"Thems as don't order their coffee but a minute before they be wanting it dunna deserve perfect timing, as ye call it." Noreen spoke with a thick Irish accent. She set the tray down. "What will ye take, young man?"

"Cream and sugar, please," Peter said.

" 'Cream,' he says! It's milk."

"Milk. Of course, thank you."

Noreen took an interminably long time to prepare Peter's cup.

"One teaspoon of sugar, please."

She dumped in several heaps. Then she hobbled over to Peter and gave his cup to him.

"Thank you."

"Hmp."

"No sugar for me, thank you, Noreen."

"Amn't I been giving you coffee every day now these thirty years? 'No sugar'!" She brusquely handed Beeche a cup with coffee and milk, and then said, "Them scones is for ye." She waved her hand at a plate on the tray. "Now if that will be all, gentlemen, I shall take me leave." She hobbled away.

As soon as she was gone, Arthur leaned over and gave himself one spoonful of sugar. "Sorry, old man, should have warned you." Arthur took a sip of his coffee, making a faint, aspirated sound of satisfaction after swallowing.

"Well, Peter," he said. "The reason I asked you to come by, and thank you very much for doing so, by the way —"

"Not at all."

Arthur smiled. "Well, you see," he said, "it's a personal matter, really. Your friend Holly, I enjoyed talking to her at dinner very much, she's charming, and I thought, well, you see, I'm having some friends to visit for the weekend, and — it was a-spur-of-the-moment idea — I thought I'd invite her along. And she agreed. So that's very nice." He took another sip of coffee. The delicate cup and saucer looked incongruous in such a large hand; he looked as if he could crush them. He looked, frankly, as if he could crush Peter, too. His personal manner was not menacing, not at all, but on account of his size, virility, kingly ease, and position in the world, he sent out waves of power that buffeted Peter, practically knocking him out of his seat. But it was all effortless; Arthur was not trying to be domineering any more than would a lion in repose.

"So, then, it occurred to me that I really don't know Holly very well and that it might make sense to find out a little more about her. And I thought you might help me in this regard, if you didn't mind?" He smiled at Peter, but didn't wait for a response. "You see, I have developed a . . . a . . . fondness for Holly, and I want the weekend to go well. I think it would be awfully helpful if I knew her likes and dislikes, what her favorite books are, for example, her favorite movies. You see, dammit, I haven't been to a movie in fifteen years. Does she have any particular interests? Does she shoot?" Arthur's expression became dreamy. "I'd like to know everything about her . . . all her joys and sorrows . . ." He stared off for a moment, then recollected himself and looked back at Peter with embarrassment.

"Well, old man, that's where you come in. How about it? Do you think you could help?"

Peter put on the calmest and most obliging expression he could manage, but inside, all was turmoil. Of course, he said to himself, of course I am up here on the seventy-seventh floor of the Beeche Building in Arthur Beeche's office talking to Arthur Beeche about a woman. And, of course, that woman would be Holly. Sure. Nothing more natural. It gave him vertigo. Then there was the question of what he should do. If Arthur Beeche thought that Peter was going to give him the keys to Holly's heart, he had another thing coming. But Arthur Beeche wasn't someone whose request you could simply refuse. The seconds ticked away as Arthur leaned toward Peter expectantly, emitting his great potent blasts.

Peter tried to think of his options. It was tempting to send Arthur down the completely wrong path: "Make sure that when you're with other people you comment on her tits. 'Hey, everybody, check out Holly. What a rack!' She loves that kind of bawdiness!" A little too obvious. Then Peter had an idea, a way he could give

Arthur some serious advice without telling him anything at all. If only he would fall for it.

"Well, Arthur, I certainly understand the position you're in. And, of course, I will help you, but not in exactly the way you have asked."

Arthur's expression darkened. "All right," he said. "Go on."

Still trying to maintain his air of calm, Peter took a sip of coffee, savoring it. Then he settled himself in his seat and cleared his throat. "Yes, Arthur," he said, "it's true. I could tell you a great deal about Holly. I could inform you on all the matters you have raised. I could tell you whether she likes to dance, if she prefers tennis to golf, what she eats for breakfast, how many pillows she sleeps with, and who among her father, mother, and sister is at any particular moment driving her most crazy. I could tell you what disappoints her in a friend and I could tell you how many subway fares she buys at a time."

"If you spend enough," Arthur said, "the discount can amount to something. The weekly card isn't a good value in comparison, I don't believe."

"I agree," said Peter. "But now, Arthur, what if I did tell you who Holly's favorite writer is? What would you do? Arrange for her to 'discover' you while reading one of his or her books? Or maybe you would have someone buy a complete set of first editions and install them in the library before she arrives. Do you think that, unless you really did know and love that writer, you would last thirty seconds in a conversation with Holly before she would know you were faking it? Then where you would be?

"Alternatively, think about what it would be like to let her teach you about some book she loves. Wonder, discovery. The point is, part of the fun is learning things about each other, finding the places where you share a border and the others where you are separated by a sea. If you force that process, it'll never come out right.

You can't climb a mountain with someone if you start three hundred feet above her. You can't enjoy a meal together if you are eating cheese and she's still having soup. You'll never learn the material if you get the test answers ahead of time."

Arthur furrowed his brow and pursed his lips and thought for a moment. "There may be something in what you say." He thought a moment longer, and his expression brightened. "Yes," he said, nodding, "I think you well may be right. I think that is the right approach."

Peter decided to go for broke. "Arthur," he said, "if I had only one piece of advice for you, it would be this: just be yourself."

Arthur looked off and took this in, murmuring "Be yourself, be yourself . . ." Then he turned back to Peter. "Thank you, Peter," he said. "You're right. It wasn't exactly what I was expecting, but it's usually the unexpected answer to a question that is the most helpful. Thank you very much."

Peter smiled back at him seraphically. "Not at all," he said.

~

On Monday morning Peter got a call from Holly. He asked her how the weekend was, and she told him that she had had an enjoyable time. They had gone to an island in the St. Lawrence Seaway that the Beeches owned and where, a hundred years ago, they had built an enormous camp. It was cold but very beautiful at this time of year, and there were huge roaring fireplaces and delicious food — roast capons and pies. There had been eight other guests. A mix — professor, socialite, old school chum.

"But, Peter," Holly said. "The real reason I'm calling is to ask you what you wanted to talk about. What's going on?"

So Peter told her all about Charlotte.

"Oh, Peter!" Holly said. "I'm so sorry! If I'd known that's what you were going through, I never would have gone away! How are you doing?"

Peter told her that he was doing fine, really. In fact, he admired Charlotte for taking such risks, offending her family and giving up her nice, unexceptional life, to go after the man of her dreams. Admittedly — ha-ha-ha — not the man of everyone's dreams. It was courageous. They would have been decently happy, he said, but he and Charlotte had never really been right for each other. They spent a while discussing various aspects of the situation — what a drag to have to tell people and put up with their nosy sympathy — with Holly saying again and again that he should please ask her if there was anything she could do. Peter imagined the pitying expression she must have been wearing as she said this, and how beautiful she must have looked, her jade eyes glistening behind tears.

"Well, Peter, I am sad," she said. "You may be right. It really may be for the best. But when people who were together aren't anymore, it's sad." She was quiet for a moment and then laughed. "But you're taking it so well, I don't want to bum you out!"

"No," Peter said, "it is sad. A lot of emotion and commitment, and it didn't work out, and maybe Charlotte has missed ten years of being happy. But all's well that ends well."

"Yes."

"Or at least, all's well that ends."

Holly laughed mirthlessly. "Yeah," she agreed, "for most things in life, that's probably true."

They talked a bit more, and then Holly said, "Well, here's something that's good news. You've really impressed your boss."

"What do you mean?"

"He told me about the conversation you and he had on Friday before the trip. You know, he was really very nervous. 'Be yourself'!

I laughed out loud when I heard that, and it embarrassed him. Apparently, no one had ever told him that before. But, you know, it really is true, and he didn't try to put on anything, and I'm sure he would never have been as likable if he had. And, yes, it was fun to discover things about each other, just as you'd said! Do you know that the first time he invited his wife out, he took her to an auction of early firearms, a very important auction. It turned that she didn't care very much for harquebuses, and I had to confess that neither did I. But if he had known that ahead of time, we never would have had a conversation about them, which was highly entertaining. I don't know, it's funny, for someone who's so stiff and so important, he actually loves to just chat, and he's sweet. I think he has a very tender heart. I like him.

"Anyway, he asked me to pass along his gratitude to you for your help and for saving him from a big mistake. You're very wise, he said. Isn't that great?"

Forget the barbiturates and all that. What Peter wanted to do now was to strangle several dozen small, defenseless mammals with his bare hands.

~

Later that morning, Peter received a call from Gregg Thropp.

"Russell," he said, "get in here, pronto."

When Peter arrived, he saw that Thropp wore a wide grin. His eyes sparkled.

"Hello, Champ," he said gleefully. "Take a seat. I want you to listen to something."

Thropp picked up the phone and dialed an extension. "Good morning, Miss Ippolito," Thropp said. "It's Gregg Thropp returning Mr. Beeche's call."

Thropp was put on hold.

"Good morning, sir," he said eventually. He listened.

"Yes, sir, the market has given a good account of itself, although we may see some late-morning profit taking."

Peter could hear only one side of the conversation.

"Yes, sir, that's what your message said, you wanted to talk about the cereal box tops?"

At this, Peter's heart leapt into his throat.

"No, sir, I'm afraid I don't know anything about it."

Thropp listened for a few minutes, interposing "Good heavens!" and "Good Lord!" here and there. Finally he said, "Use cereal box tops to take over the world! Why, that's madness!"

Thropp listened, obviously trying to restrain himself from bursting out laughing.

"Really, sir? Bullwinkle, sir? That is remarkable."

Now Arthur was talking again.

"SPITS? Oh, yes — serial partnership interest toggles. Yes, sir, I am familiar with that idea. Oh! So that's where the confusion came in, with *cereal* and *serial.* I see."

Serial. Cereal. Of course. Peter should have known it was something like that. Fortunately, at this point, he had no feelings.

Evidently, Arthur had asked a question.

"Well, sir, Peter had said he had a project he wanted to work on very badly with Mac McClernand. I asked him what it was, and he said he'd rather not tell me until they were further along. Well, you know better than anyone — it's the policy you've set for the firm, after all — that we try to let our people be independent, to push the decision making as far down as we can. So when I saw how keen he was, I thought I should give him his head, so to speak. Now don't quote me on this, but it was my impression that the basic idea was Peter's."

Arthur asked another question.

"I think Peter has always seen Mac as something of a mentor."

Peter could hear Arthur exclaim, "What?!"

"Yes, sir," Thropp said. "Peter seems to admire Mac very much."

Thropp listened briefly.

"Peter? Oh, yes, I'm sure you and Seth liked him. He's very bright, very capable. However . . ." Thropp paused. "I hate to be critical, but he does seem to have gotten off-track. There was a meeting, very poor preparation. Rich and Andrea can tell you about that. And now this business with Mac. I wouldn't want to speak prematurely, sir, but, in all honesty, I wonder if with Peter we may not have a case of someone who is a bad fit."

"A bad fit!" Oh God! "A bad fit!" Peter knew what that meant: we got to fire this sucka's ass.

"Yes, sir. Of course, sir. I'll do that, sir. Thank *you*, sir. Good-bye."

After hanging up, Thropp rocked in his chair and looked at Peter with a self-satisfied grin. He sighed with happiness. "You talked to Seth," he said, "and Seth talked to Arthur, and Arthur was quite interested so he called Mac earlier this morning, and Mac explained it all to him." Thropp chuckled. "Do you know what Arthur told me?"

Peter didn't respond.

"He told me that there had been a story line in *Rocky and Bullwinkle* in which the world went on the box-tops standard and Bullwinkle became richer than anyone else on earth because he had collected so many." Thropp chuckled quietly, shaking his head. "Why, God," he said, "why can't every day be like this?"

~

The next few weeks were not easy ones for Peter. He had draining conversations with Charlotte, who wailed about how terribly she had hurt him and begged his forgiveness. Then, whenever he ran into him, Thropp would grin mischievously and say something like "Twisting slowly in the wind, Russell? Keep up the good work!" or "Christmas Eve, I've always thought that that was a good time to fire people." Peter thought about going to Arthur and telling him the truth, but this was madness. At Beeche you didn't complain about your boss to someone higher up, you didn't act like such a baby, and going to Arthur himself to whine was unthinkable; in this case, Arthur would be especially offended if he thought that Peter was trying to take advantage of their new social connection. Anyway, Thropp would just contradict him and twirl his index finger around his ear if McClernand's testimony was introduced. Meanwhile, Arthur kept whisking Holly off someplace. She corrected exams while cruising the Mediterranean on his yacht. And when she was back in New York, she and Arthur were together. And when Peter was with Holly, Arthur was there, too! Trying to keep him from brooding by himself, Holly asked Peter to come out with them a few times. This was excruciating for Peter, naturally, but Arthur was very kind: he treated Peter like some backward cousin for whom he had affection. Miss Harrison, who was also present, discussed the weather with him.

Peter was absolutely determined to tell Holly everything, absolutely determined, and yet, well, time passed and he didn't do it. In truth, he was simply scared. What did he have to go on, anyway, as far as Holly was concerned? A glance. A glance! He was going to declare his love for somebody on the basis of a glance? It was sure to be humiliating. Throw in Arthur Beeche and you had a real disaster. Oh, man, Arthur Beeche! Only the richest and most powerful man in the world, practically. Only the owner of a large proportion of all the most beautiful objects of human fashioning in existence. Only a nice and somehow endearing guy. What were Peter's chances against him? And what would Arthur's reaction be if he learned that Peter was trying to move in on his honey? People can be touchy about these things, and Arthur could probably arrange for Peter to spend the rest of his life jobless, homeless, and covered with sores. Also, Arthur was a large man. Well, no matter! Holly might say she didn't care for him, Arthur might destroy him, he might gouge out Peter's eyes. He was still going to forge ahead, fearlessly, just as soon as ... as soon as, well, as soon as he got Holly alone and it was a good moment.

~

On a snowy day about a month after Arthur Beeche's dinner party, Peter received an unexpected phone call at the office. It was from Graham Edwards, Holly's father. He was in town to visit Holly, and he wanted to talk with Peter about something; he was having dinner downtown with friends that evening, would it be convenient for them to get together afterward? Sure, Peter said, I'll be here late. He thought if he could accomplish a couple of things before the axe fell, he might be able to save his neck, and he didn't have anywhere he wanted to go other than the office anyway. At about ten o'clock, he got a call from the desk, and Graham came up.

"Hello!"

"Hi, Graham!" said Peter.

Graham shook his hand with animation, grabbing Peter's shoulder at the same time. "Great to see you, Peter, great to see you!"

Tall and broad-shouldered, Graham was wearing a suede sport coat, a denim shirt open to the sternum, and cowboy boots. His long blond-and-white hair framed his features, which were a squarer, more robust version of Holly's. Still handsome, Graham's face showed no signs of sagging, no double chin, but it was weathered and lined, and, it appeared, of a permanently red complexion. There was a suggestion of defeat in his green eyes. He looked like an aging Viking, an aging Viking who had lost his nerve.

"It's great to see you, too. Are you here long?"

"Just a couple of days. I'm spending Christmas with Alex and my granddaughter, but I thought I could get a little visit in with Holly." He paused. "I'm also here to meet this fellow that Holly has been seeing. We're all having dinner."

"That's great!" Peter said cheerily. "That's great! Well!" He motioned to his desk. "So, well — if you'll just give me a second, I'll be right with you." Peter sat in his desk chair and began clicking on his keyboard. "How are Alex and Clementine?"

Graham had walked over to the window and was leaning against the wall with one hand as he looked out. Large white snowflakes drifted down, lit from below. "Oh, they're great. Clemmie comes up with the most amazing things. The other day she said something was 'most absurd.' What kind of kid says 'most absurd'?"

"That's funny," Peter said, still tapping away.

Graham stared out the window. "Fifty-eight stories," he said. "You're right in the middle of it, aren't you? They always say that compared with people here, the people in Los Angeles are shallow and two-dimensional. Well, there is another dimension here. Up."

Peter had finished and turned to look at Graham and saw his ghostly reflection in the glass. Graham's eyes were scanning the view through the window. Holly had once mentioned that her father would often be arrested by a scene — any scene, someone's kitchen or a parking lot at twilight — and he would study it, his eyes darting to and fro. It seemed that he had never lost the habit.

"You know, this place has always made me sort of nervous," Graham said. "Look at all those windows. I always imagined it to be like a huge lab, with all these drawers containing people." He tapped on the wall with his hand in time as he spoke-sung softly, "'The great big city's a wondrous toy, just made for a girl and boy . . .'" He laughed a little to himself and turned to Peter.

"All done," Peter said. "Please sit down." Graham sat opposite him.

"Well," Peter said. "It's great to see you."

Graham nodded and smiled. "It's great to see you, too," he said.

"So! I . . . uh . . . um. Well!"

Graham bailed Peter out. "I guess that you have no idea what I'm doing here," he said.

Peter thought for a moment. "To borrow money?"

Graham laughed. "Well, now that you mention it . . . But, no, actually. That's not the reason." He shifted in his seat. "Let me ask you something, Peter."

"Shoot."

"How are you doing?"

"How am I doing?"

"Yes. How are you doing?"

"Oh," Peter said. "I'm doing fine. Maybe you know what happened with my wife?"

"Yes, Holly mentioned that."

"Well," Peter said, "it's all very difficult and all that, but actually — I don't say this to everyone — but actually I'm not unhappy about it. I'm not just trying to pretend to be okay."

"It wasn't true of me," Graham said, "at least not the first time, but most men I know are ecstatic when their wives leave. They work overtime to try to get them to."

"Right," Peter said. "So all things considered, I'm doing well."

"You like all this?" Graham asked, looking around the room. "You like the work?"

"Yes," said Peter. "I like it a lot. Sure there are one or two things that I could live without, but I like it a lot."

"There are billions and billions of dollars swirling through here, and you just put your pan down and scoop some of it up."

"It's not quite that easy, but sure."

"What you really want to do isn't to direct?"

"No."

"And your family," Graham asked, "they are well?"

"Yes, everyone is fine, very well, thank you."

"Mm-hmmm."

Graham leaned back. He held his hands with the fingers spread apart and the fingertips touching. "So you're fine," he said.

"Pretty much," answered Peter.

"Is there anything that you'd say was *not* going so well? That's disturbing? That's causing you any pain? I'm sorry if I'm getting too personal."

"Not at all," Peter said brightly. "Let's see. No, I can't think of anything. I'm okay, really."

Graham nodded. Some his tresses fell forward, and he ran his hand through them, training them back. "Well, then, I guess there isn't any truth to what it says in this letter I got. If there were, then I would think that you'd be pretty miserable right now."

"What letter is that?" Peter asked.

Graham reached into his back pocket and pulled out a pale blue envelope. From this he extracted a letter of three or four sheets folded over. It was written in a skittering hand. "It's from Julia Dyer."

"Julia?"

"Yes."

"Charlotte's — my wife's — stepmother? Julia Montague?"

"Yes. She signs it Dyer."

"But how do you —?"

"We met at Jonathan's funeral. We talked a little bit."

"Oh, right."

Graham took his half-glasses from his shirt pocket and put them
on. He unfolded the letter and smoothed it out, making a crack-
ling noise, and, with his lips pursed, began to read it silently. "You
know," he said, still studying the letter, "what she writes is really
quite interesting." He looked over his lenses at Peter. "It isn't very
long. Would you like me to read it to you?"

Peter found that his knuckles had gone white as he gripped the
arms of his desk chair.

"Sure."

"Okay." Graham did a lot of stage business adjusting his glasses
and getting settled in his chair, making sure the pages were in order
and lining them up, clearing his throat. "Okay, here we go:

Dear Mr. Edwards,

*I am (for the time being, at least) the stepmother of Charlotte Russell, the
bride at whose wedding Jonathan had his accident. You may remember me as
the woman who was so upset at Jonathan's funeral and whom you comforted.
I remain very grateful to you for that.*

*I remember vividly what you said that day about your daughter Holly.
Your love for her came through strongly. I am writing you now about a
matter that concerns her happiness in a very important way. What I have to
say may sound strange, but I beg you to take it seriously and to take action.
It is urgent.*

*Gossip has reached me from New York that Holly has been seeing Arthur
Beeche and that matters seem to be racing ahead. It sounds like what my
grandmother would have called a "whirlwind romance." However, I have*

reason to believe that Holly is in love with Peter Russell, Jonathan's best friend and Charlotte's soon-to-be-former husband, and that Peter is in love with Holly. I don't have absolute proof of this — to be honest, I don't even have any hard evidence, and I have to keep the sources of the evidence I do have secret — but in my heart I know it's true. The problem is that neither of them knows about the other, and now with Arthur Beeche's involvement, it looks as if there's a chance that they never will.

I am in no position to pursue this matter, but I couldn't keep this knowledge to myself, so I am writing you. You probably doubt my sanity, and even if you believe me, I don't know what you can or should do. But there is nothing worse in the movies than for the girl to end up with the wrong guy. You said yourself that there had to be a happy ending. Please, please do what you can to make sure that for Holly and Peter there is one.

Yours truly,
Julia Dyer

"So there it is," Graham said. "Oh, yeah, she added a P.S. Not really relevant: 'By the way, I never got a chance to tell you what a fan I am. Even though it wasn't my cup of tea, I thought *Apostle's Run* was terrific, the sequence in the Chinese restaurant was amazing, and *Forever and a Day* is one of my favorite movies ever. I even thought *Tamerlane* was underrated!' "

Graham whipped off his glasses. "*Tamerlane!* What a disaster. Everything went wrong, sandstorms, the whole bit. A huge cast and a huge crew and we were rewriting the script every night. And those damn goats! Ten thousand of them. God, I loved making the battle scenes, but the whole thing ended up as a bloated mess and it didn't make a dime. Someday, if I could get my hands on the footage and recut it —" He shuddered. "But I can't let myself start thinking about that."

Out of the corner of his eye, Graham had been watching Peter closely during this speech. "So anyway," he said now, looking at Peter directly, "what do you think?"

Burning with embarrassment, Peter blushed deeply. He was being confronted for the first time ever about Holly and the one doing the confronting was her father, of all people. Then, Julia's letter baffled him. Julia could not possibly have discussed Holly and Peter with anyone but Charlotte and conceivably—dear God—Jonathan. But what could they know? Peter was certain that he had never betrayed the feelings that Julia ascribed to him, and he found it inconceivable, just about, that Holly had ever done so. The letter was bizarre, absurd, demented, a weird product of Julia's distressed state and certainly not a document in which to place any confidence. Yet something must have prompted it, and it was accurate about him, and what it said about Holly was thrilling! Blushing and with his heart in tumult, Peter tried to restrain his emotions. He wanted to believe Julia, but he didn't want to allow himself to believe her, and with Graham, of all people, his ego required that he play it cool.

"It sounds pretty far-fetched," he said as calmly as he could.

Graham shrugged. He tapped the letter with his finger. "Maybe you'd like to take a look yourself," he said

"Sure."

Graham handed over the letter and continued to study Peter. Peter, meanwhile, looked at the letter intently, turning over the sheets, holding them up, hunching over them, and generally playing for as much time as he could. Julia's linear, elongated writing looked like Arabic, but Peter managed to decipher the word "please." Then, suddenly, it began to blur. A drop of water had fallen on it. Another one fell, and another. Peter now realized that his chin was trembling and that he was crying. The tears made jagged circles of ink that looked like bullet holes. Peter put his hand up to rest his forehead on it and to shield Graham from a view of what was happening. He wiped tears away with his other hand and then reached into his pocket and retrieved a handkerchief. He dried his eyes and blew his nose.

After a minute, Peter organized the sheets, evened them out, and handed them back to Graham, who folded them and put them in the envelope. Graham could play quiet and still. He leaned back in his chair, holding the envelope in his lap with both hands. He neither spoke nor gave any indication that he wished to speak, nor did he move.

Peter's face was damp and hot. He had placed his elbows on the arms of his chair and he was resting his chin on his clasped hands. He stared down at his desk, at the fancy calculator the possession of which had made him feel so foolishly proud when he had bought it years before. Then his shoulders heaved a couple of times. Putting his hands to his forehead again to shield his eyes, he cried some more. Eventually, he managed to compose himself, and, after attending to his eyes and nose with his handkerchief, he raised his head and looked at Graham.

Graham didn't say anything as he turned the letter over edgewise several times. Finally, he spoke. "Okay, so that settles at least half the question. What's the next step?"

Peter looked away, out the window. The snowflakes twirled downward. In an office across the street, a maintenance woman was vacuuming. In another, a woman had her shoeless feet up on her desk and was drinking bottled water while talking on the phone. The lab samples.

Peter looked at Graham. "The problem is — all right, I've given you a hint of how I feel about things. But what about Holly? Has she ever said anything to you?"

"No."

"Me neither. So there you are. Julia's ESP or whatever it is may tell her all sorts of things — maybe I should ask her where the stock market is going — but there's no reason to think that she's right about this."

"She was right about you," Graham said.

Peter rocked from side to side in his chair. "Yeah, I know. She got lucky."

"All right," Graham said. "Do you believe in love at first sight?"

"I do, but please don't ever tell anybody."

"Okay. So you were the guy on the plane, right? Years ago, when Holly flew out to see the baby?"

"Yes. You know about that?"

"Sure. I was there, after all. I remember it very well. She met this guy on the plane, he was going to call. Holly tried to play it cool, but Alex was beside herself. Every time the phone rang she jumped out of her skin, and if she answered she would say hello brightly, listen for a moment, and then say, in the tone of a mental patient full of Thorazine, 'Dad, it's for you.' After a couple of days it became clear that this guy would not be calling after all. Holly did some sniffling, and Alex was outraged. Me, too, actually. I was ridiculously heartbroken and angry and I wanted to kneecap the bastard."

"Would you be interested in knowing why I never called?"

"Of course."

Peter rocked in his chair for a moment before finally saying, "I lost the number."

"You lost the number?"

"Yes. Holly wrote it on a piece of paper and I put it in my shirt pocket, and when I got to my hotel, it was gone. I didn't even know her last name."

"You lost the number?"

"Yes."

"You lost the number?"

"Yes! Yes! All right? I lost the number!"

"How idiotic."

"Thanks. I know."

Graham leaned forward. "But you see the point. You could tell that Holly was kind of devastated. Something had happened on the plane, she thought. She really thought that there had been something between her and this guy. Now, if that isn't love at first sight, I don't know what is. You know, I've heard Holly talk about you once in a while, and now that I think about it, it's always been with a tone of voice you don't use when you're talking about just anybody. Then there's what Julia says." He leaned back in his chair again and folded his arms. "So: case closed."

" 'Case closed,' " Peter repeated under his breath. He spoke quietly, his eyes downcast. "Look, Graham. I'd like to believe you, I really would. I'd like to believe Julia. Somebody must have told her something — I can't imagine what — and, yeah, maybe Holly and I do have this special affectionate vibe. As far as I know, though, Holly had a brief little crush on the guy on the plane and then totally forgot about him, and this special affectionate vibe is exactly that, and exactly *not* something else." Now he looked at Graham. "But do you know what? Even so, after Charlotte took off, I was ready to take my chances anyway. I had it all planned out how I was going to tell Holly all about how I feel about her. I know she would have said that she was deeply moved and that she loved me, too, but that she loved me as a friend, a *dear* friend. After that, I was going to rampage through this floor killing everyone before finally turning the gun on myself. But I was willing to risk it." He paused. "But then another element came into it."

Graham rolled his eyes. "Okay, here we go. Your rival. You know what I have to say about your rival? Pfah!"

Peter laughed. "'Pfah.' Let me try that: pfah." He shook his head. "No, it's not working. You see, first of all, it certainly looks an awful lot like love at first sight between Holly and Arthur Beeche. How am I supposed to believe that she is really in . . . uh . . . in —?"

"In love with you."

"Right, that. How am I supposed to believe that when she and Arthur seem so crazy about each other? It's not just that Arthur is incredibly rich. There's something about him — he's a really good guy, actually. Then, second of all, do you really think that Arthur would let *me* keep him from getting anything he wanted, especially a woman? Yeah, he's a good guy, but so was Othello. Combine jealousy with the power Arthur's got, and there's no limit to what he might do. It's not just losing my job. Bankruptcy, starvation, madness, death. These are all possible." He frowned. "Also, have you ever seen Arthur?"

"No."

"Well," Peter said, "he's big. And he looks very fit." After contemplating this for a moment, Peter continued. "But, Graham, I am going to tell Holly. I am. I really am. I've been planning on it. Whatever happens, whatever the consequences. I'm going to do it. I'm going to tell her."

Graham clapped his hands together and got a big grin on his face. "You are? Peter, that's terrific! That's wonderful! You're going to tell her!" He paused. *"When?"*

Peter coughed and cleared his throat. "When. When. Well, you know, the timing, it's tricky, and I've hardly had a chance to talk to Holly the past few weeks . . . and, well, I'm waiting for, you know . . . uh, the right elements to come together . . ."

With a thoughtful expression, Graham looked off above Peter's head and nodded slowly. "I see," he said. He sat up straight and drummed his hands on his thighs. "Well, thank you for your time, Peter. I know how busy you are. I won't detain you any further." With a slap, he put his hands on the arms of the chair and began pushing himself out of it. But then he stopped, waited a second, and sat down again. He looked Peter directly in the eye. "I have just one question for you." Graham paused dramatically. "Are you in love with my daughter?"

"Yes," Peter answered.

Graham leapt out of his chair and began waving his hands. "Well, then, for God's sake! What are you waiting for? Are you just going to sit there while somebody steals her away from you? Look, Peter, what I care about is Holly's happiness. I wouldn't actually mind if you were happy, too, but that's not as important. If you two belong together, and I have a feeling you do, then I want you to be together. But if you don't have the courage to do something about it, then Holly is better off with Arthur Beeche — or anyone else *but* you."

"Are you calling me a coward?" Peter asked hotly.

"Yes."

"Are you saying that I'm too much of a coward to deserve Holly?"

"Yes!"

Peter slumped in his chair. "You're probably right."

Graham threw up his hands in exasperation. Then he sat and just stared at Peter. Eventually he leaned forward and spoke in a forceful whisper. Graham's resonant voice had a roughness that made it very effective at this volume. "Look, Peter," he said, "you can take this guy. Oh, he's got a couple of trivial advantages, but you go out there, you do your best, and I'm sure you can wipe up the floor with him. Is Holly really going to choose some old stiff who's spent his entire life counting money over you, a guy she's had a thing for for a long time? So he's got a couple of shekels! Come on, Peter! Arthur Beeche, he's nobody. He's nothing!"

Graham leaned back in his chair and allowed this encouragement to sink in. Then he reached into his second shirt pocket, the one without the glasses, and took out a soft cigarette pack. He looked inside and shook it and extracted a hand-rolled cigarette that was the size of a toothpick. "Is it okay? Just a little pin joint, a little hash mixed with tobacco."

"Well, they're very strict, I mean about the smoking —"

"Christ! I forgot. I'm really sorry. Not anywhere inside the building? Sorry, never mind."

"What the hell," said Peter. "Go ahead."

Graham lit the joint and offered it to Peter, who drew on it. The hash tasted like coffee and dark chocolate. Peter and Graham passed the joint back and forth a couple of times and Peter felt the cables holding up his eyebrows go slack. He and Graham remained silent while entering a sort of mild, mutual trance. It was amazing about Julia, Peter was thinking. How could she possibly know that he was in love with Holly? But this was an important point: if she was right about one side of it, maybe she was right about the other one. It was amazing. Maybe Julia had learned something from somebody somehow. He was taking a last drag and drifting off into a pleasant reverie when he and Graham were shocked by the sound of two light raps on the door. Peter looked up and saw a form through the ripply glass. He doused the roach on his desk and waved his hands, trying to disperse the smoke.

"Come in!" he called.

The door opened and the large head of Arthur Beeche poked through it.

Peter had still not exhaled, not even when he'd said "Come in," and a coughing fit seized him.

"I'm so sorry," Arthur said. "Am I interrupting anything?"

"Arthur, hello!" said Peter through his coughing. "Not at all! Not at all!" He shot to his feet and ran over to the door and opened it further. "Please come in!"

Arthur entered. He was beaming and wore a beautiful gray suit and highly polished shoes. Peter coughed quite dramatically.

"Goodness, Peter," Arthur said, "are you all right?"

"Yes," Peter said with a gasp. "I'm fine." He coughed again but was finally able to speak. "We were just . . . uh . . . uh . . . uh . . ."

By this time, Graham had also stood up.

"Uh . . . uh . . . uh . . ." Peter continued. He swallowed. He tried to smile graciously. "Graham, this is Arthur Beeche, and Arthur, let me introduce you to Graham Edwards."

"Graham Edwards!" Arthur said. "Well! This is a delightful surprise!"

The two men shook hands.

"It's a nice surprise for me as well," said Graham. "I wasn't expecting to see you until tomorrow night."

"No! Nor was I! I've been looking forward to our dinner very much."

"Me too."

"Your daughter is a wonderful person," said Arthur.

"Yes. Yes she is."

"But," Arthur said, taking a step backward and looking from Peter to Graham, "I fear I am intruding."

"Oh! Not at all!" said Peter. "Not at all!"

Arthur gave a slight nod of his head and came forward again. His face was flushed and it appeared that he was tipsy. Suddenly he lifted his nose in the air and began to sniff.

"That's strange," he said. "It smells as if something is burning. Do you smell it?" He looked at Peter and Graham, who looked at each other, and did not answer. Arthur sniffed again.

"Funny," he said, "to me it smells like a mixture of tobacco and hashish." He considered this with a quizzical expression. "Well," he said abruptly, "if there is a smell of smoke that we can't identify, then we had better call the building fire marshal."

"Uh . . . uh . . . uh . . ." said Peter.

"We've been having a little smoke," Graham said. "I'm afraid I'm to blame. Peter was too good a host to forbid it."

"Oh, I see!" said Arthur. "Well, well. Would there be any chance of my joining you?"

"Of course!" said Graham.

They all sat, and Graham lit another pin joint and handed it to Arthur, who took a puff. Exhaling, he wore a relaxed smile, as if his skull were thawing.

"Good heavens," he said, after passing the joint to Peter, "Graham Edwards. You know, it really is an honor to meet you, and not just because of Holly. I have always been a tremendous fan. *Apostle's Run*, that was terrific. The Chinese restaurant — I'll never forget that! And the romantic one — *Forever and a Day*? I swear, I cried. You know, I also quite liked — what was it? Oh, come on, the conqueror."

"*Tamerlane,*" Peter said.

"*Tamerlane!* Of course! Fantastic battles." Arthur frowned. "I seem to recall that that one didn't do quite as well."

"It sure didn't," said Graham.

"Oh, but, please. I didn't mean to be rude!"

"Not at all, not at all. I'm glad you liked it, and the others."

"Oh, yes. Indeed, indeed," Arthur said. Then he gestured to Peter. "Well, now, I see you have paid a call on my trusted and valued colleague here."

"We're old friends, aren't we, Peter?" said Graham. Peter nodded. "Yep, I was in the neighborhood, and I thought that I'd drop in on old Peter." The joint had made a couple of circuits, and after taking the last drag Graham stubbed it out on the sole of his boot and tossed it toward the wastebasket, missing. "As a matter of fact, Arthur — may I call you Arthur?"

"Of course."

"Well, Arthur, I hate to admit that I've been talking about some-one behind his back, but as a matter of fact, the reason I wanted to see Peter was to ask him about you."

"Really?"

"Yes," said Graham. "A father always has a temptation to check up on the people his daughter is seeing. No one knows Holly bet-ter or cares about her more than old Peter, and he knows you, of course, so he seemed like a logical person to consult."

"Well, well," said Arthur, looking embarrassed. "I — of course, I understand." Then he turned to Peter and smiled. "In fact, I've tried to use Peter for a similar purpose. And I certainly expect, Peter, that you have been candid. But I also hope you have not been too harsh."

"How did you put it, Peter?" Graham asked. "'It's not just that he's incredibly rich, he's also a really good guy.' Wasn't that it?"

"Graham!" Peter cried. "Arthur —"

"Don't apologize!" said Arthur. "Don't apologize! That will do very nicely! Very nicely, indeed!" He laughed. "If I were you, Graham, I'd want to protect her too. She's a precious item."

"Yes," said Graham.

"Amazing girl."

"Yes."

Arthur looked at both of the other men with a big grin. "I was coming back to the office to do some work after having dinner with her tonight, and I thought I'd see if Peter was around. I wanted to tell him about what happened. So now I guess I'll tell both of you. Here, look at this."

He removed a square velvet jewelry case from his coat pocket, put it on the desk, and lifted the lid. Inside lay a diamond and emerald necklace that was the shape and size of a maple leaf. Light refracted among the stones following an infinity of crisscrossing paths. "It was a present for her," Arthur said dreamily. "The emeralds were for her eyes."

"It was a present," Graham said, "but you still seem to have it."

"Exactly," said Arthur. "I do. That's the story I was going to tell.

"I wanted to give this to her, an early Christmas present. So, at dessert, I pulled it out. I haven't had any practice with these things for many years, but she made a little gasp and it seemed to me that she liked it. 'Oh, it's beautiful,' she said. I asked her if she wouldn't like to try it on, and her face got an anxious look and she said, 'Oh, Arthur,' and gave me a kiss. 'Oh, Arthur,' she started again. 'It's very beautiful. But I can't accept it. Really, I can't. It's too much. I don't mean to sound old-fashioned, but it might create an expectation or a sense of obligation or . . . but can I see it again?'" Arthur chuckled. "Well, I pressed it on her. 'Please take it,' I said. I said I wanted so much to give her something as beautiful as she is." He blushed. "That sort of came to me on the spot. She looked at me and looked at it, and I could tell she was feeling torn. She closed the box and shook her head. And then she seemed to have an idea.

"'I will take it,' she said. 'But it's only fair of me to tell you that what I want to do is to give it to the hospital and let them sell it.'"

"Low-income pediatric oncology," Graham said.

"Yes," said Arthur.

"I remember," Graham said, "Holly once saying that, sure, in just about every case you could probably make an argument that you hurt people more by trying to help them than if you just left them alone, but that helping poor children with cancer might just be an exception."

"Yes," Arthur said. "Well, I told her that if she would accept the necklace, I would make a contribution that would be equal to the necklace's value. She thought about that for a moment, and then said, 'Okay, that would be great. Except then I would still give the necklace to them, so they would have twice the money.' Fine, I said, how about if I gave them twice the money, and she took the necklace? You know what she said, of course — that she'd still give them the necklace. Then I said, 'All right, I'll give you the necklace and I'll give them *three* times its value, but if you don't keep it, they don't get anything!' Then she got a solemn look on her face. 'Oh, Arthur,' she said, and she put her hand on my arm, 'you wouldn't want to put me in the position of having to make that choice and possibly deceiving you, would you?' What could I say to that but no? So then she said, 'So it's all settled. You'll contribute four times the value of the necklace.' 'Four times!' I said. 'Four times? When did I ever say four times?' Then she looked up at me with these soggy eyes. 'The three times plus the new one,' she said. So I told her, 'Okay! Okay! I better just agree before this gets even more expensive!' She thanked me and kissed me and began to laugh and cry at the same time. I've been asked for money by a lot of people in my time, but I've never been swindled quite like that." Arthur started laughing and so did Graham. Nervous as well as intoxicated, Peter laughed harder than either of them. Oh, they all three had a good laugh together.

Eventually, Arthur shook his head and became reflective. "A little while later, she got a bit serious and said she knew that I didn't just want to give her a present, but that I wanted to tell her something about my feelings for her and that she was very touched and appreciated it more than she could say." He fell silent for a moment, and Graham and Peter joined him in his wonder at this beautiful sentiment. "Well," Arthur said finally. "I'm going to hold on to this. It might come in handy later on." He snapped the lid closed and picked up the box. Then he put on a cumbersomely sly expression. "Or, then again," he said, "I may want to trade it in for something else."

After the men talked for a few minutes more, Arthur said that he had better be off. They all stood up, and Arthur shook hands with Graham, saying again how much he was anticipating their dinner together. To Peter, he said in a stage whisper, "Keep up the good work. The longer we keep the real truth about me from him, the better!" He gave a little wave with the jewelry case, which he still held in his hand, and he was gone.

Graham's and Peter's eyes lingered on the door after Arthur had closed it behind him. Then they looked at each other for a second before bursting out into laughter. Tears came to their eyes and they could barely speak. "Oh my God!" Peter managed to say, "I almost had a heart attack!" Graham clapped him on the shoulder and cried, "Arthur Beeche himself walks in!" Peter clapped Graham on the shoulder and they laughed and laughed until they seemed to be spent. But then they looked at each other and started laughing all over again.

Eventually, when they had settled down, Peter threw himself into his chair and leaned back in it. "Ah, man, unbelievable," he said.

Graham had sat, too, and said, "First I think we're totally busted, and then he asks" — he imitated Arthur's voice — " 'Would there be any chance of my joining you?' "

Graham chuckled. Peter chuckled. Graham chuckled some more. Peter chuckled some more. They both chuckled at the same time and sighed and shook their heads and said, "Oh, man . . ." Then there was silence with little punctuations of chuckling. And then there was no more chuckling.

Peter's brow began to darken and became darker and darker. After a long silence, he spoke. "Cute story," he said.

Graham cleared his throat. "Which one?"

"Holly and the necklace."

"Oh, yeah. Sure. Cute."

"And how about that necklace." Peter made a low whistle. "Gorgeous, huh?"

"I suppose. If you like that kind of thing."

"How much would it set you back, I wonder."

Graham shrugged. "Beats me."

"I figure it'd have to be a couple of million bucks. Four times two is eight, so right there that's eight million to help tiny little innocent poor children suffering from cancer. And that's a check he can write over dessert. Then it was really touching what Holly said to him, you know, about how the *feelings* meant so much to her. Honestly, I got all choked up. Oh, but wasn't Arthur sweet? That impish look and him saying, 'Or I might trade it in for something else.' A real sweetheart of a guy." Peter gnashed his teeth for a moment, and then muttered, "I hope they'll be very happy."

"Now, Peter —"

"Yes, sir. Oh boy! I sure have got it made! Arthur Beeche? He's a punk. A two-bit palooka. I can whip him easy. No problem. Like taking candy from a baby."

"Now, Peter, I don't think sarcasm —"

"Look, Graham, why pretend? It's all over. You should be happy. Only a fool would prefer me as a son-in-law to Arthur Beeche. There'll be no hard feelings if you just want to slink off, and we can forget about this whole conversation."

"Now, Peter —"

Peter gave a wave of his hand. "Go on, go on. If you play your cards right, you'll have a backer for a dozen pictures."

"Now, Peter, you don't think that I would —"

"I don't think anything but that your visit has been a complete waste of time and that from now on I wish your good friend Julia would keep her lunatic ravings to herself."

"Now, Peter —"

"Please stop saying that!"

Graham looked at Peter sympathetically. Very slowly he shook out one more little joint and held it up. "One for the road," he said.

Peter grunted.

Graham lit the joint and took a deep drag and passed it to Peter. It went back and forth a couple of times. Then Graham said quietly, "Yes, they could probably be happy."

Graham drew on the joint, handed it to Peter, and waited for him to pass it back. Graham was now holding it between his thumb and forefinger, and smoke rose from it like a wavering thread. "There's only one problem," he said.

"What's that?"

"Holly is in love with you."

Peter scowled and made no reply. They smoked awhile in silence.

12

Over the next couple of days Peter heard Holly recount and re-recount her dinner with Graham and Arthur. What fun they had had! Graham told such stories! As different as they were, he and Arthur had gotten along wonderfully. Isn't it funny how that can happen? They had become so palsy that Holly had begun to feel left out!

Peter was now spending a good deal of time staring out the window. The phone rang, the e-mail indicator blinked, the graphs on his screen skittered, and the numbers jumped. Peter ignored them. Observing him, one might have thought that before him lay an undulating sea whose ever-changing surface registered with blues and silvers the clouds above, and the sun's slow progress. Or he might have been watching the traffic in a colorful city square — the larking urchins, the lovers walking hand in hand, the elders on shady benches engaging in their voluble discourse. In fact, all he could see was the protruding grid, for that was the architectural style, of the building across the street. A few vivid images rotated in his mind as if in a continuous slide show: the words in looping script, Graham's hands moving in the air, the glistening necklace. At regular intervals, he would suspend all his thoughts and darken all other images as he remembered the way Holly looked when on the airplane so many years ago they had turned to each other for the first time and she had smiled.

Peter was staring out the window one evening in the state just described when someone from the mailroom dropped a small manila envelope on his desk. It had come from the seventy-seventh floor. Peter opened the envelope and withdrew its contents. First, he found a note from Arthur saying that his mother wanted to invite Peter and his wife to the dinner and dance she gave every December and that an invitation was enclosed; she had thought that this was the fastest way to get it to him, and she apologized for the short notice. Peter opened the invitation, addressed to Mr. and Mrs. Peter Russell, and saw an elegant card expressing Mrs. Beeche's desire for their company and providing the details. It made Peter happy that Mrs. Beeche had thought of him. But in addition to Arthur's note and the invitation, the manila envelope contained another sheet of paper. Peter unfolded it and saw the name Isabella Echevarria de Sena inscribed at the top. Isabella. How odd. Peter read what she had written:

My dearest devious Artie,

I should have known that when you invited me up to see the Beeche Venus you had an ulterior motive. I'll never be able to think about your office in quite the same way.

Thank you thank you thank you for another unforgettable night.

Counting the minutes until we are together again, and thinking of all the things I want to do to you.

Love,
Your Iz

Peter's hands trembled and his heart pounded as he read these words. When he tried to reread them, his hands shook with so much fury that he could barely do so.

Good God! he thought. Somehow this note had gotten mixed up with the others. So that was it! Isabella had been Arthur's special guest at his dinner! He was the one who wanted to put her with all the big shots. And he was screwing her all the while he was pursuing Holly as if she were the only woman on earth! They even had cute little pet names for each other! Mr. Square, Mr. Decency. What complete bullshit. Like every other man, he was really a duplicitous horn dog. Of course. That goody-goody act could never have been the whole story. Fucking Isabella all this time. The low-life scum. The dirtbag. The prick. The scoundrel! Well! We'll see about this! Peter may have stood by and watched while Jonathan cheated on Holly, but there had been reasons for that (although at the moment he couldn't think of what they were), and he would be damned if he would let Arthur Beeche get away with it! Arthur and Holly were going to have a drink at Arthur's place that night, before going out to dinner. They might not know it, but their plans had changed.

Without even stopping to put on his overcoat, Peter left his office and the building. Once on the sidewalk, he realized that at this hour by far the fastest way to get to Arthur's would be to take the subway. Somehow, that didn't seem to fit the drama of the situation, but he nevertheless walked quickly to the station, swiped his MetroCard, waited on the platform, watched two trains go by without stopping, and finally boarded a third one that soon became so crowded that Peter could have died and still been held upright by the crush of his neighbors. Forty minutes later, having transferred to the local and run eight blocks, Peter arrived at Arthur's. He rang the bell, and almost immediately a door swung open. A tall, gangly young man with red ears greeted him.

"Good evenin', sir," said the servant in a brogue.

"Good evening," Peter said. "I am Mr. Russell. Mr. Beeche is expecting me."

"Yes, sir. Very good, sir. If you would just wait here a moment, sir, I will have your name sent up." He walked a few steps to another servant, a short, chubby, Hispanic-looking man, who stood at the foot of the stairs.

"Mr. Russell to see Mr. Beeche," said the man who had greeted Peter. The second servant nodded. But in the time required for this exchange to take place, Peter had already begun to mount the staircase. The tall servant turned and called out, "Excuse me, sir, excuse me!"

Peter's step was very fast, and he quickened it in response. The servants looked at each other, looked at Peter, looked at each other again, and then began to give chase.

"Excuse me! Excuse me! Mr. Russell!"

"Escusa may! Escusa may! Meester Roossell!"

Peter looked behind him and then increased his speed. He reached the top of the stairs, turned left, and began to walk quickly down a corridor. He had a pretty good idea which room Arthur and Holly were likely to be in, the private study. The tall servant took the last few steps in one bound and hurried after Peter. Looking behind him again and seeing that the servant was catching up, Peter walked faster. Meanwhile, having rested at the top of the staircase, the shorter servant brought up the distant rear, taking sixty-fourth-note steps and covering little ground. The tall servant drew almost even with Peter, and the latter then simply broke out into a run.

"Sir! Sir!" the servants called.

Peter reached the door of the study, seized the knob, and threw it open. Within, he saw Arthur alone on the sofa. He had a drink on the table next to him. On the other side of the room Miss Harrison sat at a writing table. There was no sign of Holly.

Their faces swung around in surprise when Peter entered, and Arthur instantly rose to his feet and held out his hand. "Well, well! Peter! Hello! What a pleasant —"

Peter walked up to Arthur, reared back, and struck him a powerful blow in the face.

This action produced a sharp pain in Peter's hand; it appeared that he had broken every bone in it. Arthur reacted as impassively as if he had been a wall that Peter had punched.

"Goodness, Peter," Arthur said. "I'm not sure —"

Peter hit Arthur again, as hard as he could, pulverizing the bone fragments in his hand, and this time Arthur said, "Ow!" and stumbled backward, falling over an ottoman. A moment earlier, the tall servant had arrived at the doorway, where he had stood watching, lacking the presumption to enter. The little servant, running at full tilt, had knocked into him and bounced off, and they had both just regained their balance and taken their places when Peter punched Arthur the second time.

"Ecod! Mr. Beeche!"

"Dios mio! Señor Beeche!"

Both men ran into the room. They each went to one side of Arthur and tried to help him up. Their difference in size made this an awkward business, however.

Now Jenkins, Arthur's butler, appeared. "Mr. Beeche!" he ejaculated. "What's happened? Patrick, Manuel, what's going on here? What is the meaning of this?!"

"The gentleman," Patrick said, nodding at Peter. "He punched Mr. Beeche."

"Good heavens! Put him down!"

Manuel and Patrick let go of Arthur, who fell to the floor. "Jenkins —" he said.

"Please, sir, don't speak." Jenkins went down on one knee and leaned his face close to Arthur's. "Sir, how many fingers am I holding up?"

"Three," said Arthur.

"Very good. Now, sir, can you count backward from one hundred?"

"Jenkins, this is ridic —"

"Please, sir, try. Try to count backwards from one hundred —"

"All right," said Arthur. "Ninety-nine, ninety-eight, ninety-seven, ninety-six, ninety-five, ninety-four. Et cetera, et cetera."

Jenkins sighed with relief. "Mental faculties appear intact, thank goodness." He rose. "Patrick, Manuel, help Mr. Beeche up."

Jenkins then wheeled to face Peter. In his most minatory voice, he said, "Sir: may I help you?"

Peter pulled back his fist, causing Jenkins to cower and scream, "Help!" Patrick and Manuel let go of Arthur, who once again fell to the floor, and raced over to Peter. He had already lowered his fist, but they took him by either arm. Patrick glowered down at him as Manuel glowered up.

When Jenkins saw that Peter no longer posed any danger, he raised himself up again to his full dignity. "Mr. Beeche," he said, "I will go call the police."

Arthur had stood by now and was brushing off his clothes with his hands and straightening his jacket and tie. "No, Jenkins," Arthur said. "I don't think that will be necessary."

"But, sir —!" Jenkins protested.

"I don't think we can expect more trouble from our young friend here, but if we do I'm quite sure I can handle it."

"But the lady!"

Everyone looked over at Miss Harrison. She did not seem like someone in a state of terror, fearing that at any moment she would be ravished and murdered, and in this way she disappointed Jenkins's expectation. Rather, she seemed completely calm and self-possessed.

"She'll be all right, Jenkins," said Arthur.

Jenkins wore a look of the deepest consternation. Peter had behaved in a way that was not only actionable but also highly irregular.

"That will do, Jenkins," Arthur said.

"Very good, sir. Shall I post someone at the door?"

"No, Jenkins," said Arthur. "You needn't worry about us."

"As you wish, sir," said Jenkins, trying to bear up as best as he could under the conflicting demands of reason and his master's wishes. He made a slight bow. He turned to Miss Harrison and made another bow. "Patrick, Manuel," he said. They headed to the door, and, in a devastating show of contempt, Jenkins passed Peter without any recognition whatsoever.

Arthur and Peter stood a few feet from each other. Peter's hand throbbed, making him wince with every beat of his heart. Nevertheless, he was squared off, ready to go another round.

"Well, well," Arthur said, rubbing his chin. "Not a bad right hand. You know, I did a bit of boxing myself in college. As a matter of fact, I had some club bouts —"

Peter interrupted him. "I don't give a good goddamn about your goddamn amateur sportsman crap."

Arthur stared at Peter. "No, I don't suppose you do," he said coolly. "For your own good, I might tell you that you won't often find someone who will react so good-naturedly to a punch in the face. Now, why don't you tell us what this is all about?"

"What this is all about?" Peter spat back. "What this is all about? I'll tell you what this is all about." He took Isabella's note out of his pocket and flung it at Arthur. "How do you explain that?"

Arthur caught the note against his chest and tried to read it. "Damn," he said, "without my glasses . . ." He moved the paper toward and away from him, trying to find the best distance.

"All right, let's see . . . mmhmmm." Suddenly Arthur blushed deeply. "Peter! Where did you get this?"

"It came in the envelope with your mother's invitation."

"And you think —"

"That's exactly what I think, Artie. So all this time that you've been romancing Holly and acting as if you are deeply in love with her, all this time you've been getting some action with Isabella. Very classy, Artie, very. As if, with all that Holly's already been through, she needs someone two-timing her. To take a beautiful, sweet person like Holly, who's still recovering from something horrible, and to trick her and toy with her. Well, it's just disgusting and pathetic, and you should be tortured and shot. Artie."

With his hands in front of him, palms downward, Arthur made a patting motion. "Take it easy, Peter," he said. "Please try to take it easy. I can understand how you might have misinterpreted this. I can understand your reaction. I would feel the same way. But you must believe me when I say that this note was intended for someone else."

Peter sneered. "Oh, come on, Arthur," he said. "You've got to be able to do better than that." He folded his arms. "All right. Why don't you just tell who that someone else is?"

"It would be a violation of that person's privacy if I did so."

" 'It would be a violation of that person's privacy if I did so.' " Peter spat out the words with mockery. "Let's see: someone named Artie who works on the seventy-seventh floor and has access to your correspondence. Who else could that be besides you? Your evil twin?"

There was a very long, very awkward silence. Finally, Miss Harrison spoke. "Perhaps I can help clarify matters," she said in her low, even voice. "Mr. Russell, do you know what my first name is?"

Peter turned to her and thought for a moment.

"Uh . . . Miss?"

"No."

"Well, no, I don't know."

Miss Harrison spoke to Peter in the same polite, professional tone that she always used. "My first name, Mr. Russell," she said, "is Artemis."

Peter pondered this. "Artemis . . . the hunt . . . Hippolytos . . ."

"That's correct," said Miss Harrison.

"Artemis," Peter repeated. Then his head jerked back. "Oh! So . . . I . . . er . . . oh!"

He looked back and forth between Arthur and Miss Harrison.

Miss Harrison rose from the desk, stepped over to Arthur, and held out her hand. "I will take that from you now, please, Mr. Beeche," she said. Arthur handed the note to her and she looked at it before folding it up. "I can't imagine how I could have put this in the envelope with those other items. I am very sorry, sir. And please, sir, I hope you will forgive any unprofessional behavior on my part as may have been implied. I find that, late at night, it is sometimes more efficient to attend to personal matters in the office."

"Oh, please, Miss Harrison," said Arthur, "no apologies are necessary. I am just so grateful to you for speaking up. Thank you very much. That was above and beyond the call of duty."

"Yes, Miss Harrison," said Peter. "Thank you. I'm sorry for having caused this trouble. I misunderstood." He was in a daze. Miss Harrison's revelation astonished him and it was a shock to learn that his rage was completely unfounded. Moreover, the news about Isabella just made her even more incredibly sexy, not to mention Miss Harrison herself.

"I was only too happy to help," said Miss Harrison.

"Well! My goodness!" Arthur said. "That was a bit of drama, wasn't it!" He put one hand on Peter's shoulder and proffered the other one. "No hard feelings, I hope, dear boy? No hard feelings. I would have done the same thing myself." He moved his jaw to and fro. "Not to boast, but I always could take a punch pretty well, so we will just put that behind us, shall we?"

Peter shook Arthur's hand mechanically.

"Well, well," Arthur said, "now that we have cleared up that little problem, how about a drink?"

"All right," Peter said. "Thank you."

"Scotch is your usual tope, isn't it?"

Peter nodded and Arthur stepped over to a table where a few bottles of spirits stood. He opened an ice bucket, and, with a pair of tongs, dropped two cubes one by one into a short glass. The cubes were thick and landed in the glass with a chunk. It seemed very loud. Arthur unscrewed a bottle of scotch, making a swishy sound that also seemed unnaturally loud, and poured some. The ice cubes caused the scotch to climb up the sides in an irregular amber pattern.

"Now, just a drop of water," Arthur said to himself. He raised a glass pitcher, with a large belly and fluted mouth, and dipped it for just a second. This operation seemed unnaturally silent. He handed the glass to Peter. "Please, Peter, have a seat."

Peter sat and took a gulp of his drink. Arthur sat, sipped his own drink, and then just looked at Peter, smiling.

"Please accept my apology, Arthur," Peter said. "I assumed —"

"As I said, no hard feelings! Don't give it another thought."

Peter knit his brow. "Where is Holly, anyway?" he asked. "I thought you had plans for tonight?"

"She's at home, nursing a cold."

"Oh, I see."

They sat in silence for a moment. Arthur sipped his drink.

"Yes, indeed," he said finally, "I certainly am glad we cleared up that misunderstanding. I can well imagine your consternation,

Peter." His expression became more serious. "In fact, well, this is rather personal, but I may tell you, Peter, I am a bit old-fashioned about some things, and I still don't believe that before marriage, a man and a woman — well, you see what I mean? Now when a man has a relationship with a woman where marriage is out of the question, it's a different situation. But it would be unthinkable to put Holly in *that* category."

"Yes, I see," said Peter.

"Yes, well," Arthur said, "apparently Holly has been laid quite low. When I spoke to her a short while ago, she sounded awful."

"Yes." Peter was only half listening.

"We had planned to go skiing this weekend. But I wonder if it might not be a better thing if we headed south —"

Peter stood up. "Excuse me, Arthur," he said. "I'm afraid I must be going."

"You —?"

"Yes. I have to leave right away."

Looking baffled, Arthur stood. "Well," he said, "of course, if you must."

Peter shook his hand. "Thank you, Arthur. Sorry about earlier. Good night, Miss Harrison. Thank you."

"Good night, Mr. Russell."

Arthur opened his mouth to say something, but Peter had already reached the door. He ran down the corridor and the steps that led to the entryway.

"Good night, Manuel! Thank you!"

"Oh, jes, *buena sera, señor.*"

Patrick opened the door for him.

"Thank you, Patrick! Good night!"

"Yes, sir, good night, sir."

~

Peter had called Holly from the taxi. He had told her that there was something he needed to talk to her about right away, and she had said, by all means, come right over. Now they were sitting at either end of the sofa in the library of her aunt's apartment. Holly was wearing pajamas, a robe, and thick red socks; her legs were tucked up under her; her hair was limp, and the rims of her eyes were red, as was the area around her nose, which she had been blowing steadily; used tissues filled the pockets of the robe, and she clutched more in her hand. Peter had never seen her look more beautiful.

Only one lamp was lit, so Peter and Holly were surrounded by shadow. They sank down into the sofa's soft crimson pillows. Holly drank tea with honey, Peter had a glass of seltzer water. They chatted for a while. "How did you get your cold?" "I can't understand it. I woke up this morning feeling as if my head weighed a ton." "What's up with work?" "Nothing much, how about you?" "Vacation." "Oh, right." "I hope it snows again." "Yes, doesn't it look ugly when it's gotten so dirty?"

Holly's voice was hoarse. It had never sounded more beautiful.

"Wouldn't it be fun to go look at the store windows? I haven't done that for years." "I haven't either, and the Rockettes . . ."

They fell silent.

Holly looked at Peter's profile. "So, you said that there was something you wanted to talk to me about?"

Peter turned toward her; their eyes met.

"Yes," he said. "There is something that I wanted to talk to you about."

Peter took her hand. During the ride over, he had rehearsed his speech, the speech he had prepared a million million times. *Holly, I've wanted to tell you something for a long time . . .* Now, as he was just

401

about to say those words for real, his heart pounded deafeningly. He felt as if a receding surf were drawing him down, down into the pit of a huge wave that would soon regurgitate him onto the rocky shore. After taking a moment to compose himself, he looked into Holly's eyes.

"Holly, I —"

"What happened to your hand?!" Holly asked, examining it. "It's all swollen!"

"Oh, that," Peter said. "It's nothing. Had to take a guy down. I'll tell you about it sometime. But it's nothing."

"Oh."

Peter cleared his throat. He allowed a pause before starting again.

"Holly, I —"

"Oh God," Holly said, "just a second." She sneezed loudly and then took a clump of tissues out of her pocket and blew her nose a couple of times, wiggling it back and forth with her fingers. She needed more tissues to wipe her nose and hands; after putting these aside, she coughed and sniffled, and turned back to Peter. "Sorry," she said.

Peter shifted on the cushion. Once again, he took Holly's hand. Before speaking, he drew in and let out a deep breath. Now — the moment of truth.

"Holly, I —"

"Are you okay with your drink? Because I've got lots of seltzer, or if you wanted a beer or anything?"

While Holly asked these questions, Peter's mouth hung open, arrested in midspeech.

"I'm fine. Really."

"Okay, good."

Holly nodded, settled back, and looked at Peter with a sweet, earnest expression, but a whiff of playfulness around the eyes made him suspect that she was teasing him, and he actually began to laugh.

"Something's funny?" Holly asked.

"No. Yes. Never mind," said Peter. "Can I please just tell you what I came here to say?"

"Of course."

"Okay."

Peter looked into Holly's eyes. He waited and waited, and then finally the words seemed to flow out of him.

"Holly, I've wanted to tell you something for a long time. For a very long time. What I've wanted to say is that I'm in love with you. I am completely in love with you. I am passionately, hopelessly, totally in love with you. I always have been, since the very first moment we met, from the first moment you sat next to me on the plane, before we even spoke. When you turned and smiled at me, all the light in the universe and all the matter in the universe turned into light. It would all seem dark compared with the way your face looked to me at that moment, and looks to me right now. We started to talk, and the next few hours were the happiest of my life. I don't know why. I have no idea. But the feeling of closeness to you was like a drug, the drug made from the one thing that we are all born into the world wanting more than any other. Happiness doesn't begin to describe it. It was so much fun — to be having so much fun with and to feel so close to someone who also happened to be the most beautiful woman in the entire world, because you are the most beautiful woman in the entire world — I can't imagine anything more blissful.

"Well, you know what happened. For years I thought about you every hour, every minute. Every second! Seriously! The pain I felt every time I thought I saw you on the street or in a restaurant — or on a plane! — and whoever it was turned around and wasn't you. It was agony.

"And then you reappeared again, and lots of other stuff happened. But I never stopped loving you, or being in love with you. Never. Ever.

"I kept thinking that our meeting on the plane like that must have been the work of Fate. It had all been arranged an infinity of time before, and I thought that the purpose of infinite time — or, okay, at least one purpose — had been to bring you and me to those exact seats on that exact flight. But then, as the years passed, I thought, 'This isn't working out,' and I couldn't say that Fate had brought us together and then not say that Fate had kept us apart.

"But I love you. I love you. I love being with you. I love your brain. You make me laugh. I can't imagine ever running out of things I'd want to talk to you about. I love your heart. No one — no one — is as trustworthy or as kind. And, yes, I love the thing that your brain and heart get carried around in, because you are so beautiful — and desirable — all of you from head to toe, literally."

Peter paused, gathering himself for the big finish.

"I know we've been friends, Holly, very good friends. I know that you love me as a friend. And I'm fully prepared for you to tell me that that's just how you want things to stay. But can you give me any hope, any hope at all, that someday you might love me in the same way that I love you?"

It seemed to Peter that Holly had regarded him with great tenderness during his speech, but he wasn't sure if he had her. For a moment or two, as his question hung in the air, she simply stared at him, her lips apart. Then she lowered her eyes. After a moment, she raised them, and looked into Peter's. Looking into them ever more deeply, she leaned toward him and rested her wrist on his shoulder.

"No, Peter," she said, "there is no hope that someday I might love you in the same way that you love me." She slid her fingers around the back of Peter's head and began slowly to pull it toward her. As she did this, she spoke in a hoarse whisper, saying, "Because I will always love you so much more."

She drew him to her and their lips met, and they kissed. It was a long kiss.

It might have gone on still longer if Holly had not begun to sob. She threw both her arms around Peter's neck and hugged him tightly. "Oh, Peter!" she said. Peter returned the embrace, wrapping his arms around her back. Holly felt as light and delicate as a Chinese lantern. His eyes began to water, too. He had told her; they had kissed; they were embracing. Could all this be true? Now he seemed to be flying, flying and soaring the way you did in a dream.

Holly sneezed and sniffled.

"Sorry. Wait." She searched for some fresh tissue but found none. Peter picked up a box near him and offered it to her.

"Thanks," Holly said. She blew her nose, looked at Peter and began to laugh, blew her nose some more and dried her eyes, then looked at Peter and began to laugh all over again.

"Oh, Peter!" she said. "I'm so happy!" She hugged him and kissed him. "Let me just look at you." She leaned back and studied Peter while running her fingertips down the side of his face and along his jaw.

"Holly," Peter said in a voice that sounded strange and otherworldly. "Have I got this right? Do you mean . . . do you really mean that you are in love with me?"

"Yes! Yes! Yes!" Holly burst out laughing. "Yes, I am in love with you!"

For a moment they just looked at each other, stroking each other's hair.

"I . . . oh . . . I," Peter said, "I'm glad." He burst out laughing himself. That was the only thing he could think to say.

"Me too!" said Holly. They kissed, another long kiss, and then Holly started to tell her version.

"Everything you described is exactly what it was like for me," she said. "*Of course* I fell in love with you the moment I saw you. *Of course* I loved our flight together. I never wanted the plane to land; we were together, together — like the dancer and the dance." She laughed. "It was the happiest I've ever been, until this moment. It was so frustrating, though! Because the whole time, I kept thinking: I wonder what it would be like to kiss him, I wonder what it would be like to kiss him. The whole time, even when we were having such interesting discussions about the disappearance of vaudeville or whatever — and they *were* interesting — that's all I could think about. It was one of my immediate impressions, in fact — how kissable your lips looked." She touched them with her fingers.

"Then" — she sighed — "the heartbreak. The agony. Yes — me too — 'Oh my God, it's him!' And then it turned out to be someone who didn't look anything like you. For years and years, I thought about you every second, too.

"Then when we met again, I just didn't know about you. I dreamt and fantasized, and I thought maybe, maybe, I could say something and you'd say you felt the way I did. But I thought I was just kidding myself. And I was chicken. And there were other people involved.

"So I had my dreams and fantasies. And now they've come true."

This was followed by some more spooning and sweet murmurings. After a few minutes of that, Holly said she had to ask Peter something. She said that she wished to reiterate her previous statements to the effect that she was so happy, that she had never been happier, and that she hoped Peter would forgive her if, when she asked her question, she sounded just a little cross.

What was this?

"Of course!" Peter said. "Please go ahead. Ask me. Ask me any-thing!"

Holly leaned back and folded her arms. Her expression conveyed that she was decidedly peeved.

"Okay," she said, "here's what I don't get: if it was love at first sight, if you were happier during the plane trip than you had ever been, if neither this nor all possible universes (I flatter myself to assume that you meant to include them, too) could produce the light that shone from my face, then why, why, why, for God's sake, didn't you call me?!"

Peter stared at her blankly. "What do you mean? I told you why, ages ago. I lost the number."

"But Jonathan said you made that up to be nice."

"What?"

"Yes. He said that you told him you had gotten a little crush on me on the plane, but by the next day you were over it and then got busy and just never called."

Peter stared at Holly, stunned. He could barely speak. "Jonathan told you that? I can't believe it. Or maybe I can."

Peter took Holly's hands and looked at her intently. He explained that he really had lost the number, that their first meeting really had been exactly what she had always wished it was. Then he told her what Jonathan had claimed *she* had said about their first meeting.

"So he pulled the same thing on you!" Holly said. "It's impressive, actually. He must have seen right away that there was something between us."

They sat in silence, brooding on Jonathan's cunning and treachery.

"Well," said Peter finally, "I can't really blame him. After all, he was just trying to hold on to you."

~

Peter and Holly remained on the sofa for a long time, kissing and caressing each other, and listening over and over to a certain album that just happened to be in the CD player. Then they moved on. Now a gray glow seeped out around the edges of the curtains in Holly's bedroom. The curtains themselves, the bedclothes, the upholstery on the chaise, the high and low chests, the wallpaper, the paintings, all made for a monochromatic tableau. Holly's head, though, lying on Peter's shoulder, and her bare arm, lying across his bare chest, were close enough so that Peter could perceive their hues: the hair a muted blond with caramel top notes, the arm a pinkish beige over a white undercoat. It was about five-thirty in the morning. Oddly, it all seemed to have followed directly from that meeting on the plane all those years ago. Peter had difficulty remembering what had happened in the meantime.

Holly stirred, resettled herself while tightening her embrace of him, and let out a shallow, savoring sigh. A few minutes later, she shivered. Her eyes blinked open and she raised her head.

"Hello," Peter said.

"Hi."

Holly propped herself up on her elbow. She stroked the side of Peter's face with her other hand.

"Holly," Peter said.

"Yes?"

"Will you marry me?"

Holly wore a big smile. "Yes," she said.

They kissed tenderly and for quite a while lay awake holding on to each other tightly before falling asleep again.

~

Something had to be done about Arthur, of course. Holly called him later that morning, and, hearing that she was better, he wanted to take her out to dinner, but she said that she wanted to come by his house in the evening and discuss something with him. So, sitting in the small study, she told him then that there was someone else, and he took it well, very much the gentleman, but he couldn't hide his disappointment. "He was sweet and noble," she said to Peter later that night. Holly had predicted that he would not allow her to tell him anything about his rival, and he hadn't. "That's none of my business, Holly. I only hope that he is worthy of you."

When Peter arrived at work the morning after Holly had her conversation with Arthur, he had a message from Miss Harrison: Arthur wanted to see him. Peter sighed.

Here it comes, he thought. Now that Holly has dumped him, there's no reason to keep me around. How honorable of Arthur to do the job himself. Maybe I should beat him to it and resign. God knows, when he learns about Holly and me, he'll want my head. Well, none of it matters! Holly is in love with me! And as long as Holly loves me, I don't care if I'm fired! I don't care if I starve! I don't care if my entrails are burnt with a hot poker!

As long as Holly loves me.

Peter sneezed and blew his nose — he had come down with a bad head cold — and set off for Arthur's "aerie." Once again, Miss Harrison met him on the sixty-third floor and led him to Arthur. When they entered his office, he was leaning against his desk with his arms crossed, lost in thought.

"Mr. Beeche," Miss Harrison said. "Here is Mr. Russell."

Beeche looked up with a halfhearted smile. "Ah, Peter, yes," he said. "Thanks for coming up." He held out his hand.

"Hello, Arthur," said Peter. "I better not shake your hand. I've got a pretty bad cold."

"You sound terrible."

"I'm sure it's nothing serious."

They sat as they had before, Peter on the sofa, Arthur in an armchair. They had a brief, desultory chat about a report they had both seen on the huge number of engineering undergraduates in Mexico.

"Can I offer you anything?" Arthur asked. "Coffee? Water?"

"No, thank you."

"Peter," Arthur said, "there are a couple of things I want to discuss with you. First, I called you this morning because — and I can't help but remember the last time we sat here — because Holly and I had a talk last night. I don't know if you have spoken to her. We had a talk last night, and we've decided —" He looked up and rolled his eyes. " 'We've'! Whom am I kidding! *She* has decided that it would be best for us to be friends but no more than that." He winced. "Apparently, she's in love with somebody else." He stopped there, deep in thought.

Meanwhile, Peter's hands were sweating and his tie had begun to strangle him. He girded himself and finally managed to speak. "Yes, Arthur," he said. "Holly did mention that." He girded himself some more. "Arthur, there's something I think you should know —"

Arthur held up both hands. "No, Peter, no. I don't want to know anything."

"But —"

"Please. We'll say no more about the matter. Except this: I want to tell you how grateful I am to you for bringing Holly into my life. I will always cherish our time together, and I want to thank you."

"Arthur, really, it's kind of you to say, but I don't deserve any thanks."

"You do, Peter, you do, and I do thank you." He straightened up. "And now the subject is closed."

"But, Arthur —"

"No, Peter. I'm going to have to insist. No more on that. I shall never speak of it again." He looked at Peter sternly. Peter opened and closed his mouth a couple of times, making noises in his throat, but Arthur stared him down.

"And now," Arthur said, adopting a businesslike tone, "there is another important item on the agenda. It has to do with your future at the firm."

"Oh, that," said Peter. "I suppose you're going to fire me. If I could only explain —"

Arthur held up his hand. "I think I'd better explain first."

Surprised, Peter settled back to listen.

"When I talked to Gregg Thropp about this project you had been working on with Mac McClernand, he said some things that simply didn't jibe with what I knew about you and that seemed especially inconsistent as I've gotten to know you a bit better. I've never trusted Thropp, so I've been doing some checking. He suggested that I call Rich Hooper and Andrea Larsen to ask about a presentation you gave that apparently went poorly. Well, they did say that it was not a very good meeting."

"I know, but —"

Arthur held up his hand again. "Please, I think you will be interested in what I have to say. Well, Rich and Andrea described your idea to me, and I must say, I found it fascinating."

"You did?"

"Yes, and for all the reasons you mentioned I was particularly impressed with your analysis of the risks in the mortgage market. I've been thinking along the same lines. Certainly, implementing your idea would be a huge and complicated undertaking. But I want to pursue it."

"You do?"

"Yes. Now, as for this McClernand business. Thropp told me that the project was your idea, that you had asked to work with McClernand, and that you had kept what you were doing a secret. Well, of course, Mac is at that place up in Connecticut now and they have him under sedation most of the time, but I did manage to talk to him at a moment when he was fairly lucid." Arthur stopped and looked off. "Mac McClernand," he said. "It may be hard to believe now, but Mac once really had something. I will never forget, years ago, when Seth and I had a very big and, we thought, very clever trade going. We were short a company's bonds and long their stock. As soon as he learned of it, Mac undid our positions, and we even made a little money. But he chewed us out royally and told us all the ways it could have gone wrong. Over the next few weeks I looked on with horror as both the bonds and the stock moved in the wrong directions. We would have lost millions. If we had had to face my father . . . !" Arthur shuddered and laughed quietly, then turned back to Peter. "In any event, Mac told me that it was his brainstorm, and that Thropp had sent you to him. Mac also said that in the fall he had explained the whole idea to Thropp."

"Yes," said Peter. "That's right."

"Well, perhaps you can tell me the whole story."

Peter blew his nose and took a deep breath. "All right. Thropp hates my guts. I don't know why. Nothing accounts for it. But he decided to torment me."

"Of course. Gratuitous sadism," Arthur said. "Go on."

"At first he was very friendly. I had told him a little bit about my idea, and he said he wanted me to give a low-key, very rough presentation to just a few other people. I was shocked when I walked in and saw who was there and the expectations he had raised. A couple of his protégés had obviously been briefed ahead of time and they attacked me. Afterward, Thropp said he was assigning me to McClernand, hoping to damage my reputation further. For one reason or another, I had lost my protectors, but he still didn't think he could justify firing me, and anyway, he wanted to watch me suffer. When Mac told him what we were doing, he was ecstatic."

"I see," said Arthur. "But why didn't you find some underhanded method to get back at Thropp?"

"I — I don't know," Peter said. "I considered various options but not that one."

"You should always stab people like Thropp in the back, Peter. It's good for you, it's good for the firm, and, most important, it's good for humanity."

"Yes, sir."

"Well," Arthur said, "this is all much as I expected." He punched a button on a nearby phone.

"Sir?"

"Miss Harrison, I'm afraid that by about ten o'clock this morning, Gregg Thropp will have decided to leave Beeche and Company in order to spend more time with his family. You'll take care of the details, won't you?"

"Yes, sir."

"And let's call around. It would be dishonorable for us not to warn others about Mr. Thropp, even our competitors, isn't that right?"

"Yes, sir."

"Thank you, Miss Harrison. That's all."

"Very good, sir." She rang off.

Arthur smiled at Peter. "When we're through, Thropp won't even be able to work as a bank teller in Mud Flap, Arkansas." He laughed. "'Mud Flap.' Not bad. Quite funny, don't you think? I just made that up." Arthur chuckled again, pleased with himself. "Now, then," he continued, "with Thropp gone, it raises the question of who should replace him. I wonder if you had any ideas?"

"Let's see," Peter said. "Of course, it would be presumptuous of me even to make a suggestion, but wouldn't Kearney make sense? Or Poschl?"

"Fine choices," Arthur said. "Excellent candidates. But I had someone else in mind."

"Oh?" said Peter.

Pausing dramatically, Arthur looked at Peter with a knowing grin. "Yes, Peter, I was wondering if you would be interested in Thropp's job."

"Me?"

"Yes, you."

"Gregg Thropp's job?"

"Yes."

Gregg Thropp's job! This would be a big jump and would result in a huge increase in Peter's bonus. People like Jonathan or Charlotte, and even Holly — they could never understand how it felt to get a big promotion and raise. Peter could hardly believe what he was hearing.

"So," Arthur said. "What do you say?"

"What do I say? Yes! Definitely, of course! I'm thrilled and honored, Arthur, truly —"

"Terrific!" said Arthur. "You'll be good at it." Arthur stood up and offered his hand, and Peter stood and took it. "Congratulations!" Arthur said.

"Thank you, Arthur," said Peter, "thank you!" He tried to sound enthusiastic, but his face had suddenly fallen.

Arthur pumped Peter's arm. "And you thought you were going to be fired!" he said, laughing. "Fired!"

"Um, Arthur?"

"Yes?"

"There is something I need to tell you," Peter said. "There's something I need to tell you, and when I do, well, when I do you just might want to change your mind, about this job offer, I mean."

Arthur's smile vanished. "Whatever do you mean?" he asked.

"Maybe we'd better sit down," Peter said, and they did so.

"Sorry, just a second." Peter sneezed. "Sorry." He straightened his tie and cleared his throat. Arthur, stolid and unruffled but deeply puzzled, tilted his head to one side.

"Well, now, aherm . . . ah, Arthur, you know that subject we were talking about earlier —?"

"You mean Holly and me? I told you, Peter, I do not wish to discuss it." Arthur did not raise his voice, he did not even sharpen it, but his words came with the force of heavy ordnance.

"Yes," said Peter. "I know. And I respect that, I do. But, you see, Arthur, there is just one thing that I really think you ought to know. Believe me."

Arthur stared at Peter sternly, but after a moment, he relented. "Very well," he said. "I'll listen to what you have to say."

"Good. Well." Peter shifted in his chair and cleared his throat. "Well, now, Arthur. As you were saying, according to Holly, there is apparently a person toward whom she has feelings that are the kind of feelings . . . feelings of a romantic nature, I guess you'd call them, that, she says, she doesn't necessarily have toward you, notwithstanding her desire, her strong desire, that you and she remain the very best of friends."

"That's correct."

Peter tried to put on his most winning smile. "It's a funny thing, isn't it, how life takes its twists and turns? Quite a funny thing!" He let out a nervous laugh, then composed himself. "So, Arthur, what I wanted to say, you see, that other person? That other person Holly was talking about, the one toward whom she does have those feelings of what I guess you'd call a romantic nature?"

"Yes?"

"Well, actually, that person happens to be me, actually."

Now Peter saw all of Arthur's tremendous latent power seem to gather and concentrate within him. What a large man he was! His great brow empurpled with displeasure.

"You!" Arthur cried.

"Er . . . yes."

"You!"

"That's right, Arthur. I'm sorry. It goes back a long time. We just hadn't understood about each other until the other night. We've been in love for years."

Arthur's whole body seemed to bulge like that of a superhero in mufti preparing to switch identities. Peter braced himself, preparing to be smashed either by Arthur's fist or by a blast of gamma rays.

"The other night," Arthur said. "So that's where you ran off to?"

"Yes."

"And that's when you figured out that you'd been in love with each other all along?"

"Yes," said Peter.

"I see," said Arthur. He stared at Peter as if on the verge of attack, but then all of a sudden stood down. He leaned back in his chair, and his muscles relaxed. For a full minute he sat there nodding his head, lost in thought.

"My wife, Maria, died ten years ago," he said finally. "I loved her very much, and I was inconsolable for a long time. The fact is, I've never really gotten over it. But after a couple of years, everyone thought that I should start taking women out. 'You shouldn't be alone' and all that. I agreed. But what a miserable experience it was. So I gave up. I still missed Maria. I felt very lonely, but trying to find a new wife just made that worse. Being alone wasn't all that bad, I told myself. You can get a fantastic amount of work done, for one thing.

"Well, for a while now, I've noticed something changing inside me. I haven't stopped loving Maria, but I've begun to think that I would like to find someone. Then, when I met Holly that night, it was as if a whole side of life that had turned to ash had been rekindled." Arthur smiled at this memory.

"I've been very happy during these past few weeks," he continued. "I allowed myself to dream that it would never end. But at the same time, I think deep down I knew that Holly had committed her heart elsewhere. I certainly had no idea to whom, but if I had been more astute I might have figured it out."

He punched the button on the phone again.

"Sir?"

"Miss Harrison, I have a question for you."

"Yes, sir."

"In the time that you have known Mrs. Speedwell, who would you say is the person whom she has talked about the most?"

"That's an easy question to answer," said Miss Harrison. "It would be Mr. Russell. I have often noted this"

"I agree," said Arthur. "Broadening our inquiry, now, Miss Harrison, to consider subjects of all kinds, which would you say is the one to which Mrs. Speedwell most invariably returns?"

"Also easy: that would, again, be Mr. Russell."

"Quite so," said Arthur. "Thank you, Miss Harrison."

"Not at all."

Arthur rang off and shook his head and laughed softly. "'Peter says . . .' 'That reminds me of once when Peter . . .' 'If Peter were here . . .' Holly was always saying something like that. I never thought much about it, only that she might have been trying to give you a boost with me. That goes to show how wrapped up in yourself you become in situations like these.

"Well, Peter, I'm happy for her and I'm happy for you, too. Or I will be in about twenty years."

Peter had to blow his nose again. "Thanks, Arthur," he said when he was done. "Thanks for being so understanding."

"Oh, and about my offer," Arthur said.

"Yes?"

"You've barged into my house and assaulted me, and now I learn that you've stolen my girl. And I'm still going to give you a much bigger job and a lot more money. I'll have to ask Miss Harrison to watch me closely. I may belong with Mac McClernand."

~

Holly and Peter's wedding took place on a warm, bright day in May. It had not taken too long to settle Peter and Charlotte's divorce, as amicable and straightforward as it was. Charlotte had laughed when she finally told Peter that some of her histrionics had been for his benefit, since she did not want him to have any suspicion that she was trying to help him. (Charlotte and Maximilien-François-Marie-Isidore were married at his ancestral seat just days after the decree was final. As a wedding trip they spent a week visiting the sites of some of the bloodiest clashes during the Vendée, which was one of Maximilien-François-Marie-Isidore's passions.)

It was a uniformly happy group that gathered for the ceremony. No one could have been more enthusiastic about the union of Holly and Peter than Arthur Beeche. He insisted that the service be conducted in his private chapel and that he hold the reception at his house. Charlotte and her new husband were there. He looked like a dressed-up doll in his oversized black suit and white shirt. But he was clean-shaven and displayed rare bonhomie, a fruit of his delight over his own marriage. Peter's parents had been joyful at Peter's marriage to Charlotte because they rarely found cause to be discontent, especially on an occasion that was officially a happy one, but on this day there was an added sparkle to their grins. The prospect of having Holly as a sister-in-law rather than Charlotte had produced a mild euphoria on the part of Peter's sisters. His friends had not been able to follow the story line exactly, but they knew that Peter had split up with someone whom they considered actually to be kind of a bummer and was now married to someone who was really great (and who was a babe). Inasmuch as one always wishes the best for one's friends, they were pleased, and inasmuch as it is inevitable that one will spend time with the wives of one's friends and so prefers that those wives not be bummers (and to be babes), they were perhaps even more pleased. Alex, Holly's sister, thought the entire arc of Holly and Peter's relationship was both romantic and spiritually deep. "So you were in love all this time! The devas must have had some reason for having it go this way." Graham felt great joy and also relief. For thirty years he had suffered from anxiety over the question of whether Holly would ever find the right man; nothing was certain in life, he knew, but it seemed as if she had (he still worried about Alex in this respect). Holly's mother, meanwhile, floated easily from Jonathan to Peter but did manage to focus enough to say to Graham, "You know, Jonathan was so good-looking, but I think I like Peter more. And I wonder if he might not be a nicer person." Charlotte's mother, who had always been fond of Peter, also came. Her escort was her fiancé, Dr. Smythe, the man who had been so helpful on the night of Jonathan's death. Charlotte's brother, David, was there, with a glossy coat and meat on his bones. (Charlotte's father, an unlikely guest in any event, had a particular reason to be absent. Several clients had complained about Dick's work, but it was the threat of Beeche and Company to take all its business elsewhere that finally led to his ouster from his firm. His partnership interest was liquidated to repay the large loans he had taken.) Miss Harrison came, too, accompanied by Isabella.

Julia attended. Her baby, a boy named Peter, was now two months old. When she and Arthur were introduced, Arthur was intrigued. "There was a woman named Julia Dyer who died about thirty years ago," he said. "You must be a relation?"

"Oh, yes," said Julia, "she was my grandmother."

"How funny," said Arthur. "When I was just starting out as a collector, I bought several things from her estate. I still remember the sale. I vowed I was going to buy only one lot, but I couldn't help myself. I was very nervous bidding on a side table. It was getting so expensive!" He shook his head and laughed. "Now it's probably worth a hundred times what I paid for it."

Julia smiled, although she could not prevent a shadow from crossing her face. "Yes," she said. "She had some beautiful things. Of course, I had no idea of their value, but I remember each one of them so well. We would go to Gram-Gram's apartment every Sunday, and I can still see her living room. I think I could draw an exact picture of it: the bergères, the sculpture of the faun, the clock, that side table you mentioned with all the ormolu, the pictures. All those portraits of people who were not good-looking at all. She did have a couple of Impressionists — not very good ones — that I liked. Unfortunately, I'm afraid that just about everything was dispersed. I think my uncle still has a pair of candlesticks." She thought for a moment. "You know," she said finally, "it's too bad. My father and my uncle have both spent years and years in a mania — an intermittent mania, anyway — of trying to get rich. If they had just socked away everything they inherited from their mother and done nothing, they'd have fortunes."

"The key to life," Arthur said solemnly, "is having the liquidity to ride out bad markets."

He and Julia pondered this truth, and then Arthur realized he had made a faux pas, treating lightheartedly a subject that obviously caused Julia some sorrow.

"Forgive me," he said. "You must miss all those things." He thought a moment. "Maybe it would make it even more painful — but would you like to see some of them? They aren't here, they're mostly in a house on Long Island, and some are in storage. Maybe the memories would hurt more than be pleasant." His face lit up. "I'll tell you what! You could choose a couple and I'd be happy to let you have them."

"Oh no," said Julia. "I couldn't agree to that."

"Please," said Arthur. "We can call it a permanent loan, the way museums do. It would be a great pleasure."

"No, really, I couldn't," said Julia. "But, yes, I might like to take a look, although I might burst into tears."

"Excellent!" said Arthur. "All we need to do is fix on a weekend when you and . . . er . . . you and —"

"There's no 'and,'" Julia said. "I was married to the father of the woman Peter was married to before, Charlotte's father, but we have just gotten a divorce."

"Charlotte's father," Arthur said. "Oh, yes. Yes, I know of him, Dick Montague."

"Yes. But I would be accompanied by someone. I don't know how you'd feel about a two-month-old baby boy coming along?"

"A baby?" Arthur said. "That would be no problem at all! I love babies. That old house hasn't had any babies in it for a long time." A distant look came across his face. "Maria and I, we had no children."

"Neither did Dick and I, actually," Julia said.

It took a moment for Arthur to understand Julia's circumstances. "I see," he said. "Then the boy's father —?"

"I'm sorry to say that the father died rather suddenly several months ago."

"That's terrible!" Arthur said. "How awful. I'm so sorry."

They stood in silence for a moment.

"And what is the name of this little boy?" Arthur asked.

Julia told him it was Peter.

"Excellent name!" Arthur said, laughing. He asked what stage Peter was at. Was he holding up his head? What was his favorite toy?

Julia began describing her Peter's little ways, the cute noise he made when he sneezed, their little game when she shook a stuffed tiger on his tummy and made him laugh, how his head smelled like toast. She reddened. "I'm sorry!" she said. "This must be very boring for you! I swore I wouldn't be like every other first-time mother and go on and on about her baby as if no one had ever had one before."

Arthur looked at her warmly. "Don't apologize! It's all very interesting! I look forward to seeing Master Peter. I have to warn you, though, that there are some old women on the staff who will probably spoil him beyond all redemption."

"That sounds lovely," Julia said. "As far as I'm concerned, no one can make too much of a fuss over Peter."

"Well, then, it's settled. I'll call you and we'll arrange the date."

"It's so thoughtful of you, Arthur. I can hardly believe it. Thank you!"

Remembering her grandmother and her own old nanny, Julia began to tear up, and she sought to change the subject. "Oh," she said, "there's Holly's father, Graham Edwards. Do you know any of his movies?"

~

The minister was a youngish man with a closely trimmed beard and an annoyingly familiar manner. In his homily, he went for the laughs a few too many times. But his spirit, at least, conformed to that of the congregation. Its members had an air of particular delight that one does not find at all weddings. Holly and Peter were so obviously in love, and their match seemed so right, that no one could remain unaffected by the joy of the occasion; moreover, all the difficult, ill-willed people who of necessity are invited to first marriages were absent here, so everyone extravagantly wished the couple well.

At the appropriate moment both Holly and Peter said "I will." There were hymns and readings. Holly and Peter repeated their vows. The minister, grinning dopily, nodded to the pair. They closed their eyes and kissed. This lasted a long time and the congregation cheered and laughed. Their eyes open, the new husband and wife laughed, too.

Epilogue

Maggie O'Sullivan had just taken a shower, and with a towel around her she crept as quietly as she could through her roommate's bedroom, which lay between Maggie's room and the bath. It was a Sunday morning, and the roommate was in bed with a man whom Maggie had never seen before. A tricolor tattoo covered his upper back. Once in her own room, Maggie began to get dressed. She was a big girl, tall with broad shoulders and hips and a large bosom, and she had long, wavy, rust-colored hair, which she could feel sticking to her back. Freckles, a lighter shade of rust, covered her chest. She put on a V-neck T-shirt, flipping her hair out, and a pair of jeans.

Maggie was hungry, and she made some coffee and toasted a bagel, on which she spread "light" cream cheese. She drank her coffee and ate her bagel at the small, scarred wooden table in her bedroom, which also served as the dining room and the living room. She had started out in Manhattan with several girls paying an astronomical rent for a loft in a very depressing part of town, and she couldn't quite believe that after that arrangement came to an end the best she could do was to share a one-bedroom apartment deep into Brooklyn. The neighborhood was quiet and friendly, and relatively safe, and her apartment had a lot of light. But it was so far from Manhattan, and the whole point, after college, had been to live in Manhattan. Now she sometimes felt as if she were no better off than if she had gone back to New Jersey. (No! That was definitely not true!) People in her neighborhood talked about taking the "train" into "the city" and she had heard of old ladies who had never been there in their lives! She suspected that if she got a job out where she lived, the filament connecting her to Manhattan would be cut, and she might lose any contact with it whatsoever.

After college she really hadn't known what she wanted to do. She had gotten a degree in drama and, nominally, she was becoming an actress. Largely supported by her parents, she came to the city and lived in the loft with a friend and three girls she didn't know, took some acting classes, and mostly worked as an office temp, although she did have a job for a while behind the counter at a take-out gourmet soup place. Because it was in a hip, artsy neighborhood and because it was gourmet soup, it didn't feel the same as working behind the counter at a regular take-out place.

Naturally, what Maggie wanted to do, in the short term at least, more than taking acting classes and working as a temp, was to go out at night. She didn't have enough money to go out every night, but she didn't have so little money that it was unthinkable to go out at all. So despite her resolutions to limit her socializing to the weekends, she succumbed to temptation most nights of the week, spent more than she could afford, often arrived at work with a hangover, and lacked energy in her classes. She had fallen in love a couple of times, and, except for the phone calls to her parents asking for money and the visits home during which, like a stench, the question of how she justified her life hung in the air, it was all a lot of fun. She managed to placate her parents, and herself, with one story after another of a job at a magazine she was hoping to get, or another class she was going to take, or a non-Equity showcase that, through a connection, she might be cast in.

But she had graduated three years ago, and unbearable pressure was building on her to make some kind of plausible plan and then show evidence of carrying it out. She was certainly no further down any path now than she had been when she arrived, and, to add insult to injury, her nightlife was logistically more difficult to sustain, even though lots of her friends lived in Brooklyn, too. Nothing had come together for her, and she lived each day with a creeping sense of panic about her future.

The best idea she had was to go to graduate school in photography and get an MFA. She had taken photography courses in college and had liked them and had done well (although it was difficult to say how much it meant to get an A from the professor, a gregarious, big-bellied man in his fifties who liked his wine and his pot, since he gave one to everybody). Sometimes on a weekend she would take pictures or go to photography shows at galleries, although if she honestly reckoned up the times she had really done each of these things the number barely reached half a dozen. Without too much effort, though, she could convince herself that photography was a passion or, anyway, could really become a passion if she got deeply into it, and that getting an MFA was a serious pursuit. Lurking on the edge of her awareness was the belief that a graduate program would be an oasis that would, for a couple of years, provide her with a reason to exist — "I'm getting my master's" — and was something that her parents could be convinced to pay for while also supporting her, or mostly supporting her. It was painful, actually, to imagine the way her parents would try to be encouraging and proud when they were so obviously dubious about the value of an MFA in photography and also shocked at the cost, and within her breast Maggie felt guilty for taking advantage of them. And her grandparents, what would they think? Two of them had never gone to college, and her mother's father had paid his way by hauling goods around a warehouse and winning money at cards. What would they think of someone paying thousands of dollars to be taught how to take pictures? But she tried to keep these thoughts at bay, and when she failed, she could still successfully argue to herself that this really was something she wanted to do and that the degree was completely legitimate. After all, why would the universities offer it if it were not? The only problem was that it seemed quite daunting to fill out the applications, put together a portfolio, and collect the letters of recommendation.

At some level of consciousness Maggie was turning over these thoughts all day and all night long. Still, there was another subject that preoccupied her even more. A year and a half after she had come to New York something had happened that no one knew about, except her two best friends. Maggie had become involved with a man, a writer, who had been several years older than she. He had also been married.

~

His name was Jonathan Speedwell. One day, after she had been working at the gourmet soup place for a few weeks, he came in at lunchtime. From then on, Maggie would see him almost every day that she worked there. She had noticed him the first time because he was very, very good-looking. He was tall and thin, with curly brown hair and blue eyes and fair skin. She remembered his sensitive-looking fingers when he took the soup container from her. When he came in, he usually wore something kind of stylish, a purple scarf or a striped shirt of a type she was not familiar with (she learned later that they came from England).

Jonathan was always polite and friendly, but at first he would only smile at her and say hello. Then she caught him looking at her a few times, and when their eyes met he would quickly turn his away. Eventually, they began to chat, small talk: the weather or "What, out of chicken gumbo, again?" or "I noticed you weren't working last week." Jonathan was shy and often looked down or away when they spoke, but when he did look directly at her, his eyes seemed full of meaning. Finally, he had asked her if she would like to get some coffee later, and in time, having coffee led to having a drink, and having a drink led to having dinner.

The very first time they had had coffee, Jonathan mentioned his wife, Holly. It was not a big deal. They had been talking about Los Angeles, which Maggie had recently visited. "My wife," he said, "Holly — you'd really like her — her father has lived out there for years, and she loves it and she hates it." Jonathan had continued to mention Holly from time to time, whenever doing so seemed to flow naturally from the conversation.

It had not taken very much time before the high point of Maggie's life became her visits with Jonathan. As lunchtime approached at the shop, she would find herself swallowing hard as she wondered if she would see him that day. If they had a plan to meet, her heart would race as the appointed hour approached. He was funny, and he would listen to her so intently as she talked about her life or her ideas about things. Sometimes she felt embarrassed when she talked so much more than he did. She mentioned that once and he smiled, touched her arm, and said, "Don't worry, your thoughts are a lot more interesting than mine, especially to me. I've heard mine a million times." So she talked more. She didn't quite know what it was, but she was so relaxed that she kept telling him everything. And beyond that, he was so good-looking, and you could tell that he was slim but strong. And he was a writer! She hadn't heard of him, but she looked him up right after he told her what he did and discovered that even if they hadn't sold a lot, his two books were very well regarded. She read them and loved them and reread them; they left her in tears.

Early one evening, they were sitting at the bar of a place that had become sort of their regular hangout. They had been talking about one thing or another, but Jonathan had seemed to have his mind on something, and he was looking at her in a particularly yearning way. They fell silent for a while, and he sipped his beer, and then stared at the glass, holding it with both hands.

Finally, he spoke, without looking at Maggie. "You . . . you know what's happening, don't you?" he said.

She remained silent. She could not speak.

Jonathan turned to her. He interlaced the fingers of his right hand with the fingers of her left (she wore a silver ring with a Celtic design on the index finger of that hand, and on her middle finger, a silver ring with a piece of turquoise set in it).

He looked at her with an expression of happiness, sadness, and bravery. "What's happening," he said, "is that I am falling in love with you."

Maggie began to cry. Jonathan gripped her hand more tightly.

And so it had begun. They had both been too emotional to think through anything that night, but when they met a couple of days later they decided that they had to stop seeing each other. "I love Holly," Jonathan said, "and it's not fair to you if this keeps going." As heartbreaking as it was, Maggie agreed. She would make the sacrifice for Jonathan's sake and her own.

But, inevitably, only a few days passed before they were together again. They made love for the first time a week after Jonathan's declaration. They were in his study on a rainy day drinking wine.

For the next few months, Maggie's whole being was wrapped up with Jonathan — when she would see him, when she would hold him in her arms. She was right, he was strong, and she liked to run her hands down either side of his muscular trunk. Making love with Jonathan made her feel as if she had never made love before. All these clumsy, selfish boys she had had sex with — looking back, they disgusted her. She had never experienced the pleasure or the closeness that she did with Jonathan. He told her early on not to fall in love with him. "Don't, don't, Maggie. Don't fall in love with me, if you were thinking of doing that. Believe me, I'm not worth it." Of course, it was too late for that warning to make any difference.

She was having an "affair." It had never occurred to her that she might have an affair. And she was having this affair with a brilliant writer. He took her to good restaurants, relatively grown-up places, and also gave her presents, real presents, like an onyx and diamond pin for her birthday. She had no idea how much it cost. It was all so wonderful, she had never been happier, but because of the secrecy and the guilt, it was all so painful, too. She was in a constant state of intense yearning because, while Jonathan never stood her up, he seemed to have so little time. In its own way, though, the pain was delectable.

Then something awful had happened. Jonathan was killed in an accident. She didn't even know about it until a few days after it happened. In the meantime, she had been driven wild with despair because Jonathan had missed a date, had not called her, and had not responded to messages. She was sure that he had dumped her without a word, and she was inconsolable and furious. Gina, one of the friends to whom she had talked about Jonathan for hours and hours, called her with the news. Gina worked in publishing and had heard a couple of editors talking about Jonathan's death. There had even been a short obituary in the *New York Times*.

Maggie was at home, the loft, when she heard, and she felt as if she had had the air knocked out of her. For several frightening seconds, she could not breathe. "Maggie, Maggie, are you okay?"

Gina had asked. Maggie began to sob uncontrollably. Gina tried to comfort her, but she was at work, and after a while she said she had to get off the phone but would come to see Maggie as soon as she left the office. When she arrived she found Maggie facedown on her bed, still heaving out sobs like waves during a storm.

Maggie spent a week crying like that and barely stirring from her bed. She skipped her classes. She lost her job at the soup place.

Jonathan had been the love her life, Maggie was convinced. Since his death, hardly an hour had gone by when she had not thought of him. She didn't know what would have happened if he had lived. He was in torment over his wife, whom he loved. Maggie always insisted that she would never ever want to hurt Holly, and she knew that Jonathan would never be happy if he hurt her. They were going to have children, weren't they? This passion between Maggie and him, it might not even last. But who knows? Anyway, they would have had more time together.

~

When Maggie rose on that Sunday morning, she had a particular plan with respect to Jonathan's memory, for it was the first anniversary of his death: she was going to visit his grave. To do so, she would have to take a very long subway ride, and she wanted to leave early. She rinsed her coffee cup and plate and grabbed her keys and wallet. She looked in the mirror and fluffed out her damp hair a little. Then she looked around for her book.

After they had made love one day, they had planned to have a drink, but Jonathan had gotten a phone call. "Hey! Great to hear from you," he had said when he found out who it was. "This might take a minute," he had told Maggie. She had been sitting on the couch in the front room, and he had wandered into the interior one.

While he murmured his conversation, she had written in her journal, and then had looked around for something to read. There were stacks of books all over the place. Looking through one pile she had found a paperback copy of *The Magic Mountain* by Thomas Mann.

When Jonathan returned she had held the book up and asked, "Do you think I would like this?"

For a split second, he had seemed to be at a loss for words, but he had said, "Yes, you definitely ought to read it. It's, you know, kind of tough going at times, but definitely."

Maggie had looked the book over. "I haven't read anything by Toe-mahss Mawn. He was one of the writers in a course I was going to take but didn't."

"If you don't mind my saying so," Jonathan had said with a smile, "I'd go a little easier on the pronunciation."

Maggie had turned red.

"Don't be embarrassed about something like that," Jonathan had said gently. He sat next to her and took her in his arms.

"I got that from this show-offy girl in my dorm."

"See? We don't want you sounding like her."

Any physical contact between Jonathan and Maggie always led to their making love, and so it was this time, as they had begun to kiss and caress, and then, for the second time that day, had taken off their own and each other's clothes.

She had borrowed the book and had started to read it several times, but she just couldn't get too far in it. After Jonathan died, she put it aside. But she'd picked it up again a few days before the anniversary and had read about twelve pages. She thought it would be a good book to take with her on her long subway journey, and she finally found it under a magazine on the coffee table.

She got on her train and settled into her seat. With the bookmark placed on page twelve, the section she had read looked like the thinnest slice of salami. She opened the book and began reading: "They had reached the second floor, when Hans Castorp suddenly stopped in his tracks, mesmerized by a perfectly ghastly noise he heard coming from a dogleg in the hall — not a loud noise, but so decidedly repulsive that Hans Castorp grimaced and stared wide-eyed at his cousin. It was a cough, apparently — a man's cough, but unlike any that Hans Castorp had ever heard."

One would not hew strictly to the facts if one said that the novel in her hands held Maggie's attention throughout her journey. Indeed, at its end, the bookmark had not advanced by a single page. Maggie was lulled by the two rhythmic movements of the train, the small one as it rocked back and forth while traveling at full speed and the larger one as it stopped at regular intervals. She daydreamed. She gazed at the other passengers, in all their variety, representing the city's horizontal strata of different neighborhoods. Here and there, she dozed.

A few stops from the cemetery, the train burst into the sunlight; it was an exciting moment that Maggie had been unprepared for, and she was surprised by the indifference of those around her. She reached her station and got off with a couple of people who, incongruously, carried bags of golf clubs.

The morning had by this time become hot; the sky was clear, with a few clumpy clouds. Maggie descended a long flight of stairs from the platform and saw the entrance to the cemetery, a huge wrought-iron gate that was open. Reaching it, she realized that she had no idea where Jonathan's grave was or how to find it. A perspiring guard stood nearby and she approached him.

"How do I find where someone is buried?" she asked. She felt nervous, believing, as crazy as it sounded, that the guard would know her secret. In a Jamaican accent, and with the same brusque manner that an usher at a movie house or stadium would use, he directed her to the offices.

Maggie had never been anywhere in the city that was as still and quiet as this place. There were large, leafy trees and the grass was green and carefully cut. She was amazed by the size of the mausoleums; some were surrounded by terraces with balustrades. It all reminded her of the wealthy town a few miles from her parents' house, only with miniature stone mansions.

Like the guard, the people at the information center showed no sign that they were working at a cemetery; they were indifferent and bored. A woman behind a counter punched in Jonathan's name on a computer and, not immediately finding a corresponding grave, told Maggie, with a hint of annoyance, that he was not a resident. Maggie said that she was sure he was, she had read a death notice, and the woman searched again and finally found him. She gave Maggie a map, rapidly explained where he was, and had already turned to another task by the time Maggie was able to thank her.

The paths all had names like streets in an old-fashioned town. She strolled along Spruce Lane, waggling her book against her leg. It was delicious to pass into the shade of the trees after walking a ways on the hot path. She saw no one else; she had the whole place to herself. The experience conformed to the richness and drama that she associated with Jonathan.

She found the Speedwell plot at the intersection of Elm and Maple. In the center was a massive stone tomb. Gravestones surrounded it in concentric circles, and Maggie soon found the newest one. It showed no weathering. Crisp shadows made the letters and numbers of Jonathan's name and dates half light and half dark. There was also an inscription in Latin, Maggie was pretty sure.

Maggie stared at the gravestone and remembered Jonathan's face. She remembered his looking down into her eyes when they lay together after making love. She remembered his voice and the feel of his hands. She began to cry softly. "Oh, Jonathan!" she whispered.

She ached with love and grief. He was the only man she would ever love, she knew. What would become of her? She would never, never experience the same kind of love for someone. She would probably get married, of course she would. She would marry a nice guy, and one night, after they had been to a party where something had reminded her of Jonathan, he would come across her sobbing for no evident reason, and she would have to decide whether to tell him the truth.

What do you do at a gravesite? Maggie didn't know. She hadn't brought flowers. She was at a loss. But then she knelt. She could feel the cool earth through the knees of her jeans. She put down the book, fingered the small crucifix she wore around her neck, and put her hands together. Closing her eyes, she began to pray. She prayed for Jonathan's soul, asking God to admit it into heaven, if He had not done so; she prayed for herself and asked God's forgiveness; she prayed to Jesus, asking Him to help her carry her burden.

While she was murmuring these petitions, repeating them several times and also reciting the Our Father and Hail Mary, she was startled to hear voices. Her eyes popped open and she listened. It was a man and a woman. She listened for another moment; they were close and getting closer. She should have known that other people might come today! Maggie crept on her knees a few feet and peeked around the side of the tomb. Her heart flew into her throat: a man and woman were approaching the plot, and the woman was Holly Speedwell, Jonathan's wife! They had never met, but Maggie knew her from her photograph and had even seen her in person at a couple of Jonathan's readings, which Maggie had attended anonymously.

The sight of Holly put Maggie into a panic. She didn't know what to do. Looking around, she saw a huge sycamore behind her. If she stayed low, she could reach it while remaining out of sight. So she scuttled to the tree, darted around to the far side, then stood up, and leaned against the trunk. Her heart was pounding. With difficulty, she tried to take several deep breaths. She had calmed down just a little when she realized, Oh my God! The book! I left it! There wasn't anything she could do about it, though. The man and Holly must have arrived at the plot. They were talking and she could hear what they were saying clearly.

"So," the man said with a little sigh. "Here we are."

They were silent for a moment.

"Let's see," the man said. "'The Lord preserveth the simple.' Psalm One hundred sixteen." That was the scripture on the tomb.

"Very nice," said Holly, "although it doesn't seem to apply to this place very well."

"No."

Maggie heard one of them take a couple of steps.

"Look at that one," said Holly, "that tiny headstone. Curtis, 1887 to 1888. Here's a husband and wife, Minturn and Catherine. They both died in 1919. The flu epidemic, I suppose. You know, they're buried on top of each other, four or five deep, like an apartment building."

There was another silence. Then Holly spoke.

"All these dead people. It's so depressing. To think that they were alive once, and doing things — I don't know what — going to baseball games. And now: dead. It's so hard to fathom. When people you love die, it's so hard to believe that they're gone, but they *are* gone. No matter how much fancy footwork you do to feel better about it, that's the truth. And then to think that the universe couldn't care less. Or, forget the universe, look at those clouds wandering up there like a lonely poet. They don't know or care what's below them. Or that huge sycamore." Maggie tensed up. "It doesn't know that it's shading these graves." She paused. "Sorry. I'm being lugubrious. Is someone who's going to have a baby allowed to have these thoughts?"

"I think so," the man said quietly.

The sound of rubbing fabric suggested to Maggie that there was an embrace.

"Okay. Well," Holly said after a minute. "Where is he? I don't remember."

"Neither do I."

After they took a few slow steps, Holly called from Maggie's left, "That must be it. The new one." They moved again, more quickly, until they were right behind Maggie. They stopped, and then she heard two sharp intakes of breath.

A long time passed before either Holly or the man spoke.

"Holly," the man said, "do you see what I see?"

"I'm crying. I can't see anything."

"Just reassure me that I'm not hallucinating."

"No, you aren't."

"Uh . . . Hm. Have you been able to locate your copy?"

"No. It's been very upsetting and I keep opening boxes and expecting it to be there. But, no, I haven't found it."

"I see," said the man. "Well, it doesn't matter. I was just asking out of curiosity. Because, regardless, there is absolutely no possibility whatsoever that your old copy of that book has . . . has —"

"No. None. Absolutely not."

With her back pressed against the tree, Maggie looked across a path at another family plot, this one with a huge statue of an angel. Her whole body tingled. It was nerves, but she was also amazed by what she heard Holly and the man saying. The book — it wasn't just any book, it was important to them.

"I guess one of us should pick it up," the man said.

"I'll do it," said Holly.

"Okay."

Maggie heard a step, a sound of crunching grass, and another step.

"Here it is," Holly said.

"There it is."

"I suppose the next thing to do is to give it a careful examination."

"I suppose."

"Okay," said Holly. "Here goes. Same edition. Oh, boy, the title page is missing." Holly took a deep breath. "All right, there's one way to tell for sure." She riffled the pages. "Let's see. It should be about two thirds of the way through, the snow chapter — your favorite — somewhere around here." The pages stopped turning, and Holly gasped. "Peter," she said, "read that."

"Okay. 'Hans Castorp was fed up with such promenades.'"

"No! The other page. Look at what's written in the margin."

There was a pause. Then the man read, "'Met P.'" There was another pause.

"Oh. My. God."

"How bizarre," the man said.

"Oh, Peter!" Holly cried out. "Peter! Our magic book! It's come back to us! It's come back to us *here!* Do you know what this means?"

"I think . . . well, I think . . . well, maybe I don't know. What does it mean?"

"I have no idea. But isn't it wonderful?"

"Oh yes, Holly, it is. It's wonderful!"

"Das Zauberbuch!"

From what Maggie could hear, they seemed to be laughing and crying and embracing. This went on for a while. Met P here, she repeated to herself. P — the man's name was Peter! What did it mean? Their emotion, her own emotion, and the mystery made Maggie feel dizzy. Also, she had stopped breathing.

Eventually, Holly and the man recovered from their fit of laughter and tears. They sighed a few times.

"Do you remember this?" the man asked. Pages turned. "Here it is. *For the sake of goodness and love, man shall grant death no dominion over his thoughts.*'"

"Of course," said Holly. "In italics."

They were silent. Then Holly said, "It's amazing. Unreal."

"Unbelievable."

"The next thing you know, that title page with the phone number written on it that you idiotically lost will turn up."

"Please — this is weird enough."

"There's got to be an explanation."

"I know, but how in the world —?"

"It might have . . . or maybe . . ." Holly trailed off.

"When did you discover it was gone?" the man asked.

"Some time after I moved in with Jonathan. I used to keep it in a special box, but I don't know what happened. All of Jonathan's and my books got mixed up and I looked through all his stuff, too. Who knows? Maybe it's a message from him from beyond the grave giving us his blessing." Holly laughed. "Oh, wait. I don't believe in that kind of thing."

Now they were silent for a while. Finally, the man spoke.

"Poor guy," he said.

"Yes."

"What a horrible night that was."

"The way he looked," said Holly. "Gray. I'll never forget it."

"What's the inscription?"

"Oh, that," Holly said. "After we were married, Jonathan did his will, and he put a letter with it that gave instructions for a few things. He actually planned his funeral. You know, a Gregorian requiem, something that we couldn't quite pull off. Well, he also said he wanted that on his gravestone."

"What's it say?"

439

"'*Qui nunc iacet horrida pulvis, unius hic quondam servus amoris erat.*' 'He who now lies here as rough dust once was the slave of a single love.' It's hard to translate *horrida*. Rough, coarse, gravelly."

The slave of a single love, Maggie thought. Yes, that would be Holly. That was only right. Maggie felt a pang. Did she count at all? Yes, Jonathan did love her too, Maggie was certain of it.

Suddenly Maggie had the impulse to step out from behind the tree and tell Holly and the man everything. She wanted to help them; she wanted to explain and confess, and to cry with them about Jonathan, and she couldn't stand the tension of hiding any longer. The temptation was almost overpowering, and it took all her strength to stay where she was, pressing her back even harder against the trunk.

"You know," the man said, "I sometimes forget that without Jonathan, we might never have found each other again. He wasn't exactly perfect, and I sometimes wondered why he was my best friend, but I really do miss him."

"Me too."

"If he could see us now," said the man, "I wonder what he would be thinking? I know he'd be happy. That was one thing about Jonathan, he was always happy for his friends."

"And he wanted to have children so badly himself. He'd also be happy for us about that."

"Yes." The man paused. Then he said softly, "Here, Holly, give me your hand."

For several minutes, Maggie heard nothing and nothing stirred. There was no wind, and the leaves of the sycamore might have been ceramic; although, it was true, when she noticed it, she did hear a drone of traffic in the distance.

"Ready?" Holly asked the man finally.

"Yes," he answered.

Still they did not move. Then Maggie heard their footsteps crunching grass and scuffing on the path.

Tears rolled down Maggie's cheeks, and she shuddered, but she made no sound. She waited and waited and waited. Half an hour passed. Then Maggie stole away.

About the Author

JAMES COLLINS was formerly an editor at *Time* and has contributed to *The New Yorker* and other magazines. He grew up in New York City and now lives in Virginia with his family. This is his first novel.